BENEATH
THE TREES OF
EDEN

TIM BINDING

BLOOMSBURY PUBLISHING
LONDON · OXFORD · NEW YORK · NEW DELHI · SYDNEY

BLOOMSBURY PUBLISHING
Bloomsbury Publishing Plc
50 Bedford Square, London, WC1B 3DP, UK

BLOOMSBURY, BLOOMSBURY PUBLISHING and the Diana logo
are trademarks of Bloomsbury Publishing Plc

First published in Great Britain 2020

A catalogue record for this book is available from the British Library

ISBN: HB: 978-1-5266-1660-9
EBOOK: 978-1-5266-1656-2

2 4 6 8 10 9 7 5 3 1

Typeset by Integra Software Services Pvt. Ltd.
Printed and bound in Great Britain by CPI Group (UK) Ltd, Croydon CR0 4YY

To find out more about our authors and books visit www.bloomsbury.com
and sign up for our newsletters

For Celia

THEY'D FOLLOWED THE MOTORWAYS right from the start, Alice and Louis, upping sticks, moving every six month or thereabouts, going to where the work lay or when they grew tired of their digs. Up and down the north–south axis they moved, ever since the Baldock bypass (Junction 8–10 as Alice later thought of it), six point four miles of chalk and subsidence and the public house down in Clothall where Alice worked pulling in a little money, the months after college, and where Louis ran his fingers through his hair and did that thing with his eyes like he was searching for a trace of something on her face, like he could read her, the secret in her she had never known existed until then, that had her fumbling with the first pint she ever drew him. There was a finality to him, the way he stood before her, like there was nothing she could do about it, like she'd been waiting for him. Could that be true?

'You working on the road then?' What else could he be working on, with hands like that? His mouth twisted into contempt.

'This? This is like laying a garden path, something for your granny to totter up and down on, a bunch of flowers in her basket.'

'There's nothing wrong with flowers. In a basket or out.'

'There's a truth in that.' He turned his glass round. 'It's a fill-in, see, in between proper work. I've just come from working on what you could call the road of roads, over the Scammonden Dam.'

He said it proudly, saw the incomprehension on her face.

'You never heard of the Scammonden Dam?'

'Should I have done?'

'Biggest engineering job in the country, up on the M62. Six hundred men we were up on that moor, like a settlement. Two summers and the second year it snowed eight months out of twelve. No phones, no food, even the generators packed up. That's road building. What I'm doing now ... it's what the pikeys do. Lay a little tarmac and get the hell out of it. Least it's not the M1. I don't care for the M1 at all. A rotten road, full of rotten drivers.'

'No more than any other surely.'

He raised the glass to his eye. Examined the colour.

'Ah, but that's the thing, see. A good road can make a good driver even out of a novice like you. Can you drive yet?'

She felt the question rush inside her, intimate, like it was an examination, like it was a switch. She knew what he was asking. Suddenly she knew it all.

'I cannot. Dad won't cough up for the driving lessons.'

'Lessons! It's a question of character, driving. A good road looks you in the eye, asks you to take a look at yourself. You'd come out colours flying.'

He thanked her and walked over to join his friends, never once looking back in her direction, save when he left, stepping over to say he'd be round to pick her up Sunday evening, ten minutes before opening time. Ten minutes before opening time he was there, walked her to the car, opened the door, waited until she was settled in, before getting in himself. He started the car, said nothing, drove it out on to the road, said nothing still. She sat not daring to move, hands by her side, conscious of his hands moving over the wheel and the sour taste in the air. The front seats were almost like a bench, they were fitted so close together. She hadn't expected that, didn't know what to think about it. It was a big car, a lot of room in the back.

'Do you know what sort of car this is?' he said.

'I wasn't looking.' He cleared his throat, inhaled.

'Cars are important. How they respond, the traps they lead you in. This …' he tapped the wheel, 'this is an A55 Cambridge Farina Mark II.'

'With a fringe on top.'

'You saw that then, the red. Gives it a bit of dash, don't you think, that and the fins.'

'Fins.'

'As big as a shark. I'd have thought a woman like you would have noticed the fins.'

A woman! Had anyone ever called her that before? She kept her voice steady.

'My dad had a Zephyr. That had fins.'

'The later Zephyr, excess chrome and a bonnet the size of Rutland. This is a lighter car than the Zephyr, but there's still a weight to it, too heavy for a woman to drive some would venture. That is, if a woman should wish to …'

He let it drift. He was waiting for her. She'd never been more sure of anything in her life, that he was waiting for her.

'… chance her arm?'

He nodded, grateful.

'Something like that.'

'Depends on the arm, I would say.'

'Would you now?' He was looking at her while driving. 'Would the arm chance a drink?'

'As long as it isn't by candlelight.' He laughed.

'Open the glove compartment, see what's on offer.'

It was stiff. She yanked it open.

'Are they all whisky?'

'Blended. Miniatures I've picked up, dens of iniquity and such. I don't go for all that malt snobbery. There's a half-bottle somewhere in the back.' He caught her eye. 'For longer journeys.'

'And this?'

She'd pulled out an old cough-mixture bottle lying on its side, an old wine cork for a stopper ...

'That's holy water,' he said.

'From a church?' She liked the idea, him stealing from a church.

'From a place of worship,' he said. 'From a font the size of a man's soul. Scammonden waters. Do you take water with your whisky?'

'I don't believe so, no.'

He took the bottle from her, stuck it in his pocket.

'Just the one miniature then. I don't want you tipsy on your first lesson.'

That was just the start of it, the drives he took her on, her stuttering down the road in the pitch-dark and him so calm and clever, and all the later times, telling her of the places he'd been, the work he'd done, the eye it had given him, always the eye, she spellbound, like he was Vasco da Gama, master of the oceans, and she just wet behind the wheel, her father despairing she might throw everything up for a man, who would scupper any chances of using her talent, bettering herself. So what? What did she care? He was so, what was it, connected to what she knew she wanted, the way he moved among these wayward men, the way his hands drew shapes when he talked, if he talked, that stare of his when he didn't, like he could read every word lit up in her head, could repeat them back to her if he wanted, like he was waiting for her to cross the line, reveal herself, and when she did, the only time, light from the three-quarter moon shining through the windscreen like she was on offer, spread out and ready, he did nothing but stare out on to the gorse bush.

'Looks like a wig,' she said, tired of waiting, 'all grey and fuzz, something bald underneath.'

He turned.

'I'm not laying a finger on you,' he said, 'not until the meat's falling off the bone,' and started the engine again, she not knowing where to look, and he was true to his word, nothing but a terrible propriety, opening doors, brushing down her seat, warning the men to watch their language when in company, nothing until the night he placed his hand between her breasts (in between them, would you believe, like they were not there, like he couldn't sense the heavy fruit hanging on them, like she was Eve, wholly corruptive in her thoughts), saying as he spread his fingers on the bone, 'I'm off Durham way. Before first light. Two years minimum I reckon. Nothing for you but empty hours and the sweat running off me like rain in a gutter. You coming or what?' Of course she was coming, lay awake that night knowing this was it, that her father was right, she was throwing everything away, everything for a man and the unknown his hard, restless hands would fashion into God knows what. But wasn't it wonderful, not knowing, having no future, not giving a toss, just the bare floor of his car rattling under her feet, and her college bag thrown in the back as they cracked the dawn open heading north, making their tracks on the Great North Road, or what was left of it. A great road, he said, a fine road, a road full of dignity and temperament, Christ he was full of it, its history, ribbons of the stuff he could reel off, they hardly had to pass a signpost but he didn't know the wherewithal, how the Black Death had decimated that village back knows when, the crossroads where Dick Turpin held up the stagecoach, the roadside inn where Queen Elizabeth stopped off for a quick banquet (Wasn't she the educated one? Wasn't she the one with qualifications and an education and a smattering of Spanish?), going on and on like a jackhammer, spewing facts and figures out like she was on the wrong end of a production line. Halfway through some story about the Jarrow March, she could take it no longer.

'Are they never going to stop?' she demanded.

'What?'

'The stories? I can't take them any more,' and no sooner had she said it than he gave the wheel a sudden yank, sending them lurching like a drunk across the lanes, bouncing into the lay-by. She knew what was coming even before he'd walked round and torn her door open, knew what was coming as she rose up finding his mouth, his hand running up her legs, the flesh of her pressed against the heat of the engine, her dress up over her hips now and her underwear kicked into the dirt along with his trousers (no underwear!), their first fucking breaking over them like a dam had burst, wild and difficult and uncomfortable, a truck going past, sounding its horn, like it could see them at it, and the both of them glad, riotously so, that it had happened that way, on the road, in the morning, in full view, like it sped them on, like it started them off like they meant to carry on, not giving a monkey's what anybody thought, she back in the car soon enough, smoothing down the folds of the flower print as if she were waiting in church for the service to begin, he sitting up dead straight, his hands holding the wheel at a quarter to three, like he was a Sunday driver out for a morning run, the stuff running out of her on to the seat thick, like it was top of the milk, like he'd been saving it up for weeks, just for this. It was finished now, their beginning. Now they were known to each other, had sealed the pact. This is how it would be, the two of them, no precautions, no second thoughts, not the cars they drove, not the lodgings they lived in, not the work he had to follow, asking for nothing than the friction between them and their need for uncertainty, the rub of it. The history lessons exhausted, she sat quiet beside him, her future disappearing fast.

They drove for long, slow hours, stuck in the inside lane, her eyes gritty from the lack of sleep, buttocks aching from the busted seat, the gaze of the road hypnotic. She'd never thought of a motorway before, its strange effect, never appreciated the magnetic pull of it, how it emptied you out then filled you up with a sort of nothing. You could be anyone on a motorway, whatever you wanted. Traffic came and went, bunched around them for ten minutes and then left them quite alone; cars, coaches, lorries, huge flapping cliffs of tarpaulin thundering past inches away, like vast untroubled liners.

'How old are you?' She spoke suddenly, not knowing quite where her voice came from. 'Not that it matters to me.'

Almost straight away he swung off the road again, pulling off into a field like he knew where it was, the way he unlatched the gate and drove in behind a clump of trees, where there was a little dell falling away to the left of them, where the ground was moss, where he took a rug that smelt of damp and laid it down, where they lay side by side, where he fell asleep, instantaneously, like a dog, and where, when she woke (an hour, she thought, though she had forgotten her watch, the one thing she had wanted to keep, left it lying on the shelf by her bed), he brought out a pair of eggs, hard-boiled, from a little canvas bag by his side, cracked the shells and rolled them loose on his thigh, holding them out for inspection, white and bare.

'This is how it is,' he said. 'You and me. Thick like cream. Perfect like an egg.'

'Like an egg.'

'That's it. You and me and wherever we want. You seen this country? Know anything of it.' She shook her head.

'You will. I'm thirty-five,' he said. 'Just so you know.' He saw her working the age difference, adding, 'Older than any man you knew at college, I'll be bound.'

She picked the egg from his hand, fed it into his mouth, then her own. Her fingers had never handled anything so naked.

'They weren't men,' she said. 'They weren't anything. Save one.'

'And he would be … don't tell me, a teacher.'

'A tutor. Spanish. He had a cloak, like a matador.' She didn't need to say any more. It was enough. He thought about it for a moment, then took her hand.

'Like that, was it? I'd snap his Spanish back for him, if you wanted.'

'No need for that now.'

'But once you wouldn't have minded ... "*Ay, qué trabajo me cuesta quererte como te quiero!*"'

She looked at him astonished.

'We had a Spaniard. He drove an RB10, two years back. Wrote poetry in his lunch break about his fascist father. He said it all the time. The women he cored because of it. Barely decent.' He brushed egg shell from his trousers. 'Shall we be off?'

'Not yet.'

One of his trouser buttons was showing. She eased it out from the eye, her skill amusing him.

'Like you were churning butter, please,' she said.

'What does a woman like you know of churning butter?'

There it was, the woman again. Every time he said it.

'My grandmother churned butter, when she wasn't tottering up the path with a basket of flowers. Eighty years old and she could turn the handle slow and steady, hour after hour, as long as it took, never missing a beat. You up to that?'

Thick like cream. Perfect like an egg. She wasn't worried what might happen, not this time, not yet. Nothing would, not while they embraced their irresponsibility so fiercely. There would be a life of travelling and upping sticks and this feeling of the two of them falling through the earth, like there was no one to catch them but themselves.

They arrived late. She did not know where they were, and he did not tell her the name of the place (and she made a point of not asking, a mark of her indifference to everything but him and her), but it was waiting for her, prepared, a ground-floor rent, a yard at the back, across which they walked into a kitchenette and then two rooms, one with a table and chairs, the other with a bed; flowers on the table, roadside stuff, wilting in a jar, and by the bed a candle stuck in a candlestick shaped like a snake, the flat head the candle holder, the curled tail the base.

'The landlady's,' he said, disowning it. 'She threatened as much.'

'And the flowers?'

'There was a crop of them, Stamford way. I drove here and back the day before yesterday, to sort it all out. Surprised you didn't notice, the bags under my eyes.'

'Before you asked me even?'

She stood in the passageway taking in the two rooms, thrilled. The plain wooden table, the two upright chairs, the naked light bulb over the mattress, its aversion to comfort, to permanence, the faith it was asking of her, she loved it all. There was nothing to hide behind here, no props, no distractions, nothing to bind them, nothing to keep them.

'I could get a sofa in, if you like, for the front room,' he said, watching her closely. 'Though it's just bricks and mortar.'

'Where would it go?' she laughed. 'On the table?'

She moved back out into the yard. It was dark, the sky hidden. It was 1967. She was three months off twenty-one. The things she had known, the friends she had made, the expectations of her time (*her* time, she'd been told) had blown away. They had no call on her now.

This was how it started, their two rooms and the shared bathroom with the perilous flooring on the first landing, the couple above them burdened with a young boy, Finley, never at school, who would race up and down all day until sleep felled him, nine-thirty sharp. That first full day, the Saturday, Louis was gone first light, money from the last job wrapped in a rubber band and stuffed into the back pocket of her jeans draped over the foot of their bed. It was scary, the way they had folded their clothes carefully before getting into bed, the formality of it, like they had been together for years, like the newness had already rubbed off, like they knew everything about each other. She had laid hers across the end nearest the window, he the end near the door. They had stood facing each other across the divide. One pillow. One sheet. One blanket.

'The pillow's for you,' he had said. 'I'm not one for pillows.'

She nodded, an extraordinary lightness suddenly blossoming within her, realising that she had no need for them either. Or anything. She took it and dropped it on the floor.

'A redundancy of pillows, then,' she said.

And that had been that.

Sitting up she reached out and snapped the rubber band clean out the window and laid the money on her lap. Hundreds of pounds she counted. Hundreds.

She walked up to the bathroom, washed herself where it mattered with the flannel she had brought (cold water, for she had no change for the meter), dressed in yesterday's clothes and went out herself after eating a tin of peaches she found in the kitchen cupboard. Tinned peaches, tinned peas, tinned meat and tinned puddings. There was no fridge. Outside, it was colder than she had expected, so she returned for the one jacket she possessed, a second-hand, dark blue, striped affair, like a businessman's jacket, but with a bust and declamatory badges down the left lapel. Walking into town she noticed any number of women of her own age, preoccupied as she had been with their youth, their manner, the flick of their eyes, on their way to work or elsewhere, waiting for buses, talking amongst themselves, elbowing their way into their future, but she felt no affinity with them, rather the opposite, a sort of distaste, and she thought, hurrying through, she would get rid of it, this little jacket and its student history as soon as she could. Even the music she had loved, her record collection, imported soul, the forty-fives protected in their dust covers, the most precious things that had been hers and hers alone, meant nothing to her now. Not for a moment had she considered bringing them with her. They would have been as weights around her neck. They could have drowned her.

He was back at eight. She had the corned beef shredded and mashed into the potato, a tinned steam pudding simmering in the one pan and four bottles of brown ale she'd bought at the nearest off-licence floating in a sink of cold water. They had milk now too, and bread and jam and Irish butter. Irish butter and Irish whisky he had once told her, quite drunk, can't be beaten, and she had bought a bottle of Paddy, the brand she had known from the pub, and had stood it on the table in place of the faded flowers. The rest of the money and the change was laid out next to it. He opened up the Paddy and put his hat over the money, like he didn't want to see it. He poured a shot of whisky into the cap, one for her, one for him: they shot them back like they were medicine. They went up to the first floor where she ran the bath while he banged two beer caps free on the windowsill. She sat on the edge drinking, watching him undress, lower himself in, the first time she had seen the skin on his back. Three times she had been with him and this the first time she'd taken a proper look at his back.

'What is it,' she said, 'bits of snake?' thinking of the candlestick, thinking there might be a message here, something she didn't know, like he belonged to a secret society, like in one of those Sherlock Holmes stories she'd read. Her dad had all the Sherlock Holmes at home. Her dad.

'Bits of snake!' He half-turned to show her, water lapping over the sides. 'It's the road, can't you see, the Great North, the sections I've been a part of. I'll end up with a tattoo from my arse to Edinburgh, if God wills it. God or McAlpine. There's a man in Worksop who does them, Eddie, Eddie the Squint. Better than a cartographer. Passports too, driving licences, he can do anything. It's to scale, see. Don't you think it adds something to a man's back?'

'And the gaps would be … where you've yet to work on it? Jesus.' She followed her fingers down it, a tremor of thought running up her spine. 'Why just a man's? Could he not fix something suitable on a woman's?'

'Yours you mean? Your skin's too … Christ, you've a woman's skin. What do you want a tattoo for? What would you be having, any road?' She gave it a poke.

'Not an unfinished jigsaw puzzle, that's for sure. And not on my back. Somewhere I could see it. Do you all have tattoos like this? Or is it just you who's crazy?'

'Crazy?' He handed her the soap, lifted his leg. 'We're the sanest men you'll ever know. We build tunnels for the badgers. The updraught gives falcons and buzzards fresh hunting ground. Those flowers? Half the men working with me can name them. All the time you're digging, you're learning about what went where, different rocks and soils, not to mention Romans and Gauls and Iron Age forts, just beneath your feet, wherever you go. And it ends up a motorway, floating over it all, easing the rider through. Wait until you've seen one finished, you'll see, laid out like a virgin bride on her marriage bed, not a mark on her, aching for the first touch.'

He drank from his bottle, desperate to relieve his throat. She doubted he had ever spoken longer.

'So that's what it was,' she said.

'What?'

'The gorse bush. That's your dream, is it?'

'What you on about?'

She soaped his foot. He knew all right.

'And this rider on the road? On a horse now, is he?' He swallowed the last of it the wrong way, waved the bottle in the air, choking on his words.

'He might be driving a car, but he's stuck in the saddle, riding the motorway. We have to think of everything, how it's done, the consequences, where the water runs off, where the fog might come down or the snow might drift. It's a rough life, 'cause you have to work it, whatever the weather, whatever's thrown at you. We had a swarm of flies once, coming out of nowhere like a herd of buffalo, you wouldn't believe it the noise they made, swarming into every hole going, sending us all running like Egyptians, like the Red Sea was closing in on us.'

'Well, no flies on you today.'

She told him. How she had gone to the bus station, learnt the number of the bus that would take her closest to where she wanted, sat there impatient, waiting for the driver to climb in and turn the engine over, how it took her there eventually, the town stuttering to a halt like an old man out of breath, setting her down within a mile of it, how she'd walked until she found a vantage point, a field, from where she could see it all, where he was working, the new section of the A1, Bowburn to Bradbury, spread out before her like an army preparing for battle, the sprawl of Portakabins and generators, the broad, metalled track seared into the land to the rear, a convoy of giant, what were they, twelve-wheelers? tortuous in their approach, belching towards an area ahead of the camp, great flattened monsters roped on to their backs. She'd sat there, caught by the scope of it, waiting for the machines to start up, for something to happen, to drink in the noise of these men, the sound of their work, but nothing did. She wasn't disappointed. She had glimpsed the measure of it, its size, its implacability, its tenacious, orchestrated power, and it had excited her.

'Keeping an eye on me?'

She shook her head. She was fearless now.

'It's mine too now, this road you're so proud of. And this Eddie of yours. Fuck the cartography. He can do me a proper snake, a cobra running up the front of me, tail round my belly button, head poking out the top, with his little tongue darting out, like he was going to come all over me.'

She had never promised herself anything as intense. It was just the start. It was like she'd lain down on one of his blessed roads, been driven right over it, sort of flattened out by one of the Euclids or RB10s he went on about, like she'd been pressed through the softened skin of it into its solid core, become part of its structure. Soon, she knew all about motorways, how they were built and the men who built them. She learnt that Louis had the bead on it, this stripping of the earth, understood the surveyor's eye and the engineer's requirements, could read the land, its layers of difficulty, as good as any professional. They always hired Louis if they could. It made her proud, the way he took things on, wrestled them to the ground. They put it down to the Celt in him, though he professed to have none. He was a muck-shifter that was all, clearing the land, levelling it out, cutting through hills, building up escarpments, fashioning the gradient. The thing about muck, he explained, was that it didn't lie still. It was like a sea, vast, full of wind and treachery, inventive in its troubles; quicksand, marshland, floodplains, hard indigestible rock. Muck could have you sliding about on your forty-ton shoveller like a one-day foal on ice. Muck could open up and swallow you whole.

It wasn't long before she got to know them too, the men that worked with him, men who followed him if they could, like he was a scout taking a wagon train across the Great Plains, with a frontier folklore of their own. Heroes and villains and the road they travelled. Not like the men she'd known up till then, this wild, motley crew; proud, antagonistic to outsiders, irrational, drawn together by the thing itself, the motorway and the machines upon it: Hogan, the bare-knuckle boxer from County Mayo; Pete Harris, the country-and-western fanatic; the twins, Brummie One and Brummie Two; and Gil from Pontypridd, with his gold watch and his Jack Russell who could balance a cooked sausage on his snout and not move a muscle until Gil gave him the nod. Others came and went, but always Hogan, Pete, the Brummies and Gil, men with selective pasts, all of them. The vagaries of their work, the intransigence of their lodging houses, the unforgiving deadline, they cared not a jot for any of it. They found happiness on the machines they drove, that was all. They were in love with them, their simple stubborn ways. Taken away from them, they were like widowers or bitter divorcees, cut loose from the regulated ease of what they knew, what they wanted to know, what they expected, their routine, their unhealthy cabins of comfort. Torn loose, they would grow irritable, would drink too much, and take to brawling and losing money.

She met them first on the following Friday, their shift finished at four-thirty, in the pub by six, all of them washed and brushed up for the occasion, sitting in a line along a set of tables, not one of them trying to hide their curiosity. She was curious too, sensed the long camaraderie that bound them all. Louis introduced them with a sweep of the hand. She sat down, conscious of the thin straps on her shoulders, what they held. They were men, these men. She'd never sat with a bunch of men before. She liked it.

Pete patted the sides of his silver hair, adjusted his tie. It wasn't like a proper tie. It had little tassels hanging down. She tried not to look.

'He never said, you know, the coyote. If he had I'd have hitched up the wagon, driven down to warn you.'

He beckoned with a nicotine-stained finger. She put her head close.

'Did he not tell you,' he said, looking up back at him, 'the years on the old horse?'

'He did.'

'And it didn't put you right off? It puts me off just thinking about it.'

'Do what I do. Don't think about it. The wrinkles just fade away.'

'Fade away!' Brummie One said. 'That's a good one.'

Pete wasn't finished.

'And his history lessons. Worse than a teacher with a bent ruler. Did he warn you of that?'

'I had a double dose, coming up. It's like having the measles. I'm immune now. It just rolls off me, nothing taken in.'

The twins spoke in unison.

'Nothing taken in!'

Pete cleared a little path through the strew of glasses, as if he wanted no obstructions.

'But the women? Did he tell you about the other women? McAlpine usually has a slip road built special, for Louis's women.'

'Peter,' Louis warned. Alice raised her glass.

'It was a relief to hear he'd had so many. I've had it with amateurs. And who's the ultimate beneficiary? Them or me? Ask yourself that. Here's to them all. The Practice Ground.'

They raised their glasses. All except Hogan.

'The Practice Ground!'

'Sod the other women,' said Hogan. He held his glass in the air. 'Here's to our Alice. The cream of the crop.'

They drained their glasses in silence. Louis got to his feet.

'My round then.' He bent forward, one hand on her bare shoulder as he leant over to pick up her glass.

'You're in,' he said, and laid his lips on her head.

Three months they stayed in that flat, but the Durham bypass lasted a good deal longer than that. Aycliffe to Chester-le-Street, Chester-le-Street to Carrville, Carrville to Bowburn, Bowburn to Bradbury. What a time they had of it. He'd be away working when he had to be, back when the day or the drinking was done, it didn't matter. Didn't matter where they stayed either, up and left as the fancy took them, if he found digs closer to where he was working, or they fell out with the landlady or the baby downstairs cried too much. There was always a reason for leaving, for stuffing what they had into a couple of bags and fucking off out of it. 'Let's fuck off out of it,' he would say and they could be gone in ten minutes, sod the rent paid or the rent due. Out in ten minutes! Who else had she known who could do that! And the money he was earning! They spent it on nothing. Friday night drinking with the boys through to Saturday afternoon, then it was off themselves, ripping round the countryside, the drink on his breath, hers too, out to the coast, or up on the moors, damn the weather, walking along the northern sands, stripping for freezing hill pools, fiercely suspicious, giving nothing to no one, sniffing the world out. Those early years, they could barely keep still. He was the most animal creature she'd ever met. When driving he insisted she read the routes for him, wouldn't turn right or left until she told him when.

'Why, for God's sake? They got signs, telling you where to go.'

'And we're supposed to obey them, is that it? You need to learn, girl, learn how to read a map, read a road, keep your eyes peeled. Otherwise God knows where we'll end up.'

No fear of that. He seemed to have memorised every road in Great Britain, could draw her a map of almost any county he'd been to, roads running like veins on a leaf. He knew them all, the M this, the A that. You take the A something, turn left on the B whatever, stabbing the route out with his finger. Later he taught her to drive for real. Taught her to drive and taught her the names of wild flowers and she learnt the first quicker than she learnt the second. He'd bring back a paper most nights and she'd read it the next day, but nothing of it seemed to matter, what was happening. How was that? It was like she had stepped into a different time zone, and was watching it from afar, like an observer, not mixed up in it at all. Her jacket with its labels had long gone. She'd left it behind somewhere, a pub most likely, or a sea wall. A Woman's Right to Choose. What did it mean? What did it mean more than this? What about a woman's right to change a wheel, or a woman's right to bypass the electricity meter? A woman's right to skin a rabbit? A woman's right to shoot a twelve-bore? He had one of those too, under the front seat of whatever he was driving, showed it to her the third week they were together, took her out into the hills, walked a way on to the moor with this overnight bag she had never seen before, like you see at airports. She thought they were going for a picnic, or he'd brought a sleeping bag so they could stay out all night, until he asked her to open it up. Her eyes went all pinball, like when they were making love, like he was taking her somewhere unexpected.

'Take it out,' he said. 'You do it, so you won't be frightened.'

'Of what?'

'Of me. That I should bring you up here with that in my bag.'

She gave him a look and took it out. It was folded up, in half almost.

'There's cartridges in the side pocket. You put them in, one by one, the soft end in first. Go on.'

She slotted them in, her fingers perfect steady. She was surprised at her calm.

'Now snap it together,' he told her. 'You must have seen it in the films.'

She shook her head, but did it anyway.

'Now hold it up, the butt pressed into your shoulder. It feels heavy but it's not really. It only seems that way, the way the barrel only seems long. It isn't really. You put your right eye up to the sight, don't close the other, and look down. Now swing it about a bit, to get the feel of it, out and up like you were brushing cobwebs off a ceiling, left to right, in an arc. Feel how light it is really, how it wants to move with you, like it's thick, like cream. Now. See that sheep up there? That's your target. Don't worry. You won't hit her, not at this distance. Just look at twelve o'clock to her three, and then, when you feel it right, when you see the booby move, swing it over and let it go. Just swing over and give it all a squeeze, like from your cunt upwards, like you want to make both of you come. Don't tense your shoulder, or you'll dislocate something. You'll get a terrible bang in your ear but it won't be as bad as you think it is. Go on. Shoot the Brebis.'

'Brebis?'

'That's what the French call them. It sounds better than sheep. Go on now.'

She looked away. She could see cars in the distance below. Police cars most probably coming up to arrest them. Or farmers with shotguns of their own. The Brebis looked up. She swung and let it go, the jolt running through her body. She felt fizzy inside, like someone had shaken her. The Brebis had disappeared.

'Can I try again? I like it. The way it jumps in your hands.'

'Don't talk filthy.' He moved in close, handed her two more.

'Empty the first, then slot in these. That's it. Just let them drop to the ground. It's a good smell, don't you think. Hangs nice in the air. Like in our room after an afternoon of it.'

She did it again, the Brebis only in her imagination. He was right. The gun was heavy and yet it wasn't. It sort of fitted, felt natural.

'I could do this all day,' she said.

'Can you say that in Spanish?'

'That's unworthy of you,' she said.

'Once more then. And then every weekend until that Brebis would run at the very sight of you.'

'And then what will I be shooting?'

'Whatever you need to. It's a necessity, see, denied to most.'

'Not legal then, this gun that you've kept hid from me all this time?' He slipped the cartridges on to her palm.

'And your driving licence is where, madam?'

It thrilled her again, to hear him talk like that, like they were outlaws, outside of everything. A streak, a shadow, slipped up by the rock where the ewe had stood. A fox, crossing the scrub skyline. She lifted the gun. Straight away his hand came out, pushing the barrel down.

'Not him,' he said. 'Never him, not even in jest. He's one of us.'

She could do so many things. She could make jam out of wild roses, out of nettles; she knew what mushrooms to pick, what to feed hedgehogs with. She could sink pints, drink whisky chasers, brew lager in a bucket, play cards, throw a decent dart and subtract from 501. She could jack up a wheel, change a tyre, clean the spark plugs, drain the oil. She could fashion a slip knot, lay a rabbit snare, shave a man with a cut-throat razor and raise not a drop of blood. No ironing though. Whenever he needed an ironed shirt for going out, for he liked to look smart going out, he did his own, wouldn't let her within a mile of the iron, was a miracle worker with the thing (he owned one, would you credit it, a little black snub-nosed object, almost foreign-looking, heavy as fuck), spitting on its flat surface, slapping it with his hand, testing the temperature, shaking water from his fingertips over the collar like he was a priest at the altar. 'You're better than my mother,' she told him. 'I'm better than anybody's mother,' he said. 'I had to be.' A year after she could drive, he bought a delivery van from a bankrupt furniture store, and she learnt to manhandle that too, lived in the back of it for three months that summer, was better than him at reversing, judging spaces, which was strange considering his line of work. It was where they gained the habit of washing each other down, standing outside the back of the van in a tin bath, while the other went to work with a bucket and a flannel. The soap was scentless, almost gritty, the flannel rough. It was a serious business washing another person's body, and it was done without frivolity, methodically, a hygienic examination of one another's skin. She saw the age in his muscle then, how under the surface his work had taken its toll, older flesh welded on to a younger man's bones. And he, he washed her in small circular movements, like he was cleaning silver, a patch at a time. He could take an hour at it if he had a mind to, sent her into a sort of trance, like she was somewhere else while he attended to what was left. It drew them close, who they were not, what they did not want to do. Even when they had use of a bathroom, they would wash themselves this way, him particularly after a day's work. And if they had use of a yard, bathroom or no bathroom, he preferred to be washed there, even in the winter months, arms by his side, standing patiently, while steam from the water rose up in clouds, like a hot spring.

And what did she do, while he was not there? To begin with, if you had asked her she could not have been able to tell you. She was not aware of it, the separation of time.

23

She must have been suspended, preparing for his return, not cleaning their room or getting his food ready – for she discovered that they did not care for food much, save for the sight and sound of it on fish and chips or greasy sausages or, the treasure of travelling, cold meat pies with a surfeit of jelly – but living somewhere distant in her head, of what he was and what they would be, of the uncharted waters she had ventured upon, how he was both the sea and the land, the unknown and the proven, that she knew nothing of him and little of herself either, save she was young and brave and certain of what she had done. The hours came and went and at the end of it he returned, and she was dependable in both, never wavering, never bored, never doubting. At some stage, without asking, she bought a bicycle, a man's bike, straight handlebars, a fraction too big, which she rode, not to discover the countryside, but to work her legs and her upper torso, to become strong and physical like him, to work sweat upon her muscle, to enjoy the sensation of exertion, of leaving things behind. In time she could cycle for hours and not know where she had been, not care, barely notice. And all this time, all the words they spoke, the acts of their bodies within and without, she learnt nothing of his history. He was a stranger then, with a stranger's face, but what of it? What did they need of memory, her and Louis? He was he and she was she and that was the end to it. It gave them the room they needed. They would become, that was it. What it was, she couldn't say.

When the Carrville to Bowburn section was ready for traffic, 1969, Chester-le-Street to Carrville but a few months away, Louis took her there a week before it opened, midnight, half a bottle of whisky under the front seat and the remains of a fish-and-chip supper screwed up on the floor, the road cleared of all the working detritus, ghosts in the air. It was like what a theatre must look like when they pulled the curtain back, she thought, an idea painted on the set with a set of brushes, waiting for the dancers to come along. She had learnt ballet at school until she was thirteen, until a thickness had come upon her frame that had her ballet teacher looking the other way whenever she saw her dancing. He drove the van on and parked it across the two lanes, switched off the engine.

'Look at it,' he said. 'Is that not the most beautiful sight you have ever seen?'

And it was so. She had never seen anything so pure, like a poem on a page, gathering the world up in its wake. She wanted to dance on it, pirouette up and down the lane, walk on her hands ...

'That's where you swam aboard, you freeloader,' she later told the child, when he understood nothing but the tone of her voice, but she didn't tell him the whole story, their bed he had waiting there, smack in the middle of the fast lane, the way they walked down towards it, the way they'd undressed standing either side of it, as if they were home, deliberately hanging their clothes over the edge, hers to the right, his to the left, the feathery warmth of the night, the slow, deliberate care they took, the way he lay down, the way she covered him, the way his hands spread out as he lifted himself high in the air, like he was almost floating inside her, more a thought than a body, not a bed nor a road at all.

'You got your dream after all,' she said. 'Do you think they can see us?'

'Who?'

'Neil Armstrong and the other one.'

'Is it tonight?'

'You know it is. If we had a television we could have watched it, like the rest of the world.'

'Would you rather be sat watching a couple of Yanks scuffing up moon dust than being here?' He ran his hands up into the pits of her arms, took the weight of her into his.

'It's historic.'

'This isn't? There'll be other men on the moon, but no one will ever do this again. And all we needed was a clapped-out Bedford and a drop of petrol.' He tilted his head back. 'Besides, they've probably left by now. No stamina the Yanks, no sense of permanence. Everything's a plaything to them.'

She knew they hadn't. She could see the moon and the moon could see her. She could feel the glow of it on her breasts, feel the light from her body beaming through space, feel Armstrong's eyes full upon her as she leant back, showed him how to make love in the luminous dark. It was like Armstrong had landed there just so he could stand in her shadow, see it all from the great length of space, the white virgin territory of the road, her body radiant upon it and a presence reaching up underneath. It was almost as if she could stretch out and touch this brave American, he in his hermetic and swaddled suit, and she, uncoiled and naked, raised up in the arms of the earth. The whole of heaven was watching her, the whole of life itself. She was the beginning and the end, the journey and the destination and for a moment she saw it all.

'Holy Mary, Mother of God,' she said. 'Touch me.'

And who it was who did it, touched her, touched her like it was the first footprint on her soul, Armstrong, Louis or the

Archangel Gabriel, she never knew. A drop of all three, she imagined, thick like cream, perfect like an egg.

Louis's work on the motorway finished, they drove down to Worksop, he to have Junctions 59 to 63 inked upon his back and she to have a snake wrought upon her front. Louis had sat in the room while she had lain, reclining on a raised cushion, surrounded by anglepoise lamps. It had taken three days to complete, three days of discomfort and drink, Eddie the Squint with his one good eye hovering over every inch of her, Louis sitting in a deckchair, sipping bottled beer. The trickiest part was the snake's head. Eddie had to hold her right breast aside while Alice had pulled at the other. Louis was up on his feet, watching.

'Not many you've pricked with skin like that, Eddie, I'll be bound.'

Eddie the Squint held the needle to the light.

'It's the best tone I've seen this side of the Atlantic, though the tattooed woman is not as rare a sight as it once was. Bikers,' he explained. 'Shoulders usually or something on the ankle.'

'Ankle? What bloody use is that?'

'My sentiments entirely. This now. What could be more fitting on the body of a young woman than a venomous snake coiling up from you-know-where. Are you going to give it a name?'

'We are not. And don't make his head too big. I don't want any unfortunate comparisons going on there, do you understand me?'

Eddie understood, though it had a presence, the snake, rising up out of her cleavage like it was coming up for air. The head was flat and flecked with black and green. There was no tongue. The tongue, Eddie had explained, would become an irritant, like a fly she'd want to swat but never could. Instead the head was twisted round so that it was staring straight at you with its eyes.

To celebrate that night they went to a nightclub, three miles outside Worksop. A working men's club with a scrupulously stocked bar, tables with Cinzano lampshades on them. A crooner in a bow tie, a comedy act peppered with jokes concerning the Irish, which neither approved. But there was dancing on the dance floor. For the first time in two and a half years she felt the pull of it. He sensed it too.

'You should dance,' he said. 'A woman like you.'

'Dance with who?'

'Not me. Anyone you care to. The devil if needs be. It was wrong of me not to think of it. A woman of your disposition.'

She touched the top button of her blouse, an act of bare containment. She would like to dance. They knew their soul in Worksop. No crap white bands aping their betters. Just the business. She knew all the records, could name the B sides of most of them had anyone the nerve to ask. There was a lad watching her from the dance floor. Intense face. Thin like he never ate. Danced with tight, controlled energy, like he could fornicate for hours and never drop a stitch. She tore her eyes away.

'I got most of these back ...' She nearly said it. 'Back at Mum and Dad's. 'Best collection in the county, I had.'

'But you didn't bring them with you.'

'You know why.'

He nodded.

'No room for them then.'

'No room for them now, Louis.'

'There's a truth in that.'

The lad came over. Slim shirt, well-cut pair of trousers, slightly feminine shoes. His hair was clipped tidy too. She liked the look of him. She'd never liked long hair. Not on a man. He hooked a thumb in his belt, chancing it.

'Your dad let you dance with strangers?'

Louis laughed.

'Take her then. Mind you bring her back a virgin.'

Once on the floor she took her own path. Dancing to her music again, it was like she'd never left. The lad let her go her own way, following her with a predatory patience that was just right, then moved in closer, showing what he'd got.

'That's a nice snake you got there,' he said. 'Does it go all the way?'

She stopped him right there, the pleasure gone.

'Don't,' she said. 'Be a man next time. Accept it. A woman's right to choose.'

She walked back to the table. She had just made herself a new rule. Only the ones who didn't comment on it. The rest could go fuck themselves.

───────

'Do you think about your mum and dad at all?'

It was early September, the same year. The work was over and they were driving down towards Scotch Corner, a little convoy of them, she and Louis in their two-door, 1963 Ford

Consul Capri, Pete and the Brummie twins wedged in Pete's Morris 1100, and Hogan on his 1962 Triumph Tiger, Gil on pillion with his Jack Russell tucked inside his overcoat, all making for the hotel and an afternoon session before the run down to Huddersfield, the M62 and the Scammonden Dam. Word had it they were laying the top down, and Hogan's brother was working on a spreading machine. There'd be other men there they knew. She'd never seen a bunch of men so fired up.

Scammonden Dam, Scammonden Dam. Hadn't she heard the lot of it, all those years' work, seven miles across the moor from Lancashire to the edge of Huddersfield, for what would be just six minutes of driving. Hadn't she heard about the landslides, and the snowstorms and the rainfall and the clouds that swept down without warning, Hogan wrestling with a forty-ton 54 RB, worse than white-out on a 707. Then there was the Scammonden Arch itself, longest single span in Europe, slim like a longbow, strong enough for winds over a hundred miles an hour. Now, after all the talk, she was finally getting to see it, though they had been slow to start, Louis fussing with the car, wiping the headlights, filling the radiator with antifreeze, loading the boot up with a bag of sand and a shovel.

'The North Pole has nothing on that place,' he said, as she watched him stuff a torch and a compass into the glove compartment, and she'd let it pass as she settled down behind the wheel. Truth was she enjoyed hearing him tell the same stories over and over again, noting the differences in the telling depending on his mood, the amount of drink inside him, the audience. 'No wonder it's taken longer than expected. Straight from hell, that weather, pitiless ... it had a spirit to it, you know, what with the howling and the ceaseless stretch of it. It could turn a man to terrible things …' He'd pulled at the memory. 'You won't understand, when you see it, what we went through. It'll be all smoothed out, like a fucking billiard table, like the battle was never fought. Still, I suppose you're going to see it before …'

He never liked to say it. She'd goaded him. It was part of the equation he could never reconcile.

'Yes?'

'All right. Before it gets driven on.'

'Listen to yourself.'

'So, I admit it. I'm jealous when it comes to roads I've had a hand in, those bastards who drive on them. What do they know, rushing over it like they were in a race, like they don't give a damn. It's the paradox of the motorway, the neglect it must suffer. If I had my way …' He moved in his seat.

'Go on, out with it …'

'You know what. They should set a proper speed limit, forty miles an hour. Forty miles an hour is an ideal speed for travelling. Gives you time to think, to see what you're passing through, make sense of it.' He'd spread his hand on her belly. 'Gives you time for a lot of things.'

'We were on a bed, Louis. We weren't going anywhere.'

'But I drove you there at a proper speed, without your insides all shaken up.'

So now they were finally on their way to Scammonden Dam, she was near two months pregnant and he was talking about her parents. He'd been nonplussed about the pregnancy, like he didn't expect it, like he thought he must have done something out of kilter, eaten something, drunk something, made himself unusually potent. 'What do you think it was,' he'd said when first told, 'the fish? I had haddock that night, not the cod, don't ask me why. Is there more oomph to a haddock, do you think?' and she'd tried not to laugh, seeing the serious expression on his face. He had an unlikely faith in superstitions and old wives' tales, despite the practicalities of their life. Driving a scraper under a thunderstorm gave him no bother, but should they be indoors when lightning lit the sky, he'd scuttle over and cover up the mirror (if they had one). Did she think about them? Hardly at all.

'Do you think they're happy?'

'With me gone, you mean?'

'That's exactly it. With you gone. I mean brothers and sisters. Do you have any?'

It was the first time he'd asked. It was extraordinary, what they didn't want to know of each other. She shook her head, eyes stuck to the road. It had taken some getting used to, driving at this forty miles an hour, for once she'd learnt, she'd taken to the feel of it, speed, putting the foot down, swinging the car out and overtaking. He'd soon put a stop to that. The fallacy of the indicator, he called it, and for a time banned her from using it, save for turning, so that she learnt how to drive as they should be driven. 'Drive faster if you must, but keep to this and after six months, it'll be like giving up sugar. You'll never want to taste speed again.' Now, there seemed no point in going any faster and it was only by accident that she exceeded it. There was great comfort in forty miles an hour, great purpose. It was as if you were refusing to be deflected, like the regularity of a heartbeat or a footstep, plain and solid and simple. On a long drive forty miles an hour was like a spell of elongated lovemaking, slow and steady and immensely satisfying. Thick like cream. Perfect like an egg.

She stuck her hand into the recess where the radio had been (he ripped out the radio of every car they had: 'It's either you and me or the wailing wall of conjugal silence' was how he put it) and dug out a handful of raisins from the bag. They'd be leaving the North East soon, now his work was done. He might hear of something from one of the crews still working the dam, and if he didn't, he'd make a few calls. There was loose change under the dashboard.

'How close were you then?'

She thought he was referring to her driving, for momentarily she had let the needle drift up to forty-five, but, as he dismissed her quick touch of brake with an almost imperceptible wave of his hand, she understood. Had she been close to them, her mum, her dad? She'd believed she had been, right up till the hour he had appeared and then everything had dropped away and she had realised she was not, neither of them, perhaps hadn't been for years. Her ability to cut loose had been as simple as crossing the road. Going to college had been harder than leaving for good, living in those communal quarters, making friends she didn't need. It had been a fabrication, someone else's life.

'I was thinking,' he continued, not waiting for her to answer, 'you might like to go and see them. Maybe we could find room for those records of yours. You could dance to them. I'd like that, the snake weaving about like a hypnotist.'

She looked down at herself. Underneath her clothes, the snake's lower half had taken on a sort of glow, like he'd been recently fed. His expression had changed too. He looked surprised now. How was that possible?

'Forget the records. You don't mean it anyway. You'd hate them here. Why all this about my parents all of a sudden?'

'I don't give a fuck about your parents, Alice, understand? I mean not a fuck. I was thinking, rather than Scammonden you might ...'

He let the sentence fall, uncompleted.

Scotch Corner was what it looked like, a railway hotel without a railway, but convinced of its self-importance. They'd stopped there once before, on their way back from Worksop, the first time she'd ever been in a hotel. She didn't like it much, wide, empty corridors and nothing to write home about at the end of them. Louis knew it well. A right Piccadilly Circus, he said, and the spot it marks, a junction, Cumbria, the North East, Scotland. You get all sorts, salesmen, lorry drivers, runaways making for Gretna Green, folk turning off on to the A66 to Glasgow or stopping off before the run up the A1 to Edinburgh. It was like a dog lifting his leg, Scotch Corner. It made its mark.

Hogan was sat in the big lounge, at one of the drinking tables, surrounded by red leather chairs and potted plants, Gil's little dog on his lap. He had a plate of torn crusts on the table and a squad of empty glasses, all different sizes.

'Where's Gil?' Louis said, walking in. 'Did he fall off then?'

'He's calling his mother. You should have put your foot down, we're three drinks ahead of you already.'

Louis sat himself down at the table. Alice went to the bar. The woman behind it was wiping down the surface with a grey dishcloth. Gil drank lager, the Brummie twins brown ale, bottled. Louis drank pints, straight glasses. So did she. Louis liked to tip a packet of salted peanuts into his, let them ferment a while before eating them. Hogan, there was no knowing what he drank. He went from one drink to another.

'What you drinking, Hogan?' she sang out.

'Yes please,' he said. Louis laughed. The woman behind the bar smiled with him, threw the rag into a little sink under her hands, then called right across her, as if Alice weren't there.

'How's it going, Louis?' Louis hardly turned in his seat.

'We're taking a break.'

'Scarborough, is it? I hear they've been having cracking weather the last few weeks.'

'Scammonden.'

'Jesus,' the woman said. 'I'd have thought you'd have had your fill of that.'

She dealt out the first two pints. She was a striking woman, forty, forty-five, not good-looking, but with a sense of the impact she made. She had big, fleshy arms and big, ringed hands and her hair was fiercely dyed, a kind of fiery dark brown, piled up in a messy heap, her eyes sunk in black eyeshadow. She looked like a nightclub singer, or a saloon-bar hostess, strong and sassy and difficult. She'd hit a man if she had a mind to, Alice thought, lay him out, no questions asked. Her make-up was crude, heavy under the eyes, thick under the chin. She was strongly perfumed, with an underlying sourness lying beneath it, as if she was the sort of woman who needed to wash more often than she did, more often than she could be bothered.

'Scarborough's nothing special,' Louis told her. 'Kiss Me Quick stuff, that's all.'

'Thanks very much,' the woman said.

'Don't mention it.'

Alice ordered Hogan a brandy and soda, carried the tray back.

'You know her?' she asked Louis, sitting opposite. Louis moved his pint about, like the first time they'd met.

'She used to run a little mobile café,' Louis said, 'the Pot Hole, followed the gangs about, all hours. Isn't that right, Lot. You were our administering angel.'

'No saving you devils.'

Louis tipped his peanuts in, watched them sink to the bottom. The woman had the dishcloth back in her hand, working it up and down like the bar was made out of brass.

'So, how do you find it here, under the cosh all day?' Louis asked. He wasn't looking at her at all. Like he was just being polite.

'Cosy,' she said. 'Like I said at the time, if I ever got off that damn dam alive, that was an end of it, freezing my arse off just so you boys could have a bacon butty. And you're going back?'

Hogan examined his brandy.

'My brother's gone up in the world, working on the spreader, Lot. Says he's found a man who can lay a line as true as Louis here.'

'That'll be the day.'

'And the van?' Hogan said. 'You got rid of it?'

'It's up on bricks. Couldn't even find a buyer. These motorway stations, they've got it all sewn up, even for the likes of you.'

Gil came through the big doors. The Jack Russell began wiping Hogan's face with his tail. Hogan didn't seem to mind.

'Pete's just parked up,' Gil announced. 'Says you drove straight past him, Louis, could hardly see you for the blur.' He tapped his watch. 'Record time.'

More laughter, the woman too. She seemed to know everything about them.

Pete Harris came in, combing back his white hair, the twins following. He wore a black shirt with country-and-western sequins stitched round the collar. The twins wore matching blue jerseys and loose trousers. They looked older than they were, russet-apple cheeks like pensioners, but tough little bodies underneath. They could go a whole evening without saying a word, but it was like you didn't even notice, the way they joined in, got their rounds in and went with the mood wherever it was going. They were good in a fight, the twins. It disconcerted the opposition, seeing two of them up for it. Alice went back up to the bar, got the extra beer in. They were all beer drinkers when it came down to it.

'Have you heard the weather?' Pete said. 'It's not looking good. Rain coming in from the west. Fog too. They might have to postpone it for a day or two.'

Louis stuck his hand in, drew out a clutch of peanuts.

'There's no point in going if they're not laying,' he said.

Gil clicked his tongue, loud like a clock. The Jack Russell kicked Hogan in the face and jumped into Gil's arms.

'Why don't we swing by the coast, a couple of days at the beach,' he said, brightening to the idea. 'You'd like that, wouldn't you, darling?' He tickled his dog behind the ears. 'What are the women like in Scarborough, Lot? Would they have seen a black man before, be prepared to try one out?'

'Scarborough?' The twins spoke as one. Pete nodded.

'They've been having some plum weather there.'

'Scarborough?' they repeated. Brummie One said, 'We've no objection to Scarborough. Fact is, we've never been to the sea.'

'Not even dipped a bunion in,' added his brother. 'Seen it from a train once.'

Hogan opened his hands out, like they were claws.

'You can swim in the sodding dam, if you're that desperate.' Louis was adamant.

'Dead water,' he objected. 'Water's got to be on the move for it to be any good.'

Hogan's hands rose high in the air, like he was holding weights.

'What's got into you?' he demanded. 'Here's my brother laying his first topping and you don't want us to see him? I know what you think of him, Louis, don't you think I don't, but he's as good a man as any here, and that's a fact.'

Hogan swept up the empties and set off for the bar.

'We ought to go,' Pete muttered. The Brummie twins nodded. Every time she saw them, Alice never failed to marvel at it, the way they could do things like they'd rehearsed it, like they were in a chorus line. Gil lifted one of the dog's ears.

'Another time, sweetheart. Promise. It is his brother after all.' Louis tipped the glass to his lips.

'So we what, stand in the rain and wait for the fog to lift so we can watch him toss himself off. Where's the sense in that?' Hogan turned.

'I heard that. We're going and that's that. Blow that up your clanky arse.'

'Boys. Language please. You're not in the Klondike now.' Lot's smile had gone. Hogan carried the tray back carefully, set the drinks down one by one, a glass in front of each man, then Alice's. It happened that way all the time. She could never work out whether she should be pleased or affronted.

'Now just to make it clear about whether we're going or not,' he said, sitting down, rubbing his hands together like he was washing them. 'Who'd like their drink over their fucking heads?'

They laughed. They were going now, though other arguments went back and forth, drink piling up. It was that kind of session. There'd be no more travelling today, east or west. At some point, Alice went to the cloakroom and, coming back, stood in the doorway. She saw them huddled and fuzzy, their words popping out their mouths like little fireworks, their heads bobbing back and forth like ping-pong balls floating on the surface of some water, drawn closer, then apart, closer then apart, like there was no real division between them, save the tide that ran within them. They were riding something they had ridden many times before, like they all knew what to do, what should be done, like they knew it was unpredictable, that it could take a sudden turn for the bad, but they loved it. She couldn't change it, whatever happened, couldn't save them, couldn't alter course or land them or throw them a line; they couldn't hear her, hadn't been able to for the last two or three hours. She fought her way through it and told them she was off to bed. There was a room taken, but when Louis had booked it she couldn't remember. It was small and covered in a sort of seasick tartan, with a basin in the corner of the room about the size of her foot, where she jammed her head and turned on the cold tap just for the sensation of something fresh. Out of the window, traffic was coming from all sides, like she was in the middle of a web, all the cars running up and down the mesh, lives caught, lives stretched out, lives tugging to break free. It was like she saw cars for the first time.

She woke, still clothed, to find Louis sitting on the edge of the bed, rolling up.

'What's the time?' she said.

'What's the time got to do with anything,' he said. 'You shouldn't have left me there.'

'I'd been there for fucking hours. I don't understand why we're going at all, if it's going to cause this much fuss. Give me some water. I shouldn't have drunk so much, the baby and all.'

He handed her a glass.

'Do him good, a bit of beer inside him.'

She drank it, then another. Then another.

'I don't want to go,' he said, his back to her.

'For Christ sake, Louis. I've been listening to nothing else for the last two years.'

'There was foul work afoot on that moor, did you know?'

She did know. The whole country knew. It was part of the nation's memory.

'And now the motorway will go thundering by. It's a wonder the earth doesn't swallow us all up, a thing like that.'

She put her hand to his head.

'Your hair needs cutting,' she said. 'Shall I do it now?'

'And Hogan's brother's a fool. Never had him anywhere near my gang ... Ah.' The roll-up fell from his hands on to the carpet. He was in a worse state than she thought. She sat beside him.

'We won't go then.'

It took him by surprise.

'Not at all?'

'Not if you don't want to.'

'But the boys? They expect it of me.'

'They can go by themselves. They don't need you to hold their hand.'

'Alice.'

'I mean, it's just a dam, Louis.'

'Alice.'

'A fucking dam. What's happened to your shirt? Is that blood?'

'Hogan fooling about.' He stood up, pulled it off, slapped his stomach. Not an ounce of fat on him. Never had been by the look of things.

'You're right. Scammonden Dam. God, you're right.' He went to the window, flung it open, leant out, far as his body could go. 'Sorry, boys,' he shouted. 'The trip's off. Alice and me, we're fucking off to Scarborough. Fuck the dam. What use is that to anybody, save the people of Manchester, and who cares two rats about them? Not me. Damn the people of Manchester. Damn them all to hell.'

He fell back on the bed, overwhelmed. She took the scissors out her bag and, cradling his head, cut his hair. When he woke, the day had long broken. She had a fresh shirt hanging from the curtain rail, and was stood by an ironing board, shaking water on a loose, blue calico dress of hers. He sat up, rubbed his scalp. He pointed.

'Where did you get that lot from?'

'The manager. It's his wife's.'

'You don't need to tart yourself up for Scarborough. I thought you'd have known that.'

'We're not going to Scarborough. We're going …' She stood the iron up. 'You'd know where, if you put your mind to it. You put it in my head, Louis. The baby doesn't help either.

I'll see them and that's it. We go now, we'll be there in four hours. You don't have to do anything at all.'

They were there in five, the land peeling back behind her like it was her skin, the raw fruit of her exposed. Louis slept half the journey and, even awake, he was dead to the world. She parked the car a few streets away, to give herself time. Her mother was always looking out the window.

'If you came with me, they'd know I was all right.'

He said nothing, just pushed open her door.

She collected the bunch of wild flowers she had picked up on the way, began the walk to the house, streets she had once lived upon, their familiarity tainted by a growing unease, like the houses, the roads, the pavements she knew had lost a dimension or been drained of colour or the ground underneath them had shifted in her absence, like they shrank from her, what she had done, what she had become. A giddiness crept upon her, not from the pregnancy (for she never had a moment's discomfort, and never did the whole nine month, no morning sickness, no swollen ankles or dicky blood pressure, nothing, drinking, smoking up to the last minute, no one told her any different), but like the perspective was out of kilter, like she was unable to make sense of what lay in front of her. Names swam out at her like flotsam at the water's edge, Becky Anderson who was queen genius at science, the weird Bartle boy, Andrew who fancied Maisy's mum. Maisy and her were friends for ever, everyone knew that. The last time they met up, she'd promised to try to get Maisy a job behind the bar too, so they could be together again. Then Louis had come along, and Maisy, like everyone else, had been blown away.

She reached her old home, semi-detached, cracked stained glass over the door mantel, cyclamen in the bay window, but the car in the drive a different make from what she had expected. She knew cars now, knew the measure of them, their roadworthiness, their petrol consumption, their depreciation value. She attended car auctions, knew what to look for, did the bidding when Louis had work on. A Vauxhall stood in the drive, a 1959 four-door Vauxhall Victor F, 1.5-litre engine, three-speed manual gearbox, bench seats front and rear, chrome trim around the windows and a horrible shade of blue, like a tank rucked up in a pinafore. Second-hand, of course, and dirt cheap most likely, because no one with any nous would buy a second-hand Vauxhall Victor, or any Vauxhall of that time. Louis had come back with a '63 Vauxhall Viva a year ago, won in a card game, and they'd got shot of it within the week, what with the petrol it drank, and its tail end taking corners like a drunk, and the rainwater running into the boot from the crap capping round the edge. 'We're not putting up with this a minute longer,' he'd said and they'd jumped out and tipped it head first into a ditch, laughing all the hitched way home.

She edged round it, up along the side wall, and on to the steps to the kitchen, her pregnancy for the first time lying heavy in her, her heart beating wild, like she'd made a mistake, been caught out, like they were waiting for her. She shoved her hair back, conscious of the mangled state of it and the dirt under her fingernails. She should have done something about it. Louis could have made sure.

She pushed the door open. She knew the house was empty the moment she called out, knew it from the echo it made.

It hadn't occurred to her that they wouldn't be in and, now that they were not, she was relieved. It made a sense to her, to see the house, her home, on her own terms, without their influence. The kitchen was the same, the stove, the sink, the refrigerator that shuddered every few minutes. Even her mug, the one with her name stamped on it she'd bought at that fair, was hanging from the hook. Why shouldn't it be? Why shouldn't it all be the same? She sat down on what used to be her chair, the shape in the wood suddenly familiar, then rose discomfited and walked through into the main room, glancing up the stairs as she passed to the closed door of her bedroom staring back down. She was seized with alarm just to see it, remembering what sort of girl hid behind it, someone she no longer recognised nor had any time for, someone almost not human, an invention, made for others by others. She hurried into the front room. There was something new there too, preposterous like the Vauxhall outside, disagreeable and heavy like it too, a gas fire, sat in the fireplace like a stubborn growth, six fluted columns of gas mantles set in a block of silver chrome and stuck behind a row of massive bars, like a prison-cell window. She could hardly imagine either of them, her mum, her dad, sitting by this thing at her feet, yet there were their chairs, like the cushion she saw in the Vauxhall propped up on the passenger seat for her mum's back, and seat belts there too, wicked things, like Donald Campbell wore, carrying you to oblivion. You'd go to hell wearing a seat belt, the gas fire turned to level ten, ready to roast the soles of your feet.

She went back into the hall, caught sight of herself in the mirror. She was unused to mirrors, least three-quarter-length ones that gave her a sense of her body. If she used make-up at all, it was done in the rear-view mirror of whatever car they possessed, a smear of lipstick, a smudge of eyeshadow. In that regard the snake had become her spokesman. But now, surprised by a mirror she had known was there, she saw herself for the first time in years, and saw, not the badly ironed dress with the tear on the left breast, or the scuffed boots and the knotted hair, but the straight simplicity of her, the breadth on her shoulders, the strength in her arms, the clarity in her eyes. How steadfast she appeared, with her wide, capable hands and her feet anchored to the ground, like no one could divert her from the course she had taken. Even her skin was transformed, the hue of brown possessed of a depth no swimsuit could ever attain. It ran over her whole body, deep like currents in a river, rippling through her sinews, the snake swimming over it, leaping up and over her. She pulled the buttons of the dress apart. Yes there it was, slightly fatter now, half-hidden between her pink and purple flesh, the head reared up, revelling in what was happening, and his part in it. It gave her pleasure to see it all, more than pleasure, a joy almost. She wished Louis there, to gaze upon her with him, for her to look back at them, his hands on her, and for her to see how she'd been taken away from here. There was him and there was her and what else there was was the mystery that lay between them. That was all it could be, all she wanted. Suddenly she became afraid. Suddenly she could stay no longer.

She returned to the kitchen, fastening back the buttons. She took down the mug with her name upon it, her hand shaking, the first time that had happened since she had left, filled it with water, stuck in the wild flowers and laid it centre table. That was it. Nothing more.

'Hello?'

Her father's voice from upstairs. He'd been up there all the time. Was he sick? She stood perfectly still.

'Margaret? Is that you?'

Her hand went to her mouth, like her breath would give her away. He took a nap now?

'You're early. How did it go?'

She took a step back, knocking into her stool. Her father would come downstairs and her mother would walk through the back door and she would be caught. The question came again.

'Margaret?'

Their bedroom door opened. He was standing on the landing. She moved to the door, quickly, her boots huge and clumsy, a terrible weight hanging on her legs. She lifted the latch. It rattled like a snake ready to strike.

'Who's there?'

She jumped down the steps, squirmed past the Vauxhall and ran down the street, ran the next, ran all the way, her mind in front, her body pounding after her, desperate to keep up. She flung the car door open and sank back into her seat. Louis looked at her, surprised.

'What happened to you?' he said. 'Your dress is all crooked.'

'Is it?' She looked down. In her haste she'd slotted the buttons into the wrong holes. She started the car, revved the engine.

'I need a drink,' she said.

He pulled a half-bottle of Haig out of his pocket. She unscrewed it, let it run down her throat.

'I'd thought you'd be there longer,' he said. 'Did they have nothing to say?' She shook her head, took another gulp, handed the bottle back.

'I didn't know what to do. I mean look at me.'

'What's wrong with you?'

'Nothing's wrong with me. That's the whole point.' She stuck the car in gear, let the clutch out hard. 'I feel like driving all night.'

'And where would we be going?'

'How the fuck should I know? What about Devon or Cornwall, or Wales? I've never been to Wales. We could do the lot. Devon, Wales, Cornwall, what's that county where the cider is, Somerset, live off our wits for a while, buy a Volkswagen camper. What do you think?'

'Like we're eloping, two fingers up to the lot of them, the flat, our bits and pieces, and everything?'

'Everything. Thick like cream. Perfect like an egg.'

It was the language he loved to hear. He leant across, undid the buttons, did them back up in the right order, his face alive again. It was marvellously powerful, that brief caress to her body in those familial streets.

'Not a camper van,' he said. 'It's what hippies drive.'

'What about a Volvo? You've always fancied a Volvo.'

'Too pricey, even third-hand. I know a man outside Aylesbury, Charlie Hicks, God's own mechanic. He'd fix us up. Something we can kick loose in.'

'They drive a Vauxhall, would you believe, my parents, a fucking Vauxhall.'

She began to laugh. By the time they reached the main road, and she'd told him the whole story, he was laughing too.

TWO

I T WAS AROUND LUDLOW, and later in Wales, where
she grew to love it, that Louis taught her how to drive at
night without any lights. It took some getting used to, but as
he said, it was only the headlamps that prevented you from
seeing. What you had to do was to sit in the dark without
moving for half an hour, sit in the car or stand outside, it didn't
matter which, just so long as you let go and told your eyes
to stop looking and let the dark sweep in. In that way there
was a sexual element to it, like an embrace, like an entice-
ment to the night, a promise of coming pleasure, excitement.
They had to do it, he said, for the poaching, lamp-lighting for
hares and rabbits and fucking off out of it, or a farm chicken
grabbed in a sack, the collie or whatever barking in the yard
and she freewheeling the Humber down the hill, while he
knocked the squawking on the head, but it was more than
expedience, that was obvious to both of them. There was still
the gun, but they were loath to use it. Everyone knew when
a gun had been fired, the shot smacking into the air like a
great fist. It was safer, what they did in the dark. It became,
for those miraculous weeks, a way of life, an expression of who
they were, reaching far beyond the confines of the road. Ten
minutes with a chicken and they'd have it plucked and gutted

and no one could prove otherwise. They could chop it up and stuff it in a pan, chuck in beer, onions, carrots and put it on the camp stove they had, eat it with dripping hands, revelling in the juice. They ate well, found a taste for it, better on the move than stuck in a flat, Louis claimed, brewing up in a clearing or parked up in a field. Louis had even fashioned the means for a Sunday roast, wrapping whatever in foil and cooking it in a biscuit tin punched with holes, set in a bank of earth, a fire stoked underneath (though they tried it only the once – three hours that chicken took and still it was raw). It was amazing what farmers left around at night, what their fields contained. Meals on Fields, that's what they called it. One night they stripped Taffy of what felt like half an acre of potatoes, had them rolling in the back for weeks, big misshapen brutes they cooked whole and ate cold in their skins. They loved thieving from farms, their kitchen gardens, beans, tomatoes, leeks, cabbage, beetroot, stealing away in the dark. It was erotic. The whole trip was erotic, her with her belly fermenting and Louis like a pirate, rapacious, and ready for anything.

It was a big car, the Humber Hawk, 1956, eighty-seven thousand miles on the clock, clean tears in the back seat like the scene of a cat-fight, the facing gone on both front doors. Big engine, big room, big headlights, lazy to drive, disreputable-looking, a tin bath bought from the same junkyard stuck in the boot, a decent spade and a length of good rope. What else? They had what they needed, torches, tin openers, a set of steel knives. The Humber was their home, their first real one, Alice would say, their *only* real one. Some days they hardly left it, the back seat laid out with cushions, where she could stretch out and swing over the road like a hammock on a ship, but she preferred it up front, behind the wheel, Louis leaning up against the passenger door, the space between them like a conspiracy, maps and money and food and drink. Travelling from place to place, driving around, Louis would read aloud from the local papers, reports of meetings, of village-hall gatherings, what the farmers were doing, interviews with school prizewinners and race runners, stories of accidents and magistrates' court, things for sale, addresses, telling everyone what they were up to, what was available and how to get there. It was like a personal invitation.

'You know why we do this?' he once said.

'Because we can.'

'And soon we won't be able to.'

'You mean the baby?'

'Not as simple as that. Years back we used not to have to be anybody. We could be whatever we wanted. No one gave a tinkers, how we lived or died. Now, the questions they ask, just so we can walk the streets, pull in a day's pay. One day we're going to have to take off, fuck the lot of them.'

'I thought that's what we're doing now.'

'I mean take off for good, like we were never here, like we could never be found. It's harder with a child though.'

She nodded, but did not fully understand

It was a lawless time, money running through their hands like they didn't care what was coming, them living in the night as much as the day. It was gradual, how they moved across, but there was so much more energy outside normal hours, like a pub lock-in or copulation in the afternoon, time itself setting it off. And driving without lights, it was like nothing else, any sort of road, it didn't matter, though the bigger the road, the more likelihood of traffic, the greater the thrill. It was the only time Louis did not object to speed, looming up behind some luckless soul, giving them the shock of their lives when she flicked on the headlights, or cruising past them like they were phantom drivers of the past. You were like kings without lights, kings in a different country, where the laws were different. You could drive anyhow you wanted without lights. It was like you had found a new means of propulsion, like the air was black fuel, like you were just sucking it all in. You could sit with the engine idling, while Louis jumped over a wall or set off down a blackened path, a duffel bag slung over his back. You could tour a residential street real slow, like you were on night patrol or drive half-naked with the windows open, drinking whisky, an owl calling out up ahead. Two months and a half of her pregnancy they did, no check-ups, no special diets, sleeping when she felt tired, eating when she felt hungry, moving on when they felt randy. Only once did she flag, for five days halfway through, when Louis rented an out-of-season flat, worked for a week in a coal yard, shovelling coke into sacks, while she slept, slept like she'd just discovered it, discovered it and couldn't get enough.

The Brebis put an end to it, somewhere outside Brecon, a full moon at three in the morning, a goose in the back, Louis struggling with its anatomy, and she rolling with the steep bends, the road blotted abruptly to a state of invisibility, the baby restless within her, like it was reaching for light too. She flicked them on, the headlights, the world suddenly dazzled and blinking, the Brebis standing blonde and broadside on, smack in the middle of the road, her dark face turned in to her. Alice stamped on the brake and, pulling a sharp curve, slammed the car into a wall, before bouncing back on the road, the Humber tailing and straightening and tailing once again before skidding to a stop.

'That was a bit risky,' Louis said. 'Have you seen the drop on the other side?'

'Have you seen what's ahead?' She flashed the headlights full on. Fifty yards on, part of the right-hand side of the road had been washed away. They'd never have seen it, only felt the lurch and the fall.

She took the torch from the glove compartment and got out. Louis followed. He had the gun by his side. The Brebis was still stood in the centre of the road, her head swivelled, facing them. Other than that, she hadn't moved.

'Did you not hit her?' Louis said, checking the breech.

She played the torch up and down the Brebis's length.

'Does it look like I hit her?'

'I was sure you'd hit her. There was an awful wallop. Jesus, look at her, standing like butter wouldn't melt.'

The Brebis remained static, eyes fixed upon them.

'Perhaps she's a ghost,' Alice suggested. 'Perhaps I ran right through her.'

'She's no ghost. Ghosts don't stand around like dummies. Ghosts weave about like mist. Look.' He raised the gun.

'Louis.'

'If you'd hit her I'd have had to. If you'd hit her like you were supposed to, we could have chopped her up, sold the joints on to pubs and restaurants, no questions asked. Why do you think we got a car like the Humber? So it could take on something like this. And you chucked it against a wall.'

'You couldn't chop that up. She's bloody enormous.'

'I've done goats. She can't be much different.'

'She's completely different. Look at her.'

The Brebis stood there, motionless, as if she was waiting for them to decide, like they were at a crossroads all three of them, life or death, an opening up or a closing down, whether they'd leave this country unscarred or whether they'd pay a price. There was light on her now, not from their torch, but like she was illuminated from above, or maybe from inside. It seemed to Alice like she must have been standing there since time began, carrying these minutes like a child, waiting for them to blossom forth, complete.

Louis shifted the gun in his arms.

'What's it to be then?' Alice said.

Louis turned to her.

'Is it my decision then?'

'Don't look at me. Keep your eyes on her. Otherwise she'll vanish and then we'll never know.'

'Never know what?'

'If you did the right thing.'

He ran his hand down the length of the barrel, his face pale set and, she thought, the most beautiful she had ever seen. 'And when did I not do the right thing, Alice? Tell me that.'

She was still there, the Brebis, when they rolled off, edging past the collapse, the last living thing they saw of that country. Alice could still see her, a ghost in the mirror, when she took the road to Hereford, still see her when they neared the outskirts of the town. Where she was making for she did not know. It was a road that was all, and she was struck, the first time driving she had been struck by such a thought, that it had no destination, this road they were on, no purpose. It was drained of reason, flat and glittery black and unwritten upon, like a slate. She should have asked the Brebis where to go. The Brebis would have known.

'How did we get away with it for so long?' she said. 'Living like that.'

'We had the eye for it.'

'Maybe not any more. It's time you looked for work anyway.'

He was half out of his seat, tucking the gun under the blanket, searching in the back, bringing out the whisky, unscrewing the cap, letting it run into his mouth.

'No need,' he said, wiping his chin. 'I found it two month back. There's work coming on Scotch Corner. Might cover us for six month or more, a two-level interchange.'

'That woman told you, I suppose. At the bar. Lot.'

He offered her the bottle. She shook her head. Silence overtook them. She did not volunteer where they might be heading. He did not question her. Neither of them knew. There was no traffic, the world emptied of everyone but themselves. A roundabout loomed up. She turned on it hard. There was a terrible scraping from outside.

'Did you hear that?'

'Stop the car. I'll take a look.'

The Humber's right-hand side was buckled where it had met the wall, the mirror snapped off, the front bumper crumpled, the right wing bent in against the tyre. Alice put her arm out, shone the torch on it while Louis took a hammer, fell to his knees and clawed it free. He had developed a bald patch on the top of his head, she noticed. It was the first time she had seen it, the first time she had seen evidence of his ageing, the passing of his time, this man who she still did not know. It was like discovering a closely held secret, as if he had betrayed himself, his coming frailty, without him knowing. She hadn't known another man's body like his, the years on it, the hard graft, the smoking, the drinking, the stubborn indifference to health, and now there he was, on his knees, an older man, with a bald patch, shaped like an egg.

He got back in the car, shaking his head at what he'd seen.

'I was going to sell it back to Charlie when we were done,' he said. 'It was a favour, him putting it our way in the first place. He'll have a fit when he sees it now.'

She kissed him direct, surprised him with her mouth, its fierce search.

'Let's keep it then. Let's clean it up, put a baby seat in. Between them, this car and the Brebis saved our lives. All three of them.'

She took his hand, laid it close on her lap. She had asked him to feel the child only once, lain down on a rock like it was an examination couch, he with his long coat flapping like a hospital doctor's, the sun weak upon her, the swell rising, the sky almost touching it they were so high up, and when he did so, ran his hand over and back like it was blown glass, the fields and pastures lying far below them like in an old painting, she saw that he was frightened, unsettled, the strange unseen stirrings inside his and not his, unable to see where he fitted into this landscape, the dimensions of it, its smallness, its enormity, the great uncertainty of it all. Her lap and the rim of the drum was the nearest he could go.

'And is there not any more work for you round Durham still? He's making demands on me now, this boy of yours. I want somewhere I know, while we all get used to each other. I'd like him to see it too, where he came to life …'

'He's a he, is he?'

'What else, with you for a father? Even if you are going bald.'

'What?'

'Do you not know? Oh Louis. Thirty-seven and going bald. Almost makes me sad. So, where's it to be?'

Louis let the question hang in the air, rubbed the window with his sleeve, sank back into his seat.

'What do I know?' he said. 'I'm going bald. You're in the driving seat now.'

He closed his eyes. She pressed down, the Humber picking up speed. It felt grand to be heading up north again, grand to be in this battered car. She'd drive the whole way, like on a mission, with Louis half-asleep and the baby kicking against the steering wheel, like nothing would stop her, up towards the cold country, Tamworth to Worksop, barrel on the straight, barrel on the curve, barrel past Scotch Corner in the blink of an eye, see it come and see it go. There would be a home of sorts in Durham or wherever, a place of brief permanence, where she could stand immovable like the Brebis, stand immovable, look out on the road and take it all in.

'What about Huddersfield?' she said. 'Didn't Hogan say there's still work on the M62?'

Louis said nothing.

'Or the other side of Newcastle, round Morpeth? We don't have to stay put for very long. See him born, let him get used to our ways. After that,' she drummed the wheel, 'I'm thinking, nine months in and nine months out. He should be ready to move by then.'

The words stirred him.

'Not staying put for good then?'

'Course not for good. Jesus, Louis. For good? What do you take me for? My fucking mother?'

'No. No. It's just ... babies ... I don't ...'

He sat forward. The sky was beginning to open up, slashes of silver light and the clouds broody dark.

'The Birtley bypass isn't finished yet,' he offered. 'I might get work there, and then … I was thinking we could head down south. There's work there, gobs of it, all over. It's Cambridge I'm counting on. Epping Forest all the way up, and then upgrading the A14 to the you-know-what.' He rubbed his back against his seat, like a dog on a post. 'It's a link.'

'Have you got room there for a link?' she joked.

'So I'll have it done on a buttock,' he said. 'Or on the little fellow. Why not? He has the minor roads, I have the major.'

They were back into their old ways and they were both glad.

'Talking of needles,' he said, pointing to the speedometer. 'Looks like we're running a fever.'

She took the bottle from him.

'Nothing you can do about it, but let it burn itself out.'

He folded his hands into his lap, resigned.

'You'll be wanting a radio next.'

So Durham way it was, outside, not far from the coast, Louis finding work where he could, odd stuff, patching up, tarmacking minor roads, even temporary council rubbish. They had two rooms again, two rooms and the smudge of a back garden just big enough for a rusty swing he found in a skip.

And he'd come home dirty and complaining.

'It's like a bank robber snatching old ladies' handbags,' he'd say, and she, wrapped up on the swing as often as not, soothing the child to rest, for he did move so in the early evening, she would hardly listen, so intense was it within her and the memory of the Brebis staring. And in bed, two months on, his head on her great veined breast, his body angled away, the snake growing huge and bloated, he said:

'Pete says there's shift work likely down Sheffield way soon.' She could feel his lips shape the words on her, feel them roll down like little boulders into the steep of her body, weights on her skin.

'Go then.'

'Not yet. I don't need to go yet. But if it's offered in a month or so, the money it might bring, maybe …'

There they were, the stones, a sort of dam between them, or perhaps a sort of stepping-stone path to lead him away. She stroked his bald patch, as potent as her breast now, feeding him small thoughts of mortality. She kissed it feeling comforted that he wanted to explain, that he wanted to share it with her, his tremulous uncertainty.

'It's all right, Louis,' she said. 'It's all right.'

———

When the child came he was a hundred miles away or more, as she knew he would be. She'd been to the doctor but once, in her sixth month, and after that evaded all appointments until she had no choice. She trusted no one. If Louis had been there, she would not have gone to the hospital at all, she would have had it at home, and put her faith in him and a neighbour, who claimed she knew about these things. As it was, Hogan drove her there on the back of his bike, she clenching with contractions and he gripped to his handlebars, terrified.

'I'll go and fetch the bastard when I've dropped you off,' he said, helping her on, furious at the imposition. 'Strap him to the pillion.'

'Just let him know after it's over. Leave him be until then. He hasn't worked for a while, not proper stuff. He needs it, you know, so he can come back like he was.'

'My brother's down there, did he say, Lot cooking for the whole tribe of them, like in the old days.'

She closed her eyes and tightened her arms around him, the child urgent upon her. Twenty-five minutes to get there, she leaning with him as he took the corners too fast. It was difficult, her belly the way it was, the clutching pain, but she was glad of it too, the rushing of it, the movement, the wind and the speed, and the bellow of the engine.

There were seven women in the ward. The contractions increasing in intensity, they made ready to take her into the labour room. The woman next to her, stuck to her radio, was all excited.

'Have you heard,' she said, 'them American astronauts on the way to the frigging moon? They got blown up or some-thing. Halfway there and no breakdown van to tow them back.'

As soon as she learnt of it, she could feel her body magnify, the baby retreat, the contractions cease, a cavern open up within her, as if, Lord help her, she had to make room for others. For the first time since she'd left with him, she was caught up in the news and the tale of these men marooned in their broken mother ship, the moon voyage aborted, the only way home for the three of them to squeeze through the narrow ribbed tube into the lunar module, and with a four-minute push of the descent engine, have it sling itself round the moon's gravity and slide down the space chute to home. And she knew right away, she wouldn't hear from the child again, not until they were returned. She was carrying them all, Lovell and Swigert and Haise, this little man in her womb, carrying them all to safety. Nine months it had been since Armstrong had stood there, gazing down upon her child's conception, and now, it was time for his successors to return, splash down upon the ocean's waters and bear witness to his birth. Was he saving them, this child, or had he summoned them? It was difficult for her to comprehend the complexity of what was happening, but she knew this. Without him lying within her, the three Americans would have never returned, but died on the moon or in the vast deep above it. Now the four of them were hurtling through fields of logic beyond her understanding, travelling at the same speed over the same distance to the same hallowed place.

She settled down. Nurses came and nurses examined her, suspicious of the sudden cessation of activity, perturbed, as if the child had no manners. She liked the idea of that: rude Louis's boy. Doctors threatened her with epidurals and Caesareans, but she had learnt one thing from Louis above all, which was how not to listen to others, especially those who knew better. The third day was the most tense, for they expected the baby to show signs of distress, linked her up to heartbeat monitors, peered up inside her more times than was necessary, but he did not, and she knew he would not, for his focus was on the Americans. She listened to every bulletin, for his sake as much as hers, Lovell and the crew fashioning makeshift apparatus for their survival, the little ship holding good, her body scarcely any weight at all, as if she too was moving through unknown matter. That night she took to her feet, walked the green corridor past the closed refectory, past the reception desk, to outside, where the air was cool, and where, the news had had it, a quarter-moon hung. She walked to the parking area, but there was no sign of it, no sign of the stars either. The sky was dark and empty, dark like in Wales. It was then that she saw them, Lovell, Swigert and Haise, staring out their little bubble-car window, racing towards them, the eyes of a heavenly Brebis lighting the way. She was mad, she knew it, mad with their demands, mad from her months of travelling, mad with this child turning the heavens inside her, but she was glad of it, this derangement, how it separated her from normality. Normality, how she dreaded that. How did people describe it? Coming down to earth with a bump?

The following morning she woke rested, Lovell and his companions well on course. She informed the nurse re-examining her inactive cervix, that the child would arrive early evening, and they should prepare for it to happen suddenly, without warning. The nurse straightened up, amused again by this wilful woman's certainty.

'What, like a popped cork?' she suggested.

'More like something falling out the sky,' Alice answered.

And that is how it was, a little after seven, the splashdown confirmed, the crew safe on the USS *Iwo Jima*, there came a rapid rush to her head, a great space rolling her aside as she cried out in a moment of intense pain, like a bright light, almost fainting with the sharp intensity, and he slipped out there and then as if he'd been greased with goose fat, the staff caught short, the others envious, and she triumphant, a cup of tea and two biscuits on her bedside table, the child lying upon the deflated snake.

Gil was the first to visit, a day later, walked down the ward with a bunch of tulips wrapped in the *Daily Mirror*. The other mothers looked at him askance.

'Which roundabout are they from?' Alice said, laughing. She'd never liked tulips. He stuck them in her water jug and pulled up the one chair.

'I told him. Spoke to him only yesterday, telephoned his digs, told him where his place was.'

She unveiled the baby's head, a pink thing the size of Louis's bald patch, sleeping now.

'He's got a thing about experts, you know that. I'm glad he's not here. He'd have only got in the way. Where's your playmate?'

Gil opened his coat. The Jack Russell poked his head out.

'They told me to tie him up outside, but I thought you'd both like him to see him. Say hello, Patch.' He held him forward. The dog leant down, sniffed warily, then began licking the baby's head.

'See?' Gil said. 'Patch has made him one of the family now. Did you hear about those Americans? It was touch and go.'

'No it wasn't,' she said and pushed the little dog away. He had done enough baptising.

Hogan was next, Hogan and Pete Harris. Pete had the same gear on as in Scotch Corner but had also brought his guitar. Hogan had a striped black and yellow blazer that he'd bought in a jumble sale with the words 'Lacrosse Captain' on a badge stitched to the breast pocket. It was a woman's blazer, a schoolgirl's. They admired the baby. Pete liked the look of his hands, carpenter's hands he said, strong fingers, a good wrist. Hogan took the courage to hold him, tipped him this way and that, like a spirit level. Pete asked if she'd given him a name. Alice shook her head. Not yet.

'What about Louis the Second?' Pete said. 'You know, like a what-you-call-it.'

'A king?' Hogan offered.

'A dynasty,' Pete replied. 'Shall I sing him a song?'

Hogan begged him not to, but Alice insisted. They'd been a closed book to her, country-and-western songs, until she'd heard Pete sing.

'Sing the one about the moon,' she said. 'The moon shining through the trees.'

'You mean "Blue Shadows on the Trail"?' he said. 'Roy Rogers and the Sons of the Pioneers?'

'That's the one.'

Pete stood up, tipped his hat back, put one foot up on the edge of the bed, rested the guitar on his calf. It was how the cowboys played. Alice closed her eyes to the blue shadows moving along.

Brummie One and Brummie Two were the last to turn up, ties and blue shirts and clean jerseys, one either side of the bed. They brought a box of barley sugar. They barely spoke a word, but that was all right. She didn't expect them to. It was enough to have them there. She showed them the baby and they clapped their hands as if he were their own. After twenty minutes, the child agitated, she pointed to her right breast, indicating what he required. They understood at once, but made no attempt to leave. She didn't mind, in fact she was glad, glad to show someone what she and this child were capable of. She lifted him up and, pulling the gown aside, waited as his tiny mouth enveloped her bold, fat nipple, so proud of him, so proud of her bared womanly flesh. The twins watched intently, entranced, their eyes going from her to him to each other, from her to him to each other. It was something they had experienced themselves, she thought, their first memory most likely, buried deep, now returned, tender on their faces.

'Would you cast your eye on that,' said Brummie One. Brummie Two took a closer look.

'God, but wouldn't I like to paint that,' he said. 'The mechanics of it. And beyond.'

Alice had a sudden vision of the pair of them, as they were now, fully clothed, hair brushed and best jerseys, busy at her breasts. She'd have enough milk for them and the baby, she thought. For Lovell, Swigert and Haise too if they needed it. She'd have enough for everyone. God, she felt huge.

'When he's older,' Brummie One said, 'we'll take him to Scammonden, sail a toy boat on the water.'

'Feed him dandelion and burdock.'

'I don't know about Scammonden,' Alice said, slowly tucking herself away. 'He might prefer the seaside.' Brummie One stood up.

'Scarborough then. The four of us. Right, Gerry?'

'Scarborough it is. Dandelion and burdock, a ride on a donkey and a paddle in the sand,' and they were out the swing doors, occupied by the prospect.

———

Louis came the fourth day. They had kept her in because of it and because they had the beds to spare. He came straight from the site, straight from the drive up, pushing the doors open like he was master of the house, the first time, he said, he'd ever visited a hospital, yet he knew their etiquette, addressed the nurses with courtesy, understood the grading, seemed perfectly at home. He was a marvel, the way he carried it off, his trousers crumpled, his shirt collarless and his boots big, but the swing of him pure thoroughbred, like he was a film star gliding through the set. He'd been working hard, the trim on his body told her that. His colour was back. She could smell it too, the work, hanging on him like aftershave. She thought he looked brilliant, better than any other man that had done the cockerel walk about the ward. For a moment she felt a pang of something fearful inside her, that the spirit between them, that high-proofed astringency that had sliced through like a razor blade, had been diluted. He was looking down at them, trying to gauge what he saw.

'He's quite ragged, isn't he?' he said.

'How do you mean?'

'His skin. It's rougher than I thought. Did he put up a fight then?'

What was it he was hoping for? she thought. She tried to find words to help him.

'He's like a wild flower, Louis, found by the roadside. Where he came from and everything.'

'That must be it.' He pulled something green and cloudy out of his pocket, pulled at the cork with his teeth. She knew what it was right away, Scammonden holy water. She held the baby firm while Louis poured the water out over his head. The baby blinked, unmoved. Alice patted him dry.

'Shall I take him then?' Louis said.

He gathered him up, the dark shine of his jacket and the soft white of the blanket.

'Weighs a ton,' he said. 'Never felt anything so heavy. You never said.'

'He was weightless then,' she said. 'Like in space. He's our space baby, Louis, from the moon.'

She was still mad with it, she knew it. But it was true. He was from the moon, twisting and turning through a great hole in space, just to get here. No wonder he looked ragged. Louis nodded, eyes staring down.

'The moon, is it now?'

'Maybe. Somewhere in heaven, that's for sure.'

He pulled the blanket back with his finger.

'Do you have a name in mind?'

'Nothing to do with your blessed road.'

'Or the moon,' he said, adding, 'as if I'd think of such a thing.'

But he had thought of it, she could tell, had it whirring in his head from the moment he knew, probably had Eddie the Squint tattoo it somewhere unlikely while he'd been away, as a talisman.

'You'll be wanting to be driven home then,' he said.

'At the speed of your choice.' He scratched his head.

'I've got us a new car,' he told her. Alice shifted her pillow.

'What was wrong with the Humber? I thought we were going to keep the Humber.'

He shrugged his shoulders.

The car was a 1962 Rover 80, two-tone, ivory and grey, twenty-nine thousand miles, sat up on its axle like a pocket battleship. Of course, he had ditched their old car. Hadn't Lovell done exactly the same? She got in the back, held the child on her lap. It was a cold vehicle, stiff, censorious. There'd be no fun had in this car. It didn't allow for it. The seats were like you were in someone's office, somewhere where you shouldn't so much as let a fart out.

'Didn't expect this. A cunting magistrate's car was how you once described Rovers,' she said.

'We're respectable now,' he said.

She looked out the window. You sat high up in a Rover, like you were royalty, like it expected you to wave at the rabble outside.

'No, we're not,' she said. 'Not if I have anything to do with it. Come on, Louis, out with it.'

'Out with what?'

'The name. His precious name.'

Louis turned in his seat, one hand on the wheel. It looked heavy to drive too, she thought. He had a smile on his face as big as a zip.

'Chester has a ring to it, don't you think?'

And she agreed. It had a ring to it, Chester.

They kept to it though, the staying put, not even a hint of moving for the first nine months, though the work around Durham did not go the full distance, Louis forced to go away for two-, three-week stretches, that look upon him whenever he returned, Chester twisting in his lap, like the two of them couldn't wait to throw the lot into a bag and fuck off out of it. But there was an order to things now, a requirement of objects, checklists, timetables, an unwelcome hierarchy of possessions. He was a big baby, big head, big eyes, big hands, slow to walk, slower to talk, could lie on his back for hours, staring up.

Alice couldn't keep away from the Rover, found herself sitting in front of the steering wheel at all times of the day. Its interior was red, seat, floor, doors, everywhere but the dash-board and the walnut-finish front. It reminded her of eating Sunday lunch at home, hands on the side of the table and chewing twenty times before swallowing. There had been a sort of motion to the meal, as if she was strapped to the chair but hurtling away from the table with the speed of thought. The Rover had the same effect. She wanted to escape but could not. She saw it from the window, her and Chester on the inside, the Rover outside, demanding their presence. It was like it was a messenger come down from above. It had a reason, was working towards it, she didn't know what. Next thing, Chester would be laid out next to her on the bench seat and the key stuck in the ignition. She'd look in the mirror and realise she had brushed her hair, exchanged her torn shirt for a fresh one, done it both consciously and unconsciously, like in a science-fiction film, like the Rover had sent out signals beyond her control. This is how she found herself time and again, her hair in place and driving with no thought to it. 'Damn near empty again,' Louis would complain. 'Where do you go?' She had no reply.

Strange, troubling car. Could she fuck in the Rover? She never had the desire to, but her and Chester couldn't get enough of it. She drove, one hand on the wheel, Chester beside her on a bed of blankets, his head nearest the door, her other hand ready to tickle his stomach. She placed a bed of eiderdowns on the floor, so that if the car stopped suddenly, he would roll down on to the feathers. The first time it had happened it had gone exactly to plan. He had lain there kick-ing his legs, gurgling at the adventure. He was a voracious baby, constant for her milk. While she might pull over, give him his needs, other times she would pick him up in one hand, balance him unsteadily on the spoke of the steering wheel, yank her clothing aside, angle her breast forward, manoeuvring herself until her nipple had found its mark and she could settle in, one hand steadying Chester, his bottom on the wheel, his body tipped to her breast, the other ready with the steering wheel and the gear change. She couldn't help but look down. It was full of desire, an action carried out against the Rover's wishes, all flesh and womanhood and abundance.

Six months in, Louis off with Hogan, a quick three-day job on a new housing estate, money in the pocket and no questions asked, she was riding the Rover in between the A1, the A691 and the A693, a triangle with Chester-le-Street at its right-hand base. She liked flirting with Chester-le-Street, liked driving the Rover over the very spot where she and Louis had fucked Chester into being. That day there was a mist rolling about the Rover's bonnet, like it was ploughing a ghostly sea. Chester was wonderful hungry. She held him on the wheel, the milk bubbling in his mouth, running down her fingers, the wheel slippery wet, the Rover driving noiseless. She felt like she was floating, pumping life, alone and not alone, tied down and barely there. She had filled the spaces. His mouth withdrew. He needed more. One breast was not enough. She rearranged her clothing, shifted in her seat as the Rover neared a narrow corner and a sudden hump-backed bridge. Taken by surprise, her hands were outnumbered, a gear to change, a child to steady, a wheel to direct. She saw the shadow of something, pulled over hard, felt a glance, Chester tipping clumsy into her lap. She jammed the brakes, stopped the car, placed Chester on his blanket. Walking back, she looked down over the low wall of the bridge. A man was sprawled below, spread out like a starfish.

She ran round, slithered down the embankment, nettles on her arse. He was older than she'd thought, and his hair was parted flawless, like it had taken hours. He smelt sweet, of lotion. His eyes were staring wide, not understanding.

'Are you hurt? Say something to me.'

She squatted down, waited for him to respond. He had a woman's mouth, too pretty for a man. She wondered what he was doing, dressed in a proper pinstripe and miles from anywhere. He was perfect, perfect brushed and perfect clean, a Roman nose and brilliantined hair, black shoes to match. He stirred.

'That's better,' she said. 'What's your name?'

She eased her hand between his shoulder blades, raised him up. His fingers clawed at the earth, afraid to leave. A bunch of chrysanthemums wrapped in blue tissue paper lay on the ground next to him, half the heads broken.

'Off courting, were we,' she said, 'all butter wouldn't melt …' She picked them up, pulled out the broken stalks, jammed the bouquet into his jacket pocket.

'You had a nasty fall,' she said. 'I've got a car up there. Feel like getting up?'

She pulled him to his feet. He stood unsteadily, as though he was trying to keep his balance on a boat. She hadn't noticed it before, but there was a steep path running up to the road. She could hear Chester crying.

'Think you're up to it?' she said. 'She's waiting for you.'

She stuck her hand deep into his armpit. There was blood coming from his ear. He took a couple of steps forward, his legs remembering what to do.

'That's the ticket.'

She wrapped her arm around him, hauled him up the bank, pleased to feel how muscle ran so easy in her. It was great to be strong. Once back on the road, he walked towards the car, his legs moving promptly, one after the other, but without comprehension. The heavy-headed flowers batted up and down, their purpose forgotten, their tranquillity destroyed. She felt sorry for them. Once by the car he collapsed in a heap.

'Nearly there.'

She opened the back door, lifted him on to the edge of the seat. His head was running with little rivers of blood. She took one of Chester's spare nappies, wrapped it tight round his forehead, her breast falling loose as she knotted the nappy ends round the back, brushing against his face.

'Romeo with the pirate look,' she said. 'Weak at the knees she'll be.'

She swung his legs over, his lips and cheeks pale and flaccid. His hand clutched at her thigh.

'Easy, boy,' she said. 'Not there yet.'

She leant him back, closed the door, a sudden sweat running down her. Chester was flailing, wanting more. She climbed in, lifted him up. There was blood on her. She wiped herself clean with the sleeve of her dress, gave him what he wanted. Behind them the man was sat upright, fists clenched and his breath coming short. In the mirror she could see that his tie was crooked. She wanted to straighten it, make it right for him. Chester wouldn't let go, his little hands and mouth insistent, his eyes gazed upon her. The thought came to her that she should lay him down, let her milk work its miracle on the man instead, let him tap into the wonder of her womanly strength and power. It was how she had felt in the delivery ward. Feeding, the constant flow of it, was the most wonderful sensation she had ever known. What was it, motherhood, but the earth and an affinity with the stars? It was like time travelling, moments of weightlessness and being everywhere. She had enough for everyone.

She lay Chester down. Straight away, he fell asleep. She eased the Rover into gear, her eyes moving from the road to her passenger. She drove slowly, fearful that he might keel over. The bleeding had stopped, but his breath was sucking in and out like pebbles on the beach. If he would only wake up, she could drive him somewhere. She should have gone through his pockets, found out who he was.

'Where do you live?' she said. 'Can you tell me that?'

She drove on. The road remained merciful, narrow and clear of traffic. She didn't know what to do with him. Knock on the door of the next house? But what about the attention it would bring, the questions that would be asked? No one had seen her yet. As for the Rover, if there had been a mark, she hadn't noticed it. If she could put him somewhere safe … A minute later she passed a country telephone box. She slowed down, reversed.

'I can't take you all the way,' she said. 'But I'll get help. You can wait here.'

She helped him out, led him to the phone box, sat him down, leant him against the door jamb. She dialled 999 with the door propped open. The hair on the back of his head stuck wet against the glass When they answered she said:

'I found this man. He's fallen, hurt his head. I can't stay. I got a baby to get back to.'

She gave the address above the coin box, hung up. Back outside, she crouched down, straightened his tie.

'You'll be all right. They're bloody good, these ambulance people.'

She got no reply. She took the flowers out of his pocket, laid them on his lap. Did his eyes move? She wasn't sure. She put her hand to his neck, felt nothing. It frightened her, the lack of life in it. She thought of Lovell and Swigert and Haise hurtling back to earth, imagined the darkness surrounding this fellow human as his life searched for light.

'Come on, darling, you can do it.'

She pulled the flap wide, held her breast to his lips. His mouth fluttered at her flesh. What was happening? His skin was as smooth as her own, shaved and perfumed, but bathed in innocence and want. She pressed herself, held his head close, squeezed milk on his lips and teeth and tongue. She saw the old youth in him discover itself, take her nipple in full, the longing he had for his future bubbling up, sucking hard. He was a man she had never met, dressed in a suit and tie. Not young, but a man, and a baby now. His shoes were polished and all she had to give lay plentiful in his mouth.

Then it was over. She eased his head back against the glass. She put herself away, stood up over him, biting her nails. Was he alive, was he dead? She had no idea. She decided to go. She didn't see another car until she got back on to the A road. She blamed the Rover for the accident. A lighter car and she would have been able to swerve quicker. The stem to the wing mirror was all that was damaged. He'd put his hand out, been caught by it, spun over the bridge like a dancer. Anywhere else and he would have landed on grass. She twisted it back as best she could.

73

Louis spotted it the moment he saw the car again, his whole body bending to it, like he'd stumbled on a clue. He ran his finger over the top.

'What's this then?'

Alice put her hands in her pockets. She knew it wouldn't escape his attention, however well she'd done it.

'I had an accident.'

'Driving too fast, no doubt.' He tugged at it. 'What you hit?'

'A man.'

'Your eyes on his arse and not the road.' He tapped the wing again. 'How could you hit a man and leave only this?'

'It caught his hand. He must have had it stretched out. He fell off a bridge, banged his head.'

'He has your name then, the car's licence number.'

'Nothing like that. I put him in the car until I found the phone box. I sat him outside, dialled 999. I thought he might be dead.'

'And was he?'

'I don't know. I don't think so. I don't know.'

'Did you leave anything?'

'Only one of Chester's nappies round his head. It was quite a drop, Louis.'

Louis worked on the wing mirror, got rid of the car a week later, only the faintest crease in the stem visible. Seeing it go, she said a prayer.

So began their life with Chester, Louis changing cars more often than before, every two months it seemed to her, and she, irked that he should change them so often and her not so involved, outlandish efforts for the most, nothing like their sturdy Humber, wheels jacked up, innards laid out on the scrappy drive, getting them ready for the road. Whatever Chester's needs, whatever pleasure she took from him, she couldn't wait to get moving again, though she never mentioned it, felt she shouldn't, though that in itself went against the grain, holding things in like that, not wanting to admit being her. So she held it in her mouth, kept the restlessness tight within her body.

When they left for the first time, a year and a bit after he was born, a long drive down to Beaconsfield, Louis going to work on the Gerrards Cross bypass on the M40, it was like that first drive up north with him, like she was escaping again, young and bold and brimming with unconsecrated sex. She couldn't wait to get her hands on him, the very first night there, Chester dog-tired, parked up and sleeping in the back of the car, and her and Louis lively with the beer and the chat and that familiar, unknown, pillow-less bed. She took all she could from him. Thick like cream. Perfect like an egg.

She always remembered Beaconsfield. Beaconsfield was where Chester learned to crawl up the stairs, where he played peek-a-boo in the Corsair Estate, a really good-value car, really practical, no nonsense, but after Beaconsfield it was difficult to keep track of the where and when: work on the M23, work on the M5, crap digs, Chester growing all the time, second year, third. Nothing seemed to suit them, until Ellen Road and the basement. Chester had got used to moving by then. Louis would come home with the news, new digs, new job, time to fuck off out of it, and she'd tell him, 'We're moving on out, cowboy, ten minutes to pack that saddlebag,' and quick as a fly Chester would fetch his little suitcase, like a little dog really, the way he trotted over, opened it up, putting his things in. He was comical like that, the seriousness with which he did it, pulling his little shoes on, talking to himself like he was urging himself on, the studied care he took, packing his animals away. Pete had been right. Chester was good with his hands: slow in other ways, but good with his hands. He had curly hair now, golden like an angel's, heavy for his age, nothing like Louis at all. It had surprised them both. She'd look at his fair head and tell him stories she remembered, though no fairy tales, no princesses. Princesses were out. No Sleeping Beauty, no Cinderella, no prince and no fucking slipper.

Her days were long now, longer than they had been before. Money was tight, Chester growing all the time, the food he needed, the clothes. Sometimes Louis and she ate egg and chips four days running. Louis spent what spare cash they had on another Corsair that year, a de luxe, over a hundred and twenty on the clock, but with two-speed wipers and original carpets in the load space where Chester made a little den with his stuffed giraffe, his camel and his rabbit. It was perfect when Louis took time off with a decent wage packet in his pocket, even better than the Humber. They could ride anywhere with Chester in the back like that. He never gave them any bother. In the car it was like he was in a little time capsule of his own, her and Louis sitting up front like the early days, rolling cigarettes, bouncing about the roads, ending up in a pub, sleeping it off on the beach, or fooling around up on the downs.

Then that last time, Gloucester way, Louis found the basement flat in Ellen Road. A real find, he announced, and that much was true, like a stately home it was, with a piss-long corridor and rooms running off it left and right, high ceilings you couldn't even jump to, French windows at the back with a landing strip for a garden, clumps of giant bamboo at the end of it. Chester's Forest they called it, where he played all day if the weather held, with his donkey and his camel and all the others he'd been given (for the boys had brought something every time they visited, she almost wished they wouldn't, the menagerie they were accumulating), and Alice not being able to find him.

Louis was proud of the flat, the big bathroom and the tall, stand-up fireplace in the front room, brought stuff back from skips he'd passed they could burn in the grate. It was kind of magic for a time, when the fire was blazing, the room quite bare and the shadows on the wall flickering like you were in a clearing, but the thing was, it was so spacious, so dry, so bloody perfect there was no good reason to leave at all. They had a proper bedroom with a proper bed, Chester's room a thankful way's off, a bathroom with a fuck-off bath stuck in the middle: everything. Whenever Louis came back after two or three days away, he walked around it like he owned the place, like it meant something to him, like it mattered. He started bringing back bits of furniture he'd found, armchairs with the stuffing hanging out, lampstands with frayed cords, even an electric clock for the kitchen (what, so she could cook their meals on time?), wouldn't even let her knitting-needle the meter like she usually did. It wasn't that Louis wanted a home. It wasn't as simple as that. It was as though the flat itself had a say in how they lived, that it was more than a set of stuck-up walls and doors and windows. It was important. The balance of power had shifted away from her, away from them, to somewhere else, somewhere she couldn't quite fathom, couldn't get a hold of, somewhere unseen, somewhere oppressive. Every time she went out, the thought of the flat started to drag her back, the great empty rooms, the bare walls, the weird light that seeped in through the windows and under the doors. It got so she thought she'd never leave, Chester babbling away in his forest, Louis out with the gang, and she let loose in this space she didn't need, like she was supposed to do something with it. She thought of Lovell and Swigert and Haise baling out, jettisoning the whole caboodle without a moment's thought. They'd done it to save their lives. She wished she could do the same. It was killing her, this flat, sucking the breath out of her. She could feel herself slowing up, her mind going sort of cloudy like she was being drugged or poisoned. Even her colour started to change, her skin turning a kind of fatty white, like a corpse, her flesh dead. That's what it was, she was rotting from the inside. That would account for the smell on her, wafting up from out under, the vacancy lodged in her head like a lump of concrete, the lost appetite for sex stretching out vast like a desert. She was dying there, organ by organ, limb by limb, and she had no right to. What was wrong with it? Then Louis came back with the news that he'd blagged fourteen solid days' work up in Glasgow, double time, top pay, and that he had to leave right away. She couldn't believe it, put her arms round his neck, pressed her body up hard, the words busting into her mouth.

'I'll tell Chess. We can be off in an hour.'

Louis had unfolded her arms, his face set.

'It's fourteen days. It's not worth the effort, for fourteen days.'

He was gone three hours later, the car as well.

Putting Chester to bed that night, she felt it like she had never felt before, just her and Chester and her man gone she hardly knew where, and she left behind in the long corridor and the big bedroom and a bath you could drown in. She thought of the car, travelling without her, Louis in the brilliant dark and the road he was on, with lights up ahead and the cars that would pass him, not knowing who they overtook, not a clue to his singular power, his untouchable determination. She could sense herself in the car with him, the heat stealing up her legs, the hum of the engine rolling up the miles to Scotch Corner, the turn-off to Glasgow and the meagre room at the end of it, the hard, sparkling bed and the chipped washstand afterwards and the thin curtains that kept out nothing, the simplicity of it all like an altar. It was what she needed too, a place to worship, a shrine to who she was.

Resolute, she abandoned the idea of sleep, flung the closed doors open, began restoring order, dragging Louis's unwanted furniture into the fireplace: the wooden bookcase that he'd never put up, the pair of dining chairs they never used, the three-legged table under Chester's window, the bamboo blinds, two pictures they'd found in an empty house, a busted umbrella, Louis's lampstands, three of them, jammed them up the chimney's innards. She rolled two great balls of newspaper, as big as watermelons, stuffed them under the contraption. For the first time in months she felt happy. It looked like a kind of ballsy giant, ready to stick her under his arm, carry her off, fuck her for his tea. She pulled her dress off, sat down cross-legged on the rug before it, matches in hand.

'Mum?'

Chester stood in the doorway. Her hand went to her throat, dislocated. She'd imagined herself masturbating into the flames.

'There you are,' she said. 'I was just coming to get you. It's just you and me now.'

He stepped forward, hesitant, staring at the strange wooden statue. It had a smashed face, the cuckoo clock Chester had broken weeks back, pulling the bird out of its house.

'Dad's gone away,' she said. 'Doesn't need us any more. So I've made a bonfire. All the things we don't need, see?'

He came in closer, standing by her side in his little pyjamas. She snaked her arm around, pulled him in.

'Would you like to light it?'

He shook his head, pointing to the cuckoo, the bird hanging down like a busted eye.

'Time for him to go, Chester. Time for him to flap his wings, fly away. Go on, you do it.' She pushed the box open, took out the spindle. 'You've seen Mum do it, haven't you? Hold it away from you, strike it towards me. Like this, see. Go on.'

The boy took it from her, uncertain. He had the dexterity to know what to do, but not the conviction with which to do it. The match skittered along the surface, broke in his hand. He turned and ran back down the dark corridor to his room, his feet slapping against the tiles, like they were wet. Alice jumped up, followed. When she got there, he was back in bed, his blanket pulled over his head, shoulders heaving. Alice lay down beside him, waiting for his breath to calm. His head smelt sweet, intoxicating. It drifted into her like a sleeping gas. When she woke the next morning, his body tucked into hers still, she was surprised that she had stayed the whole night, surprised the more when the following night and the nights after she found herself back in his narrow bed, her fire unlit, desire abated. The flat was hardly there at all and, when she was in it, she barely moved.

Louis came back from Glasgow four days early, tired and dirty, smelling like he hadn't washed for a week. Chester was asleep. They didn't wake him. Louis did what he always did, made straight for the bathroom. She pulled two beers out, determined to have it out with him, walked down in her bare feet. Louis was standing there, the big taps gushing.

'How you been?' he said.

'I've been shit. I thought you'd never come back, like I was trapped here, never see the light of day. I made a bonfire of it all.'

'What all?'

'All the crap, Louis. All the stuff you've been bringing back.'

He put his hand under her chin.

'Aren't you the clever one?'

'What do you mean?' He ignored the question, took off his shirt, went to the mirror, examined his chin.

'You didn't go out then?' he said.

'Course I went out, but I had to come back, didn't I. Felt like day release from prison.' He went back to the bath, turned the cold off.

'Don't talk daft. We've more room than we know what to do with. Look at this bath. Princess Margaret would be happy to be washed in this bath.'

'I bet she would. The legs on it look like she's just been screwed by the footman.'

'Two footmen,' he corrected. He moved the water round. 'Loads of water, this bath takes.'

'And money. It's a bath for cunts, Louis. How much did you make?'

'Not a single penny.'

'For fuck's sake.'

'That's because I didn't go to Glasgow.' He stepped out of his trousers, kissed her on the head. 'I lied to you.'

'How do you mean?'

'I mean, I told you an untruth.' He turned his back on her, lifted his leg, stuck a foot in.

'The M11, that's what the trip was about. It's finally coming off. Signed up first day there, spent the rest of the time looking for somewhere to stay. Epping Forest. It's nothing like here, but we won't be there long.'

She felt the colour run back into her.

'Jesus, Louis.'

'And here you were, clearing out before I'd even told you. It's a worrying trait, you know, clairvoyance. Means I can't trust myself to pull the wool over your eyes at all.'

He slipped in, his head and body under the water, his hair waving about like seaweed. He stayed down there, not moving. God how she loved looking at him, the dark swim of his body. He'd reclaimed her. He'd gone away and come back, everything changed. It was religious almost, what he'd done, like a pilgrimage, like a journey to salvation. He came up, the water streaming down his face. He wasn't going anywhere again, not without her. That was the whole point of it.

'When can we go?' she said, her chest wild.

'What?' He stuck a finger into his ear, wiggled the water out.

'I said when can we go?'

'Whenever we want.' He lifted a leg. 'Are you going to wash me or what?'

'I am not.'

She raked the shirt off, glad to be rid of it.

'I am going to fuck you until the footmen get cramp, until we fall through the ceiling.'

He put his hands on the bath's side, smiling.

'We're on the ground floor, Alice.'

'Fall through to Australia then, I don't care, as long as we split the bastard wide open. Then in the morning ...'

She stepped in, her breasts heavy over him.

'We're up first thing and fucking off out of it. And two other things. I'm doing the meter and I'm driving. All the way.'

They woke late, what with the bath, and the drink they had and the fire. The fire had taken the greater toll, kept them active through the night. The fire had hardly given them any sleep at all, the sight of its fury driving them on. She couldn't remember when she had last felt so drenched. Ten o'clock they were ready, the Corsair down on the suspension, Chester's hideaway ready in the back. Chester hadn't packed his suitcase at all. Alice had done it all while he'd taken refuge with his animals in the forest. It was how she wanted it, just her and Louis scraping their lives clean again. They brewed a last pot, then, twenty-five past, she stood at the French window and called.

'Come on, Chester, time to head on out.'

She saw his little head disappear like someone had jerked him back. Louis was sitting in the passenger seat, rolling a cigarette. They hadn't told the landlord. She loved that, not telling the landlord. If it had just been her and him, now that they were all set, she'd have gone at him again, nice and quick, just to put them in the travelling mood, but with Chester on the loose ... She walked to the end of the garden, impatient.

'Come on, Chester,' she said. 'Time to go.'

He stood in the thicket, his little fists clutched around the canes. He had one of his animals tucked under his arm, the giraffe. There was a deliberation to his face, like he wasn't a little boy at all, like he was an old man, hanging on to his future. He pulled the canes across him, like she couldn't see him.

'Come on now. There's a sweetheart. Don't you want to see your new home? It's in a proper forest, Dad says, trees and everything. He'll make you a tree-house, right at the top.'

The horn sounded, two quick bursts. Louis was right. They couldn't hang around for long, not if they wanted to get away unnoticed.

'Now, Chester. Your father's waiting.'

As soon as she'd said it she wished she hadn't. It was what her mother used to say, your father's waiting. He was always waiting, waiting for her to make a mistake, to fail his expectations. That's what she loved about what she'd done. Her father was going to stand at the top of the stairs and wait for ever now. The boy gripped the bamboo ever more tight, the canes shaking feathery, like he was standing on a raft.

'We'll go without you then. Leave you here.'

He blinked, a long deliberate thing, a slow-speed shutter imprinting the memory of the moment, a shadow on his life. He was blond and big and his eyes were wide and blue and unsettled, like a stone had been dropped in.

'Go on,' he said. 'I don't care.'

There was a moment, in the turning of her heel, in the stride to the French window, the walk down the corridor, before she heard his running feet and his little voice, before he grasped her hand and stumbled alongside, trying to match her unforgiving pace, when it crossed her mind how much easier it would be if she could leave him, if it could be as simple as that, and if she could do it, how what had been lost would be restored. Nights like the last night had proved that it was still there for the taking, just her and Louis, thick like cream, perfect like an egg; that the thrill of movement, discomfort, suspicion, was the fuel of it all. Chester was the weakness. Chester required a different sort of need, not hard and intolerant like hers and Louis's. He was small and incapable, could do nothing without them, and she wished for that instant, a wish that had her jerking Chester forward in her distaste for the dark measure of it, his feet hauled along the tiles like a scolded dog, that she could leave him, pretend he didn't exist, jump into the car with her man and head out, not because she didn't love him, or want him, or even need him, but because she longed for the charm of irresponsibility to envelop her once again, Louis dangerous at her side.

She opened the door, pushed Chester into the back.

'What's up with you two?' Louis said.

She checked the mirror, grabbed the gear stick, threw it into first. The Corsair bucked forward, Louis looking at her askance.

'Don't say it,' she said. 'Just tell me where I'm going.'

Louis reeled off the route. Chester began pulling his animals out of his rucksack. She closed conversation down, she needed the room. She felt out of control, needed to corral it. Nearing the motorway, she started up again. They were on their way now.

'Last night,' she said, 'what with the fire and everything, I forgot to ask. Are the boys going to be there?'

He ran his hand along the inside of her leg. He'd had the same thoughts as her earlier, she could tell. He had such a touch.

'Hogan's already there,' he said. 'Pete too. Gil's having woman trouble again.' His hand lingered in the muscle. 'I don't know about the twins.'

She swung out on to the motorway. A thin voice came from the back, troubled. She'd almost forgotten he was there.

'Where's Horace? Horace not here.'

Louis spoke softly.

'Horace?'

'His donkey.' Alice shifted in her seat, settled in lane.

'I thought he was called Algy.'

'That's the camel. Christ, Louis, keep up will you. He must have left it behind.'

Chester was squirming amongst his things.

'He's not here,' he said. 'He's not here.' She glanced back. The car shifted a fraction.

'We can't go back, sweetheart. Horace will be all right. He likes it there, in the forest. It's where he belongs.'

She flicked the indicator, unsettled by the distraction. She was going to overtake, whether Louis liked it or not. Still it came.

'I want Horace. Can't leave without Horace.'

His voice was shrill now, rising. Louis had his eyes shut.

'This is the trouble with all these things,' Alice told him, her voice low. 'That's why I had the fire. We don't want it to get like that again.' She called over her shoulder. 'We can't go back, Chester. Anyway he won't be there now. He'll have left, packed his bag, like we have.'

'Not there?' It made no sense to the boy.

'Walking the roads, that's what donkeys are best at, trudge, trudge, steady as a rock. He's probably walking to our new place right now.'

'But he's all alone.'

'That doesn't matter. They're loners, donkeys. They like it best on their own. Tell you what. You make a special den for him when we get there. Then one day you'll wake up and there he'll be out by the back door, waiting for his new home.'

Silence. Chester was trying to work it out. He knew Horace was a stuffed animal, but he was full of love and animation too. Hadn't he walked in amongst the forest, in and out of the den?

'Will he know the way?'

She smiled. It was nearly done.

'All donkeys know the way. Just like your dad.'

Crisis over, she picked up Louis's hand, kissed it, let it drop back and settled it in. Chester set his animals in a row, the camel, the giraffe, the fox, the two hedgehogs that the twins had given him.

'Horace has gone,' he told them, his voice solemn. 'Fucked off out of it.'

Louis started to laugh.

'Did I hear right? Fucked off out of it?'

She pushed his hand away.

'You shouldn't encourage him, Louis. If he starts up like that when he's at school ...' Her voice trailed off, her heart not in it.

'What if he does? It's what we do, isn't it? You take after your old man, don't you, Chester? If that isn't the best thing of all.'

He had turned round to face his son, his other hand sudden on her bone. She felt wonderful, like they could drive for ever, do anything they wanted, like it would never stop. And Chester, thrilled with his audience, threw his camel up against the roof.

'Horace has fucked off out of it, Algy! Fucked off out of it!'

It was nothing more than a shack down a sunken lane, slap bang in the middle of nowhere. God knows how he'd found it. It had a low roof, guttering hanging down like a tipped hat, an extension squirrelled away at the back. It smelt three-quarters rotten.

'A hovel,' she said. 'Not even bricks and mortar.'

'Creosote, that's all it needs,' Louis said. 'We don't have to stay here long.'

She looked out the window.

'See that?'

Chester was running down the garden path and out towards the trees, his camel hanging by his legs. 'It's not what he needs, moving about, no one to play with. If we were travellers, it would be different. He'd have boys his own age.'

'We're not travellers. God forbid.'

'Should have seen him hanging on to the bamboo. He's after somewhere fixed, Louis, somewhere where he can ...' the words were difficult for her '... settle in, where you come home to after work.'

'Like to slippers and such.'

She stepped up, took his hands, clenched them to her belly.

'Listen to me, Louis. I'm the same as you. This is good for him. But not for me. Not all the time.' She paused, got her thoughts in order. 'We need to stay put for his sake, but I need the other too. I'll go mad if not. When did we last go for a real drive? When did we last …?' She sighed the unspoken list.

'Not him, you mean?'

'Of course him. But not all the time. I want to fuck off out of it, Louis. Just like you do. You fuck off out of it all the time.'

'I could get someone,' he said. 'Someone to stay with him, when you want it. Someone you could trust.'

She knew who it was even before she appeared. She'd seen it in her eyes, that she'd find a way. He drove up there and back in a day, a month later. The hour he was gone she went to Chester's room and painted the Brebis, just as she had seen her, only in daylight, the Brebis standing on the road white and still, as big as the wall could take, the road on which she stood climbing into the distance like a medieval painting, the hills at the back and with a donkey in the foreground, tied up to a tree. It was a good likeness, she thought, of the Brebis, her immobility, her eyes. With luck, she might see her again.

'What do you think of her?' she said, pleased.

Chester walked to the wall, pointed to the donkey.

'Horace,' he said.

She wished she had painted it in her room, not his.

Louis was back before the moon was out. She stood at the open door, waiting for both. He stepped out like the gravity was different, like it was new territory.

'Well?'

'She'll do it.'

'What about money?' Alice asked, the ground slipping under her. Of course she'd do it.

'She'll find work, don't worry. There's just one thing. She wants something in return.'

Louis held her straight, not a flicker on his face.

'Here it comes.'

'She'd like it if sometimes, than rather you go away with me, and she stays here, we could do it the other way round. You'll be with Chester and she'll …'

'… go with you.'

'That's the condition. I don't mind if you don't.'

Alice found herself laughing.

'If it's intimacy you're worried about, there'd be precious little on that score. She was never that bothered. It's just … I'm the only one to get near her at all. It's always been like that with her.'

'Goes back a long way then?' He threw it off.

'No harm will come from it, Alice. She will be good with him. She is a good woman.'

'Would she live here then?'

'I thought we'd get a caravan, put it round the back. And if I got the Pot Hole working again, drove that down, she could start up the café again, you too if you want. It was a nice little money-earner, that van of hers.'

She tried to find reasons to object, couldn't find them. There was nothing dishonest about this, no deception. An older woman was offering her the key to the door.

He went to fetch her six weeks later, she and Chester waiting for them all afternoon. She had flour on her jersey, her jeans greasy where Chester had wiped his fingers. They'd made some scones for tea, herb scones, a bit of parsley, a bit of thyme, sage. She stuck them in the oven when the car came bouncing down the track. The woman stepped out, sniffed the air. She was wearing the same dress that she had on up at Scotch Corner, heels on too. Alice felt like a homesteader watching the glamour riding in. The woman walked up the path to the open door, Louis fishing two bags out the back.

'So,' Alice said, trying not to notice the nails, the slightly chipped scarlet. 'You're a childminder now.'

Lot looked down.

'Is this the fellow?' she said. 'Looks as if he hardly needs minding at all.'

'Shirking your duties already.'

Louis pushed past, putting the bags down.

'Now, now, girls. Let's not get off on the wrong foot.'

'Chester is it?' Lot said, in a good way Alice had to admit, straightforward.

Chester nodded. It was important, this meeting, he knew it, the way they were all standing.

'This is Aunty Lot,' Louis said.

Chester looked up at her carefully and then across to his mother.

'Aunty Lot is coming to stay, to help Mum out with this and that. Isn't that right.'

'So it would appear.'

'We're all going to get on fine, me and Mum and Aunty Lot. She's brought her television, see? We can stick it on the sideboard.'

Chester looked again. She was tall, Aunty Lot, taller than Dad, taller than Mum. Loads of perfume, like a toilet.

'Aunty Lot is going to stay with you when Mum has to come with me.' He looked nervous.

'Leave me like Horace? In the wood.'

'Not like Horace, Chester. Not like Horace at all. It won't always be like that, anyway. Sometimes it will be Mum who has to go away, and sometimes ...'

'Yes? Go on, say it.' Alice's voice was hard.

'Sometimes Aunty Lot will come with me, and Mum will stay behind with you.'

'Won't that be fun,' said Aunty Lot. 'Do you've a den or something? Out in the wood?'

He didn't reply. She put out a hand. 'I know you do. Come and show Aunty Lot.'

And Chester took her hand. Alice and Louis stood still while they walked down the path and out the gate. He touched her on the shoulder, twisted her round. They had a mirror now. He tucked her hair back.

'See? Nothing has changed,' he said.

'No?'

He covered her breasts, sought the pulse in them.

'Thick like cream,' he said, his voice soft on her neck. 'Perfect like an egg.'

'Oh, Louis.'

Chester showed Aunty Lot his den, hidden like a smuggler's cave, showed her where the stuffed animals lived, the hidey-hole where the food was kept, and the secret road leading out from it, through the brambles and under the branches, for when they fucked off out of it. She was still laughing when they returned, half an hour later, Alice in a clean jumper and a fresh skirt, the television and aerial up on the sideboard, the scones burnt and Louis glutinous down her leg.

THREE

IT WAS LIKE EDEN for them, Epping Forest, and they Adam and Eve with a bastard family cocking a snoop at God and the Bible and all his effing rules. There was nothing to the Hovel really, the trees pressed in at the back, and the pubic scrub at the front, and they wanted to keep it that way. It was never said but it was understood. The only thing Louis had to do was to hack down a space round the back where he could screen off the motor, one of the first things they did, Louis bare-chested and Alice in boots and a dirty bra, blood scratched up all over as they bent two lines of striplings over the cleared ground. No cars in Eden. Cars were for outer regions, fierce extremes. Like a nave in a church, Louis said, reviewing the work. Like a fucking cathedral, said Alice, and raised the boy to the roof, proud to have carved out space for their own responsibilities. Afterwards, with the Corsair driven in, they turned the hose on each other, blood and dirt washed into the soil.

How big was their Eden? Sure, it had a beginning and an end, but on occasions it appeared without end, from the warped windows and walls across the stubborn grass to the sentinel walk of the trees and the hidden heart that lay a foot-fall away, could they but find it. There was the four of them,

Alice and Louis and Chester and Aunty Lot, and to Alice it seemed like they were the only ones really alive, sailing out on a leaky raft, bumping up against strange shapes and queer customs. Those who came and went were different, didn't smell of the forest like they did, didn't move in the forest like they did, couldn't see the forest for what it was – the brazen, two-fingered gamble of it all. But Alice and Louis could always see it, see it clear like it was strung out from the branches in big shiny letters, felt the excitement of it every time they opened the door. Lot took a while longer, but once she was settled in, there was hardly any call for her to step outside it at all, save the fortnightly run to the shops, and the monthly visit to the beauty salon, where she'd get the hair back up to strength, pick through the magazines and realise once more why Louis had trashed her television within a fortnight of her arrival. Television had no place in their Eden. Their Eden was switched on all the time and, despite what God had hoped, vastly pagan. There was nothing innocent about this Eden, not within the man, not within the woman, not in their grasp of knowledge, nor in their understanding of nakedness. Nakedness was to be relished in all its parts. Nakedness was like knowledge, it was what it was: banal, necessary, sexual, it didn't matter which. The forest would let them be as they wanted to be. They were the forest's and the forest was theirs.

Not that they were alone. It was a good place to meet, everyone knew that, was almost sacred that way. Its skin was light and dappled, its core a darker hue: sunken ponds, abandoned cars, a world of undergrowth and crooked paths. People brought things to the forest, cargo, emotions. Goods were exchanged, guns were buried, marriages too, betrayal laid out on a rug, bushes limp with underwear and exhausted rubbers. Hooligans visited the forest, rival gangs with hold-alls full of Stella, the drinking polite and visceral while they planned their pandemonium. The fresh-air enthusiasts gave them a wide berth, but came all the same. The air was like everything else in the forest, there for the taking.

Louis bedded Lot in permanent within the year. He rode up to Scotch Corner on the back of Hogan's Triumph, fixed the van's wheels, drove the Pot Hole down three days later. It was ugly like the Hovel was ugly, vulgar, unashamed. Louis scraped it smack against the Hovel's side wall, its black nose poking out the front.

'Like a dog sniffing out his dinner,' Hogan said. They were stood back in the clearing, a beer apiece in their hands. Chester was holding Aunty Lot's hand. He had to reach up for it, was getting to like it. Alice stood next to Hogan's bike. It was one of the things she hadn't yet learnt, how to ride a serious bike. Hogan had offered but she didn't know if she wanted the bother. Cars were everything to her. Louis shook his empty can.

'Just the job, if there's any cooking to be done,' he said. Lot handed him hers. She wasn't drinking, not holding the boy.

'How am I going to get in?' she said. 'Out the front door, round the back, up the steps? I've done with all that.'

Louis pulled at the tab, turned his head from the sudden spray.

'We'll cut a space through. It's only wood and tin. Hogan and me can do it next time we're off.'

Alice jumped across, prised the can out his hands.

'What am I doing? Painting my fucking nails?' She worked the drink down her throat. 'Just leave the car, that's all.'

Next day Alice measured up, found the timber yard, drove back with Chester hung over the rear seat, staring at the mad flapping of Alice's jersey, its arms wrapped round the joist ends tied to the Corsair roof. Three days she worked at it, pulling Hovel shelves down, wading into the sanctity of the Pot Hole, marking up the needs of the cut, Chester holding the pencil and the paper, and later, when the work began, the drill or the hammer or the Allen key, whatever he hoped she might need. He knew the names of things, knew where things were kept, the toolbox in Mum and Dad's bedroom, the chair he had to stand on for the saws and drills hung up on their wall, the lean-to out the back with the padlock, where the heavy-duty stuff was stacked, the jacks and batteries, and the box of oily rags where the smell came from. He was part of it, something new and thrilling, and he watched his mother like she was a circus act, her arms brown and strong, opening up the Hovel wall, cutting slices out the van, a bandana round her head and goggles on her face, the metal jagged and bright, Alice pulling the flaps free, bending back the edges, her fingers in a grunt, and the back of her bare legs taut and true. No door at first (that came later, before the second winter set in) but a blocked-off gangway joining the two, like the Hovel was the quay and the Pot Hole a boat all tied up. It moved when you stepped on to it, moved like a boat might, and once aboard had a front, not like the nose of a dog at all, but like a prow busting for the sea. Alice did it all, not banged in haphazard with teeth and nails, but drilled and dovetailed and bevelled, a piece of work, she said, when it was finished, a girly piece of cock and balls, wouldn't you say, Chess, and Chester nodded and hugged her leg. He was young but he knew she had a way of looking at things unlike other mothers, made her not quite natural, made her strange, kind of separate. It drew him to her. It kept him apart.

Finished, they all saw the point of it, not just for what it would do for Lot, but for who they were, what they thought. It was like a statement, a deliberate blot on the landscape, rubbish on the outside and a health hazard in, with fryers like long-handled bedpans and a kettle the size of a Kraut sea-mine, intimidating hideous and ready to blow. For Louis, it was like breaking in a stretch of open country, bringing the forest to heel. It had a beauty all of their making now. Alice sort of hoped that now they were attached, when it all got too much, she could turn the engine over, flip it in gear and fuck off out of it, Hovel, Pot Hole, the whole shebang. She loved the idea of that.

Meanwhile they were staying put. It was larger than it looked, the Hovel, went back a bit, the rooms wooden and sloped on the floor. It had a long, covered porch at the front and was raised up from the ground by blocks of cracked concrete. At night they could hear the company wild below, rats, rabbits, foxes, who knew what. Alice revelled in it, never dreamt of interfering, made her want to fuck Louis sometimes, make her own noises back. Louis kept the gun under the bed now, for when he was away, but she wasn't fearful of that, never occurred to her to be so. The forest could be whatever it wanted to be. She would let it all swim in.

After the porch came the main room, running the whole length of the place, where the black range smoked, where the table with the scuffed top stood, where they'd eat and bang about, later where Chester worked on his schooling, his eyes searching for the light coming from the one bulb hanging up by the alcove where the sink sat, right next to the new door.

Behind him, beside the mirror, stood the big sideboard, plates and cups, knives and forks and a drawer full of cartridges. Three rooms at the back, bare floors, no heating, cut off from the front by the spine of a passageway, Alice and Louis's room on the left, then Chester's, then Aunty Lot's, which was no bigger than the bed they manhandled in. In between hers and Chester's, the bell-pull toilet and washbasin. That was the sum of it. They had water, they had electricity (a generator) and they had a cesspit. What more could they want?

Like on the motorway, Louis soon became known to the forest, the measure of the man. There'd been dog-fights when they came, could hear them on the weekend, the cars coming and going and the noise of the men with their blood up. Alice didn't like it, none of them did. Now and again they'd find parts of a dog left behind. Louis would bury whatever it was, Chester planting a sprig, a root, a handful of fern. He was good with his hands that way. One Sunday Louis found a badger with her back broken and her jaw smashed in, like with a spade. He carried her to the clearing in his arms, laid her out on the ground.

'Bastards wouldn't even let her fight fair,' he said, trouble in his eyes. 'Men like that hate badgers. They're an affront to them, living so clean and independent, better than they ever could. They're afraid of them, afraid of us too. It's like a badgers' sett to them, this house, do you see that, Chess? Would you help me, here?'

They took her to the deepest part of the forest. Alice held the spade. Louis wrapped her in an old overcoat of his, tied it up with baler twine, the body wet and heavy and rank. Chester had brought his stuffed rabbit, put her in one of the big pockets of the coat, to keep her company. Louis laid a hand on the badger's broken muzzle, closing the mouth as best he could before enveloping the shroud. Alice finished the grave in clean-cut digs, four feet down by her reckoning. Louis jumped in.

'Hand her to me careful,' he said, 'like she was a brother.'

'A sister,' Alice said.

'Sow or boar, they're all brothers to me,' Louis said, and held out his arms. Alice took the back legs, Chester the shoulders. As Louis accepted the weight, the badger's head slipped free of the coat. Louis turned away in a groan.

They packed the earth down. Alice squatted, pissed over it to keep the foxes away. Back at the Hovel, Lot had made a sausage pie. They ate in silence, boiled potatoes hard in their mouths. Louis was off the next morning, ten days.

'It won't happen again,' he said, and went to bed, the only words he spoke.

The boys arrived unannounced. Pete and Hogan and Gil, Brummies One and Two, came in quiet late one Saturday afternoon, sat in the Hovel quiet, bottles on the table, smoke flattened against the windows, a pickaxe handle apiece stacked in the corner by the door.

'Will you look after Patch?' Gil asked Chester. 'While we're gone.'

'Gone?'

'It's no place for a dog, where we're going,' and they laughed. Alice stood up and held Gil to her breast. It amazed them all.

'There's not many of you,' she said, letting him go.

'They'll be fraidy-cats,' Hogan said, rubbing his big hands. 'One more before we go, I think.'

Lot sent Chester to his room. He heard the boys clink bottles, Patch sat up on his bed, attentive.

99

'If you'd brought another handle ...' he heard his mother say.

Chester put his hand to Patch, the dog shaking inside, the little trembles rapid like a motor. He heard the benches scraped back, and the clatter of the wood and Alice saying, 'Here, one for you too,' and a silence and the soft shuffle of feet. He heard the door opened and the boys troop out, heard Alice say, 'I still don't see why not,' and Lot answering, 'Oh for heaven's sake, Alice, of course you do, that's why you kissed them.' Chester put his hand to his lips to the dog, like he'd seen Gil do, looped a scarf round Patch's collar and pulled him through the window, no shoes. The dark was thick as fur, but the boys were moving light and quick, fluttered torch-lights on the forest floor. Chester followed. He knew how to move at night, knew how to see a path when you weren't looking. For a while he lost them, nothing but the forest, endless like the stars. He was glad he was barefoot, wished he had nothing on at all. He didn't know why he wished it, what it meant, but it came on him strong, a call – turn aside, walk into the thickest dark. Live like that, and never come back. He was a boy but a stranger too. What more was there but the forest? What more could there be? Then he saw them, Hogan and the others outlined by a little thicket of tree, and beyond them, a circle of light coming up from the ground, like it was dug in, and within it, a body of men spread out in a ring. How many men Chester did not know, more than Gil and Pete and Hogan and the Brummies, but as he worried at the thought, the boys were running through the lot of them, smooth and rolling, knocking them down like in a bowling alley, not a word spoken, the blows coming out of the blue, like pirates swinging down from a rope, everything wild and wonderful. He pulled the dog close, hearts hammering rib to rib, men doubling up, falling to the ground, cries like startled birds panicked through the bracken and the fizz inside him enormous. But the boys wouldn't stop. On and on it went, even when it was finished they wouldn't stop, Gil and Pete and Hogan and the Brummies, arms flailing up and down like toys wound up too tight, the fizz stuck in Chester's throat, like he couldn't swallow, like he was going to choke, up and down, up and down ...

It was harder climbing back in, Patch wriggling as he pushed him through. By the time they were back on the bed, Gil had his door open.

'Give you any trouble?' Gil asked. Chester shook his head, aware of the vastness of the man, what a man like that could hide.

'I was asking the dog,' Gil said and picked him up, tapered fingers long round the belly. 'He's all wet,' he said. 'What you been doing? Spying on us, Louis's little drummer boy?'

He dropped the dog and lifted Chester up by his waist, carried him head first into the front room.

'We had an audience,' he said. 'Front-row seat.'

He stood him down. Alice was sat on the table, swinging her bare legs. The boys were clustered round, passing a big bottle of Paddy between them, long gulps like they were thirsty. They had a smell on them too, overpowering, like a rabbit on the turn. He could taste the stink of it in his mouth, in his stomach. He felt sick, excited, like he'd eaten something forbidden, something wrong. Alice had her head back, breathing it in.

'Give him a go then,' she said, and then Brummie One was tipping the neck to his teeth. He took it straight to the back of his throat, swallowed it whole like Alice and Louis did, felt the whisky whoosh down inside, like someone was pulling it through from the other end, pulling it like it was a length of knotted string. He shut his eyes to the heat. Then he was burning, a bonfire boy dazzled in their midst, everything lit up, wonderful again. He jumped up on the bench.

'They've fucked off out of it!' he shouted and he leapt on Hogan's back and went round and round until he couldn't see any more.

Life in Paradise. Louis worked the M11 in thick slabs of time, got picked up by Pete or Hogan, left Alice with the car, not that she used it much. It lay under the trees mostly, waiting for Louis's return and the box of oily rags. He rented a lock-up under the railway bridge a mile away: car parts, chains and pulleys for lifting engines out. They spent time together there, making their cars go the distance. When Chester was around five, Alice walked him through to the stop where the bus would ferry him to the all-day primary school, pick him up in the morning, set him down at night. She did it for the first week to clock the driver, but after that, he was on his own. Come winter, Aunty Lot waited by the stop to walk him home, but as often as not he'd run on ahead, lose himself in the wind and the dark and the great alone, so after a while she didn't bother. Some days he'd take longer than others. No one thought about it much. When he was there, he was there, and when he wasn't, he wasn't, just like everybody else. Alice did what she had always done, whatever it was. Some days she'd walk out the door and not return until Lot and Chester were long in bed. Some days she'd come back hands full, a sack of mushrooms, a roll of netting, one time a big rubber tyre she hung up for a swing, sat in it hours on end, swaying at the moon. Some days she'd hardly move at all, sit in the porch with her crayons, draw pictures of the clearing, the trees, draw them relentlessly, hang them on the walls, tear them down, no escape. They drew the hut further in, added protection. Rainy afternoons, like as not she'd take the gun out from under the bed, lay it on the table and clean it. She missed the gun.

When Louis returned it was different. Alice would have polished the car. There'd be beer on the table, beer and hard-boiled eggs. Louis would throw his boots into the corner of the room, plant Chester on his knee, jiggle him this way and that, set him on the floor, hand him a sherbet lemon from his gritty pocket. Alice would lead Louis out the back, take the hose and a bar of soap to him, Louis standing there, hair plastered, bottle in hand, Chester sucking out the powder, fascinated by what he saw. Other times Alice would knock the top off one of the bottles, take a swig, walk straight into their room. If the weather was good Aunty Lot would take Chester out on to the porch, or down to his den. If not, she turned on the radio. They were allowed a radio for that, and besides, when Louis was away, Lot liked to have it on for the music, something she could tap her foot to. After supper, they'd sit on the porch, watch the foxes come out. Winter, Louis would leave a bowl of bread and milk at the edge of the clearing. September he'd put down a bowl of blackberries. Alice had never known about foxes and blackberries before. Louis was right. Foxes were just like them.

So it went. Louis in top form, Alice aglow, Chester like he was bouncing on bed-springs. Night begat morning and morning begat a deliberate uncertainty. Sure, they had a routine, but it was theirs and could be broken any time. Journeys! There were so many of them, so many cars, so many rides for Chester in the back, Alice and Louis travelling in the dark, two o'clock, three, their preferred hours, the trip like in space, lights distant, outside a vast emptiness, the rumble of the road the mother-ship's turbulence. Chester wanted to tell school about those journeys – but he knew he must not. They were under a spell, the moment they jumped into the car, everything suspended and them moving in and out untouched. They'd end up always in the same sort of place, a town, a square, a market, somewhere big, where Alice would park the car and let him out. 'See you back here in a couple of hours, all right?' she'd say, and Chester would nod, waiting for the money that she would slip into his hand 'just in case', and the ruffle of his hair as Louis leant over and opened the door for him. He'd watch them drive off, the turn of the wheel always quick, like they were slipping the leash, couldn't wait, and he felt it too, alone, like in the forest, stone and brick soaring up in trunks. He'd move through them, sucked into their orbit, hollow churches, old libraries, town halls with cold staircases, statues when he could find them, figures with clasped hands and eyes looking to where they could not see. He liked the big churches best, cathedrals when he got to know the word, could tell the difference quick enough. Cathedrals were like cars, there to take you somewhere. When he stood in a cathedral, he could imagine the whole thing taking off like a spaceship. He would stand feet planted on the flagging, no feeling of time, only passage, the coloured windows and the robed figures flying and the roof impossible, tempting him with wings. No one noticed him. He never looked lost or worried, always purposeful, always glad, always content, which he was. Then his time would be up, and he'd know it, not by any clock but by the mechanism deep in his gut, the same place as Alice and Louis had theirs – so long, and no more.

And where did they go? He had no idea, knew better than to ask. Not that there was much to tell. They never took anything, never left a mess, rarely stayed more than sixty minutes. They had a nose for the empty ones, stood back or out of sight. They'd find a way in (upstairs windows were often the easiest), wander around, touching fabrics, looking at photographs, taking pictures of their own with the Polaroid Alice had bought, all grainy colour and bad lighting, Louis dolled up in golfing trousers and DJs, Alice hand-standing on the kitchen table, the evidence pasted on the bedroom ceiling, better than any television. They were claiming a territory outside the law, wanted their space marked, like Billy the Kid had his marked, like the Quantrills.

Only once did Chester falter with the timing, caused by the appearance of a stuffed giraffe astride a flatbed truck as it teased its way through the narrow streets. They'd dropped him as usual by the steps of what looked like a library. He'd wandered about, the streets hugging him in, the crowds pressed along the pavements, the world all squashed up. Then he saw the giraffe floating down like he was at sea, inexplicable. His head was level with upper windows, the old houses crouched like they were whispering. He was stuffed, Chester could see that, and tied down to the truck, but he was still a giraffe. He started to follow him, fascinated by the way the animal was staring ahead, how far he seemed to see into the future he was being driven to. He ran alongside, hopping on and off the pavement, knowing it was taking him further away, no choice in the matter. Then the street broadened and there was no pavement left, only the main road and the flatbed winking its way on to it. On the corner, in a shop doorway, stood a man with a dress over one arm, naked mannequins clustered in the window next to him. As the lorry swung out, the man gave the giraffe a wave, but catching sight of Chester, wiped his hands on his trousers, embarrassed.

'He's off to the museum,' he said. 'There's a glass cage there, as big as my bungalow, with trees and flamingos and all sorts. Life of Riley that giraffe from now on.'

He had a bag of sweets in his hand, offered him one.

'Liquorice,' he said. 'Don't tell your mum. Stains the teeth.' Chester shook his head. He knew that much.

'Can he see it,' he said, 'up there, where he's going?'

'I daresay he can,' the man said, and worked a sweet into his mouth. 'He was eyeing my madams up well enough. I should have chucked him one in. That would liven him up, wouldn't it.'

Chester ran back. Alice and Louis were sat on county steps, Louis beer in his hand. Alice leant back between his legs, her arms draped over.

'You're cutting it a bit fine,' Louis said. 'Alice and me were worried you'd up and left us.'

Chester pointed down the street.

'There was a giraffe,' he said. 'Tall as a house.'

'Pull the other one.'

'There was, Dad. On a lorry. He was going home. A glass cage, as big as a bungalow.'

Louis laughed.

'Everything's a cage, son. You, your mother, this beer.'

He held the can out.

'Here. You finish it off.'

By the time they got back he was fast asleep. Louis carried him in his arms. Later he woke, remembered it all. There were sounds coming from their room, like he imagined a pillow fight.

Word got out about the Pot Hole right after the Calor gas had been laid in. Lot was frying up a mess of onions, showing Alice how to cook them slow.

'That's the trick,' she said, 'to keep this going all day. One waft on the air and …' – and there it was, a rap at the hatch. Lot propped it open, her hair fully serviced and lips startling crimson, Alice behind her. Two men in baggy shorts stood in front of them, tall and bony like frantic spurts of willow. Louis was away muck-shifting.

'Only in Epping,' the one with the hat said, his eyes working hard to avoid the snake. 'If we was in a desert I'd call this an oasis. A deliverance of some sort, any road.'

Lot stirred the pan with a wooden spoon, blissfully at home.

'Postman, are you?' she said.

'Miners,' the man said. 'We come here on our days off.'

'Miners? I thought …'

'We'd be too tall for miners, yes I know.' He shifted in his boots, wished the snake would go away. 'The name's Miles. This here is Ken.'

Ken put his hand up. He hadn't spoken yet.

'I'm Lot,' Lot said. 'That one's Alice. Her house, my van. So, a proper pair of pixies …'

Miles pushed his hat back. He had a tall forehead, like there was a lot of brain stuffed behind it.

'That's us,' he said. 'Take the air whenever we can. Isn't that right, Ken?' His friend said nothing. 'Ken's a Communist,' Miles explained.

'A communist!' Lot said it like he'd won first prize.

'A Stalinist,' Ken said. His voice was serious. 'It's not the same thing at all.'

'I daresay it isn't.' Lot turned back to his companion. 'And are you a Communist too?'

'He's an idiot,' Ken said. 'Believes in the TUC and Uncle Jim Callaghan. Are they onions?'

Lot looked down, smiling.

'I do believe they are.'

Ken patted his stomach. There was no flesh on either of them.

'And they come with …?'

'Onions. We're not really open for business yet, are we?'

Alice shook her head. She had only seen it once before, how Lot could work a bunch of men. She had the flesh and the snake, but Lot's call was on a different wavelength altogether. Lot lifted the pan.

'Seeing as it's our first time and your first time,' she said, 'how about a pot of tea, a plate of onions and some fried bread? On the house.'

Miles looked to his friend.

'That would be, what would you say, Ken?'

'Comradely.'

'And I'd say generous,' and he lifted his hat.

Lot took two plates down from the rack.

'Just one question,' she said. 'The fried bread. You want it cooked in lard or dripping?'

After that, Ken and Miles called in any time they were there. They'd spend the morning giving their legs an airing, then sit at the trestle, tucking in, Ken with his mouth full of egg and politics, Miles chewing on exasperation. Others came regular too; Wednesday afternoons meant Amy, a woman the long side of fifty, with her younger belle. They'd hold hands across the table, unable to keep themselves apart. The lad in the mohair coat, played football with Chester most Sunday afternoons, in the hope of impressing Chester's mother. Louis encouraged the pursuit. It reminded him of Worksop, the strength Alice had shown him. Floyd was with the police, Flying Squad, Drugs, no one was sure. He'd park his white Zephyr down the road some, stir his tea and gaze into Lot's eyes while she wiped the table and avoided his questions. It was Floyd who saw off the health inspectors when news of the Pot Hole filtered through. 'Best fry-up south of the tunnel,' he told her, 'I'll not let them scupper that,' though they both knew the real reason. Rogue, villain, lover, walker, Lot prized them all. She'd stand, arms folded, tapping her foot in mock-impatience. Lard or dripping, she'd ask, though she only had the lard. Lard was solid. She liked its adipocerous colour, liked the smell of it, the way it slid over the pan. It was cooking as cooking was meant to be, guilt swimming on the plate. Money changed hands, but it was a secondary transaction. The sums she charged were arbitrary, big round numbers dreamt up on the spur of the moment: fifty pence, one pound fifty, three pounds. Spring and summer, in the dying days of autumn, Chester would turn into the clearing wondering who would be sat by the table or slouched in one of the deckchairs strung out along the back wall, drinking tea, smoking cigarettes, idling the hours away like fighter pilots waiting for the off.

Chester's time at school didn't last long. There were spelling tests, projects to complete. They were too interested in him, wanted to know about his home, why he missed so many days. Alice and Louis would get letters inviting them to meet the staff. Alice could see it stretching before her.

'He'll start bringing it all back soon,' she said. 'Not just homework, but everything else, attendance records, ties, boys asking him what car his father drives, like it matters …'

It was morning. Louis had come back the night before. He was eating the cold rice pudding Alice had made over the weekend, treacle on the top. He had braces over his bare chest, braces and a pair of trousers. Lot was off somewhere.

'You care very much what his father drives,' Louis said, adding the cream. 'I've never known a woman like it.' Alice felt the colour run up. It still got to her, Louis calling her a woman.

'Not that way. You know not that way.'

'What then? If not attendance and ties?'

'We'll take him out. We had this yesterday.' She waved a badly smudged handout. 'Guy Fawkes Night. They want him to make a guy at home, for fun.'

'So?'

'They tortured him, Louis, tortured him so he could hardly write his name. I was taught to celebrate it, and so will he if we don't watch out.'

She laid the invitation out on the table, big jumbled lettering, stars and exclamation marks. Louis smoothed the paper down. There was the man himself.

'He was born in York,' she said, 'travelled the continent, fought for Catholic Spain against the Dutch. Guido was the Italian version of his name, not Spanish.'

She hadn't expected it, the history that had come.

'Catholic?' Louis said, as if he didn't know.

'Outlaws then,' Alice said. Louis stared at the picture, feathers in the man's hat, a hand on the beard, conspiracy wrapped in a cloak.

'If we take him out, they'll come at us even more,' he said. Alice pulled at the hem of her jersey, the fierceness welling up.

'Let them. It's not a fight I'm afraid of, Louis, it's the contamination. He's going to be bringing back this sort of crap every bloody day. I can teach him, you can, teach him what he needs.'

Louis swung his legs round, patted his knee. That's what he loved about her, the tidal waves that washed in and out of her, saw something else too, that if they set to it, they could breed a new race. She sat down, slung an arm around, body heavy. He brushed her hair back, studied her face. They rarely did this sort of thing.

'There's Lot too,' he said.

'Lot?' He felt the tension ripple through her. She bit his neck. 'OK. Lot can teach him domestic. We'll teach him how to fuck it up.'

They took Chester out of school. She began to teach him herself. She was surprised. She had thought she'd had no use of it, what she had learnt, and now she found she had. And she could teach things her own way, the way she thought

Chester should learn, ideas and interests swimming in and out in no perceptible order. She was practical, could do so much. He learnt about electricity, the positive and negative, how magnets worked. She held him up to the setting sun, showed him how the earth was hurtling round it like a spaceship, the sun so still, and the planet so fast. History was about the land he lived on. A land of tribes, that's how she and Louis saw it, a land of rebellions, people rising up when they got pressed down too hard, Luddites, Wat Tyler, the Tolpuddle Martyrs, the constant struggle to be who you wanted to be. She took out library books, travel, adventures, discoveries, geography and science rolled into one – Thor Heyerdahl, Madame Curie, Scott of the Antarctic – started reading to him whatever took her fancy, his eyes trying to comprehend. She didn't care if he didn't understand it all, not understanding was an important lesson in itself. There'd been a book she'd liked as a child, *Barboche* by Henri Bosco, about a boy travelling across the French country with the dog and his cantankerous aunt, read it to him time and time again, so that the idea of travelling, being apart, seemed entirely natural to him. She taught him Spanish too, a word, a phrase. Spain had always meant something to her, the long heat of it, the clatter of the tongue, and the first fully-fledged man in her arms. History, Spanish, writing proper sentences and then mathematics. It was what she had taken at Reading, what had turned her away from the students there, who had thought it a perverse subject for a young woman. Men had thought less of her, the women puzzled. Even her lover had made a show of flinging her textbooks to the corner of his bedroom before undressing her, a blatant show of contempt as to the abilities of her brain. But now she found pleasure in it, the smell of his head and the row of his pencils and the clean simplicity of the task. Nothing was organised, nothing was judged. Weeks could go by and nothing done. What did it matter? He would learn well enough. They had found their universe and they circled within.

One week, Louis drove to London, came back with a sheaf of maps: geological, Roman roads, battlefields. Unsure where to begin, he stretched the most colourful out on the table: ancient walkways, burial mounds, stones, fathoms of untouched terrain.

'Your mother's history,' he said. 'Did she tell you that what happened is as much about the terrain as anything else? Earth and stones, that's what we stand on. Stones are like roots. You put down a stone and …' He caught sight of the name, jabbed at it with his finger. 'See here? First proper road to it, first proper gods for it, first proper clock to make sure they got it right. Time you knew about these things.'

Alice was taking a nap. Louis walked in, kicked the bed.

'Stonehenge. You ever been there?'

She was on her feet in an instant, worked a sweater over her head.

They arrived late, parked a mile away, waited until the guards had closed the gates and walked back, Louis ahead, Alice's arm swinging against Chester's face. The fence was no trouble. Louis pushed a post down with the mould of his hands. Alice guided Chester through. There was a ditch and then a flatness, the shapes arranged like in a gathering, private.

'They're here for everybody,' Louis said. 'You make the journey, you move around them as you please. Got that? They put us on the right path, these stones, your intimates and mine.'

They walked towards them, the stones, watchful, waiting, like some of them had turned, were looking in their direction. Then they were standing in amongst them, under a momentous opening, overwhelming, like a crack in a cathedral, a huge stone hanging above them, and inside a night of secrets.

'Can you feel it?' Louis said. 'Men and women thousands of years ago, hopping about in fur skins, yet all this mathematics and geography. Forty-ton stones and not a plumb line between them. But they nailed the sun and moon, inch perfect. Nailed it till the end of time. These are our ancestors, our real guardians, Chess, not those uniforms down the road.'

Alice dropped her hands, forgetting him.

'Perfect like an egg, then,' she said.

Louis arranged the hair out of her eyes.

'Something like that. Something very near holy, something very near outside it all, something near you and me.'

Alice jumped up on one of the stones, her shoes banging against the rock. Louis put a hand out to steady himself. It came to him that there were things he could never tell the boy, things that he had done, things that he had not. He could teach the boy everything he knew, set him out on the road, but there would be a no man's land of untelling, questions and answers buried. Still, he would have to push him out.

'This is what movement means,' he said. 'It takes you away from yourself, to what's under your feet, what's above. When I see something like this, it makes me want to chuck it all in and fuck off for good.'

He sat Chester next to his mother, eased Alice's trainers one by one from her feet, handed them to his son like they were frankincense and myrrh.

'I need to occupy your mother for a while. Matters of moment, Chester, matters of men.'

He took Alice's hand, held her as she jumped down. Out here on the old stone, who knew who they could create? Another son, he thought, and Alice shuddering with intensity. Later he'd build a vehicle for them all, have it moving over the land, like they were roaming on water in an ark.

Chester wasn't listening. The stones didn't look fixed at all. They looked like long cloaked ancients in a gathering. His voice cut into the night.

'Is this where they're buried then,' he said, 'your mum and dad, Mum's?'

'Jesus,' Alice turned away. 'My mum and dad,' she said. 'My fucking mum and dad.'

Louis looked through the stones. Wasn't that what they were about, ancestors, lines that reach out beyond? Hadn't he been telling Chester exactly that? The stones were telling the boy something. Louis took the shoes back.

'He has a point,' he said, 'and he's raised it up, planted it down. I know it didn't work last time, but it's different now. We could go right away, check them out first. If you don't like the look of it, they wouldn't even know. And if you think it's OK we can ...'

'Say hello ... take morning coffee? She makes lovely finger biscuits, you know.'

'Alice.' His voice was patient, infuriating. 'He might have to live there if ever ...'

Alice pulled Chester to his feet.

'Fuck me, Louis, I thought that was why you brought Lot in.'

'What, and she's immortal, like our friends here?'

He held out her shoes. Alice turned her back on them, marched to the car. How old she'd been when first she knew she had to get away, soon as she could, she couldn't say, but coming through the front door after school was the start of it, the hall dark and still like religion, and the telephone in the alcove untouched like a Buddha. She drove non-stop, save for the petrol. Once on the road her mood changed. Last time she'd gone, the house had conquered her. This time she'd walk right through it.

'It's like a different planet in there,' she said. 'Only objects have meaning. Every afternoon I was given a glass of milk to drink, told not to drink it fast or it would curdle in my stomach, and every afternoon I wanted to bite on the glass, fill my mouth with blood.'

'But you never did?' Alice was surprised at Louis's question. They never talked about families, not hers, not his.

'Once, by accident. Spat it out on the tablecloth, milk all streaky with blood.' She wiped her mouth with the back of her hand. 'They looked good together.'

They arrived in the early hours, parked opposite. Alice turned off the engine, pulled the handbrake tight.

'God, gives me the creeps just looking at it. See what they're driving now? A Cavalier. The worst dashboard in the world.'

She lit a cigarette, impatient, angry.

'You really want him to end up like this?' she said. 'I can hardly breathe, my chest is so tight. They got a sprinkler on the front lawn for fuck's sake.'

Louis threw up his hands.

'OK. I give in. From now on, it's just us, Chester, your mother and me. And Aunty Lot of course.' He opened up the glove compartment, took out a quarter-bottle, let the cap drop into his lap. 'Ride us home then, girl.'

Alice pushed open the door, flicked the stub over the hedge.

'Fuck that. Now that we're here, I'm going to get my singles back. It won't take long. They'll be dead to the world.'

She turned in her seat.

'Come on, Chess. Fancy helping?'

They skirted round the Cavalier, stopped by a gate at the side. She knelt in front of him.

'See those steps at the end of the path? I used to keep a rabbit in a hutch there, used to take him inside, so he could shit on the carpet.' She flashed a key in front of him. 'Once inside, don't say a dicky bird, just follow me up the stairs. They're all in boxes under the bed, least they better be. You can manage a box can't you?'

Chester filled his lungs, followed her in. The hall smelt like a swimming bath, carpets up to the walls. The stairs went one way then the other, the smell rising with them. He wished he'd taken his shoes off. He'd never walked on a carpet before. Alice stopped by a door with a tile with her name on it, pulled the knob towards her, opened it up slow. Her other hand was clamped over her mouth. Once inside, she shut the door, let her breath out.

'God, that smell. What day is it, Thursday?'

He had no idea but he nodded anyway.

'She cleans the house Thursday. And they wondered why I started smoking early.'

She walked to the window. Light shone in from the street lamp. Louis was round the rear of the car, the boot open. He had one foot on the bumper, bottle dangling in his hand.

'Isn't he brilliant,' she said. 'I mean isn't your father just fucking brilliant. When I see him like that ...'

There were three boxes under the bed. Alice pulled them out approvingly.

'Here. Hold out your arms.'

He held out his arms. She was smiling. She placed a box in his hands.

'Take this one down. No dropping it on the way, mind.'

No dropping it on the way was going to be difficult. He couldn't see his feet for the box tilted up against his chest. There was light in the corridor, blue like a distant star. It made the walls look far away. He walked down the landing feeling his feet. The cardboard flap rubbed against his nose. He turned, shifting the box to see better, the stairs somewhere ahead. At the end of the passageway a man in pyjamas stood in an open door. His hair was white, stuck up sparky like a crazy man's.

A noise came from the room he'd left, like something dropped. The man's eyes rolled across then bounced back. He was staring at him, eyes bulging, like they were going to jump out on to the carpet. His neck was scraggy and white. There were dark openings in his pyjama bottoms, and his toes were horny, spread out like a chicken's. The man stared at him and he stared at the man, a kind of static buzzing between them. The man knew him and he knew the man. This was his grandfather, weird and bony and spooky white. How it was so, Chester could not understand, but he knew it to be so.

The box grew heavier. His arms began to ache. It was deep and shapeless behind the man, like the entrance to a cave. He wondered what lay beyond, could only think of the great stones bent in their cloaks, like the man had flown from there, his hair wild and his toes clutching at broken lumps of earth. They'd never speak, never touch, never … Chasms of thought opened up between them. Only words could bridge it, yet neither dared speak.

A waft of cold air made him look round. Alice was backing out of the bedroom, one arm holding the two other boxes, the other working the handle. He turned back. The man was gone, the door was closed, the cavern sealed. Then Alice was behind him, poking the boxes against his head, pushing him along.

Louis was waiting by the boot. He took Chester's box, pushed it right back.

'How'd it go?'

'Not a peep.' She dumped her load down, put her arms around his neck. 'I got such a kick out of it … I've half a mind to go back, take you with me. There's a full-length mirror in the hallway.'

'Alice.'

'OK, OK.' She wedged the boxes up against each other, ran her fingers over the top. 'It was all I wanted, play my singles, backcomb my hair, look a little black.' She pulled one out. 'See this? Max Romeo, 1968, "Wet Dream". That one went down well. Tell you what. Why don't I go back in, put it on the turntable, run like fuck.'

She started singing, enjoying the obscenity and the shape of her lips.

The stones stayed with them all. Alice remembered them as messengers from the sky. Louis could not rid himself of the men who had hauled them there. The stones held Chester, not for the stars or the men, but his ancestor living in a cave, scrabbling the earth with his toes, uncovering what lay beneath, bones and badgers and ... and Rabbit. It would not leave him, the idea of Rabbit in the overcoat. He imagined his head popping out of dark pyjama openings, desperate to breathe. The badger was dead and the ancestors were dead but Rabbit was not dead. Rabbit had never been alive but he was not dead. He lived and he didn't live, like grandfather. Rabbit never spoke, never averted his gaze and he had thrust him away, sealed him in a tomb. He found it troubling to think of it. He was old enough to know better, but he found it troubling. Months later, one cloud-heavy afternoon, Louis and Alice off somewhere, he took a spade down from their bedroom wall, carried it to the spot. He had no choice. The boy inside refused to leave him there. He hung his jersey up, dug the cut in, worked quickly, despite the foolishness. It had been raining the week before and the soil came out in wetted chunks. He laid them out like tiles on a roof. He had a way to go.

'What the fuck are you doing? Burying a body?'

He looked up. There was a girl, as tall as him, tall with freckles and a crooked mouth.

'I remember you,' she said. 'You sat two rows in front, couldn't take it. Everyone says your mum's loco.'

He remembered her too. Her name was Angela. She had a gap between her front two teeth.

'They can say what they like.' He stuck the spade in again. She watched the movement. He was just a kid but he knew what he was doing.

'What's down there then, treasure or something?'

'A badger,' he said. He turned his back to her, lifted out another slice.

'Haven't you heard, that's where they live, Dumbo.' She was laughing at him.

'She's dead. Something else got buried with her. I want to get it back.' He stopped. She'd been good at skipping, could run too. He remembered her sticking out her tongue at him, had enjoyed it. 'I've seen you down by the pond, with the older boys.'

'My sicko brothers. They're around somewhere. Where do you go to school then?'

'Here.'

'In the forest?'

'Pretty much.'

'What, like, under the trees?'

She was laughing at him again. He stuck the spade full into the earth, stood it free. It was a long time since he'd spoken to someone of his own age, or so it seemed. It was hard to know what to say, how to say it. He could say what he liked to Alice and Louis, and yet there were acres in his head left unploughed. He was a boy, wanted to be a boy. It wasn't only Rabbit that was buried alive. What was she doing here anyway? Her hair had a streak in it, crimson like a slash of blade. Unexpected sunlight swept across the little clearing, the forest quickly bright and alive. Sudden mischief rattled up his spine.

'That's right. I sit on a toadstool and get taught by owls.' He jumped up and down, flapped his arms. 'Twit-twoo. Twit-twoo.'

Her hands flew to her nose. She shrieked, eyes glittering upon him, spoke muffled through her fingers, laughing.

'And what do they teach best?'

'Hooting. They teach hooting best. After that catching mice, and after that ...'

'Yes?'

'Angie!' someone called. 'Where the fuck are you?' She held a warning to her lips.

'You better scoot,' she said. 'They'll do you if they catch you here. They're cunts my brothers.' She slapped her hand to her mouth. He stood, unwilling to give ground. Forgotten years lay at her feet.

'Go on. They know it was your dad what did the dog-fights.' She pointed to the ground. 'We'll dig it up Sunday. After dinner.'

She left, not him, ducked down back on to the path, calling out. He heard her catching up with her brothers, heard her leading them away.

He walked back to the Hovel. Hogan's bike was parked in front of the Brummies' long-bonneted Reliant Scimitar. Alice and Louis and Lot were sat with the Brummies at the table. Hogan was by the stove, shirtsleeves rolled, and a waistcoat, shiny with wear.

'You're just in time,' he said, as Chester came through the door. 'Me and Gil been fishing. Do you like mackerel?'

Chester looked round for the dog.

'Just gone round the back,' Hogan explained. 'That man has a terrible weak bladder.'

Louis patted the bench for him to sit down. Chester wiped his hands on the back of his trousers.

'What's with the spade?' Louis said.

'I went to the grave,' he said. 'It needs more planting.'

Louis took his tobacco tin out of his jacket pocket, prised open the lid. Alice was wearing a dress Chester hadn't seen before, big flowers pink and yellow. She caught him looking at it.

'Louis insisted,' she said. 'Oxfam shop. What do you think?'

She stood up, smoothed it down. The black pan was sizzling. Hogan jumped back, avoiding the spit.

'Is that the badger I heard tell about?' he said.

'Chester planted hawthorn over,' Louis said, the dress ignored, 'but it still shows. God, Hogan, how many you got there?'

Hogan was holding a clutch by the mouth.

'I thought two apiece might do us. Be a while though, the size of this pan.'

Lot stood up, adjusted the dress on Alice's shoulders.

'I'd fire up the gas if it wasn't for the smell. Will you hold still.'

Alice wriggled, impatient to be rid of the fuss. Louis twisted round, grabbed her by the waist, lips friendly on her stomach.

'Seeing how you're all frocked up, we'll make a night of it. Chester'll light a fire and we'll cook the bastards in foil. Bangers and stuff, eh Lot. Is there any beer?'

Was there any beer. Alice went into the passageway, brought out a crate stacked at the back. Chester went to the lean-to, took a bundle of brushwood, laid it out on the fire circle, built the wood up, struck the match. Gil gutted the catch, Hogan stuffed the bellies with wild garlic, Louis bound them up. Lot cooked a string of sausages in the frying pan. She wasn't comfortable with fish. Alice found some bamboo torches, pushed them into the ground, in a wide circle. The fire's strength grew. Hogan lay the fish parcels around the periphery. Chester sat with Gil's dog Patch, faced his hands to the heat.

'When's Sunday?' he said, idly as he could muster. Alice was on him in a moment.

'What do you mean, when's Sunday? Sunday?'

She held the word out poised, like it was the law asking. Chester saw the faces waiting, held his hands firm.

'I mean when does the next Sunday come?' he said, keeping his voice level. 'In how many days?'

'Sunday!' Alice turned on her heel, swivelling her hips as she called them out. 'What, like Saturday, Sunday, Monday, Tuesday?'

Chester thought of the girl. She had been wearing striped trousers, quite wrong for the forest. At school her skipping rope had ended in pink handles, matched the ankle socks.

'I just wanted to know, that's all,' he said. 'I don't know what day it is today.'

Hogan sucked on his fingers, turned the mackerel over.

'God, Louis. Who's bringing this boy up, a wolf? Today's Sunday, Chess. The next Sunday will be, guess what, in seven days' time. Is that good enough?'

Chester put his hand out, pleased that it was over. Alice kicked the fire, went down on her haunches in front of him, not done.

'And who knows what will have happened by then, Chess, or where we'll be.' She pulled at his ear. 'Why do you want to know? Your life got a little timetable we don't know about?'

Chester shrugged his shoulders.

'Is it Stonehenge?' Louis asked. 'You know, the religious thing?' Hogan had had enough.

'Stonehenge, my arse. He wants to know because there are seven days in a week, fifty-two weeks in a year, ten years in a decade. You should get the boy a watch. One day, he might want to ask someone out for a date. Might come in handy then, isn't that right, Chess?'

Chester thrust his face forward, hoping the heat might hide the blood running up. Everyone could see it, the mark Hogan had hit.

'Is that it?' Alice said, falling back on the grass. 'You're meeting someone?'

'Just a girl,' he said, still looking to the flames. 'She was at that school I went to.' Alice was back on her feet.

'She has a name?'

'Angela. She has brothers. They know all about you and the dogs, Dad.'

'And you're seeing her, like on a date?' Louis looked at Alice but her attention was out by the pathway, two figures in shorts, approaching.

Lot jumped to her feet, happy to see them.

'What time do you call this?' she sang out.

They came into the clearing, their pace slowing when they saw the men within.

'Forgot ourselves,' Miles said. 'What a day!'

Lot beckoned them in. Alice had her eyes on Louis. Hogan kept busy with his fish.

'Someone's left a pile of crap by the phone box, did you see?' Miles said. 'I don't know how they do it.'

'The how or the why?'

Louis held his gaze firm to the table, his territory marked. There was animal in his stillness. Lot moved between them, anxious.

'This is Ken and Miles, Louis. You know, from Betteshanger. Haven't seen you two for a while.'

Alice put her hand on Louis's head, the big fleshy flowers pressed warm against him again.

'Things are a bit bloody at the moment,' Miles admitted. He cleared his throat. 'You've been working on the M11, Lot tells me. I've always wondered how it must be, working up top.'

Louis acknowledged the sentiment.

'Not like it was. We're skimping where we shouldn't be. It'll bite them in the arse ten years from now, but what do they care?' He held out his hand. 'Louis. You're Ken, right?'

'I'm Miles. That's Ken.'

'Lot's spoken about you two. That's Hogan cooking the fish. Works with me, has done, what, twenty years off and on. We're like you in that way, kind of a family, only we can stretch our legs.'

'I'm not like you at all,' Hogan corrected. 'My old man dug tunnels in the Six Counties, took me down once. That was enough to last me a lifetime, though it was a sight, seeing the layers of it, like a cake.'

'Never thought of it as a cake before. Have you, Ken?'

'Why not?' he said. 'Very Marie Antoinette, the mining industry. You don't have any unions at all, is that right?'

Miles put his hands up in despair.

'Not now, Ken. You've only just been introduced.'

'I was just interested to know, that's all.' Louis spat the bait out.

'Rolling stones, that's the trouble with us. Do you like fish? We got a boatload.' He pulled one of the mackerel free, rolled it out on to the grass. Ken wasn't letting go.

'British Leyland, British Steel, the lights are going out all over industry, to misquote our elders and betters. There's money sloshing around, but not for us.'

Louis nodded, determined to head the topic away.

'Hence the free fish. Have a beer, enjoy it. We're celebrating. My son here has got his first date, a frolic in the forest.'

He unwrapped the fish, parcelled them out on to tin plates. Louis sat at the head of the table. Miles sat next to Chester, Alice on the other side.

'This date then, Chester,' Hogan said. 'Next Sunday. Is it like, a day out? That'll cost you, boy.' He rubbed his hands.

'After tea,' Chester said. 'Maybe.'

'You must check the diary, Alice,' Louis said. 'Do we know what time we're eating that day?'

Alice didn't reply. It was a strange gathering before her, all the men and Aunty Lot, a sort of tableau of the possessed: firelight in a forest clearing and, in the distance, the traffic hum. Meetings could be held here, she thought, clandestine, dangerous. Location was often a key player in revolution-ary movements – a railway carriage, a winter dacha – now they had a motorway connecting this forest to the rest of the country … which meant access, speed, dispersal …

Light sank away. The trees grew tall. Chester took a match, lit the four bamboo torches, Hogan's bike flickering fiery like a mythical horse. The men joked and slapped their thighs. Alice brought out the record player she had bought, put on a forty-five, danced by herself, feet working in a space no bigger than a phone box, her body pleased, pushing back the years. One three-minute blast and she closed the lid. She could play as many as she liked, but they weren't that sort of men. Another beer crate emerged, unexpected visitors too, the lad who played football with a girl in tow, then Pete and his guitar, and another man no one else knew. The clearing grew noisy. Chester looked from one to the other, all alive in a different world from him, a world that he was being asked to join. He didn't know if he could, or what part of it lay open to him. Pete was on the steps singing, Lot was teaching Miles the waltz. Ken was arguing politics with Hogan. Alice had plucked Pete's hat from his head, was flapping the hem of her dress around a bemused Louis, while Gil was showing off Patch's party tricks to the unknown girl, the mohair lad left out and fed up. Chester saw it all, argument and love, display and jealousy, all playing out in the mysterious world of existence. We are humans, he thought, like in the books I've read, hands and skills and brains that surpass all others, but display, animal display and our reliance on it, still counts for much.

Around midnight Floyd appeared, his white Zephyr poking into the clearing and Floyd stepping out in a pressed blue suit and peek-a-boo black shoes. Chester was sent off to the outhouse for more beer. Coming back he saw Pete sat on his own bed, holding his friend's cock, saw the flesh big and purple, slipping back and forth into Pete's mouth like an engine part. He wondered at it, whether it was strange or whether it made perfect sense, couldn't decide which. It was fit for a mouth, yet to have to sit down for it, was that right? The things he saw carrying boxes. Back at the table, Floyd was clinking the last of the bottles with Alice and Louis.

'There's been complaints about tonight,' Floyd was saying. He tipped his bottle to his lips. 'Your average suburban has a mortal fear of pikeys.'

'We're not …' Louis objected.

'I know. But think what they see, that painted wagon on wheels, the lad running wild and all of you dressed like you've just got off a horse.'

Louis stiffened.

'Why do you say horse? No horses here. Not in a million years. Have you ever seen their eyes?'

'Horse … cart … you change motors too often for their liking. There's not a week goes by but … Have you heard about the new Morris? Like a Marina, but with a front-wheel drive.'

Alice put an arm round the policeman's neck. She liked Floyd. Floyd was different, reptilian, like his blood was only pretend.

'Last time round,' she said, 'the Marina had the same chassis as a 1948 Morris Minor. You hoped for something young and virile but found yourself riding an old-aged pensioner who'd just survived the war.'

Louis and Floyd burst into laughter.

'The cars you two must have got through over the years,' Floyd said. 'What's been your favourite then?'

'The Humber.' Alice spoke right away, the memory of it full in her mouth, like it had never gone. 'We had the time of our lives in the Humber, fucked Wales completely. And Louis got rid of it. I came out of hospital to find he'd traded it in for a fucking Rover 80. Never understood that.'

She wiped her mouth like she'd swallowed something unpleasant. Louis looked aggrieved.

'I thought you might want to settle down, whatever you said. Thought it might make it easier.' Alice leant across the table, pulled his nose.

'You got that wrong, didn't you?' Louis reached out, held her there.

'It was a good car,' he said. 'And guess what … ?' He let her sit back. 'Hogan and me saw it again, driving up to get Lot's old heap. Did we never tell you?'

Alice took one of Chester's beers off the table.

'No, you didn't,' she said. 'Funny that.'

FOUR

Mrs Calvert stood for forty minutes before the luggage appeared, forty minutes and the man who'd sat next to her on the flight over trying to catch her eye from the other side of the carousel. She was a woman of mystery, always had been, couldn't help it. Forty minutes and the carousel empty and the man looking at her and her right foot hooking up like an egret on the shore. She could feel the tide coming in, the flotsam of history washing over her. Forty minutes and the conveyer belt empty and the throng of feet and elbows and the man looking over, still fishing, and she standing on the edge of the emptied space of winter, hoping for the sun. Then the motor started and the belt lurched and she turned to face the shifting current. A minute she was held, the motor turning, the belt rolling over the cold, and then, right at the head, her cases nosed through the rubber curtain – her former life making its last appearance. They wobbled forward, tipped down, belly-flopped on their sides, moving towards her as she trembled within. She felt it all, the chill of the hall and the lethargy of the movement and the shiver of the wait, as if any minute there was going to be some grasp of direction for her to hold on to, the welcome hand of heat, whereas ahead lay ... No matter. She was here. She'd left by sea and she'd returned by air, journeys to the unknown both. It had taken seven days, the passage out; the flight back seven hours, but this had been the slower, the plane dragging her through the cotton wool of her past, all abilities blurred and dulled and muffled. She'd hoped for a sense of exhilaration, a seizure of momentum, but had found none. There'd been no dimension to the plane, no form attached, no physic to confront the enormity of her decision. She'd had that on the way out, taken hold of what had happened and thrown it overboard, spent the nights out on deck, feeding her former self to the vast swallow of the sea. In the daytime she'd hidden away in her cabin, food and drink brought in on trays by a steward who'd backed out of her room as if she were the Queen. Apart from one incident before they'd even sailed, there had been no harassment, no intrusions, no more of men and their needs whatsoever until she'd bumped up against Carl six months later, hauled ashore by his big red hands. She'd been working up the courage to buy a car. He'd been visiting the same dealership, looking round for a truck of some sort. Cars were not easy for her then, but in Canada, a body had no choice. He'd showed her round the forecourt, explained the pros and cons of the cars on offer. She'd warmed to the way he'd opened the drivers' doors for her, stepped aside while she peered in, his body large and awkward, his voice filling the foreign interiors with old-fashioned stories, the similar models friends and he had driven, episodes of youth and maturity, of escapades and foolishness and Canadian weather, all the while lowering her gently into the waters of her new time. Big, slow, generous Carl, who'd taught her to drive, who'd courted her and married her, who had given her a child of her own, a boy, not eight years old when drowned in the lake behind the house, his body sodden on the grass and Carl breaking his ribs as he pumped at his heart with those same red hands. Suddenly she found herself crying, stupid tears running down her face, the man from the flight seizing his opportunity, moving towards her, his face screwed up in a disgusting approximation of concern. Panicked, she barged her luggage into the ladies, panting from the effort of evasion, as if she had returned to England only for all that had happened to her once to rear into shape again.

She splashed cold water on her face, held a paper towel under the tap, pressed it to the back of her neck. She was a woman schooled in stern abilities. She had driven farm equipment the size of a bungalow, held her ground not forty metres from a brown grizzly, lain with Carl every night in a bed that he had fashioned with his own hands, big enough for everything he'd said, even the livestock listings in the auction sales, even the cancer that killed him. She patted herself dry, wondering at what she saw in the mirror, a face longing for a freshness of air and the space to breathe it in. She waited until she judged the coast clear, held herself back, knowing the implacable tenacity of such men on the move. But when she emerged, she found herself smiling. He was gone.

She wheeled her luggage through customs. Now there were queues to contend with, a customs inspection to pass through. She held her eye as compass to the exit, determined, but – the woman of mystery again – the uniform behind the counter had other ideas, beckoned her over.

'Anything to declare?' the woman said, indicating where she should place her cases, and she thought, sister, you don't know the half of it.

'Just relief,' she said. 'To be back in one piece.'

She hauled the luggage up, wishing she'd only brought the one or, better still, none at all. What did she need from Brandon, Manitoba, now?

The woman turned the cases around.

'Been away long?' she said.

'Best part of twenty years,' Mrs Calvert said, thinking of the impossibility of the words, her life wiped away, chalk on a blackboard, dust.

The woman looked at the suitcases, her lips gathering.

'That's right,' Mrs Calvert said. 'That's all I got to show for it. That and the stretch marks.'

She folded her arms, unwilling to talk further. The woman examined the contents – the good dresses, the sensible outdoor wear, even the photographs loose in their folder: Neil on his first horse; Ezra, their prizewinning Romney; Carl standing in the back of his brand-new Dodge. None of them affected her, but then came the fleeting sight of Theo waiting for his evening biscuit, and she wondered whether he'd settled in with his new owners. He'd be happy with the children, he was that sort of dog. Most likely he wouldn't miss her at all. Nobody would.

Then she was done, wheeling the suitcases through the concourse and out into the mid-morning damp and the untidy taxi rank.

'London awaits. Shall we share the ride?'

She turned. Him again. She *was* going to London, had booked a suite of rooms in a hotel in the Strand, had paid a deposit. She'd imagined herself with days of shopping, seats at the theatre, savouring her nation's capital before making any decisions, but the man's smile had taken an axe to all that. What on earth was she going to London for? The only time she'd gone to London had been the night with her dental-assistant friend, Jill …

'No,' she said, brittle with determination, 'I'm going to Aylesbury,' and, as soon as she said it, knew it made perfect sense. The man was put out.

'Aylesbury? I thought you said …'

'Never mind what you thought. Now back off, mister, and leave me alone.'

It had taken the driver a while to work out the fare.

'Could you stay the night, drive me around in the morning? I might need to go somewhere.' She was thinking on her feet and it amazed her, the path she was cleaving. 'I'll pay in cash. I've got a bit.'

So she did, part of the proceeds realised from the sale of the farm and the machinery and the three hundred head of Romney sheep, all transferred to Williams & Glyn's Bank, Birchin Lane, London. She had cash coming out of her ears.

'Any particular route?' he asked, as if she was going to know.

'Not a clue,' she said. 'We'll buy a map at the first petrol station we see. I'll need one for later on, where I am going.'

Where was she going? The solidity of her arrangements had evaporated, yet she felt invigorated, her lungs gorging on the late-morning air, as if she'd just inhaled medicinal vapour. She'd done with Canada, wanted the spread of England to breathe in, wherever it might lie. Aylesbury? She doubted it. Canada had expanded the level of her eye. But she'd got here, gone through customs. Now for the last barrier. Then all her baggage would be sent on its way.

The map was bought. The driver was curious, but she slid the glass partition shut. The two suitcases sat in the front as she had imagined. She looked to the road, cars in a profusion she'd never believed possible. She shook her head at the intensity of it. They had highways in Manitoba, but they were broad and quiet and sent you to sleep. She'd arrived to a homeland gone mad, everything squeezed together, furious, as if packed in a hurry. Later the driver veered off. Familiarity asserted itself, sights and rhythms she recognised. Colours filled the window. She'd forgotten the strength of them, the blocks of varied green, the wedges of brown, the splashes of yellow, the English memory that seeped through this land, found its tenderness almost unbearable, as if she had been robbed of it, as a child might be denied affection and grown the poorer for it. Yet she could not say that she had missed what she now saw, and wondered why that might be. 'Perhaps,' she said to herself, 'I had never really seen it before. Before, I'd been a young woman living with a watchful mother and working in a solicitor's office six days a week. Before, I'd taken up with a married man. Everything had been coloured by that.'

'What you say, lady?'

She waved his question away, her eyes filled with hunger.

———

They found a hotel near the town centre, a white sprawl of a building that she had no memory of. Hotels hadn't figured much in her life there. They had a single and a double spare. She took the single. She had not come to rest yet, needed her bed to be narrow, as if she was spending the night in a couchette or a cabin, not yet come to her journey's end. She gave her credit-card number, handed the driver his key.

'Tomorrow morning you can take me to a reputable car dealer,' she told him. 'Ask around for me. Have whatever you want for dinner. Drinks too. It's on me.' She walked out feeling freed. She'd never been so generous in her life.

It took her thirty minutes to retrace the old walk home. She stood at the top of the road, unwilling to progress, saw the tube flicker to life from the lamp post by their gate. She used to read by that light every night, read until her eyes grew sore. It had been the first inclination of her own strength. Her mother had distrusted books, favoured practicality in all things. Light had shone sparingly where they lived. She could not imagine the house any different, whoever lived there now. Her mother had been carried through that gate on the way to her grave. She'd only learnt of her death a year later, the heart attack in the kitchen and the shopping bags unpacked on the kitchen table and the body not discovered for a month. When she'd been given the news, she couldn't get to sleep for wondering what had been in the shopping bags, how much of it had gone off. Meat, fish, she couldn't get it out of her head, had taken to stripping her own refrigerator bare every week, starting anew. 'But, honey, what's a fridge for?' Carl said eventually, tired of the expense, and looking at their big table and everything stacked up ready to be thrown away, she'd woken up to the absurdity of it, and put it all back, the fixation finally broken. Her mother had given her life, and she had given life, yet what was left of them? Nothing but blame.

In the centre, the town was much as she had left it. She walked, her breath coming strange. The printing works had closed (how was that possible? Aylesbury *was* printing), the cinema gone too. The block where her friend Jill had worked had been turned into a cut-price carpet centre. 'You've got a lovely set in there,' Jill had said, that first time they'd met, and so it was still, not a filling amongst them. Her old firm was there, though the frontage had changed, and new names on the brass. Over the road stood the pub. She turned to move away, but thought better of it, plunged across, pushed open the door. The bar was as it was, but half the drinking area had been given over to food, a blackboard propped up in the corner listing the day's dishes.

'I'll have a gin and tonic,' she said, her voice louder than she'd wanted. 'And a pint of beer, straight glass.'

'Certainly, madam.' He was a young, particular man, poured the tonic with unnecessary elaboration. 'Will you be eating with us?'

She hadn't planned to, hadn't planned any of it. That was the beauty of being there.

'Why not?' she said, suddenly ravenous. 'Out of the way a bit.'

'Certainly, madam. May I suggest the table by the window. That should suit both you and your ...' He nodded to the pint glass.

'Just me,' she said, and carried them over. It was fine being here, where so much of it had started. She turned the glass in her hand, lifted it to the light.

'Beer,' she said, and drank it down in one.

The man came to take her order a quarter of an hour later. His name was Philip. She ordered the chicken in a basket.

'Are you staying long, madam,' he said, 'or just visiting?'

'Passing through,' she said, hoping he'd go away, and then, trying to remember exactly, said, 'If I wanted to go to Ivinghoe Beacon, I'd take the road to …'

'Aston Clinton,' he said. 'Through the town and look for the signpost on the left. Can't miss it. It's a famous beauty spot, though I wouldn't go myself. Only last summer someone got robbed at knifepoint in broad daylight. Lot of drug dealing, after dark. Then there was that murder, the man shot and the woman … well, not at the dinner table, eh?'

Mrs Calvert acknowledged his propriety.

'When was this?' she said.

'Years ago. She crawled on her hands and knees for miles before they found her. Lost an eye. Course everyone's forgotten about it now. My father knew him, the man who got killed.'

'And her?'

'Not to speak of. She emigrated. New Zealand. Married a sheep farmer.'

Mrs Calvert turned her head, trying not to laugh. Well, he got that right.

Later she sat him down, had him tell the whole story, held her second glass of beer and sipped it calmly listening to his description of this town in the sixties and her love affair, the clandestine meetings by the Beacon, in the car, the man who changed her life, thinking that although it was she he was talking about, it was impossible to slot herself back into the story. What he didn't understand, what no one had ever understood, was that it was not exceptional, nor wild, nor extraordinary at all. It was ordinary, commonplace, and very brief, even though then it had seemed to take up all her time in the world. But when the gun was fired and Colin lay dead in the front, it had vanished, practically all of it, in a puff of gun smoke, and that was something she could admit to no one, least of all the jury. She remembered giving evidence, the star witness in a black dress, holding on to the rail as if the court was a car and she the driver determining the pace and measure of it. She remembered the beauty of that feeling, having the ability to guide it all into such a place, so that when it was over and the accused was taken down, she could leave in one piece.

She ordered a brandy with her coffee, and walked back, knowing she'd never visit Aylesbury again.

Next morning, she came down to the foyer wearing her grey-flecked two-piece and a blouse of sombre green. Distance, that was what she wanted to impart, had stood in the mirror, ensuring that it was so, Carl's gold crucifix tucked in out of sight. Some days she believed in the Resurrection, other days she did not. She'd resurrected her own life enough times to think it possible. But why not her boy? What was the breaking of his breast for, if not for that? The driver hadn't discovered the name of a car dealer, but she had, courtesy of Philip. She'd asked him while settling the bill. He knew of one, had called him up then and there, fixed a meet. The taxi driver was put out. He'd been hoping for another extravagant day's pay. He drove her the three miles, set her suitcases down outside the forecourt gates in a peevish twitch. She was glad to see the back of him.

Charlie Hicks was waiting in blue overalls. He was big like Carl, had hands like him, but with a pot belly. Carl had been an outdoor man, had known how to hold something living. All Charlie knew how to hold was a spanner. He fidgeted his fingers across the front of his trousers. He wasn't used to dealing with women.

'You're the lady looking for something nice and regular. Been away some, Philip said.'

'Never driven here either, not properly. I have a licence, though, all the necessary papers.'

Charlie shrugged his shoulders. He picked up her suitcases, weighed them in his hands, carried them to where a Portakabin stood, laid them at the foot of the steps. Through the window she could see pictures of cars stuck to the wall. She was surprised. She'd expected quite a different type of pin-ups.

'It's not often a customer comes to me like this,' he said, 'with no way of leaving except …'

They looked across to the cars. The roofs dazzled in the sun. She pulled at the luggage labels, snapped them free, scrunched them in her hand.

'If I don't find anything,' she said, 'the least you can do is drive me back to town. There must be other garages. You have a bin?'

'If I don't find you anything,' he said, 'I'm emigrating.' He took the labels from her, stuffed them in his overalls. 'Fancy a cuppa first, biscuits? All my clients get biscuits.'

'Not this one. I'm anxious to get on.' Charlie nodded. All his clients ate biscuits, but then they were all men.

'You'll be driving round town in the main then?' he said.

'More than that to begin with. Now, show me what you got.'

He showed her. He liked his motors, every one of them, patted them on the roof while reeling off their history. Back and forth they went, an hour's worth of monologue. She found them all wanting, headlights staring through years of hopelessness: Dolomites, Cavaliers, Chevettes, Hunters, ludicrous names, incapable cars. Claustrophobia crept upon her, as if she might die in any one of them. So this was England. They were standing over a Mark 1V Sunbeam Alpine.

'If it's vim you're looking for,' he said, 'this is it. V8 engine, perfect trim, lovely to handle.'

'I'm not,' she said. 'I need something that suggests stability, forgotten times.'

She spoke the words as a door to unlock. He studied her face, then her hands. She was conscious of being appraised, felt no apprehension in it. In his pocket the labels lay screwed up in a ball, the mess and mangle of them, how she'd pulled them off, eager to cut strings.

'I might have something,' he said. 'It's been here a while, though it has a value now.'

He led her through the yard, past open-ended sheds to a small padlocked garage at the back, the wooden doors closed awry and damaged at the foot. They took some pulling, his body unfit. Carl would have barely drawn breath. There was a shape inside, a proud rigidity, and a tarpaulin slung over.

'Here,' he said. 'Help me pull it off.'

The car stood face on, incongruous like a dodo, two-tone, cream on top, dark grey below. It reminded her of the time Carl came back with their thirty-foot cruiser, the sense of a craft made for another domain. Mrs Calvert put her hands on her hips. The wing mirrors seemed gratuitously vulnerable.

'It's a statement, I'll give you that.'

'It's a Rover 80. Eighteen years old, only five thousand or so ever made. Thirty-four thousand on the clock. The last owner brought it back after nine months. Since then, I've loaned it out to a fellow who does weddings. There's not everyone suited to a car like this.'

She did a rapid calculation. The year it had all started, 1962.

'I must have seen one then, though I don't remember.'

'Women don't as a whole, remember cars. Though the markings here might have held your eye.'

'Not mine.' She walked round it, peered inside to the red leather seat and the wooden facia.

'Almost racy, that steering wheel.'

'You're the first person to call a Rover 80 racy.'

'What would you call it?'

'Unperturbable, as if the years don't matter.'

She drew her head out.

'I like that. Does it go?'

'Treat it with respect and she'll do sixty-five steady as a rock. You wouldn't want to go much faster. She's a collector's car really. But, with you here, maybe not.'

'It won't be sitting in a garage. Britain's covered in motorways now, my taxi driver told me.'

He held his left index finger to her observation.

'This is a sign, that you should say this. The man who owned her before you works on the motorways. Lives and breathes them. Fancy a spin?'

He ran the car out, stood aside. She looked puzzled, then said, 'The door opens ...' She didn't know how to put it.

'The wrong way. Lovely, isn't it. You get used to it.'

He sat her in the driving seat, showed her the gears. She mastered them right away. He was impressed.

'Farm machinery,' she explained. 'Now, let's see how she likes me.'

The road was long and straight and empty. Ruined green-houses stood on one side, smashed lines of them. She tried not to look. After a while he asked her to pull over. She pulled over.

'Do you see what side of the road we're parked on?' he said. She nodded.

'I know. I've been driving on the right.' She turned and smiled. 'Don't worry. I'm simply saying goodbye. Do you have a cigarette?'

Back at the garage, she opened her handbag, paid Charlie Hicks out in cash. The suitcases fitted perfectly. She remembered to call it the boot. She tucked the registration papers in the glove compartment, laid her jacket on the back seat and the road atlas out on the passenger seat next to her.

Charlie Hicks stood by the gate, his feet planted apart, as if he was on duty.

'Let me know how she gets on,' he said. 'She's been a long time going.'

He stepped forward, rubbed the windscreen with his sleeve.

'I should have a flag or something,' he said. 'It feels official, like a ship's launch.'

'It has a prow,' she said, 'that's why.'

———

She drove to the Beacon. The chief inspector in charge of the case, Alcott, had driven her about these roads once, to see if she could remember the route they'd taken, Colin lying broken in the morgue and the bandage stiff around her head. She couldn't then, and she couldn't now. It was all a jumble of insignificant country lanes: narrow hedges, small fields and the odd industrial plant. It had been dark anyway, the journey the man had forced them on, nothing but flashes of brilliant green and the huge eyes of the headlight animals. There had been no point in going over it again. Alcott had wanted to get close to her, that was all. She had sensed that right away, the hold she had on him, an abused and wounded woman, and him with his perfumed hair and his hand desperate for hers.

The Beacon stood scrubby, lacking the vigour she'd remembered it by. The lay-by was a smear. She got out. This was where the man had tapped on the glass. This was where he'd climbed in, ridden them all to hell. There was nothing to show for it.

She walked to the top, stubborn over the grass. Years ago, she'd wanted to run down this slope, kick off her shoes, lift up her skirt and run, a young woman's run, as if her life would be waiting for her at the end of it, flushed and full of hope and giving. She was a different woman now. There was nothing to be gained by running. She breathed in, held herself deep over the view. Down there lay the Vale of Aylesbury. Down there she barely existed at all.

She took care in her descent, brushed her legs free of grass at the end of it. She sat in the driver's seat, fingers on the ignition key. The Rover was firm upon it, not simply the smudge of gravel, but everything, the hill, the road ahead, the vast emptiness of where she was going.

'We could all go for a nice drive up the A1,' the man had said. 'Stop at Scotch Corner, have a bite to eat …'

There had been cruelty in the remark and a terrible mocking. Round and round they'd gone, back and forth beneath the Beacon, first one direction then another, a night of dark elasticity. By dawn they'd been parked up in a field not half a mile from where they'd started, Colin fast asleep, both of them unscathed. She'd stretched her legs, got in the back as the man had demanded. Did he mean to kill Colin? Did he want to kill her? 'Don't be afraid,' he'd said. 'Look straight ahead.' She saw it now, the road running up the length of England, saw the need for it, how it might lead her into the heart of where she needed to be. Once she had been so certain as to what had happened, who had done it and why. Once it had mattered. Now it didn't matter at all. The Rover was trembling, its bonnet sturdy and its sense of time implacable. She eased up the clutch. There was a murmur. Hers, the Rover's? Look straight ahead! Look straight ahead! That was it.

A sweetness to it, the way they moved.

Did she stop? Stretch her legs? Did she think about the ride she was running from, or was it that she'd turned the tables on it, was back in the old country, in the driving seat now? The Rover sped as if on air, the car heavy but the wheels light. Where she joined the A1 she could not say. The map was her memory. She swung in and joined it, felt it settle beneath her. Houses, cars, fields glided by, the land stretching riderless like an empty plain. Lines of geometry ran before her, curves and angles and points of perspective. She saw roundabouts. Roundabouts brought her back. She gripped the lick of the leather seat and let the Rover take the curve, its purr unwavering, the bonnet moving in front of her in tranquillity. Where the hell was she going? The road wound by, speed fixed on a needle point. There were cars and lorries and the sudden light of brakes, yet the Rover moved amongst them as if through wreckage. Its colour was like no other, long and creamy-grey, the wing mirrors poised like little sails and behind her the boot, as dependable as a stern.

Somewhere, a long way up, she pulled in for petrol. She got out, her legs welcoming the break. The air was fresh and cold. She had travelled a long way and was glad. She would drive to this Scotch Corner and find somewhere to stay. After that … England was opening up, stuff coming in from the north and the east, sea and wind and a land mass twenty-five times its size. Aylesbury wouldn't fit in here, nor the Beacon. The Beacon was a pimple.

She touched the Rover's bonnet, taking cheer in the engine's heat. She'd grown to appreciate engines in Canada, the parade of flatbeds and station wagons, the great funnels of the balers and tractors, the flood of fumes in the yard. The Rover was from another world. She took a tour round, her hand trailing along its length, the front passenger door, the left-hand back door, the boot, amused by the antics in the interior, its fussy respectability. She thought, when she got there, wherever it was, she might hang curtains in the back, if such a thing was possible. Not that she'd ever sit in the back, but having them there would set the picture off nicely. Her tour completed, she lifted her eyes, found a man standing in front of her, a motor-bike helmet in his hand and a woman's scarf about his neck, a pattern of petals. There was a bike parked up at a distance, and in the café a man dressed in leathers was queuing up for drinks.

'Forgive me for staring,' the man said, 'but would this be yours?'

Mrs Calvert had a sudden thought that England had sold her down the river once more, that she'd returned to a country still weighed down by false promise. She put her hand to the bonnet again, preparing herself for the worst, but the car's warmth restored her faith. She felt guilty, as if she'd betrayed the Rover's constancy.

'What of it?' she said. The man rubbed his chin.

'Well I'm damned,' he said. He took a step closer, peered at the bonnet. 'Do you see that little twist there on the wing mirror? A tree did that. Well I'm damned. Hogan!'

He beckoned furiously. The man in leathers came out, chewing on a roll.

'What's up?'

'Can you believe it? It's my bloody car, the one I collected Alice and Chester in.' He turned back to her. 'I owned this car, years back, my wife had just given birth, but …'

'His woman couldn't stand it,' the bigger man said, swallowing his bite. 'Never known anyone hate a motor as much as she took against this. It was not right, the amount of energy she expended.'

Mrs Calvert studied the man still gripped by the Rover. He was thin, but not underfed, composed but with a tension within him that informed his whole being. Caution should have governed her, the draw she felt towards him, the way he stood, pulling on the folds of his ear in a kind of rapture, but it did not, for she saw as well the nature of his commit-ment – his open-neck shirt and his weathered neck and the state of his hands, endured like an oak's skin is endured, wise to the throws of the weather. He'd ridden on the back of his friend's motorbike like that: one shirt, one jacket, and a scarf smelling of a woman's soap. How many times had she scolded Carl for going out in a similar state, and how many times had he ignored her? She knew right away who he was.

'You're the motorway man then,' she said.

The man was pulled out of his dream.

'The what?'

'Charlie Hicks, the gentleman I just bought it from, told me the previous owner had been someone who worked on the motorways. I'm figuring that's you.'

He looked at her wary, as if she might be uncovering a trick, laying a snare to trap him by. He stepped back, replied carefully.

'He still had it then?'

'Just bought it from him this morning. This is our maiden voyage, you might say.'

The man hesitated for a moment. Mrs Calvert nodded her permission. He laid his hand flat on the bonnet. If she had not been there, it would have been a caress, but the car was hers now. A gesture of remembrance was enough. The caress came in his throat.

'I always knew there was something special about this one,' he said. 'Where are you heading, if you don't mind me asking?'

She knew she should mind, but she didn't, felt marvellously free in telling him.

'Somewhere called Scotch Corner. There's a hotel there, I understand.'

She stopped. The man was jumping up and down, smacking his head.

They offered her an escort all the way up, the bike in front or settled in the rear-view mirror, on occasions, when the coast was clear, running alongside her, as if the man were sitting right next to her. On the third such visit, she waved at him, indicating that she was about to pull in, required him to do the same, watched him walk back on the hard shoulder, thinking herself a fool for even thinking it.

'Anything wrong?' the man said.

'I was wondering,' she said, 'if you'd like to keep me company. Until we get there.'

He looked to his boots, then back to where the bike was idling.

'It's what I used to do,' she added, wishing she hadn't said it the moment it sprang out, 'drive my husband around the farm and places.'

It wasn't strictly true. What she meant was that, in the early days, Carl would sit with her while she became used to cars and Canada. After that …

'Alice wouldn't like it,' he said. 'She thought this car a bad influence.'

'And was it?'

He laughed.

'Most likely. Yes, I'll ride with you, happy to do it.'

He walked back, spoke to his companion, Mrs Calvert in her driver's seat, arms straight to the wheel. She was excited, could feel her nervousness pumping. She was taking a strange man into her strange car. There was a wealth of madness to it, and yet it was completely sensible and good. She watched him talk to the other man for a while. Were they arguing, laughing, planning something? It was impossible to tell. A wealth of madness. The bike roared off.

'He'll meet us up there,' he said, opening the door. 'Wants to let rip, now that I'm not cramping his style.'

He climbed in. He sat upright, as a small boy might, on his best behaviour.

'Would you mind very much if I neglected to wear the seat belt?' he said.

'Aren't they compulsory round here?'

'Not yet. It'll come though, sure as the Indians got put on reservations.' He paused. 'It's a pattern of civilisation,' he said, by way of explanation. 'Finding new ways to lock us up. The name's Louis, by the way.'

'And I'm Mrs Calvert.' She put her right arm across her body, held her hand out. 'Good to meet you, Louis.'

Louis took it with his left.

'And you, Mrs Calvert.'

'One thing,' she said. 'I'm new to these roads. I'd be very grateful if you told me when I've been doing anything I shouldn't, road etiquette I might not be aware of.'

Her hand was back on the wheel and her accelerator foot was shaking. She'd been behind the wheel for hours and only now was she shaking.

'Trust the Rover,' he said. 'It's a sensible car, makes the driver do sensible things. Just take it steady, like you were buttering toast.'

They set off, Mrs Calvert back in the inside lane. She was conscious of the number of cars that passed them, thought it might unsettle him, but Louis sat serene, hands in his lap, quite still. Whenever Carl had sat next to her, his feet would move like an organ player's.

'I hope I'm not too slow for you …' she said.

'I never go much more than forty myself. Any tension that's out there or in the car just leaks away. Time slips by much quicker, that's the lovely part. You're there before you know it.'

She dropped down. Back in Brandon, on those long journeys, she'd set the car on cruise control, relax into the drive ahead. Forty miles an hour was like that. The car ran on and on and on, no one bothering them. The Rover liked it too, she could hear. A Rover 80 doing forty. She'd made a vow, never to drive any faster.

'You had a farm then,' he said, the pace well established. 'Not here though, not in England.'

'Canada. I suppose you'd call it a farm. Farm or a ranch.'

'Cattle?'

'Sheep. And wheat some.'

'Sheep?' Louis repeated.

'Over three hundred. You like sheep?'

'I like them on the moorland, scrambling about, chewing on not a lot. Were they for the table, your sheep?'

'Wool in the main. And breeding stock. Though we sold a little meat locally.'

'If I had a little land, a little livestock would be handy,' he said.

'Add a few chickens, hoe that garden, and you could feed yourselves all the year round. Do you have children?' She banged on the wheel, correcting herself. 'Of course, you do, you said you got this when … what I meant was …' She stopped, unsure how to carry on.

'Just the one,' Louis said. 'Chester.'

'After the town?'

'After the road,' Louis said, 'the section I was working on at the time. This road.'

'Well I never. Do we drive over it? I could toot the horn or something. No, I shouldn't do that, should I?' Louis was trying not to look horrified.

'It's a way up, near Newcastle.'

Mrs Calvert nodded, uncertain as to where Newcastle was. The Rover rolled on impervious. He had the one child. She tried to think of something to say, trying to get her thoughts behind her, hoping that the determination of the Rover 80 would be enough. Then they passed, what was it, a reservoir, a lake? Whatever it was, there was a boy in a canoe and she feared she could hold back no longer.

'How old is he, your boy?'

Louis hesitated. She could have sworn he was counting.

'Born the day the moon men came back, you know the ones that didn't make it.'

'Sounds like a lucky lad.'

She willed her foot calm. God, how she wanted to tell this man. There was always the hope that if she let it flood out, she'd have done with it once and for all, but knew that it would never be so. Talking was an illusion. They travelled on. She could think of nothing else to say. The interior was filling up with her inabilities. She was beginning to feel tired.

'Is it easy?' he said. She started, as if the question had been spoken into some great hollow space, a vast boom of it.

'Easy?'

'Keeping sheep, looking after them.' She gathered herself. Sheep.

'No more than most. They get on with it, like most animals. Lambing, that can take a while. There's diseases to look out for, but nothing that good husbandry won't account for. Some breeds are tougher than others. Your moorland sheep, for example, just take it on the chin.'

'I would like a couple. If I could.'

'You don't have the room?'

'It's not as simple as that.' Mrs Calvert nodded again. Here was a man who gave up information as a winkle gives up its flesh.

'Building roads, I suppose you move about a lot.'

'Not as much as I used to.'

'But it's in your blood. That's what your friend said, the car dealer.'

Louis stared ahead of him.

'My blood's thinner now.'

'Getting older, you mean.'

'Not that at all. It's … all this.' He gestured to the traffic ahead. 'I used to love the roads. In their prime it was like sailing on the open sea, but now … I mean look at it. Now it's like …'

'I've only been on a British motorway once before … years ago. Must have been … '63?'

Louis sat up, interested.

'Where were you going?'

'The Lake District. Colin, the young man I was with, was desperate to get on the M1 and then across country to another bit … I can't remember …'

'M6 most likely,' Louis said. ''Sixty-three, you say. Not fully complete then.' He stopped, gathered his breath. 'It was the first motorway I worked on. We'd finished the Stafford bypass the winter before. I built it. You rode over it.' He patted the seat. 'I wonder what this was doing then?'

Mrs Calvert wiggled the wheel a moment, latching on to the idea.

'Colin got fantastically worked up about it. I think he was more excited about driving on the motorways than he was going away with me. And, you know, it was our first time together, my mother in blissful ignorance ...'

She stopped. They both did, sudden thoughts about younger days, the simple splendour of it, hopes that had led them on.

'You can't blame him for that,' Louis said. 'For a driver it was a first time too. That's what the motorways were then, the way they looked, spread out before you, nothing in your way, who couldn't be excited? It's difficult to remember it now, what motorways were like, the release they offered, the sense that life wasn't all hemmed in. No speed limit, no hold-ups, hardly any other cars, just this marvellous young thing taking you, not to a destination but to a state of mind. That was it ... I bet you had a good holiday ...'

It was the nearest he could get to it, the words he wanted to say but could not. Motorways were like flesh then, flowing easy like a long slippery fuck, tactile and endless, animal in their joy, like they were lying there just for you, beautiful and willing, whispering all the things you wanted to hear, how great you were, how no one had felt or known it quite like this ever before. It wasn't the car that fed your longing, it was the motorway. It opened you up, brought you close to touching what was out there, a state of near bliss, unencumbered by thought. Now all you had were the cars that had taken you there ...

Mrs Calvert was hauling him back.

'Yes, a good holiday, although we met someone ... who made it not so good in the end.'

She cleared her throat, the story brought to a close. Louis understood.

'No use in complaining. It was life in the raw then. Now, it's just rules every second of the way, traffic jams and speed limits and seat belts.' He juggled the catch with contempt. 'And travelling to what, for what? It should be a mystery, travelling.'

'Does this mean that me then and my Rover … are we beyond the pale?'

'You?' Louis ran his fingers through his hair. He was going to grow it long, he thought. Or maybe cut it altogether. One or the other. 'Not likely. There's a mystery to you, and the car and where you're going. If I could, I'd clear this lot out the way, so you could travel this road as you were meant to – a proper purpose in your heart.'

'What is my proper purpose then?' she asked.

'I haven't a clue …' he turned to her '… and I'm thinking that you don't have a clue either.'

She laughed, her first laugh back in the old country, a laugh that she'd never heard before, not the woman from Brandon, Manitoba, nor the girl from Aylesbury, someone else, in charge of this car and with this man, travelling towards a definite uncertainty, chosen and true. And with it came a sense of arrival, of dislocated place, and a touch of pure happiness. She wanted to kiss him. She knew she wouldn't, but she wanted to kiss him, take his hands in hers and thank him with all her heart. Now she had to tell him. It was her duty, what she could pass on to this liberating man.

'It's not for me to say,' she said, her heart crazy down her ribs and her toes agitated, 'and I know I shouldn't say it, not knowing your circumstance, and even if I did, there's no excuse, but I am going to say it anyway. If you can, have more.'

Louis looked at her surprised. The Rover hit sixty.

'Sheep?'

She gulped, the word momentarily stuck.

'Children. Just in case. It's a terrible thing to even think, but if it's possible, you should … just in case. I lost mine. It was too late then. In every way, it was too late.'

There, it was said. She could breathe again. The Rover dropped back.

'Was that why you left?' There was no false sympathy in his voice, just a straight, direct question. She liked that.

'No. He was the hardest to leave behind.'

'Chester's a strong lad,' Louis told her.

'I don't doubt any different,' Mrs Calvert said, 'but, as I said … Besides …' she took a hand from the wheel, her thoughts uncontrolled '… why have one when you can have twenty?'

'Twenty!'

'What I mean is …' She made to put her foot down again, resisted it. 'They'll be all yours, won't they? What's to say, if you do have sheep and goats and a little holding, they won't be needed.'

Louis looked to the passing land. They were running alongside Robin Hood country. How strange that she should say such things now, near the remnants of the old forest. He thought, when he got back, he'd buy Chester a bow and arrow, and a green cloak for Alice, if such a thing existed. He almost never bought her clothes, yet when he did, they were near perfect. She would look glorious in a green cloak on some empty moorland, like no one could touch her, like she was the earth and the sky and the air that hung in between, like if he ever found a place like that, there'd be no stopping them; just him and Chester and Alice in her green cloak and her hair hacked back with a knife and the gun under her arm.

'You got it wrong, Mrs Calvert,' he said. 'I'm not planning a settlement.'

'No?' Mrs Calvert reached out, patted his hand. 'I thought perhaps you were.'

FIVE

CHESTER WAITED FOR ANGELA that next Sunday, but she never came. He waited for her the following Sunday and the Sunday after that, and then he forgot all about her, forgot too about Rabbit buried in the ground. The forest was like that. It budded and flowered and died back in seasons of forgetting, showering him with a constant present, never asleep, always stirring. Familiarity was a sort of remembered dream, not quite belonging to what he found in front of him. It lived somewhere else, and his feet moved forward, away from it. A month later, Alice came back from a day's wanderings with an armful of old paperbacks she had picked up from a skip, the books ragged and damp, but otherwise intact.

'Look what I found,' she said, 'absolute gold mine, this lot,' and laid them down, one by one like she was dealing from a pack of cards. Her lessons were drying up apace and she was sensing her limits. They'd been fun to begin with, like an expedition, all eyes and concentration, but the more there was for Chester to learn, the less time she had to teach. Chester read the titles. Only two of them made any sense. *Watching Birds* and *A Book of English Poetry.* The others – *Lives of Great Composers Volume One, The Islandman, Elizabeth and Essex,*

Those Greenland Days, *The Ancient World* and *Son to Susanna* – what was he supposed to do with them?

Aunty Lot picked one out, turned it in her hand.

'Is this the end of your responsibilities then?' she said.

'What do you know about books?' Alice said, sudden and angry. 'He'll learn just as much from this lot as from me.'

She stacked them up by the stove pipes. There they stayed, Alice shuffling the pile as they began to dry out. She'd leave one out on the table, the colours faded yet bright. Chester ate his food. Forest or no forest he felt disappointed, like the fairground music had stopped, like there were no rides any more. The titles were in big black letters, clean and clear.

'Like signposts, those are,' Aunty Lot said, seeing his fingers trace one of the covers. 'And once you're in them, Chess, they're just like roads, taking you all sorts.'

Chester took one to the forest. He liked the small weight of it in his pocket as he walked along. It was his own, this paper book, not like the library books that Alice brought back, all protected and stamped inside. So he began his reading. He skipped over pages until he found a sentence he could follow, and then he read until the following left him. He read the books in snatches, as the fancy took him, like one day he might want a dark blue book and another, one of the cherry-coloured ones, like Dad and Mum woke up some days and fucked off out of it, like they changed cars. Fancy took him, nothing else. He picked up a blue book and read about Handel and Mozart with never a note between them in his ear. When he was a child, Handel's father told him off for playing the piano. Mozart's father was so proud of his five-year-old son that he copied the music the boy wrote into his sister's exercise book. In *The Islandman*, Tomás O'Crohan had a son who died falling from the cliff into the sea while collecting gulls' eggs. Essex flung his hat into the water, sailed into Cadiz and stormed ashore while Raleigh burnt the Spanish boats. Tomás O'Crohan was a good dancer, so was Essex. Queen Elizabeth was bewitched by Essex until she chopped off his head. John Wesley was small and serious, and was frightened of taking the fire of love into his bosom. All these things he read alone in the forest, under a tree, by the pond, where the badger was buried, finding the right place with a book under his arm and the time to read them slowly, as if they mattered, as if they were telling him things that he needed to know. There was no reason for him to read any of them, were old and fuzzy-printed and had nothing to do with the forest or Alice and Louis and Aunty Lot, but as he read them and puzzled over them, he found that they did matter to him, that they meant something, though he couldn't say what. Learning was about wonder, nothing else. The Greeks made buildings out of sun-dried bricks, while the best bricks for an igloo came from snow about eighteen inches down and the dogs pulling the sledges got so hungry they ate their snowshoes and harness and pieces of tent. Imagine a dog eating a tent! Other books came, no order, no sense, but with acute timing, each one of them slotting into exactly what he needed. There was one about the colour and pattern of birds and animals, another about Göring and Hess and Ribbentrop, and the things they had done, things beyond his comprehension. *With Mystics and Magicians in Tibet* had stories about monasteries and lamas and a special meditation seat, where the ascetic dozed but never fell asleep. The books were full of such tales. In Greece they didn't have books, they told stories instead. Pericles made a speech about cities, what they should be. Cities teach the man, the book said, and Chester wondered if he, who had never lived in a city, would ever learn anything if he never went. London was where the angels visited John Wesley in a little room in Aldersgate Street. Wandering was good though. Heroes wandered everywhere in Greece. John Wesley wandered, the country echoing with his song and prayer. In Tibet the monks wandered almost non-stop, until they stayed put and then they hardly moved at all. What became clear to him was that the world was full of people, people who had lived and breathed and who lived in these pages now, right in front of him. Everything was about people. When it wasn't about people it kind of wasn't there. Even the book about birds was written by a person who was telling him about how the birds lived. The more he read the more he came to see the eternal fix of things. The male doves bowed and paid court to their mates like Essex bowed and paid court to his queen. *A Book of English Poetry* had a poem about a baby scorched and burning bright, just like six-year-old John Wesley, who was nearly burnt alive before a neighbour saved him from the fire. When he was grown up, John Wesley dreamt of saving everybody. Alexander the Great dreamt of ruling one kingdom for all the world. The Nile was a mighty thought threading a dream. What did it all mean? Images floated from the pages, rumbled in his head, like it was all together, the whole lot of it, part of the world and part of the forest, all mixed in, mountains of thought, rivers of history, people together as in a ship or an army, or alone watching birds or writing poems. In this way he learnt, scavenging, not understanding, but picking stuff up as it washed up on the shore, some wonderful things, others so full of dread the touch of them kept him awake: the dead boy floating on the water until a canoe full of lobsters carried his body home; the faithful dogs all shot after the Greenland expedition was finished; a child cooing with delight in the tickling arms of a white-haired woman, her husband holding the hand of his young son, pointing to sky, all of them standing naked at the edge of a huge pit, waiting to be shot.

Alice's lessons were reduced to a trickle. She taught him to drive instead, standing on the porch steps as he drove up and down over the potholes, the wheel bouncing in and out of his grasp. When she thought he was ready, she let him loose when there was hardly any traffic, when he could swerve and wobble like crazy and get a feel for the magic he had in his hands. It was the most fun they ever had.

Louis kept his lessons more regular, testing Chester on the big map, not just the roads, but the things that spread out from them. Chester began not to mind. This knowing was a fresh thing, growing inside him without any help from anybody, just like his arms and legs. Aunty Lot tried to read one of the books once to keep him company, but gave up. That was all right. The only thing he missed was the forest. He was out there, but his nose and his eyes and ears were far away. He began to visit the forest at night. He would steal out, not that there was any need to, not that they didn't know, Alice and Louis, hearing his window pushed open and the rustle of leaves as his feet touched the ground, but it was good that he did it alone, good that he wanted to keep it that way. He would steal out and he would walk and he would sit. Sometimes he would swim in Wake Valley Pond, long, lonely strokes. Later, when the water grew too cold, he wheeled down the big tyre, paddled out and span, ice-boxed and breathing like a dragon, burning up alone but amongst the most vigorous company.

That winter, before the spring had come, Louis left on Hogan's bike for a month-long stint to finish his section, the longest time he'd been away for years. The Hovel went into a state of semi-suspension. Chester wrapped up, took to one of his forest dens. Lot spent her time in the Pot Hole, brewed soup, big mugs of it for perished walkers. Alice bridled at the sight of them, enjoying themselves outside, Lot dolled up laconic, looking like a cut-price Liz Taylor. She missed Louis in a way she had never done before, not like she'd felt in the big flat back in Ellen Road, lost in the empty spaces, but bursting at the seams. There was something deadly about it, like a crack running up the length of her, like she could fall apart. She took to driving. They had a Cortina again, in homage to its imminent demise. She'd get up at the break of light and drive, come back dusk or later. Where she went they didn't ask, and if they had, she couldn't have told them. It was driving unconscious, not having to look anywhere but ahead. She'd come back and lie down in their bed, wanting more. She wished her hands could bring her peace but they could not. She wanted the emptiness to fill up, didn't know with what. One night she got up, opened his door. Chester was at the table.

'How old are you now, Chess?' she said. It didn't surprise him, the question. He didn't answer, felt it wrong. Alice stuck her hand in her pocket, threw him the keys.

'Old enough,' she said. 'Start her up. We're going for a spin.'

He felt the thrill of it, even as he caught them. Something was going to happen.

She drove him out of the forest and on to the road that Louis had built. They drove for an hour or more, silence queen, the traffic thinning out, the roads widening not in size but in scope, everything extended, slowed down. Then, off the M11 and on the B1052, north of Saffron Walden, she stopped, walked round, and pulled open his door.

'Shift over, cowboy,' she said. 'You're driving.'

He eased himself under the wheel, and because of the dark, because he knew something was about to happen, reached for the buckle on the seat belt. She slapped his hand, hard.

'This is our car. You drive by our rules. No child of ours is going to wear one of those deathtraps.'

He drove up to Linton, his right foot shaking as he tried to maintain a constant speed, before she had him turn off, roads filed down to lanes, then on to something more substantial, the A143, until they turned again, digging into deeper, unknown territory. The road came long and silent and bounded by fields of calm.

'Hold steady now,' she said, and leant over and switched off the headlights.

His foot pumped down on the clutch, but her left hand was already over his, holding the wheel firm, her right spread out above his right knee, urging his foot back down. He touched the pedal, lightly, felt the pulse underneath. The Cortina had hardly lost any speed at all. Alice took her hand away, settled back.

'Any other child, I would have parked on the field back there, made you sit until you got used to it, like Louis did to me, but you know about the dark. You sneak out your window all hours, come back your clothes all damp. Don't look all surprised. We let you do it because that's the way we are. Look at it, Chess. Can't you feel it, the whole night lit up for you.'

He looked. The windscreen was opening up like a cinema curtain, the road bleeding into the sky and shapes coming up like they were moving with him, everything fluid. The wheel grew into his hands. He felt emptied, as if who he was was spreading out through the car and into the darkness, and the darkness was spreading back into him.

The Cortina rolled on, the dark parting before them like a sea. There was a resistance to the dark, a solidity. Alice cleared her throat.

'I'm going to say something now. Don't look at me. Just listen.'

He couldn't speak.

'I'm not a good mum. I know that. It's not that I don't love you or anything. It's just ... it's as if I need to be somewhere else, somewhere here in the dark, racing into the unknown. I look in the mirror and I don't know who I am. I look at you and know that you don't know who I am either. But you know who you are. I look at you and see something in you I can't see in me, a sort of peace. It's like a wedge between us. I want to give you everything but I feel I have nothing to give ... except this. If I can make you see this, taste it, get used to it when you're young, before it eats you up ...'

Then there came a light, red and distant, swaying with a bobbing motion as if on water. Then, as the gap closed, it separated into two. Tail lights then, growing steadier as they hauled in. The Cortina was almost silent, its voice hushed, Chester's foot barely on the pedal. They drew near, the car before them insensible to their presence. They could see it now, swaying with the roll of the road, large and lumbering. Alice leant forward, a strange sensation of stealth and movement swirling between them.

'Do you see what it is?' she said, gnawing at her fingers. 'God, do you see? A three-litre piece of shit.' She put her face to the screen. 'What colour is that? Grey?'

Green, Chester thought, but what matter the colour? The road was hardly moving now, neither the Cortina nor the car ahead, just the space in between and the world fallen away. He could hear his mother's breath.

'Go on,' she said. 'Land the fucking Eagle.'

'What do you mean?'

'Like you do in dodgems. Let him know you're there, then drop away. It's almost better than ...' she stopped '... almost anything.'

He pressed down, felt the engine pick up, neither of them breathing, gliding in close, no sound, no road, nothing.

'Go on, Chess. One small step.'

He eased forward. It was different now, the black air soaked red, his eyes blurred with tailgate haze, the car quite clear, but colourless. Its driver stared ahead into the light, oblivious, the dark left far behind. That's what they did, drivers at night. They travelled away from the dark. Not Alice, not Louis, not this lad. They held the wheel solid, plunged in. He was there now, his face hot, his hands glowing. He rolled up easy, touched the bumper lip to lip and fell back, no hesitation, just closed eyes and the drop in his stomach and the noises in his mother's throat.

The car swung across the road, then settled back. Alice shifted in her seat. It was hard to say whether the driver had noticed them at all.

'Do it again.'

'Mum.'

'Just do it, Chester.'

It took longer this time, the Rover picking up speed, blowing the dark away, the Cortina straining at the pace, beginning to shake. Chess changed down, then back up again, his foot held to the floor, Alice half out her seat, urging him on.

'Come on, Chess, touch him! Sweet Jesus. Touch him!'

He came again, harder. Alice flicked on the headlights.

The Rover lurched forward, thrashed from side to side tanked up on fear and uncertainty, then caught on the lip of the right-hand ditch, bucking along on the rough, wild and angry. They drew alongside, the driver's face turned towards them, words spilling down his front. Then they were past him, his hold on them gone, spurts of lights spilling over them, jolted arcs over the fields and the road. Alice sank back in her seat, consumed.

'Did you feel that?' she was saying. 'Holy Mary, did you feel that?'

The lights fluttered, went out, the Rover swallowed up.

'Where'd he go?' he said. His mother's voice was hardly there.

'That's what we used to do all the time, your dad and me. Humbers, Renaults, Corsairs. Corsairs were the best. Even on the motorways.'

'He's gone,' he said, anxious now. Alice opened her eyes.

'Who?'

'The Rover. What's happened to him?'

'Who fucking cares? Keep driving.'

A little later, back on the A road, she felt under the dashboard, pulled out a packet of nuts and raisins, tore it open, stuffed them into her mouth.

'Pull over. I'll drive back.'

She drove back, Chess glancing over, looking for his mother's sanity.

Louis came back ten days later, the work finished. He stood on the porch, bare-chested, looking to the clearing like an enemy might lie hidden. Light was washing away. Lot had caught the bus into town. It had never happened, Louis and Lot going off together. It never would.

'Where's Chester?' he said. 'I'd like him to be here when I get back.'

Alice was by the door. She'd soaped her hair, flannelled her body. She hadn't seen much of Chester after the drive.

'You know Chester,' she said, anticipation rippling through her. 'Him and his books …' She stepped forward, brought her voice closer. It frightened her, how much she wanted only him. 'Come to bed, Louis.'

His shoulders tensed in the back. He took a step down, still staring out.

'It's closing in on us, can't you feel it?'

She jumped down. This was why she was here. Louis hadn't finished. It was storming inside him.

'I thought we might still be free of it – three lanes of freedom to call on. But they won't be any use much longer. The more we build, the quicker they fill up. I …'

He stopped, unable to voice it. She pulled him round, her eyes willing it out. This was important, they both knew it.

'What is it, Louis?'

'It's been coming a while, years if I admit it, but I don't want to build them any more, can't see the point of it. They'll never be enough.'

He turned to face the trees again. She kissed the tattoos, went inside, dropped her clothes to the floor, lay down. The sun had quite vanished before he joined her. He stood by the bed. Alice's eyes were wandering, her breasts big under the dark window. He sat down, touched her forehead.

'You remember that woman I told you about,' he said, 'the one driving your favourite car. The thing that struck me was that she had a purpose, She didn't know what it was, but it was driving her along that road like she was an explorer, hoping to find that unknown passage through. Once we had the Brebis. The Brebis was just the dress rehearsal, showing us the way. Soon only night will count and our ability to prosper in it.'

She looked at him hard, taking it in. He had a plan afoot.

'We have to do more,' he said. 'You could have children, three, four, five. Sons. A tribe.'

'Sons?' Her lungs expanded at the thought of it. She felt huge, limitless, all of her unguarded and free. A tribe. He laid his hand flat on her stomach.

'They would grow, take wives of their own,' he said, confident in his prediction. 'We'd never stop, find a sweat of land, make a shape, a settlement, our own laws and customs, never stop.'

They fell silent. On the wall opposite Alice counted the saws and hammers and the rows of scythes and spare blades.

There was enough there for a tribe. She could imagine them, their broad backs hacking down scrub, clearing land, filling the air with their sweated bulk. Her sons! She could feel their magnetism, see them bringing back women, entranced like she had been entranced, hear them rutting, nothing in front of them, nothing behind, just trust in the certainty of it. There was nothing else that counted. And she saw her pregnancies like a series of huge paintings, hanging over them for all to see, the luminous sheen on her drum-stretched skin lighting the faces in the room, her belly shining brass, the eyes of men feasting on the wonder of her fertility.

'Chester was conceived on the road,' she said. 'Our new sons ... not here surely?'

'On the motorway again?' It took him by surprise that she would want to repeat it. Alice sat up, her face wide awake. She was there already.

'Where the earth tells us to,' she said, 'where worship lives, holy tors, ancient stones, mountain tops, so what you flood into me is who we are, you and me, all that we feel.'

'How about pulpits?' he said, eyes ablaze, sounding her commitment out. 'Right in front of the pews and cassocks and the holy fucking ghost.'

She slung her arms about his neck, willing him on.

'We'll seek them out, all over England, Louis, break into new life, the gods looking down on us. Same as the motor-way, same as Armstrong on the moon. Son after son after son, thick like cream, perfect like an egg. I've got a few years left in me.'

She rested her lips on his, her body hung on the moment. His hands slipped down to the cradle of her bone. He could feel her churning inside. He thought of carrying her brazen to the car right then and there, driving blind until they found the first place. She wasn't finished.

'We'll need the car for it. It must *know*. We'll travel in the dark. At dawn you'll fill me up. It'll be like the start of a new religion, our right to choose. Go and give Charlie a call. We can set off …'

She stopped, drew back. There were footfalls on the wooden steps.

'Chester?'

Alice pulled a hasty blanket across her lap as he appeared, his hair ragged. He had a couple of horse mushrooms in his hand.

'Look at you,' she said. 'Come on, chuck it over, I'm hungry.'

He broke off a wedge, threw it over. She caught it, bit into it. 'Your father has fresh plans,' she said. 'We might do a spot of travelling again. You got your wings ready?'

Pink spittle ran down her chin, dripping on to her. She brushed it off, like it was rain or an accident from a spoon, the whole of her sudden suppressed, and the snake rising up from the depths, telling it all. Chester's eyes refused to move, like they were glued, like he dare not add to what he saw, was seeing, the meaning of her flesh burrowing into his own. There was a new kind of nakedness unveiled before him. Alice could see it too. There was heft to him now and it was growing. Once she had produced a boy, but since the drive she had seen that it was a man who had sprung out from her, a man with a darkness between his legs she could never see. A terrible thought assaulted her. It would be Chester who would bring back the first wife, Chester thick like cream and the woman's womb like a ploughed field, rich and ready for sowing. If they didn't get a move on, it wouldn't be her who produced five sons.

She picked the corner of the blanket, patted herself dry, used the motion to cover herself further. Louis was right. There were traffic jams everywhere.

They drove to Aylesbury the next day, Louis dozing, Chester in the back with a book. Alice was hoping for another Cortina. The Cortina had received a major facelift, wider-slatted grille, flattened roof, more glass. Charlie had three cars lined up for them: a Wolseley 18/Eighty-five, an old beast of a car; a Brylcreemed Vauxhall Cresta; and a Riley 4/Seventy-two, sedate and respectable. All were duo-tone, the Wolseley crimson and black, the Cresta sky-blue and navy, the Riley with blues like the Cresta, but with the darker shade above. Charlie left them alone for forty minutes, came back with mugs of tea and a packet of biscuits.

'They come up nice, don't they, after a good blow job,' Charlie said. 'I was up at six doing these up.'

'Very nice,' Louis said. 'Different approaches to our needs.'

'Which are?'

'Unpredictability,' Alice offered. She was wearing loose dungarees, her hands stuffed in the big front pocket. With the cars in front of her and the kick of driving off in one of them ahead, she wished Chester wasn't there. This was a time for her and Louis and their new companion. She fingered her belly button under the cloth. 'Unpredictability and excess. We might have to sleep in it.'

'What about a camper van then?' Charlie said. Alice spat her tea on to the ground. Louis held up a finger.

'Charlie,' he said. 'You must never use that word in front of us again.'

They were leaning towards the Wolseley. The livery reminded Alice of coach rides she used to take, journeys away from home, school outings, back-seat dares in blazers and skirts. The Wolseley would manage all manner of licence.

'You and Chess take it down the road a while,' Louis suggested. 'I'll talk money here.'

Alice settled in, adjusted the driver's seat, found the catch point, turned the engine over twice before setting off. Chester rolled the window down, put his hand out, waved as they pulled on to the road.

'She sure knows how to drive,' Charlie said. 'Another cuppa?'

They walked to the office, a Portakabin up on railway sleepers. Pictures of Charlie with his five TR4s were pinned to the walls. Louis sat on the inadequate sofa, waited while Charlie boiled the kettle.

'Did you know I sold the Rover at last?' Charlie said, pouring in too much milk.

'Did you now.' Louis held his face impassive, helped himself to another biscuit. He knew who Charlie was talking about. There was no reason for it, but he felt a sense of ownership where Mrs Calvert was concerned.

'This woman comes in, past her prime, but ... bag full of money she had, not a clue what she wants, but kind of does, if you follow me.'

'I follow you fine. There's something about the older woman ...'

'Exactly!' Charlie dropped the sugar in from a height, like he was on a bombing run. 'It's like they know everything, even when they don't. Anyway, she comes in, by taxi would you believe, so there's no escape, and blow me if she doesn't buy the 80, just like that.'

His feet gave a little shuffle, still dancing with it.

'Well,' Louis said, remembering. 'It has a presence.' Charlie hadn't finished.

'What's more, she takes off to this beauty spot up the road, driving as good as your Alice, perfect gear change, the Rover purring down the road like a big pussycat ...' His voice drifted off. He'd never had a customer like Mrs Calvert, the measure she had brought to her uncertainty, the rubber-banded bundles of banknotes pressed into the bottom of her bag, the mystery smile she gave him driving off. He had always hoped that somewhere in his yard stood the four-wheeled magnet that would draw in the woman of his dreams, but he'd never imagined it would be the Rover 80, nor that she'd look like Mrs Calvert. He couldn't stop thinking about her.

'How old would you say?' Louis said. Charlie slopped his tea in frustration. It was exasperating, the amount he didn't know.

'Could be forty, could be a hundred and forty, it was impossible to tell. And see here ...' he stuck his hand in the desk drawer, pulled out a postcard '... got this from her last week. Living on a farm now, said for me to drop in, if ever I was in the area. Do you think she's after me, or something ... ?'

Louis took the card. York Minster. She'd bought the farm then, despite what she'd said.

'Off the A64, she says,' Charlie said, looking over his shoulder. 'Where is that exactly?'

Louis handed the card back.

'Runs from York to Scarborough,' he said, and dipped his biscuit into the new brew. 'Now, the Wolseley. Are we talking a sensible figure here?'

———

Yes, the A64, but before Scarborough, the Rover had taken them back down to York to pick up the keys, Louis with a tie that he'd borrowed from the hall porter, Mrs Calvert in a grey silk blouse with a choirboy bow up front. A pot of tea and cake at Betty's and then out on the A64, empty and still shiny from the night's rain, through Malton and up into the Wolds, Louis reading out loud from the estate agent's brochure: the farmhouse (in need of renovation), living room, sitting room, kitchen, pantry, utility room, toilet; first floor, main bedroom front, second bedroom rear, box room, bathroom, airing cupboard; second floor, third bedroom and kitchenette; outbuildings, general-purpose barn, hay store (three of the four bays open to all sides), coal bunker, greenhouse; flagstone yard, garden at rear; the land consisting of a total of 35.10 acres, including three principal field enclosures.

'All fields,' he read, 'have livestock fencing and access to a water trough from a main water supply. Sounds a lot for …' His voice trailed off.

'Don't you dare say it,' she said, fingers drumming the wheel. 'Besides, you forget where I've come from. That amount of land … nothing but a pocket handkerchief to a woman like me. Still, I agree. It's madness, even to contemplate.'

Louis laid the brochure flat on his knee. This was going to be a different ride from the day before. They'd been quiet then, after her outburst, quiet but not easy, both of them wanting to talk more, not knowing how to go about it. Stupid stuff – life on the motorway, Canadian cars – got in the way. Coming up to Scotch Corner changed all that.

'A real journey-stopper,' she'd said, elated at the sight of the hotel's solid grandeur.

'Finest drop on the whole network,' Louis said. 'On its uppers now, but in its heyday … I know someone who used to cook the all-day breakfasts here. Would start you up quicker than a pair of jump leads.'

The foyer had reminded her of the liner that had taken her across, several decks high and a staircase that swept down to a non-existent ballroom. Louis had seen Hogan settled in the far bar, but stayed with her while she was found a room. He hadn't known how to take his leave of her. She'd watched as a man in faded livery struggled with her suitcases up a staircase leading to a terrible nowhere. All of a sudden she felt as if she had been lonely all her life. The arms of a good man and a difficult boy had wrapped themselves around her, and yet she had been lonely all her life. How could that be?

'Would you like dinner,' she said, 'as a sort of thank you?' Louis was embarrassed.

'Better not,' he said. 'Work to do. This van we're picking up, no telling what state it's in. The sooner we get going …' She stuck out a hand.

'Understood. Good luck then. And if you see the two of us on the road again …'

'You're going to keep it then?'

'Of course. It's my new shell.'

Louis and Hogan had ridden out to where Lot's van was parked up, a couple of miles down the A66, the old Roman road to Barnard Castle. A new battery and two front tyres and he could drive it down. They'd kipped on the floor, overnight rain tenacious on the roof, the phrase drifting over Louis all night. It was all you needed – a covering. All living creatures had one in one form or another, fur, hide, shell. Only humans needed clothes and houses and heating. If only he could grow a shell. If only it were possible. If only he needed *nothing*.

By mid-morning they'd bolted in the new battery, desperate for a fry-up, get some warmth back in their bones. Mrs Calvert was sitting in the lounge, drinking coffee beneath a potted plant. She had a newspaper on her lap and a map folded out on her table. She'd beckoned him over. Louis wiped his hands on his arse, wished he'd thought of a comb.

'I was hoping I might run into you,' she said. 'Look what I found.'

She'd ringed a notice in the local paper, a farm for sale, out in the Wolds.

'Day one you buy a car, day two a farm,' he said. 'The Almighty didn't work much quicker.'

'I know,' she said, taking it back. 'It's the last thing I want to do, get up at four in the morning again. But when I saw it …' She angled the map. 'It's not far, see … I don't suppose … it would only take half a day …'

Forty minutes later Louis was stood in the gents, trying on the tie. Estate agents, Mrs Calvert had advised him, require a nod to neatness.

The turn to the farm was overgrown, the track potholes and puddles, Louis wishing he was behind the wheel. The house stood on a rise half a mile away, tall and ugly, too big for one person. Once inside it lost its size – the rooms narrow, dark, the house's space sucked into the thick stone walls. He followed her through, up and down, bare room after bare room. There was something monstrous about a whole house, not the space it offered, but the demands it made. You gave your life over to a whole house, never got it back. Houses were not a shell. Houses were a growth, a malignancy.

'What do you think?' she had said, back down again.

'What do *I* think?'

'Yes, I know ...' She looked out to the slope of the field, and the hills beyond. 'The last time I looked across a view like this, I thought I had a future, everything in front of me. I was by a river, kneeling down, the water rippling through my fingers so strong and clear, as if it was telling me ... as if my life was going to be like that, clear and strong and never stopping ...'

'Never stopping ... that's the thing.'

'I came back down from the hill awoken. There was nothing I couldn't do, nothing that could stop me. But you do stop. Quite early on, you stop, or someone stops you.' She turned back. 'It's a bit poky, isn't it.'

'You wouldn't want it any other way,' Louis said. 'Not with the weather it catches.'

'And coal ... humping great sacks across every day.'

She flapped the prospectus limp in her hand. Outside the Rover shone solid in the wet light. Dirt was sprayed as far up as the door handles. Louis could hardly bear to look at it.

'Quite impractical,' she said, 'not to mention the draughts. Come on. Let's go. Would you care to drive?'

'I'll give her a wash first, if we can find a bucket,' he said.

And so, Louis had driven the Rover 80 one more time, back up to Scotch Corner while Mrs Calvert told him all she knew about sheep, and vowed, as he sat high and straight, never to tell Alice what he had done.

Alice returned, threw open the door, swung her legs out.

'The steering's dead in the water,' she said. 'Rolls too. Is that the best you can do?'

Charlie swept his hand over the lot.

'I got plenty others. Vauxhalls, Granadas, a nice little Chevette. There's a Marina you can have dirt cheap, otherwise ... it's digging into your pockets a little deeper.' Louis patted his inside pocket.

'I wouldn't say money is no object, but it's not the principal consideration.'

'I got something I can't get rid of ...'

'That's a recommendation.'

'There's a prejudice against it ...'

'Oh?' They were intrigued.

He led them to past the garage where the Rover once lived, where the car stood hidden behind an old Ford Transit, creamy white, nose slung to the road.

'You're trying to flog us a foreign car?' Alice said. 'French?'

'A Citroën GS Saloon,' Charlie announced. 'One-point-two-litre engine, top Pallas trim, a real beauty.'

'French,' Alice repeated.

'Put that aside. Look at the curve of that bonnet, the half-open mouth of the grille. This is one sexy car. High-pressure hydro-pneumatic system gives it one of the best rides on the road ... like you're driving one of those hippy water beds ... single-spoke steering wheel and the instrument panel ... it's what's the word ... futuristic ... like a spacecraft ...'

'Spacecraft?' Alice leant forward.

'I haven't shown you the best bit.' Charlie swung open the door, sat half inside. 'Go stand in front, while I start her up. Go on.'

They stood together, hands by their sides. Charlie thought he'd never seen such a couple so deliberately plain in their certitude. He turned the key. The exhaust growled, low and flat. Alice looked away in disgust.

'Hold your horses.'

They stood waiting, stood like they barely belonged there, like they were standing before something that held no meaning to them. Then the front started to rise, rose like it was greeting the day, ready for anything. Alice put a hand to her lip.

'You mean … ?'

'Every time,' Charlie said.

Alice pulled Louis away, spoke to him the once.

'I don't care how much it costs,' she said. 'You want five sons out of me, you buy it.'

Thus, they drove the Citroën and thus they found their places, stayed the night, walked expectant in their intent, stone circles, monoliths, battlefields, on the grassy swathe of old sheep droves, a church too, not a pulpit but a bell-tower, swaying dizzy in the breeze and the figures clothed and contemptible below, but the months went by and nothing was achieved. They had believed themselves, believed the words they had spoken were all they ever needed to do to make it real, had driven off, the sale completed, to where Charlie had told Louis Mrs Calvert had driven, left Chester to his book and pulled each other up to the Beacon, looked out. Alice leant into Louis as he promised her settlements and sons.

'Look,' he said, 'out there lies our stretch of land and our tribe. It's there, Alice. We just have to find it.'

She let his hands roam. She was a stretch of land herself. Below, a couple had parked up behind the Citroën, were busy putting on their jackets. She didn't care.

'Start us now, Louis. Sow our first one, your cock and my cunt. We'll call him Ivinghoe, fucking Ivanhoe, riding to save the world.'

But Ivinghoe never came, nor Alfred, nor Stamford, nor any of them. Louis gave up work. Months rolled into years. None of the boys came round, sensed they weren't a part of the Hovel any more. Louis thought of nothing else, impatient to see Alice's stomach growing and their vision expanded. Alice wanted the pregnancy to be theirs and theirs alone, no Lot, no midwife, no doctors. She could drop a child in a field, bite the cord clean with her teeth, skin a rabbit the next hour if it came to it. The first pregnancy would be the signal. They would load the car and fuck off to a sort of eternity, somewhere high up, fierce and difficult, where their skill and nerve and weapons would be all, the nuts and bolts of existence lying ready at their feet. Maybe they would have to leave Chester in Epping for a time. There would be space for him later, Lot too. But first must come the inception and thence the light, and thus the way. Month after month, but there was no child, just the same old leakage, clots of what was not, their attempts gleeful at first and then in turn, hopeful, diligent, hasty, anxious, sour. What could be so wrong, now that they had wished for it? The places, the season, her timing? She was fertile, she knew it, Louis too. They were nothing but fertile, had told each other time and time again. They tried under the moon. They got rid of the Citroën, ran through the lot, Vauxhalls, Fords, Austins, Louis consulting the big map, using all his knowledge setting off in hope again, Alice bewitched by the stuff spilling out his mouth like when she rode first with him, history and memory and things that had been built, Louis driving again and she sat beside him, feeling all her reason had been drained from her, like she knew nothing again, was there for one purpose, like she had no room for anything else, didn't want it, just the car and the drive and Louis spouting words and pumping fierce. Money ran through their fingers. Louis took short-term jobs before a wedge gave them a week's break. Lot and Chester would watch them go, turn, settle into their own life in the forest. Chester didn't say anything, but some days it felt like they might never come back.

And quite suddenly, it appeared to Chester that he was an older boy. Nights, he woke with mess all about him. Louis explained what had happened, but not everything, Chester thought. In his book, John Wesley had ejaculatory prayers and he wondered if his were the same. He remembered John Wesley thinking about Aspasia, her irresistible hair and clothed in glory. John Wesley meant a lot to him. What had happened to Wesley in Aldersgate was like all heaven had come down to meet him. From that moment on Wesley knew he was saved, knew how *everyone* could be saved, though saved from what Chester didn't fully comprehend, but it kept Wesley going, moving around the country, delivering his sermons like a postman might deliver letters, sermons you took into your heart's home, opened them up. Wesley's mother and father had once been something called

Dissenters. What were Alice and Louis if not Dissenters? Wasn't that what they spent their whole life doing, dissenting in one way or another, and where did that leave him? Was he a follower, or was he waiting for a bolt of fire too? Was there a purpose in him? Wesley had walked through the trackless forests lost in the energy of despair. Dissenting had held him like a sheet anchor in a sea of storms, but then he had found water, woken up, refreshed.

Then he was on the lake, reading of Essex trying to see his queen again, and he remembered Angela and the gap in her teeth and the way she looked at him. He wanted her to look at him again, didn't care in what manner, curiosity, disgust, ridicule, as long as she looked at him again. He knew where she lived, remembered the stop she used for the school bus. She'd have changed schools now, but even so … He took new routes around the forest's edges, skirted round the collecting points where boys of his age hung out, girls too. He saw many he recognised, but never her, thought that the family might have moved away, but kept on turning up in hope. He believed in that sort of thing now, how things could fall into place as though they were meant to, if you gave them enough space – not simply physical space, but the picture you had in your mind, the construct. Monks did it all the time. The Greeks too. One Saturday (he knew the days now, kept unseen track of them) he saw her brothers around the phone box, dark suits and button-down collars, one of them half in, waiting for a call. They stopped when they saw him, their hands squeezed ready for business. He was Nobody, he thought.

'What the fuck are you doing here?' the taller one said. 'You pikey shit …'

In Sparta boys went barefoot and were as loud as statues. When they met an elder, they put their hands inside clothes, looked to the ground and passed in silence. Chester slipped his hands between the buttons of his jacket, his eyes on his shoes as he walked. An empty can came by his head, a stone struck his back. He kept his ancient world close, willed the forest to cover him again. Out of sight, he broke into a run, didn't stop until the forest had run out too.

One morning he woke and picked up the book with the title *The Childhood of Animals*. There was a chapter he had read called 'Limitation of Families' and he needed to read more. Elephants were one of the slowest breeders of all the animals, and would not bring into the world more than six offspring. Yet if all the descendants of a single pair lived their full time of life and produced their six elephants, after five hundred years that one pair would be represented by fifteen million relatives. But they did not. A certain number of young elephants had to die, likewise all living creatures. Whether a species lived a short time or a long time, whether they reproduced in scarcity or abundance, arithmetic showed that unless death touched the young swiftly and often, the surface of the earth, its waters and its air, would be choked full. Dying was a part of youth's success. Chester had no brothers and sisters, and he had begun to wonder whether there had been brothers and sisters of his who had died, so that he might live. He couldn't remember any, but there was no reason why human life should be any different? Creatures made homes and gave birth. Puffins bred in rabbit holes, often turning out the rabbits from their own burrows. Rabbits lived in communities, and the mothers dug out circular chambers off the main run, with several means of exit. The harvest mouse wove a nest of narrow grasses, round like a cricket ball, suspended it to stout blades of corn. It sounded like the Hovel to him, blown and shaken about, tied to the forest. Humans made better homes, so their young survived more easily. Was that why there were wars, and famine and plagues, so humans could get rid of each other another way? Was that the reason for Nuremberg? What then was the purpose of the youth that lived? That was the title of the next chapter. He clutched the book in his hand, walked quickly to where the badger was buried, eager to start. Angela was stood by the grave, arms folded, watching him as if she'd been there the whole morning. There was an awareness to her, smooth and carved out, what she carried shining fresh on her frame. Her hair was piled up. Her eyes stared out from rituals of dark.

'You never turned up,' she said.

'I did too, two or three times.'

He was cross with himself, answering like a child.

'I didn't say which fucking Sunday, did I?'

Chester was confused. They stood, battle lines drawn. One hand went to her hip, her fingers knowing on the bone. She hadn't finished.

'How's the owl school?' she said. 'Still squatting on toad-stools?' He gestured with his book.

'Not as much.'

Angela looked away, shook her head, as if deciding what to do.

'You think no one knows, don't you?' she said. Her face, her body, returned. She took a step forward, the swell on her rising as she spoke. 'Everybody knows. A rubber tyre for fuck's sake.'

She lit a cigarette, sucked on it like she was angry. She reminded him of his mother.

'Shall we dig it up now?' she said.

Chester put his hands behind his back. Strange creation stood before him, like the mould of something he was afraid to touch.

'It doesn't matter now. It was just a toy.'

'What, like a racing car?'

He wondered whether he should tell her, risk the opportunity to feed her scorn. But there was a divide he had to cross, felt the need to do it without adornment.

'A stuffed toy, a rabbit. I put it there to … to keep the badger company.'

There, he'd said it. Angela took a drag from her smoke, held it in her lungs, the cigarette high between her fingers. She'd been smoking for years.

'I don't get it. If it was to keep her company, why'd you want to take it away?'

There was no getting away from it now. This was the path he had to tread, and he thought, quite complicated for a boy, that the main constituent of this path was to be trust.

'I missed him,' he said, waiting for the mockery.

He moved, uncomfortable. Where had she come from, looking so crisp and dangerous? The ground was slipping from beneath him. There was down on his lip and he touched it. She smiled. His sheets were drenched and she knew it.

'She have a name, this rabbit you're so fond of?'

'Just Rabbit.'

'Fuck me. I had a bed full, but they all had fucking names. They're at the back of the cupboard now. Still, I wouldn't want to bury them in the ground. That would be like murder, like really horrible, after all they'd done, when I was a kid, the grief they saw.'

This was it then, the declaration of what they were and what they had been.

'You saw me swimming then?' he said.

'Did I say that? The tyre, that's what I said. What was all that about, well past midnight?' She was dismissive but curious. They'd crossed the divide.

'You were there.'

She patted the back of her hair.

'Getting in hot water, not cold. Anyone would have thought I was twelve …'

She stopped, as he tried to work it out. He was twelve, or was it thirteen? There had been a time when his birthdays had sort of slipped by.

'I was ill for over a year, didn't you know, no school, nothing. That's why I was stuck in with you lot.'

She took out a cigarette packet, shook it, flipped the lip open, offered it up, knowing he would refuse. It annoyed her.

'What shall we do now then?' she said. 'I was meaning to go up town but …'

'We could go down the lake.'

'As long as you don't expect me to arse about on your tyre.'

'I don't have it any more. Someone nicked it.'

'These boots are suede anyway,' she said. 'We could go to my room if you like, play some records.'

Not much was said getting there, too many thoughts crowding in. Once on the pavements Chester felt like he'd stepped ashore. What was she thinking? What was he thinking? He didn't rightly know. Excitement held him, not simply her invitation, but another family home, something on a different dimension to his own. Her house stood not far from the school stop, part of a string of semi's, a garage built underneath.

She called out when she opened the door, but there was no one in. She knew there wouldn't be, he could tell by the way she had stuck the key in the lock, pretending.

'I got some vodka upstairs.'

Chester shook his head.

'Glass of milk then. Wait here.'

He stood. In the room to his left he could see a leather sofa, a bulbous television and an ashtray, silver, stuck on a pole. On the wall hung a colour photo of a man in cycling gear, head grinning like a skull.

'Ready?'

She was holding two glasses. She turned. The carpet was dirty red, scuffed on the risers. Chester followed, the climb momentous. He was nervous, full of dread. Angela was an Eskimo. She smeared her body, drank spirits, her room an igloo. At the top she stopped and faced him.

'No funny business.'

She pushed a door open. A set of blue pyjamas was folded on the pillow of a single bed, a stuffed animal on top. Angela sat down, pulled the soft toy on to her lap, fluffed up its ears. Chester stood in the doorway.

'This is Patsy. My uncle brought her back from Australia.' She held it to her face. 'They live in trees, koalas, just like you. I wouldn't mind living in a tree. Long as it had a hairdryer.'

She put the animal back on the pillow, squeezed a paw as she set it down.

'Did I ever tell you that my brothers are cunts?'

Her eyes were wet and sparkling, her voice bright as if she didn't want to be here after all.

'Come here.' She pulled him to the window. 'See that. That's your fucking tyre. Pissed themselves laughing when they brought it back. We'll just have to find it a new hiding place, won't we, soon as I get rid of these.'

She started pulling off her boots.

Angela and Chester, Alice and Louis. No one dare say it, for Alice's sake as much as Chester's, but she was there now, this girl from the outside world with friends unsuitable. Not that they met up that often. She had an Epping diary to fill, mates, men, school, volleyball, which she was good at, tall andstrong and mental. Chess might not see her for months, and then she would appear while he was waxing the car down, feeding the chickens, sometimes down by the badger or the pond, mocking him for having another book in his hand.

'Most people who come here, a book is the last thing they have in their hand,' she said once. 'What you reading now?'

It was what she wanted from him and he told her, and later, when she had had her fill, she'd tell him, not about books, for she didn't read, but the stuff she was carrying with her, stuff that leapt out into him as his books burrowed into her. And it made an inexplicable sense to them, what he had read, what she'd done, the mystery and the mess; where was the difference? It was a growing for both of them, conducted with a propriety beyond their ages. And Alice and Louis, noting the times she came and the length of the walks they took, were puzzled and, though they did not say it, relieved. The idea that those two could beat them to it was too terrible to be true. They loathed England now, a country under siege, full of rubbish and bombs and dissatisfaction: such a tired old place. They'd visit the towns and see the same weary shit piled in shopping trolleys, pushed along in prams, drunk out of bottles. They'd walk through, trying not to be noticed, but they were. They were like Sicilian peasants come down from the hill, a different race, self-contained, contemptuous, no fear, nothing to do with any of them, not the jobs they didn't have, not the dead they couldn't bury, not the picket lines they weren't standing on, none of it. It was like the nation had a cholera. If they got too close …

Chester found his first calling a month before his next birthday. Alice and Louis were driving a car they couldn't wait to get rid of, a PADX Vauxhall Cresta, cream and cherry-red, slung with the very look that Alice had objected to over at Charlie's, wrap-around windscreen, tail fins, four wheels of brashness surrounded by chrome. They'd set him down in a hurry. Louis had given him a pound, Alice a wink, like it was a prediction of a special day. They'd sped off, couldn't wait to be rid of him. He found a church right away. He stood by a pillar, looking at a stained-glass angel with rainbow-coloured wings, wondering how they might be attached, what shoulder blades might feel like with such growths. It was easy for him to see that such a thing would be possible. Possible and useful, like you could fly in and out of everything, wings flash and articulated like a convertible. No wonder the woman clasped her hand to her mouth, wonder in her eyes. Alice had that look sometimes. Was that what they did when they left him, grew wings, flew away? He could imagine them, flying in and out, no one able to catch them. When he grew up, he could join them, the three of them like swans, flapping in and out. Why not?

'Beautiful, isn't she?'

A man stood next to him, dressed like he belonged there.

'She's the Virgin Mary,' he said, 'and that's her Annunciation. You know what the Annunciation is?'

Chester's eyes remained on the window.

'Are there any more?' he said.

'Virgins? In this town?' the man said. Chester explained himself patiently.

'More churches. More paintings on the glass.'

'Depends what sort of butter you spread on your bread, doesn't it?'

Chester digested this remark, not understanding the words, but aware of the meaning, the shape of it. Understanding things, he had come to realise, was often like that, a sort of shape moving before you that, if you tried to touch, would disappear.

'John Wesley,' he said. 'Does he have a church here?'

The man fumbled in his basket, took out a Russet.

'Are your parents Methodists then?'

He bit into the fruit, staring down. Chester thought about it.

'Dissenters,' he said.

'I don't know about them. There's a Methodist chapel a couple of miles away. Do you know what a virgin is? Eve wasn't a virgin. Not by a long chalk.'

Chester left. Streets did not bother him, unknown ones, crowded ones, deserted ones. He asked for directions, was careful who he asked, kept the tone serious, made it sound like a project, which it was. He passed shoppers and shops, and a man setting up a pyramid of steel dustbins, a hairdresser winding up a striped awning; he passed houses and gardens, gates with names on them, doors with numbers, dogs on leads, a woman clipping a hedge, the streets growing quieter, the houses settled back like they had retreated from the noise too. It seemed to him that he was walking into the secret heart of somewhere. He had visited towns before, explored great tangles of buildings, but here he was pushing all that aside, the noise and flurry lifting like a mist. He could not put it into words but he could feel how a town was re-created day after day in its own image, the purpose of itself driving the life of thousands of separate men and women, all part of a gathering, all part of a motor, an intent. The town was asking something of him, but what he did not know.

The chapel was big and ugly. He had to push his weight against it to open the door. It was dark inside, but the glass in the window was bright and bold. John Wesley stood with his arms out, people all around like they were in a clearing, like it could be the forest. There was a horse stood near him, with his head bent, as though it was Wesley's horse waiting for the next journey. Wesley had ridden all over the country, carrying his message: ridden or walked. That would be the way to meet people, not cars. You never met anyone in a car. Was that why Alice and Louis were so wedded to them, that they didn't want to meet anyone? Meeting people was like his books, connections coming at you from all directions.

He looked for angels, but found none. If there were angels, their wings were hidden under their coats. It would be possible, he supposed, to fold your wings and put a coat on over them.

You could walk around without anyone getting in the way. You might look fat or like you had a hump on your back, but so what. You were an angel. You had wings. He studied Wesley again. What was he saying that everyone wanted to listen to? Chester found it difficult to move.

'What do you think he does, in town,' Alice said, 'besides the books from the charity shops?'

Alice was drinking a glass of milk on an over-cushioned sofa. Louis was wiping his cock on the heavy curtains. It had taken them an hour to find somewhere, and it was the wrong time of day.

'Not the same as us, that's for sure.'

'I wouldn't want him to be getting us into trouble.'

Louis went to stand by the fireplace.

'How do you think I look, master of the house or what?'

He laughed. His penis was long and distended, like it had been through a wringer. She picked up the Polaroid, snapped one off, Louis with one hand behind his back, like a waiter.

'The tombs of fucking Egypt this place,' she said. She flapped the print dry, stuffed the camera back in her bag. Louis took the picture from the wall, turned it round while Alice stuck the photo to the back.

'No face,' he said.

'They got plenty to look at, if they ever find it.'

Louis hung the picture back on the wall. Alice took the glass to the kitchen. It was what they did now, trying for their second son in temples of decorum. They preferred downstairs rooms, rooms where photographs of the occupants looked on. This time they'd placed Louis's boots on the mantelpiece, laid their clothes on the back of the settee, taken possession of the carpet. She'd found herself staring at the boots, imagined her new son's feet slipping along the peeled-back tongue, filling the void of where his father had gone. No words had been spoken. She'd held herself high like a cup, Louis exacting every muscle. These were the riskiest times, but they needed them. They turned their blood effervescent.

Alice rinsed the glass out, put it away.

'It's Chester's birthday a month from today,' she called out. 'We'll know if this one's come by then.'

In the Cresta outside lay a pair of boots that Louis had bought for him, bright red with black laces. Alice was making him a rope ladder.

'He will have,' Louis said.

'And if he hasn't?'

There was a large mirror in the hall. Alice straightened her dress, started pulling at her hair.

'This is like Wales,' she said. 'We can only push our luck so far.' She stuck out her tongue. 'He's asked Angela, you know. Lot's going to make a proper cake, invited half the Pot Hole, it seems.'

She walked back in. Louis was flapping his shirt to loosen up the arms, slipping it over his head.

'I don't know, Alice,' he said. 'It's getting a bit out of hand isn't it?'

'You brought her here. Your shirt's inside out.'

Louis raised his arms, peeled the shirt off, tried to pull it back the right way round. It was one of the loveliest sights she could imagine, never tired of seeing it, his head hidden and his torso, muscular and pale. It was time to go.

'What's he want a cake for anyway?' he was saying. 'He's not a baby.'

He was struggling, the shirt stuck to the sweat of his back.

'Nothing wrong with cake,' she said. 'It's all the rest of it that pisses me off, like we're part of something. I thought Lot would have … ' She stopped, a finger to her lips. The front door was opening. Louis's eyes ran wild, his trousers and jacket still on the back of the sofa.

There was a grunt as someone put a bag down. Man, woman, it was hard to tell. Alice tried to picture the layout, the stairs halfway down the hall, a dining room off to the right and the kitchen at the end. Had they left anything there? Her glass was put away, but … Louis picked up his clothes, took himself out of sight from the half-open door. The footsteps moved along, stopped where Alice thought the stairs might be. She held a finger up to Louis, noticed his boots still perched on the mantelpiece. Someone was struggling, taking off a coat perhaps, hooking it over the banisters.

'Enough!' a woman's voice said. 'I give up.'

Then a pair of wheels were being pulled down over the tiles and a blur at the door which passed and moved down.

'A thing like that!'

The voice came angry, a cupboard door flung back on its hinges. Was that where the glasses were kept? Alice couldn't remember. She pointed to the boots, tiptoed to the door. Objects were banged down on the table, Louis taking the opportunity to hurry on his jacket, his movements masked by the noise. Alice remembered the table, smack in the middle, with a drawer. The woman was unpacking the trolley bag.

'Not a blessed word, the stupid fucking cow. Shit on her coffee morning.'

Alice couldn't help but smile, this unknown woman swearing in her cleanliness. She wanted to step out, tell her to go back, tell it to the old cow's face, instead of making a cup of tea. It wasn't just about sons, what they were doing, it was a crusade, against everything.

'A thing like that!'

Alice held her hair back, edged her head out. She could see black legs in a black dress nearly down to the ankles, a glimpse of skin, then bright yellow socks and black shoes, the woman's weight moving from one foot to the other. Alice beckoned Louis near. The front door was eight, nine steps away; a Yale lock and a handle below. A rattle of bottles came, quite distinct, like a fridge door opening. Water was run, a kettle filled.

She readied herself. There was a knock at the door, a knock and then a bell ringing, a finger persistent on the buzzer. The woman cursed. Alice shrank back. Louis moved behind the sofa, still bare.

'Who could that be, Walter?'

Walter? Who the hell was Walter?

The woman walked back down the corridor, steps brusque and a finger along the balustrade. Alice could smell Louis on her, smell herself too, the presence of this stranger rippling what they'd done through her again. If it had taken this time, she'd come back, tell what they'd done and why, give the woman a heap of money – anything. She wanted to shout it out, it felt so good.

The front door opened, wind blowing down the hall. Louis slipped on his trousers.

'Yes?'

'Is my dad in here?'

'I'm sorry?'

'My dad. I saw him in the window. May I come in?'

Chester? Incomprehension propelled Alice forward. She stepped out into the hall, the woman's back framed in the light. She had golden hair, streams of it. Chester's head craned round.

'Mum?'

'It's all right, Chess.'

The woman screamed. Alice ran to the door, pushed it shut, Louis moving out, blocking the way to the kitchen, his boots swinging from his hand. Chester was staring at his father, the bulge in his back, and his bare feet. Were the tattoos markings then, like a zip, where the wings were attached or perhaps some sort of code? Wesley had seen angels. Was that what they'd been doing ... angeling? The woman's jaw was going up and down like a trap, whimpering noises in her throat.

'It's all right,' Chester said. 'They mean no harm.'

All their attention was turned to him, as if he was the only one there who could unravel what they were caught in. Chester took the woman's hand, led her to the stairs. A bomb had been thrown and it would be up to him to mend the pieces. The woman sat down, trembling. She was younger than Alice had imagined, wearing an antique dress, pulled in with a belt. She didn't look old enough for a house with furniture like this. She should be riding a bicycle, living in a flat.

'What do you want?' she said, petrified to ask.

Chester waited on his mother, to see how she would answer. In the midst of an ocean roaring with doubt and peril, John Wesley had taught a cabin boy bible stories, brought peace and calm to the whole ship.

'We want nothing,' Alice said. 'We came here ...'

'To pray,' Chester said.

The woman looked back at him.

'What the hell are you talking about?'

Chester took to the centre of the hallway, so he could be seen by everyone. He understood he wasn't small any more. The words came to him, lifted from ragged pages. 'It's the glory of their religion,' he said. 'To leave prayers to their God, where none have been asked for. They take nothing.'

'That's right …' Louis started. Chester shut him with a look.

'They take nothing,' he repeated, 'leave only the love they have sent to heaven. They bless the house with their actions and leave unseen.'

The woman shook the words away.

'Why isn't he wearing his shoes? I should call the police.'

Chester sat down beside her. Wesley told his flock plainly how they were free to choose, but choose they must. The doctrine of assurance.

'I would ask you not to,' he said. 'They have bound themselves to this pilgrimage, supplicants to salvation for a house and its occupants. It is their ministry. You are their ministry.' He took her hand. 'No need of the police,' he said. 'No need of priests. Only the offering of hearts.'

She wouldn't have it.

'This is mad. I want you to go, right now, all of you.'

'You only think we're mad because the angels have come. Look around your house. Is anything missing, anything?'

'Will you excuse me,' Louis said, and went back into the room, the woman worried again.

'What's he doing?'

'His socks,' Alice said. 'He takes his socks off, when we …'

199

They listened, the socks noisier than usual. The woman couldn't stop shaking. Louis returned, crumpling material in his pocket.

'They are going now …?' Chester ended the statement with a look.

'Sarah,' she admitted.

'I will follow, Sarah, but not until … until you have made sure.'

Alice moved quickly. No hesitation that was the trick, straight for the door, and down the path, Louis following in her slipstream. The boy and the woman watched them leave. Louis closed the door behind him. It was a peculiar touch, the woman thought, as if they were leaving the boy with her.

'What's your name?' she said.

'Chester,' he said. 'But it's better if you don't know.' He patted her hand, but left it free. Age had rushed upon him. 'Nothing will come of this, Sarah, except goodness from you.'

She ran her fingers through her hair, took him in, side on. What was he, boy, man? Her voice came calmer than she thought possible.

'My, but you're a strange one,' she said. 'How long have you been doing this? You really shouldn't.'

Chester thought for a moment, their nakedness, the times he had heard it.

'As long as I can remember. It's part of their mission.'

'Which is?'

'It's like … they want a new Eden.'

'Heaven help us. You can't just break into other people's houses. It's not right … they shouldn't make you do this. I really should call someone.'

She made to stand up. Chester lowered his head, hands between his knees.

'What will happen to them, when I am not there? What will happen to me? Without me they'd be lost, without them I would … I need the responsibility.'

He looked up at her. He was young and quite beautiful, big eyes, and a male body only just begun. A tear from his eye ran into her hand. It was like he was standing on one side of a crevice, asking for her hand in a moment of crossing. She rubbed it into her skin, her heart big. She wanted to press him to her, never let go.

———

It was ten minutes before anyone spoke, and then it was Alice.

'How did you know we were there?'

'There was a chapel down the road,' Chester said. 'I saw the car coming back. Then Dad at the window.'

Louis tried to explain.

'We're like explorers, Chess, finding out how people live.' Chester spoke back with impatience.

'You had your trousers off. I know what you were doing. It is what happens in the forest, in the bushes and cars. It must stop for you. In houses like that, it must stop. And churches. If you choose churches, you must stop that too.'

Louis laughed, forgetting the position they'd found themselves in.

'Am I hearing this? Our baby son, telling us what to do?'

'I am telling you,' Chester said, deadly serious. 'My father and my mother. I am telling you. This is not the path to walk on.'

'Right. Glad you told us.'

And Louis reached back, picked up the birthday boots, and threw them out the window.

The evening before Chester's birthday, they were lying in bed, now a place of hard refuge. To Alice, the tools opposite hung like surgical instruments, cold and intrusive, made for other hands. She had a sweatshirt on. Not in the bitterest of winters had she worn such a thing in bed before. It had ended then, their quest for sons. No more could be done. That morning Louis had driven up to see Hogan, to find if there was any decent work going, came back empty-handed. It was proving almost impossible to re-set the balance of things. Chester was watching, wherever they were, not a moment they did not feel his eyes upon them.

'Spying through the window,' he said. 'Do you think he saw it … his own mother?'

'We were on the floor, Louis. Of course he didn't. We'd finished anyway. Not that it did any good.'

'Is that it then? Is he our fucking tribe?'

She felt the possibility of tears. Failure had come to her days after the disaster, Louis greeting the news with bitter glances to the room of his only son. She had never seen his frame beaten down as she was seeing now, his limbs lifeless, a sag to his neck, like a shot swan's. He was an older man. Potency still lived in there, but it was struggling against the carry of former years. The time left to him had made itself known and he was bent with the weight of it. She shifted. She could still bring him to it. One time was all it would take. She turned on her side, determined again.

'I know where we need,' she said. 'Where you were a tribe.'

'What are you on about, woman?'

She smoothed back her resentment. He had never used that phrase to her before.

'This holy place of yours. Scammonden.'

'Holy? What makes you think …'

'You carried its water around long enough. And you've never taken me there. All the places in England, but never there. Why is that?'

She had brought something in the room with them now, big, undefined, like a shadow, like it had been in that room in Scotch Corner, the cars going past and Louis's head out the window. She'd had the one dress with her then, poppy petals scattered on cream, still had it folded in the chest. It was all they ever wanted, the bare minimum. They should have gone to Scammonden, decamped to Wales to meet the Brebis. Chester had been two months inside her. Two months!

'We could go whenever we wanted,' she said. She'd put the dress on, let him watch the big buttons slipping through the eyes.

'Go?'

He didn't seem to understand. She wanted to scream.

'Fuck off. Go. Right away.'

He reached down to the floor, lit a cigarette.

'That simple, eh?' He rolled back.

'It could be the place, Louis … and if not there …' she placed her hand on his chest, his lungs hungry for the smoke '… where the Brebis found us, the exact same spot.'

He stuck the cigarette between his lips, laced his hands behind his neck, smoke drifting up. He thought of Mrs Calvert, wondered at her sheep.

'I could do a little searching,' he said. 'The wall would be mended, so it wouldn't be too difficult to find.'

She rolled on top of him. It would be like old times, stealing from the fields and farmyards, chickens and potatoes in the back, not waiting any more, but doing, doing as the fancy took them. They were empty, that was the trouble, had been for years, everything drained out of them. She could almost taste it, the indestructible fullness she possessed.

'Why not?' she said. 'Hardly any roads in Wales at all. Be fun searching though, you and me, even if it took us years and years … you're the youngest fifty in Christendom and as for me …'

He pushed her off, sat up.

'Use your eyes, Alice. I'm sixty, ten years older than I told you.' He gestured to the wall, to the world about him. 'Sixty,' he said, turning to her, his face reddened by confession, 'and no end in sight.'

———

Alice held the bowl while Aunty Lot beat in the eggs. Chester was out in the forest. He'd been walking it, day and night, ever since they got back. She could hear him sometimes, like he was singing up and down to the trees, like they were listening. Louis was in the Cresta, driving back from Stamford. Pete had found work there. He'd gone up first light to find out what.

'Forty-five?' she'd said. 'Why didn't you tell me?'

'You were barely out of school, that's why.'

No more had been said. She'd lain awake working it out, peculiar pictures forming in her head. He'd been forty-five in the Cambridge Farina, not thirty-five. Did that make a difference? If he'd been forty-five in 1967, it meant in 1947 he'd been twenty-five, not fifteen. That made a difference, knowing women before the war made a difference, women dressed like her mother, girdles and petticoats and God knows what else. He might have been in the army too, killed Germans. The army or the navy. That could account for his love of tattoos.

'Keep the bowl still,' Lot said.

Alice studied her, her ringed fingers lifting the whisk, testing the viscosity of the mixture. It looked like a bowlful of semen in there. What did she know? More than she'd let on, that's for sure.

'Ken and Miles might turn up later if they can, bring some fireworks,' Lot said, 'though I don't know if that's a good idea, rockets in all this wood.'

Lot pushed her hair back, wiped her eye with the back of her hand. Ever since Alice had first seen her, Lot had kept herself busy, like unless she was doing something she would fall over, her nails and dyed hair no bloody use to her at all.

'What was Louis like,' Alice said, 'when you first knew him?'

'Louis?' Lot straightened up, stuck a finger in the bowl. 'Why, what's the matter with him?'

'He thinks he's getting older.'

Lot scooped up the goo, licked it off, approved of the taste.

'He'll drop dead before he gets older,' she said. 'Pass the flour, there's a pet.'

Alice left her to it, went for a walk, her gut screwed tight. Why wouldn't he have told her? Shame, uncertainty, the fear that she wouldn't be able to take it? What did he think she was made of, that he would have had to hide his age? What weakness had she *ever* shown? It was impossible to work out. Down by the lake a dark-haired boy was skimming stones across the water, not much older than Chester, strong wrists, a lovely arse fit for two hands. Mad thoughts invaded her, how she might leap upon him, straddle his body, her strength and her nakedness supreme, fucking him and fucking him, holding his head underwater while he bucked and shot the rest of his life into her, returning to the Hovel a murderess, the dead boy's child swimming inside of her, unable to escape. Louis should have told her right away, leant her up against the bonnet, whispered his age into her ear, his old cock buried in deep. She'd have been overjoyed, made what she had chosen even more right, made their first rooms bolder, every single moment of her past stripped away, pretence, pillows, everything. They'd had nothing, and they'd kept it that way, room after room after room.

When she got back, the cake was standing on a trivet, icing on the top and candles stuck all the way round like miniature barber poles. 'How old are you?' she'd asked him, and he'd bounced her off into a field and robbed himself of ten years. Forty-five then, sixty now. She had to show him how it didn't matter.

She fetched the blue dress from the bottom of the chest, slipped it on. She was still brown and flat-rounded, like a pie waiting to be filled. Back in the kitchen Lot was brushing the wire out of her hair. She was dressed in crinkly black, a dancing frock. A sharp crack came from outside. Alice went to look. Louis was standing by the open boot of the Cresta, the shotgun under his arm. Chester was staring down the sights of an air rifle.

'Thought it about time he learnt about guns,' Louis said, catching sight of her. 'Air rifle first and then … ' He tapped the stock of the shotgun. 'Better than a pair of boots, eh son.'

Alice looked down. Louis might have chucked them out the window, but she'd stopped the car, fetched them back. Louis leant the shotgun against the car, adjusted the rifle against Chester's shoulder. It had been years since she had gone shooting with him.

'Select your target,' Louis was saying, 'line the bottle up, squeeze the trigger nice and slow, like …'

He looked over to her. She was still a wonder …

'I don't know about this,' said Chester.

'It's easy …' Alice sang out, 'like you had a wire inside you, from your arse upwards, and your finger was wound round the loop at the other end, pulling it all up into place, up your spine, down your arm, and … bingo. Go on, it won't bite.'

Chester took the rifle up, reluctant in his hands. He fired, missed. Alice stepped down.

'Here,' she said, 'let me.' She took the rifle.

'When did you get this, Louis?' she asked, snapping it open, slipping in the shot.

'Dartford, this morning. Forty quid. To make up for the …'

She held it up to her cheek, stood firm, eased the trigger back. Glass flew into air. She pointed the rifle to the ground, flushed with pleasure.

'What say we have a little competition,' she said, 'me and Louis double the distance, and you a ways nearer.'

'Like "Ten Green Bottles"?' Chester said. It was easier for him, thinking of it like that. Alice kissed his head, enveloped by a sudden wave of affection. He'd got them out of trouble. He had a gun. He was the first of their tribe.

'That thing that happened in that woman's house,' she said. 'It meant a lot to us, what you did.'

'To all of us,' Chester said. 'It puts us on a path.'

'Exactly,' Alice said. 'Is your counting up to this, Louis?'

They used beer cans, not bottles. Alice went first. The cans jumped into the air like they were firecrackers, one after the other, the last bouncing off a branch, down on to the roof, landing at her feet like she had won a prize. Chester took her place, missed the first two, hit the third, missed the fourth, hit the fifth and sixth and seventh all in a row. Lot had come out to see what the noise was all about, clapped hard, thrilled to see him do so well. Chester was wearing the belt she'd bought him, real cowboy leather. Whatever he'd become was down to her too. Inside, the room was all set, plates, jam sandwiches, lemonade, the cake hidden in her room.

Then it was Louis's turn. He laid his jacket on the car roof, rolled up his sleeves, cracked off the first. No show.

'Chester probably knocked the sights,' Alice said. Louis shook his head, missed the second, his vision cloudy. He couldn't understand why. His hand was shaking.

'Here, let me look.'

Alice tipped his chin up.

'There's nothing there,' she said, brushing aside the great blob of wet.

'You said it.'

'Louis.' She kissed his forehead, held it there, Louis stiff, neither of them used to such open tenderness. Chester was growing impatient. A month ago, he'd risen above them. Now he needed to be a boy again.

'Come on, Dad. Eight more to go.'

'I can't see straight,' Louis told him. 'You carry on with your mother.'

Alice and Chester spent the rest of the afternoon shooting, stayed there until the light got bad. Then Chester went to his room, sat on his bed, waiting for Angela to arrive. They'd been seeing each other a little more regular, Angela's life unravelling by the day, Chester reading scraps from his books, half a poem, bird habits, mystics and magicians. Around seven Alice and Louis started on the beer. Louis had changed into his cleanest jacket and a white collarless shirt. Eight o'clock and Lot laid a string of chipolatas in the oven.

'When she turning up then, this girl of his?'

'She had some school game or other,' Alice said. 'She's got to get back and get changed.'

Then came the knock on the door, Louis on it like he'd been waiting all afternoon. Angela stood on the step, short black skirt, white bag, silver heels and a green sweater trained in prominence. She had sunglasses in her hair and there was perfume too, perfume everywhere. She walked in like there was glass on the floor. She'd never been into the Hovel before, had pretended she wasn't going to come, until Chester had told her about the secret cake that Lot was cooking.

'Chester!' Louis called out. He rubbed his hands, awkward. He didn't like it, the intrusion he felt this girl's body had brought, hadn't expected it. What else could she see of him but an old man, wrinkles round his neck and the back of his head bald, the meagreness of his life, nearly run. His time was past!

'Your dad works in the foundry, no?' he said.

Angela adjusted the strap on her shoulder.

'That's right, Mr Priest. Nights. We don't see him much. Ah, birthday boy.'

Her eyes swung round, the brief attention Louis had been afforded, abandoned. Chester was stood in the doorway, his blue shirt tucked into his trousers, Lot's present tight around the waist, the buckle huge and shiny ridiculous. He pulled at it, wished it wasn't there.

'What happens when you take it off?' Angela said. 'Your insides fall out?' She reached into the bag, unperturbed, the centre of attention. 'Close your eyes then. Hands out.'

He obeyed, felt the drop into his palms, looked down. A spectacle case. She tapped her foot.

'Well, open it.'

He worked the stubborn catch. Glasses. He frowned, looked back up at her.

'There's nothing wrong with my eyes,' he said.

'That's why I took the lenses out, Dumbo. It's for when you're reading. Makes you look like a real clever clogs, not just the weirdo in the woods. Go on then.'

Chester slid the arms over his ears, pushed the bridge up on to his nose.

'Brill,' she said. 'A proper professor. I'm doing you a real favour. There's girls I know who specialise in getting teachers into trouble.'

Alice and Louis looked at each other. They were very nearly not there. Chester adjusted the glasses. Thanks to the frames, everything he saw looked like pictures.

'I will use them every day,' he said. 'Not a page without them.'

He placed them back in their case with reverence, like he'd seen priests and vicars handle holy things at the altar. She pressed her hand to the swell of her young heart. It was just him and her now. How different the two of them were, how supremely different, their bodies poised and wholly exuberant, soon ready to fulfil all demands. They had life-times ahead. She was smiling at him and he was caught in the current.

Angela span round, full of it.

'Where's this cake he's not supposed to know about?'

It was like a royal instruction. Lot fished the bread knife out the sideboard. Louis left the room.

'Don't see why he has to bring it out,' Lot said. 'Who cooked the bloody thing?'

She turned out the light, the curtains all drawn, the room closed up. The four of them waited. Alice wiped the back of her neck. The purpose of the dark had changed. Louis had left the room to bring a new dark back, a dark readied for Chester and Angela. Was that the end of it then, the end of their dark, the dark they had supped on all these years? Despair rose in her throat. She swallowed it down.

'What's keeping him?' she said.

'He's lighting the candles,' Lot told her.

'Perhaps he's like my dad and bonfires,' Alice said. 'Fucking hopeless.'

Then Louis came in and Chester forgot about the word she'd used. It was just Dad and the cake and the tempting flicker of flames. Louis's hand was stretched out over the base of the plate, and he held it raised up on the points of his fingers, like the cake had no means of support at all, like it was floating, moving about the room under its own propulsion.

'Watch out for the chair,' Aunty Lot said. 'Took me hours to make.'

'Listen to her, Angela,' Louis said. 'Anyone would think she lives here.'

Alice pulled at the neck of her dress. She'd seen cakes before, but this was like it was lit from inside, the way it hovered in the air and the candles in their starburst holders, light shining up to Louis, the lines on his face blazoned away. Nineteen seventy, Lovell, Swigert and Haise had been hurtling back to earth in their capsule, Chester still wedged up her, Louis preparing to drive back in the Rover, inside his. Now, it seemed like he was showing her another universe, a planet with stars and moons and a spaceship ready to carry them off. She pulled at his free hand. The cake wobbled, flames threatened.

'Whoops!' he said. 'A bit of a crosswind there.' He faltered, unsteady.

'Here, let me.'

Angela took the cake from him as if it was her own, as if she had stirred the mixture and seen it rise and smoothed the icing over, like the cake was no different from her prepared body, all of a piece on this special day. Louis took a step back. He wanted to say something that would make her notice him again, uncertain as to what it could be. Chester was still a boy ...

'There he stands,' he said, 'a halo round his head and feet like a couple of fire engines. A man lives by his boots, did you know that, Angela? If a man hasn't got a decent pair of boots, you might as well forget it.'

Angela ignored him, took a step closer.

'Go on, Chess,' she said. 'Ring the fire bell. Blow them all out.'

She proffered it tenderly, elbows tucked into her sides, the light licking up and down the swathes of green. Chester hesitated. It was not hard to gauge the tone here. It was not something he could fail at, he knew that much. So much depended on it, not his life exactly but how it was bound up, who he was going to be. A few years older and she wouldn't have come, the year before she wouldn't have been asked, but here he understood what was expected of him, his responsibilities, the demands made on his young masculinity.

She placed the cake upon the table. He took a deep breath, as deep a breath he had ever taken, held it, like he was floating, like if she gave him a little push he might bump up to the ceiling, never come down. He wanted to close his eyes, but dared not, dared not set himself loose. He could feel what it was he could be, what he wanted to be. It was all there, dancing in front of him, a destiny, circling round and round the cake, like a hidden moon. And he could do it. He knew he could. He had been made for this moment.

He blew, blew like a hurricane bending trees, blew like wind coming off the sea, blew every part of him out all over the candles, the flames bending and quivering, struggling to keep alive before falling to his great, exhausted strength, plunging the room into a darkness.

How it thrilled him. How he loved its immensity, its closeness; how it spoke to him of all the things of which he could not speak, he did not know, how it was him and yet not him, how it seemed to surround him, envelop him, and hold him close to what lay out there, set him free. He could touch the dark, smell it, hear it rolling around his head. The dark was like the books, full of people and ideas he'd never know, would never understand, but which he might glimpse fleetingly, like night creatures in the forest. He could feel its touch, feathery and light, yet with such a weight upon him that it seemed to press him down, like he was standing underwater, gaping in a blur, like he would never see anything ever again, like he was frightened and calm at the same time. And for the rest of his life, this dark, this space, this great world was his, and his alone.

The light came on. Chester blinked. Aunty Lot was by the switch, the knife clutched in her hand, like she was ready to stab a rat. The door was wide open, and Alice and Louis were gone. A laugh rippled through the trees.

'What's going on?' Angela said.

Chester stepped out.

The clearing was pale, whispers all around.

'They've finally done it,' he said. 'As much as they could take.'

WHEN HAD SHE LAST run like that, running out on expectations, smack into life? She'd laughed, amazed at the bravery of what they had done, one hand in his and her heart skipping like she was in love for the first time, like it was happening all over again. She could have run the whole night, she felt so young. Once on the road, headlights shone into their faces.

'What you got in your hand?' Louis said. She held it up, triumphant.

'I nearly tripped over it,' she said. 'It was waiting for us, Louis.'

'Give it here.' He broke it in two, stuffed the barrel down the front of his trousers, the stock under his jacket.

'You can't hitch like that,' she said.

'What are we?' he said. 'Vagrants? There'll be no hitching on this watch. Just a walk to the lock-up.'

They hurried the streets. She had a sense of what might be going on, felt the magnitude of it physical in her chest. Only once did they stop, the street empty and lamplight shining down a pool on them, like they were on a stage spotlit and all the gods listening.

'Is it terrible, what we've done?' she said. She wanted to jump into his arms, push him on to the ground, anything.

'Pretty much.'

'This won't be for ever. We just need to …' She span round. It was frightening, how good she felt. 'That girl, Chester with his eyes on her. And you! She was so …'

She was angry with him. He rubbed her arm up and down.

'Aren't you cold in just that?'

When they got there, he unhooked the keys from his belt, started pulling at the far side of the double doors.

'Come on then.'

He stepped in, switched on the light. The car was wedged in, head first, scarce room to move around. Alice checked the make. She'd never seen wipers on the rear window of an estate before.

'A Humber?' she said. 'You got a Humber stashed here?' Louis was peeling away the ignition key taped under one of the shelves at the back.

'It was going to be a birthday present.'

'You and me don't have birthdays. Birthdays are a crock of shit.'

'Fifteen years in, I thought I might break with tradition.'

She flicked the wiper against the glass, peered in.

'You bought me a Humber. Oh, Louis.'

Louis unlocked the driver's door, stood aside.

'A 1974 Sceptre Estate Mark 3. A hundred and twenty thousand on the clock, and most likely would do the same again, anywhere you want.'

He held his hand out in invitation. She slid in behind the wheel. He walked round, got in beside her. She tried the pedals, found the catch and moved the seat forward. It sat low. He handed her the keys. She rubbed her thumb across the leather fob. It had been a man's car – more than one's most like. She could feel their old, tobacco sweat.

'Where to then?' she said. 'Scammonden?'

He shook the question off.

'When the time's right. Now, who knows? We've broken all the rules. We must be …' He didn't know how to put it. She jiggled the key in.

'A Humber. And you've left the radio in.'

She turned the engine over, worked the choke out. It spluttered and stalled. She tried again, eased the choke forward. This time the engine took. She patted herself on the chest, gave it time to settle in, found reverse. The Humber stuttered out unsteady. She worked the wheel, full lock. They were facing the road now. Louis jumped out, brought down a toolbox and a long torch, slung them in the back, put the lock-up to sleep. In the Humber, Alice was drumming her fingers against the sides of the steering wheel.

'Loads of dials,' she said. Louis ran his hand over the facia.

'Oil pressure, water temperature, amp meter. Up there, petrol light, ignition, main beam indicator. To their right, the lights. Down there are your windscreen washer and wiper switch. That next to it is the overdrive, for those empty roads you're going to be driving.' He tapped one dead centre. 'Half-decent fuel gauge, two-gallon calibrations, in litres too, for if we cross the Channel, fuck the French.'

'I bet it laps up wine like the French, too. What do we do for money?'

He smoothed back his hair to hide his shaking hand. It felt to him like they were getting away with murder.

'You've a bit of driving to do. Working on the roads, you got to thinking that your future was like that, going God knows where. Those twelve-hour shifts, sometimes I got so flush ... there's not a motorway I worked on that doesn't have an emergency fund buried away. The tramps used to do the same come wintertime, bury what they had while ...'

He had to stop, her lips on his mouth, locked in the throes of what they had done.

'We're not there yet. M11 first, then we can take our pick. You should have grabbed the spade, not the gun.'

She drove level-headed, didn't know how, but she did it, got to know this beast, the big steering wheel, the throat to the engine when she ran over four and a half thousand rpm, Louis looking the other way, like he didn't care. Maybe he didn't. Things were changing that night, the roads vacant, like they'd been emptied for them special and Louis count-ing off the slip roads and bridges, to where the first stash lay. When they got there, she pulled in on the hard shoulder, kept the engine running, thinking that he'd dig up the tin and rub it, hey presto, like Aladdin, but he couldn't find it, wouldn't believe that he'd got it wrong, tearing at the earth like it was cheating him, returning empty-handed, deflated.

'Where to now?' she said, and he just pointed up the road. Where else could she go? So she drove, not at the old forty mph, but what she and the Humber wanted. The old forty mph was out the window. She didn't know why, but it was, and the Humber handled itself pretty good at fifty-five, though when she switched on the overdrive, it jumped into it like it had been pushed. Overdrive presented fresh possi-bilities, new ways of seeing, watching the road roll down like old black-and-white film credits, but fat chance of that with Louis on the edge of his seat, trying to convince her that he'd remembered it how it was. She drove on, trying not to think of it, conjured up the forest instead, what Chess would be doing in these hours, what Lot would be saying, that girl. That girl could take her place in no time, take Chester to their bed, milk him dry. She'd do it right away if she thought she could get away with it. Chester fascinated Angela, like Louis had fascinated her, still did. How could she doubt him?

And, second time round, past Stansted, the road gave up fifty pounds, and later, where they joined the A1, a nondescript turn-off and Louis scrambled up an embankment and came back with a torn trouser and a hundred and fifty in his fist. Suddenly they had the keys to their kingdom. The sun was slicing into the corners of her eyes, and she pulled over, the first diner she saw. They sat across a small, unsteady table, ate bacon and eggs and fried tomatoes, goosebumps shivering up and down Alice's arms. They'd done it. They had two hundred pounds and Louis on a promise of more to come. They ate exuberant, the damp fold of notes stuffed in the Humber's glove compartment, like it was the Humber's money as much as theirs: a woman, a man, and a car, all welded together. Plates clean, they ordered it all over again, ate like it was a bed they were on, like they couldn't get enough.

Then, without warning, they were finished. They sat exhausted, drained of emotion and running low on reason. They parked up down a farm track, fell asleep. Hours later, Louis woke her with an iron-clad erection. Pitched to and fro, it had taken her twenty minutes to subdue it, the car riding a black ocean, like an oil rig standing in a storm. There was nothing but themselves and all they had known of each other.

Afterwards, Louis sat up, gasping for breath. She thought for a moment he might not make it.

'Might be the death of me,' he said, 'that sort of carry-on.'

She turned on the ignition, checked the dials.

'We need petrol,' she said.

'We need more than petrol. We need clothes, provisions … We've no plan, no goal, only …' He pointed out the window. 'There's a woman I know. Up north, a farm.'

'No more women you know, Louis.' He accepted the truth of what she said.

By half ten they were in Huntingdon. They loaded up the Humber, a suitcase, a tent, camping equipment, a funnel, a length of tubing, a plastic container, a penknife and a spade. Then came the charity shops: shirts, jackets, trousers, blankets, towels. Louis's highlight was a blue suit, Alice's a tweed jacket, tight around the bust, and a pair of heavy brown cords. She wore them right away.

'I could go anywhere looking like this,' she said, 'Buckingham Palace even, sit on her bed, just like …' She couldn't remember his name.

'None of this is any use,' he said, stacking the bundles in the back. 'Not in the long run. We need to think it through. We've no jobs, Alice, no papers, save what's in my wallet. You need an identity, National Insurance, a number that works. Have our pictures taken too. We're only a stone's throw from Worksop. Eddie could do the lot. A new name for you. You never know, might come in handy.'

Alice looked surprised.

'Alice someone else,' he said.

'You mean like Priest?' she said. Louis sniffed the air.

'That'd work.'

Alice drank him in, his eyes back in their sockets, and his hands familiar. He was old and she loved him, more than she should. It was flaring up like a dawn, colouring all she saw, the motorway signs, the laden lorries, the convoy of army trucks and the lads leaning out of their windows, giving her the thumbs-up. She rolled down the window, blew them kisses. It was magical the road now, like a poster. They were not twenty-four hours gone, and yet the forest was as if she had never lived there, simply been marking time, like a passenger on a railway station. She tried to raise feelings for Chester, guilt, apprehension, could not. Responsibilities, what were they? She had wanted more of Louis's sons, but she had wanted them biblical, busy begetting, adding to the sum of them. Would there be sons, now? For all they knew, she could be carrying right this minute. She laughed.

'What's so funny?' Louis said. She said nothing. May, June, July, August … she was strong, but she had to get ready.

'We've got to harden ourselves up,' she said. 'I fancy a swim.'

He turned east on to the A16 to Boston. They reached Skegness, parked overlooking the long, flat beach, got out the car, undressed. Light was stretching over the sea. They stood, water curling over their toes, the wind blowing fresh offshore. Louis's underpants looked underfed. Alice's bra was sturdy white. She pulled at his elastic.

'The current'll have those off in seconds,' she said. Louis pulled them up tight.

'I can't swim,' he said. She looked incredulous. 'Splashed about, that's all we did. And the rock pools, well they were just pools.'

He nodded to her, as if she should have known. She thought it was one of the best things she had ever heard. It blotted everything out, save them. They were their only point of reference.

'You great lummox,' she said.

She put her hand under him, and he let her pick him up. It was tough on her arms, tougher on her legs, not for the weight, but for the imbalance of him. It was hard to keep level, the sand shifting and the sea swirling and the thought that if she dropped him, the sorcery of what they had done would be broken. She took her time, stepped safe until the water was up high past her waist. She looked out. She was stood on the edge of the world, steel in her spine, Louis in her arms and Armstrong and Lovell looking down.

She lowered him in, pushed his head down, stood over him and held him there as his legs came up and his hands flailed to find her. She thought of it as more than a baptism, more a kind of birth, Louis between her legs, emerging a new man, and she a strengthened woman.

She let him go, struck out on her own.

———

Eddie was his usual self, took new passport pictures for them both, wanted to see how the snake was faring. Photos taken, she sat in the car, while he faked the rest. They came out two hours later, stinking of drink.

'I hear you're off up north,' Eddie said, and handed her new papers through the window.

She chucked them in the back, waited until Louis got in, jammed her foot down.

'Where exactly north?' she said. 'Just so I know.'

'Where we started the last time, before the Brebis,' Louis said. 'Same room if we can get it.'

It rankled, all the way up the motorway, letting him put his name on her fake card, blotted out the pleasure of two more tobacco tins and the trouble-free traffic and the long-legged bellboy who talked to them like he had a plum in his mouth. She should have chosen her own name, considering all the contraband it would be carrying.

'What is it?' he said. He was sitting on a bed, wriggling his toes. It was on the same floor as the previous room, though on a corner looking south. She was at the window. 'I know, we shouldn't be doing this. I just thought ...'

'It's not that.' She turned. It was bigger than they'd had before, separate beds. Strange, but she was glad of that.

'I didn't want your name, that's what,' she said. 'I mean, fuck me, Louis, is that what I am now, a Priest?'

'And we were getting on so well,' he said. He stood up, started pushing the beds together. 'What then?' She was back at the window, staring down.

'Hotel car parks,' she said.

'That's a name?' he said. She pressed her nose against the pane, counting.

'Petrol,' she said. 'After everyone's gone to bed. Fucking perfect. Think of all the hotel car parks, all over Britain. We'll cruise from one to the other, never pay a penny.'

He lifted her up, span her round. That night they ate in a restaurant for the first time in their lives. Louis wore his suit, Alice a big jersey, the sleeves rolled up to her elbow. She didn't know what to talk about. Louis waved his fork around, stories of the hotel and motorway madness perched on the prongs. Chester and Lot and the Hovel never got a look-in, like there'd never been any interruptions, like they were never going to look back. She listened, hoping to dream up a name on her own, even searched the menu, but nothing gelled. Later, after pudding, Louis sat in the bar while she filled their water container from a row of four-door saloons tucked round the back. It took a while, the flows steady, but with no force behind them, like Louis with his flies open. He had a double brandy waiting for her. The jersey had gone, and she'd washed her hands thorough.

'They'll never even notice,' she said. She tossed the brandy back, signalled for another. 'It's great we're here. Last time, I kept thinking of the men you were running out on, leaving them all for me. Look who you've left for me now.'

And it kicked in then, the name, bloody obvious, had been on the menu all along.

'How about Lamb?' she said. 'Like Brebis only ...'

But travelling down south, she drove past the Worksop exit without so much as a turn of her head. Another name wasn't the answer. She tapped the wheel. Was this it for them, riding the motorways, nothing behind them, nothing in front? A hollowness was burrowing inside her. They didn't have the strength for it they once possessed, least-ways not Louis. Hard ground was hard ground, damp was damp. Mornings, he preferred long johns to nudity. Time was running out.

Then, Stamford, she picked a local newspaper. The Humber was on empty. They had twenty-two pounds in the glove compartment. She'd gone to the big hotel there, thinking of theft, or something else. She'd had imaginings of the shotgun, what it could bring. A woman toting a gun had a degree of dislocation to it. She quite fancied that. In the hotel courtyard, she'd lifted a slice of cake and the paper from an abandoned table, taken them out to the meadow in the centre of town, where Louis was waiting. There was a small ad in the Sits Vacant page – kitchen staff wanted for work at a café just off the A1. They'd passed it any number of times, funny-looking place, like a bijou cinema perched on the edge of the road.

Close up, it looked more like a temple than a cinema, plumped down from the other side of the globe. She'd rung up, they'd gone together. Louis wore his blue suit. She'd put on her sturdy white, a paisley blouse and a knee-length cord skirt. Tweed wouldn't have done at all. They were interviewed together, just as she'd hoped. The manager, Mr Fish, clasped his scrubbed fingers on the other side of his undernourished desk. He sized them up. They were a couple. They sat apart like couples did. There was a washing-up situation for Louis, and a more responsible post for Alice, preparing cooked and raw food. Later, she might progress to serving customers. Their shifts might not always coincide. Was there a problem with that? Alice shook her head. Punctuality was important too, he told them. Did they live nearby? They'd just arrived in the area, she informed him, nowhere fixed. Mr Fish pulled at a drawer in his desk. As a matter of fact, there was a vacancy not a mile away, a room to let, with a kitchenette, in a property of his mother's. Shared bathroom, but fully furnished. The previous occupant had absconded with another of his food operatives, hence the two vacancies. He placed her card on the table, pushed it across. You're not planning to run off with anyone, are you? he said. Very much not, said Alice, his running-off days are over, and she grabbed Louis's hand and held it up, like a trophy. We've only recently … She brushed the slope of her tamed breasts, hid her blushes. Well, Mr Fish said, pushing his chair back, sticking his arm out, under the circs, I'll try and co-ordinate your shifts as best I can. You can both start tomorrow. Brilliant, Alice said, and stood up, shaking his hand before pulling her skirt back into place. Do I get a uniform?

Later that night, suit on the bed, Louis opened the window, aimed for the holly bush below. Alice was washing her hair in the handbasin.

'Do I get a uniform?' he said. 'Did you see his face?'

She wrapped a towel round her head.

'Don't knock him, Louis. This could be our ticket. Money, time off, a roof. We'll work behind the scenes, anonymous. We'll become a team, run the place, though no one will know. It could be like a headquarters. There'll be storage rooms where we can stash things. There'll be cars and movement. We'll hear things, opportunities. We don't make any friends, we don't make any enemies. Followers are different. You fuck the dishes, I fuck the food. We keep our noses clean, and in time …'

She came up to him, ran a hand over a buttock.

'… we'll fuck everything.'

Mr Fish showed them round the first day. It was better than she thought, empty rooms up top, outhouses round the back filled with all manner of rubbish, broken chairs, pots of paint, ladders. A second car park was round the back too. Free petrol, if she judged it right. After a week, Alice felt like she'd never been anywhere else. Louis found the work a struggle. He was used to heavy machinery, his body braced against the elements, but this … how could bending over a sink so drain a man? There was no give and take with a sink, no let-up to vary the muscle, only pans and plates, plates and pans. Two sinks, two men, Louis and Owen Mutley, a 37-year-old has-beenwith a wine-stain across his face like an old-fashioned gangland acid play. Owen lived in the ground-floor flat below them, two rooms and a passageway where he kept his bicycle. He lived on his own, played tapes of great speeches, Churchill, Kennedy, acted out Shakespeare's soliloquies, never went out and dreamt of saving the world.

Alice worked down the other end, long metal tables and a row of cookers against the wall. Out front, Denise and Rachel did the waitressing. Denise was fifty-eight and had a gummy leg which she lathered every morning with goose fat. Rachel was twenty-seven and waiting to emigrate to the other side of the world. No future here, she said, warned her against going with Fish into the storeroom. Mr Fish instructed Alice in the manning of the ropes, how to pass butter over sliced bread, how many lettuce leaves made a salad. One boiled egg equalled three sandwiches. Frying pans the size of bicycle wheels hobbled on gas rings. A machine churned out chips. Pies came in a van. Most of the stuff was cooked first thing, kept warm throughout the day. Extractor fans pushed the smell of cooking fat around the kitchen. Customers washed in and out. First surge came seven a.m., lasted an hour and a half, the second at noon. Five p.m. to half-seven was often the worst. Local families came for lunch at the beginning of the week. Quarrelling Sunday, Denise called it.

A good deal of the food came in the van, not just the pies. Wednesday was their delivery day. Mr Fish would stand by the back entrance and check the list. Hard-boiled eggs came in containers the size of distemper tins, ready-peeled and covered in brine. The first time Alice opened one up, she almost fainted, the eggs gleaming brilliant white and clustered together perfect. She rolled up her sleeve, slipped her hand in down to the bottom, the eggs slithering up and down her arm like albino eels. She wanted to take the can home, have it by their bed. If this wasn't a sign …

The boy who delivered them was called Douglas. He was thin, the way she liked men, like they were starving of something. He delivered all sorts: pies, eggs, posher stuff for the restaurants. He drove flash, stood on the brakes for the gravel spat it threw. He had a passable arse and a face with a brain behind it, as though he was biding his time. He carried a book in his pocket, just like Chester. His blond hair drooped over the back of his collar. She longed to hack away at it, watch his protests fall to the floor. For the first few weeks, she said nothing, caught his eye as he caught hers. Then, one Wednesday, when Mr Fish had a heavy cold, she offered to check the order herself.

'No point in you standing there, catching your death,' she said.

'You're an angel,' Mr Fish told her, and gave her upper arm a friendly rub. He'd been specialising in rubbed-arm situations recently. She didn't object, not while she was getting her feet firmly under. She remembered them though, every single stroke.

She stood on the steps with a clipboard in hand. She'd never held a clipboard before. It was a laugh, doing something official. Douglas pulled in and jumped out.

'Where's Fish-face?' he called.

'I've poisoned him,' she said. 'Fed him one of your steak and kidneys.'

He opened the back, started stacking the trays. She let him brush past her as he carried them in.

'You taking over then?' he said.

'All's fair in love and the catering trade,' she said.

'Is that right?'

She waited until he'd finished the job and had given her the docket to sign.

'These cans of hard-boiled,' she said, pulling her pencil out of her breast pocket, licking the point. 'Do you ever lose any, or find you have one left over? I'm just saying, if ever one did come loose ...?'

He folded his arms, watched her as she signed. He took it from her, studied her name.

'It's not for selling,' she said. 'You wouldn't lose out.'

'Except my job. It's Fort Knox back at the depot. My boss is a 22-carat cunt.'

Did he say that to test her reaction? It was like ink on blotting paper. She pushed her pencil back where it belonged, straightened it up. The lapel of her blouse parted a smidgen.

'Well, let's give the 22-carat cunt a 22-carat reason,' she said, 'say, a faulty handle. The can falls to the ground, the lid bursts open ... You'd still have the can to show him, plus a few eggs at the bottom to satisfy his genuine, 22-carat ...'

She angled her head, smiling, wondering whether she should use the word again, to show him the sort of woman he was dealing with. Instead she pointed to his back pocket. 'You read a lot?'

He took time answering. He was enjoying her little speech.

'Only when I'm driving,' he said.

She went back inside. Flirtations were new to her. All her life she'd strangled them at birth. She saw merit in them now, the opportunities that could open.

One morning, first thing, Mr Fish put his hands round her hips and steered her through to the dining area. A uniform hung on the door to the toilets, pink blouse, red skirt and a white pinafore.

'A couple of hours' prep in the kitchen, then it's out here, best breast forward,' he said. 'We're rushed off our feet, now that Miss New Zealand's gone. Think you're up to it?'

She could feel him bulging behind her. She had a moment's hesitation, but then relaxed into it. If she did it right, who would recognise her, hair up, face powdered up like a mask? Japanese, that's what it would be, with the real Alice predatory underneath.

'I'll need some new make-up,' she said. He patted her bottom, a first.

'You got an hour,' he said. 'Soon as the shops open.'

She went to the nearby department store. A salesgirl sat her down, showed her how she could make herself into someone who existed only in the mirror, came back with a new phiz waiting in the wings, immobile like Good Queen Bess, with all her Alice thoughts pancaked over. She wore perfume too, first time since fifth form, wore it heavy, all the places going. Louis didn't like it at all.

'Think Dick Turpin,' she said, when he complained. 'The perfume's the cloak, the snake's the pistol. I stand and they deliver.'

And they did – salesmen, taxi drivers, the RAC patrols, night-workers coming off shift, the bloke who stopped over on his way to Ferrybridge every Friday, visiting his dad. Ali, she let them call her, addictions forming rife. The travellers told her things. It was like squeezing spots, stuff busting out all over the table. She wiped the top clean and took it all in. In the kitchen, she'd write it down in a notebook, names, number plates, who they worked for, where they lived, age, temperament, *susceptibility*. She'd show it to Louis in the evenings. One day, she told him … He didn't go out much, not after eight hours up to his elbows in greasy water. They were fit with the money, two wages and the tips she was pocketing. They worked four weeks on the trot if they could, always volunteering for extra hours, always stepping in to save Fish's streaky. That way, after Louis got rested, they could take four days off straight, climb into the Humber, sail off in the dead of night, up as far as they wanted. They liked Scarborough, seats on a promenade, wondering what they were looking for. Alice would walk out in a long T-shirt, a towel folded over her arm like she was still waiting on table, serving herself up. She'd swim quick, would pull off her shirt, thread it through her arm to swim as she wanted to, alive in the world unencumbered, nothing in between. She couldn't stay long. The cold took hold of her right away. On the beach he'd have a double shot of whisky ready. He'd hold the towel around her, while she pulled clothes over her rubbery blue, the perfume clean gone. She smelt better that way. Driving back, he'd stop over by a farm he liked the look of, sat back on a hill, buy a dozen eggs from the clapped-out fridge that stood at the bottom of the track, free-rangers, and they'd break them into each other's mouths, an offering to a potency they no longer fully possessed. Once, when the eggs were crocked, he'd walked up to the house to get some fresh ones, tried to persuade the owner she needed a decent drive laying, he told Alice. Nothing doing, crazy old bat.

Time stacked up. They weren't bothered. It was like they were waiting. Spring '84, the place started filling up with policemen, coachloads of them, stopping on their way up to fuck the miners – Yorkshire, Northumberland, Worksop even. They'd come slyly too, unmarked cars, looking for number plates and the fifth columnists scoffing inside. The coachloads were fun, oxen boys from Wiltshire and Devon, ate like horses, hated the thought of miners. Miners were no better than badgers, fit only for baiting. The demand for fry-ups doubled. Who'd want to stick it to the burrowers with nothing but a sandwich under their truncheon? They were a rowdy lot, excited and up for it. She walked among them, intoxicated by their big hands and their cooped-up smell, their thighs spread open like it was the rutting season. She imagined their balls, heavy and sweaty and full of fuck. She'd wanted sons like that.

Midweek, April, she woke for the early shift. Chester's birthday was coming up but she'd said nothing. Louis lay on his back, eyes to the ceiling, worried, like he'd hardly slept at all. She rolled over.

'Been awake long?' she said. He put his arms full out, made his hands into a circle, squinted through it.

'What do we do when we're recognised?' he said. 'When *you're* recognised. It's bound to happen one day. The A1 for Christ's sake.'

She swept his hair back. There was almost nothing left on top, just a V at the front, so he could imagine himself as he was. The back of him had changed though. She stared at it every night. He was getting older. She hadn't noticed as much in the forest. The forest had absorbed it, like it absorbed the light, but now, out in the open … he was getting older. Every day he was getting older. It was like the drip of a tap. He couldn't turn it off. It wasn't just a matter of what she wanted now. It was the things that shouldn't matter … treading the path to the car like it was a minefield, or tapping his boiled egg as though he had a bit of Etruscan pottery stuck in his egg cup. He'd started tidying up after her, putting things away. It wasn't right. She wasn't getting older at all. There was still time, time for everything. She slipped her hand down. He was still good for one in the morning, if she paced him right.

'I'll start wearing a wig,' she said. 'High heels if it helps.'

'You'd fall over,' he said, and stumbled out of bed.

She was furious all morning, everything she touched an affront. She wanted to smash something, a plate, a window, a car. A lull in serving, she hurried to the storeroom out the back, took down a tin of hard-boileds, levered open the lid. They lay motionless in a cluster. She stood, staring at them. What did they want from her? What did she want from them? She lowered her hand in slowly, squeezed them through her fist, let them pop through, her whole body crying out. She shuddered at the cold smoothness of them, wondering how many she could take. If only she never had to think again, only to feel, every part of her immersed in sensation.

She closed the lid, walked back to the café. Ken and Miles were sitting by the window, no shorts, but lumber jackets and heavy-duty trousers. She took a steadying breath, stood over them. They barely gave her a glance, their eyes fixed on the road.

'Full English, miss,' Miles said.

'No tomatoes for me,' Ken said, then pulled at Miles's arm, adding, 'And you thought we'd got away with it.'

Outside a police van was pulling up, six uniforms piling out. One of them began taking down the number plates.

Miles stared up at her, not a flicker of recognition. Once he'd danced with her by firelight. She wanted to kiss him.

'I think you might have to cancel that,' he said, 'unless you do prison deliveries.'

She thought of Louis and the view he'd seen through his fingers that morning. Louis didn't understand the power she was accruing. She'd had enough of taking orders.

'Why would that be, Miles?' she said, standing back as his name registered. 'Epping Forest?' she said. 'The mum that got away?' She flapped her pad at the window. 'They after you, then?'

He held off, trying to adjust her face to who he'd known, then relented.

'When the car reg comes through, they will be. They've been stopping everyone at the Dartford tunnel. We thought we'd beaten them, up through Blackwall, down the M11, past … you know where.'

His hands let the forest glide by. She was thankful for that. Outside, information was coming over the radio. She moved to the window, blocking their view.

'Better follow me then.'

She took them out the rear exit and around the corner to the storeroom.

'I'll lock you in,' she said. 'Pretend you're rats. Eat the biscuits.'

Back in the café, two of the uniforms were checking out the tables.

'Can I help at all?' she said. She stood poised, pert. The shorter of the two stepped forward. His blue regulation shirt was damp under the arms. He stood with his feet apart.

'You in charge here?' he said. He was staring at her mouth, his eyes taking it all in. She wanted to smack his head with one of the frying pans, both hands.

'As good as,' she said. 'You?' He pointed to the Hillman outside.

'The owner of that heap,' he said. 'Where's he got to?'

'That still here? I didn't notice.' She looked around. 'There were two them, sat at the front, met up with a couple of others, men not girls, really pleased to see each other, embracing and that. I thought they might be … you know … disgusting, that sort of carry-on in public.' He was amused.

'It's not against the law now, more's the pity. But what they're doing is. Striking, illegal pickets. They'll have left in the other car, know we're after them, see. I don't suppose you noticed what their friends were driving, the colour, make?'

Alice tugged at her collar, looked to the car park to see if she could remember.

'I don't know anything about cars,' she confessed. 'Just get taken for a ride in them.' He nodded, man of the world.

'No problem. We'll push it round the back, make it a bit of a challenge to drive. After that …' He rubbed his hands. 'How about six fry-ups?'

'If I wasn't such a rotten cook,' she said, 'I'd do it myself.'

They pushed the car round the back, gave it a good kicking. They came in red-faced, slivers of glass stuck to their boots. She served them the Full English, doubled up on the eggs.

'My treat,' she told them, setting down his plate last. 'You show them what's what.'

She breathed in deep, held them there. His eyes shone with pleasure. They ravished the plates. When they were done she stood over him, wiped their table clean. Eating had driven him to sweat. He smelt of weedkiller. He was the sort of man, she thought, who liked to fuck holding you down. She rubbed the table hard. He tilted his chair back to get a better view.

'Might call in on the way back,' he said, 'after we've branded a few cattle.' He smacked a fist into a hand. She straightened up, ready to push her luck, stick it in his face.

'I'm not going anywhere … uh …'

'Brian,' he said. 'Plain Brian, bold as a lion.'

She stood at the window, watched them swagger out the door, hitch up their pants before they climbed back in their van. Five minutes later she had the key back in the lock. Ken was nibbling on a cream cracker. She led them blinking into the light. Outside, their car sagged on deflated wheels. The headlights had been kicked in.

'They don't like you much, do they?' she said.

'It's them or us, Alice,' Miles said, 'Scotland Yard and Number 10, working for a miner-free Britain.'

She took them back inside, sat them down at the coppers' table. They ate fastidious, on the lookout. They were working men, turned state-sponsored outlaws who used napkins. Alice grew agitated at their calm. She wanted to smash something.

'I'm off in an hour,' she said. 'I'll take you. They're not worried about my number plate. Where you making for?'

Ken laid his knife down.

'A big solidarity showing outside Worksop. Why, do you know it?'

Small wonder she could hardly keep still. She could call in at Eddie's, if she fancied it. Too late to change her name, but she could get a surprise tattoo done, an egg on each arse cheek, eggs or something.

'Stay here,' she said, and went back through. Louis was bent over his sink. She put her hands over his eyes.

'You must be clairvoyant,' she said. 'Guess who I've seen?' He shook her hold free.

'Don't tell me. Not one of mine.'

'Lot's. The miners with the legs.'

Louis turned, patted his hands on his apron.

'The geisha look didn't quite work then.'

'They hadn't a clue, but never mind that. The police were here, fucked their Hillman. Me and the Humber, we're taking them to Worksop.'

Louis rubbed his forehead, like he'd had a headache lodged inside there for years.

'After what we just said this morning?' Anger wobbled on his lip.

'They won't tell anybody, especially if I take them. It'll be a trade-off.' Louis was thinking back to what she'd told him.

'They hadn't a clue who you were, you say? So why ...?'

'It just came out. I couldn't help it. There they were, sitting there ...'

Louis turned back to his sink.

'Why don't you come too?' she said. 'We can call in on Eddie, get a pair of tattoos. I can square it.' Let Fish get his hands on her hips, is what she meant.

Louis stacked a set of plates on to the dryer. It had taken him an age, but he was locked into the rhythm of it now. There was a rhythm to everything, laying roads, drinking whisky, washing dishes ... Alice though, he was losing the rhythm of Alice.

'Three grown men in a car?' he said. 'If you want to get there unnoticed, another woman would be better.'

237

They set off without him half an hour later. Alice had changed into a dress with buttons down the front. Miles had a pork-pie hat and a short-sleeved shirt Louis had bought at Oxfam. Ken was stuck in the back in a striped golfing jacket someone had left in the café. The traffic was light, but there was an obstacle she had to negotiate before she could drive free. It took her half an hour before she found space for it, changed lanes unnecessarily, to disguise the tension in her voice.

'Been there recently,' she said, 'the forest?' A snort of disapproval came from the back.

'We've more important things to do than skipping through bluebells,' Ken said. Miles showed more understanding.

'Six months we were last there,' he said. 'Did I say six months? More than that. Another time.'

Alice swallowed. She could agree with that. How peculiarly time could change, not simply in distance and speed, but all the matter that had once lain inside it … what was forest time now, and what would be the point of asking of it, of knowing and not knowing, and knowing that you did not know? Her hands clutched at the wheel, trying to keep her voice steady.

'How were they all?' she said.

There it was, Chester in the plural.

'Much the same,' Miles said. 'Same old forest, same old Pot Hole. Lot's lost weight.' Ken couldn't resist it.

'A lot, you might say,' he said.

Was that it? Alice closed her eyes, letting the Humber drift.

'Your lad's another story,' Miles said. 'Shot up … strong as an ox, hair down to …' He tapped his shoulder. Awakened, she brought the car back.

'You mean like a hippy?' she said, disheartened. All the hippies she had known had been full of shit.

'Like he's older than he is,' Miles said, 'like he knows something.'

'Biblical,' said Ken. 'He should be in robes.'

She ate at the words. She could picture him, waiting for her by the side of the road, hair blown and in some sort of cloak. It filled her with a surge of exhilaration. He was strong and powerful, shoulders like a bull. She'd been right. Soon he would carry women to his wood-hewn bed. He would beget sons, daughters too. He would ask for her one day. She'd be ready then. The windscreen began to blur.

'He had a girl with him,' Miles said. 'Not a hippy type at all. Much more with it, make-up and stuff ... a skirt no bigger than a chamois leather.'

Angela then. Would she be the first? She hoped not, imagining all the complications that would arise, social services, family, courts. She checked herself. That was her mother talking. What was it to do with her? She brushed her eyes with the back of her hand, discouraged any more conversation.

She dropped them on a side street. They could hear the churn half a mile away.

'We did it then,' Miles said.

Alice shrugged her shoulders, waited until Ken and Miles had changed back into their picket clothes. She wasn't interested in them at all.

'How will you get back?' she said.

'Police van probably. Not to worry. We're with friends now.'

She waited until they were out of sight, climbed out, headed towards the noise. At the back of the narrow streets, a swathe of common ground. She'd come out on a slight embankment halfway along, near a line of horses, helmets to the back of them. Fifty yards away, in a sea of dishevelment, stood the miners. The horses started trotting, broke into a run, the uniforms behind banging their shields. Mud flew up as the horses thundered into the enemy. A roar went up. It rang out like a battlefield in olden times, with men and beasts and the swing of armour, as though this patch of land was determinate, and the field itself would become memorable, like Bosworth, like Naseby, a future won or lost. She'd never heard anything like it. Charging towards her, heads down like in a stampede, came the mining men, a great whoomph of them as they rushed upon the shields, the fight joined, the battle begun. She saw it in flashes, not knowing where to look, men jeering, goading, bodies grappling madly, faces looming up, vanishing as quick. The waves surged back and forward unrelenting, no quarter given, blows and cudgels and men falling to the ground. Right in front of her, brazen like a ballet dancer, a lad pirouetted to escape capture, his shirt ripped open, and his chest sweet Adonis. She found herself screaming. She wanted to be caught up in it, it didn't matter which side. She was seeing it in action, tribes at war with each other, fighting to the death. They'd been right all along, her and Louis. England was a nation that existed in a continuous state of warfare, always had been, Scots and Picts, Romans and Britons, Roundheads and Cavaliers, rich and poor, north and south, native and immigrant, us and them. Always us and them. No wonder she and Louis had tried to spawn another. A sudden surge enveloped her, feet off the ground, hair yanked stone-age, her body buffeted this way and that, hands on her legs and chest and the rump of her arse. No one knew who she was, no one cared. A fist landed on her shoulder, a glove

grabbed her waist. She lashed out, laughing. Men were looking right through her, she wanted them all. A pair of police
hands span her round, eyes widening in surprise. Brian? She
lost her footing, fell back down the embankment.

She got to her feet, swollen with excitement. If anyone
touched her again, she thought she would come right away.
The fighting had rolled off across the grass. Some way in front,
quite alone, with his back to her, stood a bare-headed policeman, helmet dangling in his hands. She picked up a broken
length of fencing, giddy at the thought. She walked up and
smashed it over his head, threw the pole down as he fell, ran
helter-skelter to where the Humber was parked.

Her foot shook all the way out of town. She had smashed
the wood against the copper's head, could have smashed
another and another, it had felt so good. Her body was
popping like crazy. And then, the Humber doing near sixty,
and one of the signs that got Louis in a lather – two geriatrics
hobbling across the road with walking sticks as bent as they
were – looming up a couple of hundred yards away, it came
upon her, what needed to be done. It wasn't a matter of driving by any more. She slammed on the brakes, mounted the
verge alongside, killed the ignition. There was a sigh to the
engine. She'd been working the Humber hard. She was a little
out of breath herself.

She climbed out, opened the back. Their toolchest was well
stocked now, a hacksaw and a set of blades just one essential.
She turned her back to the oncoming traffic, settled down on
her knees. There was no hesitation. No one took any notice.
Her arm moved like a piston. It wasn't much of a post. Ten
minutes and she pushed it clean away. She shoved it in the
back, threw a blanket over it, swung back on the road. She felt

better, but needed a drink. That was one of the great things about the A1. They had pubs up and down like it was 1955.

The place stank of drink and disinfectant. She had a double whisky. She sat at a little table next to the pinball machine. She wished Louis were here, seen the battle, seen her take the sign down. God she had a need.

The café was waiting for her in darkness. She unlocked the back door, fetched a pail of eggs from the kitchen, walked across the dining area to where Miles had been sitting. The tables were set for the morning. There was order to the room and it incited her. She placed the pail by her side, slid forward, her feet on the windowsill. The buttons were mostly loose. She let the dress fall away either side. How wonderful it felt, alone and all the power laid before her. She took an egg, rolled it down the tilt of her, until it dropped off the edge and fell to the floor. She took another, then another. They were smooth and cold and they dropped off the edge. She was dropping off the edge. Headlights swept across the window, her brain all of a tumble and the world in perpetual motion, thoughts of home looming up like a sudden fog. She felt it all so close, what she wanted, but out of reach. The eggs were looking up at her, perfect and white and full of longing. That mining lad had been beautiful, like sculpture beautiful. Where was he now? In jail? On the run? Having his wounds tended to? She let her hand fall into place, home at last. There was no stopping her now. She worked slow, deliberate, staring at the motorway beyond. It was moving and so was she, rippling through the void like in a spaceship. This was better than men. This was of her own choosing and her own time and in her own circumstances. She was queen, like Elizabeth of old was queen, like Boadicea, in command of her body and an untamed empire at her feet. This was all she needed, the power of her own glory. Let Armstrong and Lovell look down upon her in their sealed suits, let the Spaniard walk her naked in his cloak, let the boy beautiful bare his chest, let Douglas spin his tyres, and let the lad she had danced with once, when the snake was fresh, let him quicken himself over her now, as she quickened herself over him sometimes, young and confident and ready. When she called out, and she did call out, it was not in want, but an acknowledgement of the sacrifice she had made for her destiny.

She had things to do.

Louis was in bed.

'Trouble on the road?' he said. 'I thought you'd be back earlier.'

'We sailed up,' she said. 'And coming back ...'

'You got that tattoo done.'

She walked over, planted the pork-pie hat on his head.

'Eddie didn't get a look-in,' she said. 'There was a boy, a young man really, bare-chested, right in front of me, beautiful ... irresistible ... a warrior ... oh, what I saw in him.'

She knelt across him, pulled the hat down over his ears. He was waiting, not a flicker of doubt.

'We make a tribe right here, Louis,' she said. 'Not kids, grown men, women. We make a tribe, gather them to us.'

'What are you on about?' he said.

'It's us and them, Louis, all the way, like in the Bible, like I saw in Worksop. We need more, a bigger tribe. I thought about it all the way back. We might have sons, but we can't count on it. So I got you a present.'

She climbed off the bed, opened the door, brought out the road sign, stood beside it, like a school warden.

'Comes from that spot you hated. What do you think?' He scratched his head.

'What happened to the old woman?'

'I stopped off at the café, painted her out. Old sign, new warning.'

'I don't follow.'

She hauled it up, stuck it between the headrest and the wall.

'I'd have thought it was obvious,' she said. It says, DANGER. OLD MAN FUCKING.'

She got back into bed. Laughing was all she was good for, and once, in between the long, irresistible runs, it struck her that she had hardly thought about Chester and what his day might have been like, at all.

He'd woken early, and the first thing he thought of was the coming of the cake. He hadn't eaten cake for over a year, and now Angela was bringing a new one. What sort, he'd no idea, she wouldn't say. It didn't matter, because like the last one, no one was going to eat it. Last year, they had sat staring at his cake for over two hours, before Aunty Lot had drawn it towards her and said, 'Well, I don't see why we shouldn't enjoy it.'

'You can if you want,' he'd said. 'I'm not touching it.'

Aunty Lot's face crumpled. Angela had jumped to her feet.

'Why don't we bury it?' she'd said. 'Next to that badger of yours.'

Chester had carried the spade, Angela had carried the plate, Aunty Lot the torch. Chester dug the hole. Aunty Lot shone the beam in. Angela placed the cake down, licked the filling from her fingers as she stood up.

'Light it,' she'd told him. 'So she can see it with her little badger eyes.'

The cake had flickered and danced, the hole ragged with roots, like arteries disappearing back into a torn body. All around them, immersed in the earth, were living creatures, burrowing this way and that, dead creatures too, his badger and his rabbit. The badger was lying dead in the ground but part of Badger had always been alive too. Was Rabbit alive or dead? Was the thought of Rabbit enough to keep him alive? Alice and Louis had been alive in the forest, but they were gone, alive somewhere else. Did that mean they were sort of dead now? I am too young, he had said to himself, to have these thoughts.

'This is fucking stupid,' Angela had said. 'I bet badgers don't even like chocolate. Next birthday, we'll have a different sort, and we'll bury it like it was …' she searched for the right words, found them, proud that she could do it '… like it was an offering to keep us tight. I'll make it, if you like.'

Lot had laughed. Angela had turned on her.

'You think I can't make a cake? Just you wait.'

And after a while, life had got better for Chester. Lot sent him to school, told them she was his stepmother. Who knew any different? After a term of hostility, it began to work out. He started on books that everyone else carried, wrote his name on the inside, trod common ground. He could throw a ball better than most, catch it too. He had an eye. Once, the class rowdy, and the temporary fill-in's felt-tip marker thrown in malice, he caught it, his hand shooting up like *Saturday Night Fever*, walked the missile back and not a word spoken. It got around. There became a space about him, like an intent, a waiting.

Lot ran the Hovel consistent. In the morning, a proper breakfast; in the evening, always his tea waiting at one end of the table, and, on school days, a clearing at the other for his homework and his reading. He wore his glasses when he read his books. He thought he read things better with them on, like there were patterns. Lot would leave him be, sit in her squat room, listen to the radio. Later she'd come back in, chat about this and that, ask him about his lessons. They adopted a black cat with no tail, whose tongue stuck out where her teeth were missing, called her Missy because of it. The three of them watched the new television Lot bought, the cat moving from Lot's lap to Chester's as the mood took her. What they watched didn't matter. It was the triangle of three living beings that counted, separate and all connected.

First time the news of Alice and Louis got out, the boys had dropped in en masse. Hogan built a brick path, Pete and Gil tarred the roof, the Brummies stripped down the generator. None of them knew where the two of them had gone. Alice and Louis had run out on them too. They left puzzled, defeated. Later came the sightings. They'd ride in, bringing untrustworthy news sheepish, uncertain that they should be bringing it in at all. They'd been seen in Bristol, living out the back of an old post-office van; Alice had been spotted driving a Sprint outside Birmingham; Pete knew someone who'd seen Louis boarding a freighter out of Liverpool. But as time went on, the reports dwindled, and as the news fell away so did the boys' visits. They were travelling men. Leaving was what they did.

That's how it had been for Chester and Aunty Lot, growing into the new life of the Hovel, amending their ways, the trees budding in the spring, shedding their leaves in the autumn, life of the birds and the animals moving alongside them from one month to the next; always a fire in the cold, and, when the weather grew warmer, the door left open like a catch on the memory, there for the pushing. Memories of them came like that, but otherwise the Hovel kept them occupied; always logs to chop, always chickens to feed, always the allotment to husband, the car to maintain, work to be done, and the two of them to do it. It was difficult for them to see any further, or to find any reason for looking. What in the world *was* the world outside? Chester went to school, watched television, overheard conversations, but it washed over him in a blur, it was so alien. It seemed to him that beyond the forest lay a land of turmoil, mindful only of its tempests, riots in far-off cities, football fans crushed in stadiums, concrete blocks levered down on to motorways, prisoners choosing death in their prison cells, the country beset by bombs, bystanders blown apart, shovelled up like slurry from the pavement. And this was the country where Alice and Louis had fallen into. One day he might have to rescue them. He had done it before. His books had shown him that there was a shape to such things that not even a God could undo. Meanwhile there was the forest. He made no enemies, took no friends. There was only the oddity of Angela. She would find him out, sit by his side, poking sticks, listening to the fumble of his words.

And today she would come again, bearing another cake. He got to his feet, looked to the mural. One day, he thought it possible that he would wake to find the Brebis and the donkey gone, like the mother who had painted them. Transience lay in all their bones. They were still there, though the donkey had a look of impatience about him. It was all in his imagination, he knew that, but the reassurance didn't fool him for a moment. The donkey was telling him something. Things were on the move.

Aunty Lot snored in her room. Sleep was lying heavy on her these days. He dressed, took the air rifle from under the bed. Lot was going to make a pie, needed a mess of rabbit and pigeon to fill it with. He tucked the gun under his arm, walked some distance into the forest's quiet quarter. He was soft and accurate with the gun, but he didn't trust it, like he didn't trust boots or cars. He selected one bird, then another, shot both, then wished he hadn't. The Greenland dogs popped into his head, like they were panting right behind them. They had pulled the expedition, men and sledges, for thousands of miles, but when it was over, Scott had tied them to rocks and shot them one by one with a rife just like the one in his hand. What worth could their journey hold, with such thanks given? He thought of the child in Germany again, cooing at the edge of the pit, didn't understand how it could be so … Suddenly he could bear it no longer. He swung the rifle by the barrel, smashed the stock against the trunk of a tree until it fell to the ground in pieces. Back at the Hovel he laid the birds on the table, wrapped the broken rifle in a sack. Later he'd sink it in the lake.

He couldn't leave it there, plunged back in, avoiding any other company. The forest was his company. They listened to him all the time, the carry of his thoughts, caught in the branches. He wore shoes now, stout, indestructible. The day after they'd run, he'd chucked his boots away. What was the difference between boots and shoes? Not sturdiness or longevity. The attitude of a man, he'd supposed, and his purpose. He thought he would wear shoes for the rest of his life.

He kept to the paths until late afternoon, until the forest petered out, and all that stood before him was a road. He didn't know whether to trust or fear roads. Alice and Louis had left him for a road, yet there were not many boys his age who had travelled on them as exhaustively as him, or knew how they stitched themselves together. Up ahead, to his left, lay a roundabout, and a spoke of choices. On the opposite side of the road, a man was sat on a street sign, one shoe off and his sock rolled down over the instep, while he sandpapered his heel. He was dressed in a jaded pinstripe, tatty round the ankles. He had an overcoat folded at his feet and a blade of grass stuck in his mouth. Chester coughed, unable to peel the dazzling thought away. The donkey.

'First rule of the road,' the man said, without stopping. 'Always keep your feet in good order if you can. Bunions, cracked heels, ingrowing toenails, they are the curse of the traveller. I used to have a pumice stone, but ...' He looked up, his hair flopping over his eyes, dark like the eyebrows, and a prominent, aquiline nose. 'Are you from these parts or passing through like myself?'

The admission sent a surge through Chester's frame. When John Wesley preached, he had a way of stroking his hair, looking upon his flock with such intensity that their hearts had beaten like sledgehammers. There was nothing to this man but bone and cloth. Chester pointed back over his shoulder. The man eased the sock back over his foot.

'An Epping man. Excellent,' he said. Chester cleared his throat. He was such an eager boy.

'You walk the roads?' he said. He could see the course of a life running through the threads of his suit, chased by the mob, pelted with stones, his dignity frayed at the edges. The man finished lacing his shoe.

'It would be a good line for a song, don't you think?'

He sprang up, began pacing up and down, arms flung back, his coat flying up like wings.

'I walk the road, I walk the road, Bishop's Stortford, Cambridge, Huntingdon, kneading the backbone of England.' He paused. 'Kneading as in bread, you understand, not as in want. Why, dear boy, is it something I have said?'

He crossed over. Chester felt a growing excitement within him. Crowds came to hear Wesley, and when he was finished, they'd stood transfixed, unwilling to move away. A simple field had taken on the mantle of a church, a new reverence flooding over England.

'It's what my dad calls the A1,' he said, 'the backbone of ...'

His voice trailed away. It struck him then, this man might have come across Alice and Louis. It unsettled him, to have found this man on such a day. The man sensed his agitation.

'He is an engineer, your father?' the man asked.

'I suppose. He builds motorways, all over.'

The man gathered himself, took a step forward.

'And did he tell you,' he said, light streaming from his eyes, 'that motorways are the first roads ever built on which the human body is banned on pain of arrest. Never happened before, our great highways denied to the humble foot. Or hoof. What do you think that says about your father's precious roads?'

Chester didn't know what to say. The man's voice softened.

'Well, your father is not solely to blame, though his motorways have made my life exceedingly difficult. It used to be said that, if you were travelling, you could tell where you were just by looking at the architecture, the stone: limestone in the Cotswolds, flint in the southern chalklands, gritstone on the Pennines. On a motorway all you see is concrete … You wouldn't have a sandwich on you, by any chance? Jam would suffice.'

Chester took him back to the Hovel, sat him on the porch. Aunty Lot was taking an afternoon nap. He put the kettle on, cut him a sandwich, filled it with home-made. Back outside, the visitor had closed his eyes, his legs stuck out straight like broom handles. Chester set the plate down on the railing.

'I made you some tea,' he said.

The man opened an eye, took the offered mug, turned it in his hand.

'Chester?' he said.

'My name,' Chester said. 'Aunty did it.'

'Chester,' the man repeated. 'This is turning out to be quite a day.' He set the mug down.

'There's beer if you'd rather,' Chester said.

'Thank you, I would not. Alcohol can knock you off course, and I have been knocked off enough courses to last me a lifetime. One moment you're on your path to destiny, the next …'

He took the plate, balanced it on his knee. He moved the sandwich around, so that the rounded crust lay at the top. He separated the two halves, raised the lower to his mouth, bit in tentative, took his time with it. Chester could see that bread was important to him, like a prayer made physical.

'This is fairy-tale jam,' he said, his mouth full. 'Your mother's hand, no doubt?'

'My aunt's.'

'Your aunt again. I had an aunt, you know. Never made a pot of jam in her life. Have you lived in the forest long?'

'Since I was little,' Chester said. The man was looking round to the Pot Hole, the axle bricked up and the steps leading down.

'That's our little café,' Chester said. 'Quite famous in these parts.'

The man nodded, scratched at his scalp.

'Someone must have told me about it,' he said. 'There's a telegraph, you know, for men like me. People believe we leave marks, but too much is made of that. Anyone can make a mark. Word of mouth, that's the thing.'

Chester nodded, unsure of the man's ground.

'Are you headed somewhere?' he said. The man waved the crust in the air.

'Never ask a man of the road of what he has done, nor where he might be going. The past and the future do not exist for us. We only have the grammar of our feet, and they recognise only the present. As a matter of fact, I'm heading north, following the Great North as best I can. It's been straightened out over the years, which is a shame. You know what Blake said?' Chester shook his head. "Improvement makes straight roads; but crooked roads without improvement are roads of genius."'

He popped the crust in his mouth. The edge stuck out, wriggled like a frog's leg as he sucked it in. Chester fumbled with his words.

'I just thought you might be on your way to a meeting … in a church, or a field … a congregation waiting for you to speak.'

There, he'd said it. He would join him if the man asked him, become a disciple, see him clothed and fed, carry his books. The man roared with laughter.

'Out of the mouths of babes. No one is waiting for me any more, dear Chester. Even if they were, what would I tell them? That we are born to disappoint who we wanted to be? That there's no answer? That none of it will matter? Your father is working on the motorways still?'

Chester gaped. History lodged in his throat.

'Not at the moment,' he said. 'Mum and Dad are off right now.'

The man nodded, pleased at the news.

'There *is* a field,' he said, 'right in the middle of the town I'm heading for. Stamford. Many a preacher has preached there, I'll be bound, but never me. I go there for second-hand …' He pulled at his jacket. 'You need top quality for this sort of caper.' He swallowed the last of his tea, dabbed his mouth. 'Would you think me awfully rude if I took the briefest of naps? Ten minutes, then I will be out of your hair.'

Chester hesitated. How good it would be if the man took up residence for a while. Aunty Lot could fatten him up, and when he got back from school, he'd be sitting where he sat now. He'd talk and Chester would listen.

'You can stay if you want,' he said. 'We're having a feast tonight. And there'll be cake. It's a special sort of day.'

He corrected himself. 'Not that we'll eat the cake. It's not there for that.'

The man took the news in his stride.

'What will you do with your cake, if not eat it?'

What could he say? A year had gone by. Aunty Lot's cake might be still alight, flames still flickering, lighting up an underground road to where his mum and dad lived.

'We make an offering,' he said. 'To the forest, everything in the forest, and everything that leaves the forest.'

The man considered this with dignity.

'I believe in offerings. My only advice would be, don't put too much faith in it. Is it a particular type of cake you won't be eating?'

'A birthday cake.'

'I am honoured that you should invite me, but it's best to walk these light nights when you can. I need to reach places. First Spellbrook, then over to Standon, then if it allows me, the A10 and ...'

'Ermine Street ...' Chester caught the man's surprise. 'Dad taught me,' he said. 'He loves his maps.' The man spoke with care.

'As you love him.'

Chester turned his head away. How could he tell him what he felt? He did not know himself.

'If you stayed,' he said, 'I thought, when you were ready, I might come with you. I have a feeling ...' The man snapped upright.

'There is no romance to this life, Chester,' he said. 'I don't do it out of choice. I do it because I can no longer do anything else. I work part of the year, groundsman, hotel porter, farms sometimes, but then I wake up and it's as if I have to ...' He pointed to the trees. 'Things happen to people – they knock you over and you walk unbalanced for the rest of your life.' He grabbed hold of Chester's arm. 'I had a gift. I thought, one day I would be, how does it go, a contender ... ah, what does it matter. I better go.'

He shooed him away. Chester went back into the main room, cut him more sandwiches, wrapped them in a paper bag. On the porch, the man was fastening the buttons of his overcoat. Chester walked him to the edge of the clearing. Angela was coming soon. He didn't want to leave and he didn't want to stay.

'Will you come here again?' he said. The man gave him a gesture of uncertainty.

'Who knows?' He caught Chester's dejection, laid his hand on his shoulder, spoke softly. 'You are disappointed, had hoped for something more. Remember, men like me, we had visions once, as vivid as yours are now. We ran as children, came of age, boiled spaghetti, held women. It was all there. We took a wrong turn, that's all, or a wrong turn took us. Only one thing sustains us now.' He let his hand drop. 'It's time I walked upon it, discerned its mysteries again.'

Chester watched him fade into the forest. He heard the shuffle of breath behind him. Aunty Lot was stood in the doorway.

'Who was that?' she said. She'd been sleeping, woken to the sound of muffled voices.

'A traveller of some sort. I made him a sandwich. I asked him to stay the night if he wanted. You wouldn't have minded, would you?' Aunty Lot shook her head.

'It's ours now, Chess,' she said. 'Been like that a whole year.' She stared out. She wanted to chase after him, then brought herself back.

'This girl of yours. When's she coming?'

'No idea. You know what she's like.' Aunty Lot turned back inside.

'I wish,' she said.

———

Angela came two hours later, carrying a biscuit tin. Inside lay the cake. She lifted it out, placed it on the table.

'Coffee,' she said. 'Walnuts too.'

They stood staring. There were lumps round its side, like it had toothache.

'I ran out of candles,' she said. 'The dog ate them.' Lot smiled.

'Makes a change from homework. Least he didn't eat the cake.'

'And neither are we, remember?'

'We remember,' Chester said. 'I'll get the spade.'

'Before you do …'

She fixed him, effervescent. She wore a black beret, a black halter-neck top dotted with silver stars. Four inches of bare midriff followed, then a short red skirt, with black leggings underneath, finished off with pink socks and black boots. What was she doing here, Lot thought, worlds away from her boy?

'Last night I had a dream about this cake,' Angela said. 'It was floating on water, lit up like a liner, and I was on the shore, waving it goodbye.'

Lot stirred. She didn't like this conversation.

'You can't put a cake on water,' she said.

'You sure about that?' Angela put her hands on her hips. 'What do you think, prof?'

Chester went outside. The two women stood either end of the table.

'You're still at school too, I suppose,' Aunty Lot said. Angela laughed.

'That's put me in my place.' She pulled out a cigarette packet. 'Sometimes I am, sometimes I'm not. I don't mean bunking off. I can be there and not be there at all, like it's nothing to do with me, that life's the other side of the window. Other times, it's like I wish they'd look at me different, not see just this.' She tapped the unfiltered end against the packet. 'I mean why can't I sit in class looking like this, talking like this? What's so bloody wrong with swearing or having a fag if I want to.'

She struck a defiant match.

'The trouble is …' Lot began.

'I'm not worth the effort. They take one look at me and say, why bother? We know what's going to happen to her. You know it too, don't pretend you don't. Everyone knows it. *I* know it, unless I join a girl group or something. He's knows it too, don't you gorgeous?'

Chester had returned, carrying short planks of wood.

'Know what?' he said.

'How you're going to teach my cake to swim.' Chester clapped the planks together.

'These and the tyre,' he said. 'Piece of walnut.'

'Comedy act now, are you? Come on, let's do it. You coming?'

Aunty Lot shook her head.

'I'll keep something warm for when you get back,' she said.

Angela carried the cake, Chester the planks of wood. Down by the lake he pulled the tyre out of its hiding place, rolled it to the bank, lowered it in.

'You light it,' she said. 'Just be careful of my hair.'

He struck the match, shielded the flame with his other hand. His knuckles grazed against her breast as he moved the flame across.

'Mum gave me a sunlamp for my birthday,' she said. 'Couple of weeks I'll have the best all-over for miles.'

He knelt on the bank, drew the tyre in. She came up close, bent forward as best she could. He took the cake from her, balanced it on the plank, pushed the tyre away. The cake sailed out, out from under the shadow of the trees, into the open, turning as it moved. Across the water, the trees stood like silenced cranes, the pond a gathering and an unknown sea lying out of sight.

'There was a tramp back at the Hovel earlier,' he said. 'He could have done with a slice of that.'

'You could have given him the whole bloody thing if you'd wanted. I wouldn't have minded. Looks great though, doesn't it, like it's going on an adventure, can't wait.'

She gave her shoulders a shimmy, like she was on a dance floor. It was dark but he could see such living creatures moving.

'He had to go,' he said, turning his gaze back to the flickering lights. 'He walks at night when the weather's good.'

'Like you.'

'He walks on roads. I just …'

'… lurk in the forest, yes I know.' She came up behind him. The water lay still, the tyre merged into the black and the cake glided along like it had risen from the dead, like it was the other cake, reborn, like it was telling him something. Did she really make it? She might have had a hand in it, but … She put her arms over his shoulders, spoke into his neck.

'You could float me out if you like,' she said, 'set me alight.'

He said nothing. Astride the tyre, that's where he wanted to be. Odysseus had travelled the world, finding the way home to his wife and his home. He had no wife, but he had a mother and father. This is what Alice and Louis had done, sailed away. He could see it illuminated now, the wonder of what they had done, the great misshapen beauty of the unknown. Perhaps his home lay unknown too. He might never find it, but that might be what he'd have to do. His wanderings could take years, like it had in ancient times. He would come across hardships and duplicity, kindnesses too, with hearths of warmth and sustenance. He wondered where they were, Alice and Louis, could imagine them gathered by firelight, see their faces reflected, strong and untroubled.

It was an age before he could move. Angela had gone, the candles burnt out, the cake vanished to the night. He walked home. All was quiet. The man's plate lay on the porch floor, but the mug with his name on it was nowhere to be seen. The man had stuffed it into his overcoat pocket while he'd been making him extra sandwiches. He hadn't taken him, but he had taken his name.

It was the best thing that had happened to him all day.

SEVEN

T HE TRIP WITH KEN and Miles loosened Alice up, and
she worked with a new energy. Spawn a tribe? Louis had
been doing it all his life, corralling men, fixing their eyeline,
sending them out in all weathers. Alice was as single-minded
as he was. Signs were what they were looking for, signals. The
first had been standing next to Louis every café day. Louis
had grown to like Owen. He was drawn to quiet men, men
who had the capacity of holding back, and in Owen he saw
a man gripped by fury and disappointment. During the day,
Owen worked gob shut, hands busy. At night they could
hear his voice rolling up through the floorboards, could stop
them in their carnal tracks. It became as the call of an exotic
bird, something they listened out for, held their breath to, felt
aglow for the hearing of it.

One madhouse Friday, last orders taken and dirty plates
stacking like a three-lane pile-up, Louis and Owen were
working flat out, Alice and Denise bringing them grief by the
armload. Every time they walked across, Owen would turn
his face away, like he didn't want them to see it. It was getting
on Louis's nerves. They all knew what Owen's face had writ
on it. Next time he did it, Louis spluttered into life.

'For God's sake, man,' he said. 'You don't have to ...' He mimicked the action. 'No one gives a hoot.'

Owen shoved his hands in the dirty water, rubbed his face like he was using sandpaper.

'Won't come off, see?' He snatched up his apron, wiped himself dry, went back to his dishes. Louis felt the ground slipping beneath him.

'Look, I didn't mean ...' Owen stopped him with a wave of his hand.

'It's a dirty word now, handicap, but that's what this has been. Who knows what I could have done, if it wasn't for ...'

Louis took a plate.

'Not this then?' he said. He span it in the air, let it crash to the floor. Owen unlocked the semblance of a laugh.

'What about you?' he said. 'Born to juggle, were you?'

Louis looked over his shoulder. He could see Alice through the porthole, attending on table, tapping a pencil against her chin. A year and a half ago, he'd never have believed it.

'We like it here,' he said. Owen heard the tremor in his voice, caught it right away.

'Yes,' he said. 'Why is that? You don't seem the ...' He stopped short, his hands quiet in the water, held them there, summoning up the courage. 'It's as if you're hiding from something, tucked away here and the hours you spend in that room. I often wonder what you get up to in there.'

He swirled the water, almost angry. He could have been talking about himself.

'We know what you do,' Louis said. '"Friends, Romans, countrymen ..." Alice joins in sometimes.' He caught Owen's look. 'She had a proper teaching,' he explained. 'Knows heaps of stuff.'

'I wanted to stand for Parliament,' Owen said. 'But thanks to this …'

He stared down into the turmoil of the sink, as though all his life was spinning round, glimpses of sunken hopes surfacing through the murk.

'Labour?' Louis said. 'Conservative?'

Owen dropped in the next load, winced at the splashback.

'The Poet's Party,' he said, 'preparing for the Land of Dreams.'

That night, Alice and Louis lay in bed, unable to sleep. It was a sign, Alice insisted, what Owen had told him. The Poet's Party? She raised her head, conscious suddenly.

'He's crying,' she said. 'Listen.'

She sat up, leant over, switched on the lamp, her face like light itself. The trip had done something to her. Louis wasn't sure what. She'd gone up to Worksop Alice and come back Alice, but it was like she'd come back Alice Mark II, like her Alice lines had been sharpened up, sliced through the air with less resistance.

'What if we strap him to a rocket,' she said, 'land him on the moon?'

They were at his door the next morning, knocked hard, wouldn't let go. The door opened with a lurch. He was wearing a dressing gown and slippers and his hair was parted pencil perfect. He looked like groomed insanity.

'We've brought you breakfast,' Louis announced and walked through to the kitchen. It was clean, cream painted cupboards, waist-height, a stove, a sink and a little table off-centre, looking out to the yard. Only one chair. A blue mug stood upon it.

'I don't eat breakfast,' Owen said.

'It's more food for thought, than actual grub,' Louis said. 'Alice has something to show you.'

Alice faced the window, pulled her shirt apart, did the same with her breasts, turned back, hands still in place.

'This is my mark,' she said, looking down at herself. 'I had it made special, this prick Louis knows leering at me while he did it. You have yours already there.'

Owen did not speak. Not a single person had ever been in his flat before. He looked for means of escape, found none. Louis was leaning against the door. Morning sunlight sloped across Alice's arms like prison bars. He found himself wondering how she would drink tea with her hands positioned as they were. Did he have enough cups? The snake rose from her belly like a flame. There was something to grasp here. Denise had to grease her gummy leg every day to ease the torment that could erupt. His caused no discomfort at all, yet the pain it had brought had been ...

'You had a choice,' he said, his eyes not leaving her. He wanted her to remove her hands, to see the snake in situ, terrified that she might do just that.

'I'd rather have been born with it,' she said. 'I'd have learnt a lot quicker then.' She stepped closer. 'Touch it, if you like.' Owen hesitated. 'Go on. It's not me, but it is, just like your face is not you, but is.' She rolled her hands round. 'Don't worry. I got these under control.'

Louis looked out the window. Owen rubbed his mouth with the back of his hand, took a breath, like he was going to jump off a diving board. He placed a fingertip on the head, ran the back of his first finger lightly down the length. The snake gave a belly twitch. He pulled back, startled.

'You've woken him up,' she said, laughing, finding it hard to keep her hands in place. 'Do it again. He likes being stroked.'

He did it again. It was the first time he had ever touched a woman and they both knew it. She wanted to open her arms, press his head against her, so he might discover the stilled wonder of it. When he was a child, Chester had a head almost as big as Owen's. In the cars they'd had, she'd place his head against her and bask in the sensation, the engine humming and the wheels rolling and the steady sense of uncertainty floating out in front of them. Back in the Hovel, she'd sat with him the same, but with fear upon her, the birds trilling and the trees nodding and her feet nailed to the floor. She twisted away, covered the snake back up.

'My turn,' she said.

She placed her hand full upon the stain, moved her fingers over the surface. There was a roughness to it, a texture. He had never imagined such intimacy.

'This Poet's Party Louis was telling me about,' she said.

'It was a joke.'

'It was a dream,' she said, 'a want for something different. A way of seeing, if you like …'

'I'm fed up with the current view on offer, that's for sure.'

He tried to laugh but it wouldn't come. Her finger followed the edges of the shape.

'They look at you and …'

'Pretend it isn't there,' he said.

'We'll see about that,' she said. 'Put your hat on. It's all arranged. Louis called you in sick.'

She drove him to the department store, took the girl aside. The conversation flitted back and forth. The girl slapped her hand to her mouth, like she was watching a horror film. They sat him down in the tilting chair.

'You can't hide it,' he said. 'I've tried.'

'We're not going to hide it,' Alice said. 'We're going to make a feature of it, a piece of art.'

The girl held Owen's face, tipped him to the light. She followed round the edge with lip liner – the uneven coast underneath his left eye, across the bridge of his nose, down the right-hand cheekbone, across the lips, over the chin and up the other side. Owen held himself like he was at the dentist's, hands gripping hard the seat. Alice was reminded of the maps she'd drawn at junior school. When the girl had finished, Alice levered the chair back upright, considered.

'Not bold enough,' she said. 'It needs to be thicker, like a picture frame.'

The work done, Alice walked him to the mirror, stood beside him. Owen put his hands to his lips.

'A window on me,' he said.

'Like a chieftain,' Alice said, 'a man of consequence.' She turned to the girl. 'What do you think?'

'I like to boast,' she said. 'And that's the best thing I ever done.'

She stepped in between them, held out her hand. She was slender, dyed blonde hair cut short, deliberate in the dark of the roots. She was blusher perfect, but with a glitter in her eyes.

'The name's Frankie,' she said, 'and this evening I will be wearing spangled tights and drinking brandy in the Calypso Club. Cost you a fortune to keep me happy, if they let you in, that is.'

Alice lent him Louis's suit. He walked in to a gasp, like he'd boarded ship without a cutlass. He bought her five brandies and later sat her in his room and recited slabs of *Henry V* at her. She made him put on her tights and do it all over again, like he was wearing armour. She had never seen anything like it. He was a man of consequence with his codpiece in her net.

Fish fired him next morning, the moment he saw him, grabbed hold of his apron strings, started pulling him towards the door. Alice turned the gas low, walked across.

'Don't be hasty, Mr Fish,' she said. 'I've got something for you.'

She led him to the storeroom, closed the door.

'What is it?' he said.

She opened a tin of peeled eggs, held them crotch-level at an angle, so the gunk didn't run out.

'This is the nearest you'll ever get,' she said. 'Do it in there. All you've got. It'll feel fantastic, a completely new way of seeing things.'

Light came into his eyes. He did it in there, all he had. It felt fantastic. He left the storeroom with a completely new way of seeing things. Owen kept his job. The café was Alice's now, hers and Louis's. With Fish out the way, Alice and Louis took over the empty room above the restaurant, filled it with sofas and armchairs, ranged them round the window. After work, they'd troop up the stairs round the back, crack open the whisky and watch the traffic flow, like they were at the cinema, the lights out and images moving back and forth across the screen.

'You see,' Louis told Owen, 'roads are part of your imagination, if only they'd leave them alone. The only trouble with roads are the signs. Everywhere you go ...'

'Come on, Louis, you need signs.'

'You need sign*posts*. Maybe. The rest ...'

They'd fall silent, bewitched. If the moon came big, Alice would stand up by the window, put her hands to glass. One day, she and Chester would walk on that.

———

Miles came back to collect the Hillman, brought his wife Biddy with him. The mine was being closed, like the government were always going to do. End of a life. No going back.

'It was a war and we lost,' he said. 'Never thought I'd say that, but ...'

'We can't stand the sight of it,' Biddy put in. 'Out of the window ... it's like we're looking at our own guillotine.'

Alice was sat with them at the same table Ken and Miles had chosen on their way to the picket lines; Biddy carried an air of generosity worn thin, would have filled the room with it once, big and capable and light on her feet. Owen was waiting Sunday-buttered-toast on the three of them. He did a spot of serving now, when there were kids around. They got the make-up right away.

'How did it go,' Alice asked, 'the pickets?'

'Bloody war zone, no quarter given,' Miles said. 'If we'd had swords ...'

'You get hurt?'

'They claim we did a copper in a bad way, but we reckon it was one of their horses. Didn't you hear about it?'

She shook her head, conjuring up indifference.

'Never listen. It's all fucking lies.'

Had she really done that? It was hard to believe, but at night, alone in the car park, she could still feel the surge in her arm, the sheer swing of it! It had been like a blow against all her wasted years, the times that had kept her from being who she wanted to be. He'd been standing there and she'd knocked the stuffing out of him, one blow! She wanted to question Miles further, dared not.

'What now then?' she said. Ken looked to Biddy, like they'd made an agreement, what to say, how to say it.

'Ken's staying put, hoping to sign on for the Channel Tunnel,' he said. 'Me, I'm never going underground again.'

'Not unless Mr Fawkes invites him,' Biddy added. She took a piece of toast, bit it in half. She was a woman who liked her food.

'There's that,' Miles agreed. 'A bit of treason would fit me like a glove.'

Alice pressed her knees together. She'd heard from one of their regulars, there was work going in the market garden, tucked ten miles away behind high Victorian walls. Things were falling into place.

'How about the great outdoors?' Alice said. 'Not for every-one, but …'

It wasn't for Miles. Biddy went instead, was offered the job within the hour. She came back and threw her arms round Alice, plastered her with kisses. Alice had never felt anything like it, straightforward gratitude. It held her fast, feelings of affection trapped in her lungs, then she struggled free.

That autumn, Frankie took over from Denise. Denise's leg had finally given out. Alice kept her on, doing the books. Biddy and Miles found a flat above a butcher's in the village down the road. Alice and Louis moved into the café, upstairs, into the adjoining set of rooms, the other end from the entrance. The place had been a pub once, and they took over where the landlord used to live: a cramped kitchenette, a clapped-out water heater above the bath, and a room with slit windows at the back, big enough for their bed. There was a smaller room leading off it, like a sitting room. They didn't know what to make of it. What were they to do there, watch TV, listen to the radio? They took the hinges off. Every morning Alice would place the OPEN sign outside and marvel at what she saw, what they were holding in their grasp, this sprawl of a building sat dirty white on a bed of tarmac like cabins on a freighter, and they with the run of it. She and Louis didn't own a square inch, but it was theirs, and she, like a captain, handing out recompense and reward. It made her giddy just to think about it.

The café started making decent money. Alice and Frankie were good together, rude and lively. They dumped the uniforms, burnt them out the back. Fish wasn't bothered. He watched through his window, waiting for his next visit to the storeroom. Frankie started wearing antique dresses and impractical lace gloves. Alice reverted to denim overalls and boots, loose cutlery jangling in her big pocket like she was a garage hand. Weekends, Owen would stand on a chair and give the customers a taste of what he could do – 'The boy stood on the burning deck', 'Come into the garden, Maud', ''Twas brillig' – that sort of thing. Frankie got him a top hat for the occasion. There was a shop she went to in Stamford, a couple of gays flogging upmarket second-hands. She'd started painting Owen's fingernails as well as his face, each nail the same colour, but in a different shade, like there was a tune in his fingers and a world to play it on. Denise kept the café up to date with the official stuff: accounts, VAT. Alice made sure the place was run tight. No point in letting the light in. When the law came calling, Fish was there to show them what's what. Uniforms ate there like everyone else and, like everyone else, only saw what they wanted to see. The café had its quirks, but it did what it was supposed to do: steady service, steady food. It was in the big room above where Alice was hoping that all hell would break loose.

One Wednesday she took Mr Fish to the storeroom, gave the tin a shake.

'New instructions,' she said. 'From now on, you can give all our wages to Denise. We're pooling them together in one big lump.'

'One big lump,' he said, and reached for her hips.

'And five per cent more all round,' she said. 'The money you're getting. Easy now.'

'Five per cent,' he said. 'Oh God.'

Douglas drove in as they were coming out. Fish scuttled back inside. Douglas jumped down, pushed his shirtsleeves up his arms. There was vigour to it, and the hairs on his arms shone in the sunlight, like they'd been freshly mowed.

'What's up with Fish?' Douglas said. He threw open the van doors, began pulling cartons towards him. He'd loaded himself up, as many as he could. He was showing off, in good shape, but older than he let on. Alice found herself lining him up.

'Let's not talk about him,' she said. 'Let's talk about you.'
He poked his face round the stack, eyes like they were waiting
to spring a trap.

'Are you asking me out?' he said. She imagined his dreams,
how threadbare they might have become.

'Don't be foolish,' she said. 'It's just …' She nodded to the
hum of the hidden traffic. One day she would tell him about
Fish and the eggs. One day she would find him a mate. One
day … 'We're thinking of alternatives, me and Louis and …'

She pointed to the door and the stairs leading upstairs.

'Come up one night, find out. Bring the van.'

He came at the weekend, brought the van. He'd put on a
tie, hair oil too, like he was on a date. Louis had his feet up.
Owen was standing with his back to the window, rehearsing
'Once upon a midnight dreary'. Alice was showing Frankie
how to swing the shotgun at a moving target. Biddy had a
notebook on her knee, trying to put into words what had
happened during the strike, Miles next to her, no help at all.

Alice brought out the whisky, sat Douglas down in front
of a plate of hard-boiled eggs. There were always hard-boiled
eggs going in the big room. She made them special, fresh eggs
from the market, boiled them up in the kitchenette, no danger
of them getting mixed up with the café's. She introduced him,
one by one: Biddy, Owen, Miles, Frankie. Louis, he knew.
He shook hands with him, his gaze darting one to the other,
always back to Frankie and her head of blue.

'This some sort of club?' he said.

'More like a training ground,' Alice said. She nodded to the
outside. 'Fucking with that lot,' she said. 'Carrying the battle.
Isn't that right, Louis?'

Louis walked over, broke the gun in half, tucked it under his arm.

'Let's go hunting,' he said.

Months later Alice would look back on that night as the time she had thought the cement had been mixed, watered and set, when they started chopping down road signs in earnest. Later, there'd be a reckoning as to how it were done best, but that night there'd been no inkling of what lay ahead, the Humber, the Hillman and the Ford Transit driving aimless, all scooped together, no idea whatever, even when they piled out and stood, nervous in the headlights, as Louis fell to his knees and sawed the first one through.

'Is this some sort of dare?' Douglas said. Louis spoke through his exertions.

'You're driving a car,' he said. 'There's a bend up ahead. Once upon a time you took it upon yourself to understand the bend, to drive with it.' He sat back on his haunches, tapped the pole with the arm of the saw. 'What does this bastard do? It takes away your responsibility. You don't have to stay awake any more. We're being lulled into sleep, everything we do. We need to wake everyone up.'

He went back to it, energy redoubled, urgency in the air. The pole groaned as it toppled to the ground. Louis rose to his feet, wiped his hands down, breath coming short. Alice looked away.

'There's another one up ahead, warning drivers about a bridge not ten foot away from it,' Louis said. 'Any takers?'

Frankie drew her lover close, lay her lips on his bare neck. It had got her going, watching the steady working of the blade, couldn't help but think of it.

'Me and this one,' she said, and they all drove to it, stood in a cluster while Owen did his stuff. Took him fifteen minutes.

'There she blows,' Frankie said.

Six months in, it was working like Alice had always dreamt of, the seven of them getting thicker and tighter, like they didn't have to explain anything, just be and do and look out the window on the rest of the fuck-up. They began to live a kind of shorthand, like they knew the rules and the aims and who they were within them. They had a language. They had a voice. Their bodies began to move in the same way. They'd plucked forbidden fruit, fed on their sweetness. There were dreams in their mouths, riots. Obedience was for the birds. What good had it done them? They would burst free from it. The café was showing them the way, Alice and Louis and the big room above. They'd had enough of compliance.

The signs grew into quite a collection: LOW FLYING AIRCRAFT, WILD ANIMALS, FALLING ROCKS, all propped up amidst a platoon of speed limits, double bends and round-abouts. They lifted a RIVERBANK with the image of the car plunging headlong into water, in broad daylight, couldn't resist it, Frankie distracting attention with a spot of tank-top hitch-hiking twenty yards down the road. Skill was making them choosy; time, place and what they singled out, it all had to matter. Then came the month there were only two road signs left they hadn't taken the chop to, NO VEHICLE CARRYING EXPLOSIVES, which Louis had never seen, and HIDDEN DIP, famed for its fabulous markings.

'It's like a rare bird,' Louis told them one night, the café shuttered up and whisky unscrewed on the tables. 'A great big Exclamation Mark coming out of nowhere, and only a clue as to what it might be warning you of, written below, as if the road was a book. There's one eighty-odd mile away, if only I can remember the road right, if anyone fancies chancing it.'

Did anyone fancy chancing it? A restlessness was starting to lie amongst them, like their limbs weren't being stretched, like they were free in a cage. They needed more. Alice felt it herself regular, like waiting for a touch in the morning, flesh aching on the bone.

'Enough of tinkering,' she said. 'What we need …' she paused, gathering breath, 'what we need is to take out a whole stretch, ten miles, twenty, take out *everything*, like it was a communiqué … There's one spot I saw last month, back road into Lincoln, first a forty mph sign, then a quarter of a mile on a fifty, then back to forty, forty, fifty, forty, fifty, bends, double bends, tractor warnings, all rammed up your arse like you couldn't shit for the asking. Must be twenty signs either side. Let's take them all down, bring the road back to life.'

Frankie had thirst in her eyes.

'Bring them here?' she said.

'We could take some of our own,' Douglas said, 'mix them up all wrong, like the world has lost its reason.'

'The world has lost its reason,' Louis said. 'Let's not lose ours. Let's keep it simple, see how we get on. Later …'

Keep it simple! As if taking out ten miles of road signs was going to be simple! They drove the night, only two cars, Dougie behind the wheel of the van, Alice leading the way in the Humber. They wore overalls. Each of them had a pair now for work like this, kept in the room without a door, overalls and boots and thick rubber gloves. They'd stripped in the big room and zipped themselves up, certainty locked in tight. They were of a piece, mission-minded, ready to stick it.

Louis rode with Alice. Neither spoke. Minutes in, he took her hand, laid it on the length of it.

'Do you think all the others are like this in the van?' he said.

'Wouldn't surprise me,' she said. 'It's like warfare now.'

She took her hand away, pleased at the thought, what it meant for the future. Louis was too.

'What'll we do after this?' he said. Alice put her foot down, threw her hands in the air.

'Something else,' she said.

It wasn't ten miles of road they took out, but it was over three and the rain coming down before they'd started and only the headlights for guidance. Nothing on their heads, but fresh blades in the saws and half-bottles of Paddy for the chill. It was as Alice said, an innocent road, hedges, fields, houses, natural in its line and curvature, besieged by jobsworth stupidity. All it ever needed was to be left alone. They worked methodical, both sides at the same time, two teams of three and one in the Humber, flashing in case intrusion was offered up. But they could sense things like that, timing, opportunity, speed. They were pack-minded, breathed in and out animal. Three miles straight, sixteen signs chopped on either side, the van slung down on suspension it didn't possess. They hadn't counted on the gathering weight, nor the room they took, dragging them over the grass, loading them up, the poles glistening wet, and their own bodies glowing too, like it was all one, the rain and the dark and the way they were moving amongst the mute, hadn't counted on the weight, and hadn't counted on the excitement of it, as the van groaned and the signs lay orgiastic and their bodies touching in the to and fro, wanting to ring victorious. When Alice came back with FARMYARD MACHINERY, Frankie was tonguing Miles, and they were laughing, their faces busting with joy. Barriers were coming down, Alice could hear them crashing about her.

Once packed up, Owen stood by the Humber, ready for the ride back. Alice pulled him away.

'You lot get back to the café,' she said. 'Louis and me are going to bag the HIDDEN DIP. Monte Carlo or bust tonight.'

So Alice and Louis drove the forty miles, with only Louis's memory their guide. The rest drove back safe and stayed up expectant, preparing for their return. It was a mark of cohesion, the belief they had, showed without showing. Dawn hours, Louis flashed victory headlights as he turned in. They stepped out to a guard of honour, all the signs that night leaning in like an arch, Miles and Biddy holding flaming torches, Douglas blowing trumpets through a traffic cone. Alice marched up the stairs, carrying the sign like it was a Roman eagle. Owen and Frankie stood at the top, bare-chested both, thick black rings painted round the tips of Frankie's breasts to match Owen's markings, the brushwork shiny and savage, almost cruel. Owen spread his arms and chanted his home-made *Hiawatha*.

'*Homeward then they sailed exulting,*
Homeward through the black-pitch highway,
Homeward through the bastard coppers,
With the trophies of the daring,
With a shout and song of triumph.
Above the caff stood Miles and Biddy,

Above the caff stood Doug and Frankie,
And the wary sink man, Owen,
Waiting for their heroes' coming,
Listening to their song of triumph.
And the people of their parish
Welcomed them with songs and dances,
Made a joyous feast, and shouted ...'

They broke into cheering. Alice lifted the sign high.

'Parish?' she said. 'Is that what we are?' She felt pagan, reckless, encumbered by the walls and windows. She wanted to drink, fuck, wreak havoc. Fish pumped himself silly in her hands and look what had come of that.

'Like a settlement!' said Frankie. She came forward and kissed her. Her breasts were like spears. It could happen now, Alice thought, all of them fused together if she played it right. She banged the pole on the ground, like breaking down a door.

'It's the weekend,' she announced. 'We'll close the café up, get the right clobber, fuck off out of it. Scarborough. We'll ride donkeys, paddle in the sand, do whatever we want.'

They took all the cash they could find. Frankie rode in the Humber with Alice. Miles sat in the passenger seat, while Louis piloted the Hillman. Owen and Biddy were up front on the Transit bench, next to Douglas. It was deliberate on Alice's part, the seating. She waited until the journey had settled in.

'We need babies, Frankie,' she said, 'if this tribe is going to mean anything.' Frankie looked uncertain.

'You mean kidnapping?'

'I mean the regular way.'

She glanced up, Louis visible in the rear-view mirror. It had been brilliant, the ride back, passing the whisky back and forth and his hand loose upon on her. But there'd been so many times …

'You tore into everyone back there,' Alice told her. 'You looked so … so ready, you know, holding nothing back, all painted and fertile. You could try for it as soon as we get there. Drag him into your room, fuck every last drop out of him.'

She felt a power in saying it. She wanted to touch her, feel the potency.

'Jumping the gun a bit,' Frankie said. 'Everything's Thames Barrier down there. And even if I wanted to, we're not married. I'm having a white wedding, no shotgun and no bulge.'

Alice twisted, shocked in her seat. Frankie stretched her legs, admiring their length.

'Why not?' she said. 'It's what you do, make something of it. Just because we're shacked up now …' She relented. 'Maybe not a church. But some sort of ceremony, some sort of special.'

'We'd make it special,' Alice said. 'Fuck me, we'd make it special. Our own church, our own ceremony, our own way of doing. You and Owen and all your babies.'

'All of them!' Frankie blew her nose. 'Shouldn't you be setting an example, if you're so keen?'

Alice made a show of letting a Volvo 245 swing out in front of her. She had been keen. One time, the whole of her being had been given over to nothing else. She was still keen. But Louis?

'His is not Gold Top any more,' she said. 'More like semi-skimmed.'

They laughed.

Scarborough was wearing its Sunday best. They took over the top floor of a guest house round the back of the railway station. The weekend was nearly over, plenty of rooms going spare.

The rooms were airless, seaside hot. The smell of diesel drifted in through the dormer windows. Cries floated up, shrill, far away, drowned by the hiss of engine brakes and carriage doors slamming, the gears of the town fully engaged. They felt excited, a little dangerous, like they were in enemy territory. Frankie sat on Owen's cock while she touched up his stain. The mattress was thin. The bed creaked. She'd never thought of babies before.

Twenty minutes later they were all lined up outside the guest house, the women long-dressed colourful, the men in uniform dark, like they were going to the races. There was a pub nearby, old-style: frosted glass, straight glasses, no food. Time to get stuck in.

They drank steady. Unlike in the big room, they kept quiet, conscious of strangers' ears, said what they needed to say in looks and gestures, single sentences clipped short like a soldier's haircut. It was the first time they had been out together in public, and they felt the alienation stronger for it. They kept to a tempo, glass by glass, no one falling behind, no one hurrying the pace, drank close and physical, like it was a scent they were laying down, glandular and swollen, like it was a sign of ownership. Hours later, they blinked their way out into the sun. Possibilities of enjoyment swam in front of them. The beach was waiting. Alice took Douglas's arm, led them down. Louis brought up the rear, bottles clinking his pockets. Behind Alice, Biddy and Frankie held hands like it was second nature, Miles and Owen following content in a blur.

They stood by the promenade railings. Alice thought Louis looked unbeatable in his hat, the clear pick of the bunch. Times like this, he didn't look old at all. They should have had a run at it before they came out, but when they heard the springs going the other side of the wall, all they'd done was smile at each other, like they were embarrassed. It didn't seem possible, that they'd be stopped short by such a thing, but there it was, lying between them.

Down below, a line of donkeys stood roped together on the sands, eating out of feed bags. Contentment wasn't in it.

'Fancy a spin?' Louis said. He walked down. Their owner was sat by a small table, breaking buns in half.

'I remember you,' the man said. 'You ran off with Pearl. She's gone now, keeled over, no warning. Typical.'

Louis patted his pocket.

'And I'd brought her some refreshment.'

The man smiled.

'That one there, with the green halter, that's her sister, Poppy. She really hit the bottle when Pearl went.'

Louis placed the beer on the table. The donkeys lifted their heads in unison, stares from another world.

'What is it about donkeys?' Louis said. The man tipped his hat.

'If we knew that ...'

Louis nodded, stuck his hands back in his pockets, thumbs out over the top.

'We'd like to hire the whole troupe for the rest of the afternoon,' he said and took out his wallet.

'What about the kiddies?' the man said. Louis started counting.

'We're all children at heart,' he said, and beckoned the others down. 'There's seven of us, but the eighth can carry our bags. I'll take the drinker.'

They rode three abreast, three women, three men, Louis at the back again, with their porter. Halfway down the beach, Alice dropped back, rode alongside.

'We must do something about Douglas,' she said. 'I mean look at him, always alone. He needs to get interested in women.' She called out. 'Hey, Douglas. How about a swim?' She slid off. 'Come on, all of us!'

In the end, only Douglas and Alice did the sea justice. They set out together. It was thrilling, swimming alongside him, the steady breath, the pliant roll of his body, the shared stamina. She wasn't young, but she felt it rippling through her, as if she could be. They swam long and hard, with no thought of resting until they both knew the time had come and they could turn and look back at the dwindled shore. They were on their own, the laws of land irrelevant and the water vast beneath them. The sea was different here, a solid mass, living without thought. She felt deep and emboldened. They could be carried away and she almost wanted it.

'When I'm out like this,' she said, water lapping at her words, 'I make a point of …' She pulled the straps down, drew her knees up, threaded the swimsuit over her arm. 'Do you mind?'

Douglas somersaulted and disappeared. She trod the water, hoping she hadn't made a mistake. Then he was bursting through, trunks triumphant.

'Adam and Eve,' he shouted, 'as nature intended.'

Alice felt like hugging him. There was nothing else but the sea and their blubbery cold.

'That's what we should be, all the time,' she said. 'Godless fucks.'

She turned towards the open sea. On the surface they were nothing but head and shoulders, eyes and mouths, a slight flurry of hands, while underneath … icebergs of intent. To swim like this, to live in the elements, for them and through them and not knowing of anything, water running down your back, grass against your body, gnawing at food, watching strangers through slit eyes … A pack, that's what she wanted to belong to, like wolves or porpoises, running together, win or lose. Swimming out with Dougie alone wasn't the right way to go about it. Two wasn't a tribe. Two was an invitation. She didn't want him, not for a moment. It was only the possibility of reproduction that Douglas offered, his relative youth, the probable consistency of his semen, his stamina. For a tribe to work, the men would have to be treated like cars, miles on the clock, no different from the women in that respect.

She blew her nose into her hands, struggled her costume back on.

'We should start back,' she said.

On land, they dripped up the beach. The others were dried and dressed and ready to leave.

'Thought you weren't bothering to come back,' Louis said, 'you were that far out.'

'Dougie was looking for a mermaid,' said Alice.

'Never found one,' Douglas added. 'The story of my life.'

They walked the donkeys back, Dougie with his and their baggage carrier. Halfway and Frankie tugged at her reins. A man in skimpy white trunks lay stretched out in front, handsome on the sand.

'Valentino,' she said. 'What the fuck?'

The man sat up, dark locks greased and swept back. He wore mirrors. He rose, agile in his feet, his stomach brown and flat, his teeth very white.

'Val works in the shop we get Owen's gear from,' Frankie explained. 'Didn't expect to see you here.' Valentino pointed back to the promenade.

'My father is in a care home a few streets away. I visit every month, and when the sun is out ...' He ran a thumb round the band of his costume. There was a lot inside. He was film-star Italian, Alice thought, proud of it.

'You are on holiday?' he said.

'Just for the day,' she told him.

Valentino ticked them off with his index finger.

'Eight donkeys but only seven of you,' he announced. 'You have buried one?'

'She's our spare,' Frankie said. 'In case one gets a puncture.'

Valentino smiled, gathered up his towel and bag.

'I will walk with her,' he said. 'You can introduce me to your friends.'

They left him by an ice-cream stand. He bought them all cornets, said his goodbyes. They stood in a huddle.

'I'm ready for a nap,' Louis said, the meaning quite clear.

They agreed to meet up at seven. There was a room at the back of the pub where they could be private. Closing time, they'd go for a knockout curry.

Back in the guest house, the room stank of baked mothballs. Alice opened the window, closed the curtains. The salt water had stiffened on her skin. She stepped into the shower, stuck in the corner of the room like a telephone box. It had a glass door, every bit of her like on display, all chrome and lights. The soap lay untouched and strongly scented. There was a young man once, leant up against a glass door, his head beautiful in a bandage, and she wished him there, so she might see him again and he might see her. She saw his parted hair and his young lips responding to her. Had that happened, her so willing, and the miracle of him in his suit and tie? It seemed so far away, as though her breast had belonged to someone else. So fertile then, so brimming. And this afternoon, in the water …

She eased back the door, stepped out, unwashed. In the mirror, the snake's head was part-hidden by the growing spread of her. She couldn't get her mind off it. Seven of them and all useless. In the Bible, people begat like billy-o. Louis was sat on the edge of the bed, trying to get his boots off.

'I talked to Frankie this morning,' she said. 'She doesn't want babies, not yet. Biddy is past it. That leaves me.'

Louis tugged at a bootlace.

'We're doing the best we can, Alice.'

She spoke with her back to him.

'Don't take this wrong, but what if I asked Dougie to go with me every now and again, to see if it made any difference?'

She looked round. Louis was holding a boot in mid-air.

'Just for a few months,' she said. She paused, waiting for him to chuck it somewhere, her, the window. There was a picture of old Scarborough on the wall, thought he might choose that. 'It would be for all of us, you understand?'

Louis set the boot down, began tugging at the other lace, his words unbearably light.

'Douglas? Why not ask one of your customers. I'm sure …'

'I'm serious, Louis. It's not about him as such. It's about us, the tribe.'

He eased the boot off, laid it next to its partner, adjusted them parallel perfect. The two of them, no one else fitted that way, was that what he was showing her? He spoke as careful as his action.

'You already have a son, or have you forgotten?'

She faced him full on, towel clenched in her hand. He was looking at her direct, no escape. She was angry that he should say it. She hadn't forgotten.

'We had to leave,' she said. 'You know that.'

He straightened up. His hat lay on the pillow. He took it up, turned it in his lap, studying the headband. He spoke low, head bent, like the words were enough, no space for anything else. He was right. They filled the room.

'Could we not go back, fetch him?' he said. Agitation stirred in her. She wanted to draw back the curtains, let the light in, show him expanse, the distant blue, where freedom lay.

'To wash dishes?' she said. 'He doesn't belong with us, not yet.'

Was she right about that? They had carved something out at the café. She wasn't sure what.

'Don't you think about him at all?' he said.

Her hand went limp.

'I know he's all right, if that's what you mean.'

Was that what she meant? She had no idea. Everything she'd done had been because of him, ever since the seed was planted. She tried to search for clues on Louis's face, what their son meant to him. If only children could be like birds, or foxes, if only they could drop them in a field, and they'd be grown in a year or so ...

Louis stood up. She liked him in a suit, like he didn't give a shit and his bare feet poking out.

'When do you want this to start?' he said. 'Tonight?'

'Don't be silly, Louis.' Louis span his hat in his hands.

'I'm not being silly,' he said. 'I'm being practical.'

She pressed the towel close. He span his hat again. They held their ground, separate beings, breathing the same air in the same room, a whirlwind of thoughts spinning up from the floor, phrases, images, memories, seen from different angles, caught at different speeds. Their history was unsteady now and they groped for balance.

'It's not desire I'm talking about,' she said. 'You could be in the room next door, if you want, to make sure ...' she moved closer '... that's all it was.'

What should she do? Drop the towel, wrap her arms around him? How could she explain, what she wanted, the release from the order of things? Another man would be an indication of how it should be. It would be like a sign to others. She reached out for his hand, touched the back of it.

'We'd still make love, Louis,' she said. 'As many times as you wanted.'

Louis pointed across the room.

'And here you are, washing yourself by the basin, without another thought. Years ago, you wouldn't have done that, not on your own, no chance.'

He sat back down. His hands gripped the mattress, as though he had nothing more to give.

'I'm wearing thin, Alice, I know that. I'm tired in the mornings and tired in the evenings. When we drove back that other night, and I switched off the headlights, I couldn't do it like I used to. It wasn't second nature to me any more. But you are. You're second nature to me, every blemish on your skin, every word from your mouth, every stretch of my being that you ask of me.'

'Louis.'

He pulled her towards him, drew the towel aside, kissed her belly.

'Go on,' he said. 'He's just a room away. Knock on his door right now. See if he'd be willing. Set a date. Like a trial run.'

He looked up, his smile floating over her skin.

'Go on!'

She slipped the dress on, left him sitting there, closed the door behind her. Dougie's door was directly opposite. All her life she'd been crossing thresholds. That's what life demanded, to move from one uncertainty to another. Here, behind this door, lay another resetting of the compass. She knocked, loud, excited. They were being bold again. Together, she and Louis could do anything. The shotgun came to her mind. They'd never used it, except for rabbits and pigeons. Robbery would be easy, but without meaning. They needed to give it value, let it jump in their hands for a cause. She had a gun in her hand right now. She'd give it to Douglas right now, both barrels, intent and language.

The door opened, Douglas surprised, holding up a hasty pair of trousers.

'I thought we said seven,' he said.

'It's not that,' she said. 'I wanted to ask you something …'

She broke off. Reflected in the mirror, on the edge of Dougie's bed, sat the film star from the beach, no clothes and a towel over his lap. The scent in the room billowed out. Another thing she hadn't seen.

'Sorry,' she said. 'I didn't know you were ...' A voice sang out.

'... busy,' it said.

Douglas looked back, grinning. He was exuberant, glowing with the colour of fucking. Alice felt emboldened. This is where I am tested, she thought, my mouth, my words, the very core of me. Another threshold.

'I had a request to make,' she said. 'But if you're busy.'

Douglas was intrigued, stood aside, beckoned her into the room. Valentino, the towel secured, stood up. The bottom sheet had come away from the mattress. Bedding lay in a heap in the corner. A redundancy of pillows. It was what was needed. To be naked in all things. To jump right in.

'I need to get pregnant,' she said. 'But me and Louis, it just isn't working. And we thought ...'

She paused, gathering her momentum. Valentino was splashing his face with cold water, Douglas up by the door, eyes on both of them. She was standing in a simple dress, with the simplest of requests.

'We were both wondering if you'd be busy with me once a month,' she said. 'Just a normal fuck. Just to see if it made any difference.'

There, she'd said it. Valentino was blowing water through his fingers. Douglas, blinking back the surprise, pointed to the bed and the man standing on the other side of it.

'What about this? This doesn't change your view?' he said.

'If anything, it makes it better,' she said. Douglas rubbed his head.

'I don't even know if I'm able … even if I agreed.'

'I am. I'm able.'

Valentino, comb in hand, was studying his parting in the mirror.

'I have two children already,' he said. 'One look and the ladies … boom!' He exaggerated a stomach. 'When would you like to start? Mondays is a good day for me. It would be a pleasure.'

'I don't want it to be a pleasure,' she said. 'It's not about that.' Douglas scratched the back of his neck.

'And Louis would be happy with this arrangement, whether it worked or not?'

'He'd be in the next room,' she said. 'Or downstairs, if that suited you better.' Douglas shook his head.

'I don't know what to say.' Alice felt herself getting carried away.

'Don't say anything,' she said. 'It would just be a date in your diary, no different from your day job. You'd turn up, make the delivery, drive off. No paperwork either,' she added, making light of it. She bit her lip. It was the wrong thing to say.

'I'll think about it,' Douglas said.

'Tell me tonight,' she said. She pointed to his new friend. 'You can come too, if you want. We need fresh blood.'

She went back to her room, all bolshie. Louis was sat up on the bed, still suited, reading the *Reader's Digest*.

'How did it go?' he said.

'He'll think about it.'

Louis tossed the book aside, got to his feet. He traced her lips with his fingers, testing the shape.

'You know what I think about?' Her mouth grew cavernous.

'Louis.'

'Thick like cream, Alice. Perfect like an egg.'

He lifted her dress over her shoulders, led her to the basin, filled it with cold water. He dipped a corner of a towel into the bowl, began washing her in small, concentrated circles. She stood a statue. The sleeves of his suit grazed her skin. She wanted him to hasten, but knew he would not. He did it studious, unperturbed and without speech, inch by inch. She felt herself gathering in immensity.

When he was done, he dropped the pillows to the floor, folded his suit upon them. He placed his bare feet upon his jacket and trousers, invited her to do the same. They stood, face to face, holding hands. They were in a stranger's room and it had become theirs. There was no anonymity to it, only liquid intensity.

'We go back,' he said. 'We fetch our son, bring Chester to us. We teach him everything we know. Everything. If you must go with Douglas, you go with me the same day, or a day either side, so there's no telling, you understand? If you must. But for now …'

They slipped into the water, shallow streams at first, but, as their confidence grew, into deeper folds. Then they were swimming out to sea, long, steady strokes, into currents of immeasurable depth, taken away to they knew not where.

'What if we never make it back?' she said.

He said nothing. The curtain was billowing out like a raised skirt. Alice fixed her eyes on it.

A storm was coming.

———

When she rose, and they were all readied, the evening seemed to shine before her, like a glow in the sky, like it was set fair, the seven of them in the snug, stuffed seagulls peering down, the pints all lined up and packets of crisps ripped open on the table, all different flavours, like they could cut loose, any time they wanted it. It had been the best with Louis since she couldn't remember when, the smell of it still strong on her. Douglas was sat beside her, jiggling his leg like a coiled spring, Frankie laughing her head off, because the landlady hadn't let Owen pick up her Pekinese, like she thought he was going to bite its head off.

'That's us,' Alice declared, 'fucking barbarians, no quarter given,' and raised her glass, because that's what it was all about, savages, and how to become one. It was there for the taking, the night, hands around their beers and the first sip taken in unison, like they all got what it meant. She swallowed it down and looked around, in half a mind to clap her hands, announce what she and Dougie were going to do, like it was perfectly sensible and right, and what the fuck. They should all do it, take a turn on the gene-pool roundabout, different rides on different donkeys. Who knew what they might end up with? Wasn't there stuff about that in the Bible? Old Testament, not the New. The New was just Jesus and all that guilt crap.

They laid down their drinks. Louis tipped peanuts into his glass. Dougie helped himself to barbecue-flavoured crinkle-cuts, stuffed them in his mouth, like he couldn't wait. Valentino hadn't turned up yet. She'd told Louis all about him, as they'd sprawled lazy-legged afterwards, told him about the smell of complicity that had wafted out their room and the sheets all tumbled.

'We should rope in a couple of those,' she'd said. 'It's like it was no different from what we had been once, what we are.'

'A couple of *those*?' he had mocked, and she had sat up serious, because she was dead serious about the whole thing.

'There're all sorts of rules that need chopping down, Louis. We need a tribe full of everything, colours and age, sex. Weren't there any queers on the motorway?'

Louis scratched himself.

'They kept quiet about it if there were,' he said. 'No one dared admit it.'

'What about Pete?' she said.

'Pete?' he said. 'Our Pete?'

'Fuck's sake, Louis. Of course your Pete.' She bent close. 'Keeping quiet, that's the fucking problem. What do they have to go through do you think, just to be who they are, like when they're starting out, necking in the back of a bus like it was the most important thing in the world, fifteen and you didn't care and your fingers all sticky with it? We're all boxed in, Louis, whoever we are, not listened to, not wanted, put in our fucking place. It's a terrible country for that.'

He'd held her hard. When the fierce was on her like that, it came on him like a drug in his blood.

'Ask him then, this Valentino. You're right. Time is getting short.'

They'd got dressed, touching each other up, pumped at how the day was shaping up. But, no Valentino in the snug. She didn't want to ask Dougie, because then it became formal, like a who-are-you-and-what-is-he-to-you sort of bollocks. Getting older, they had to guard against that. She lifted her pint again, like she was going to make a toast, start things off, but Biddy swivelled her eyes at her like she'd been tipped upside down. Something else in the air.

'Tell them, Miles,' Biddy said.

Miles put a hand round his glass, tuned it like it was a crystal ball he was looking into.

'Biddy was talking to the landlady this afternoon. Her brother owns the chippy round the corner.' Louis patted him on the back.

'We're getting cut rates, great.'

'Not that. He's selling up, cash for a quick sale. Upstairs flat, cold storage in yard.' He paused. Vowels were coming out of his throat, like there were hands round his neck. 'Thing is, with my redundancy pay, plus a bit put aside, we could just about manage it, if he brought the price down.'

He took his glass up again, drank deep. Alice spoke first.

'What do you know about fish and chips?' she said. 'You've hardly set foot in our kitchen.' Miles put his pint down, wiped the foam away

'Best food in England, I know that much. He's promised to train me up for a month.'

'He?'

Miles hesitated. Biddy leant forward, took centre stage. This was a public performance, like they'd rehearsed it.

'Fact is,' she said, 'we went to look at it, while you were all resting, put in an offer, right then and there. Be perfect for us, a new start, working together in a strong community. The summer you got the tourist trade, the winter our regulars ...'

Our? Alice could scarce believe it.

'What about what we're doing?' she said.

There it was, out in the open. They sat, staring down at the table, like all the unformed ambitions she wanted them to corral were laid before them. Miles pushed his pint away, the crystal ball clouded over.

'What *are* we doing?' he said. 'Driving round, acting like drunken teenagers. It might be fun for a while but …'

He looked to his wife. She'd cast her eyes away, glad that he'd said it, uneasy with the consequences. Alice wanted to hit her.

'Fun?' she said. 'Is that what you think this is?'

Frankie jumped in.

'Well, isn't it?' she said. She looked fabulous, fabulous and young, and with Owen beside her, Alice saw, like it had been staring her in the face for months, that they didn't need her and Louis any more. They'd live or not live, stay together, split, without the signs or the big room upstairs having anything to do with it. The stuff on their faces, their age differences, their bold theatrics had bolted them together like rivets. Sure, they'd crash into something unforeseen, but it would be something internal that would sink them, if they sank at all, a flaw embedded inside. Alice tipped the beer back.

'It's way more than that,' she said, 'what we did last night was just the beginning. We were so together, so right. Surely we should be …' She turned to the others for support. She should tell them now, be proud of it, what she was going to do for the good of them all.

'What do you think, Dougie?'

Dougie got to his feet.

'I'm off,' he said. 'Giving that guy we met on the beach a lift back.'

The words stuck her with a stab knife. She bit on her glass. He looked at her like it didn't matter.

'He's got to be there for the shop tomorrow, me likewise, early-morning delivery and all that. Don't know what I was thinking about, staying overnight.'

Frankie was smiling at him underneath her eyelashes.

'You haven't lost much time,' she said. Dougie drained his pint.

'No.' He grinned. 'What a name, eh?'

With that he was gone, the door banging empty and it was like Miles and Biddy were empty too, and all that was left was the four of them, her and Louis and Owen and Frankie, none of them knowing what to say. It was over. A trip to Scarborough, a ride on the donkeys, a fuck in the afternoon ...

'Like sappers in the war,' Louis said.

They were driving back late, Biddy and Miles taking the lead in the Hillman, with Frankie and Owen squashed on the back seat. Alice and Louis were alone in the Humber. Everyone had slept in.

'Like sappers in the war,' he repeated, 'the rest of us oblivious in the trenches, while Miles and Biddy dug a tunnel underneath.'

'Biddy and Miles more like,' she said. 'I can't believe they're ...'

Louis balanced his tobacco tin on his knees, began rolling.

'Have you ever noticed,' he said, 'how we've all ended up waiting on tables, first Lot and the Hovel, then us and the motorway caff, now ...?' He finished the roll-up, stuck it in his mouth. 'At least they'll own it. What do we own?'

Alice stared ahead. What treachery were they planning in the Hillman? She dropped back apace.

'So where do we go now?' she said. He leant forward, steadying the flame.

'You know where,' he said. 'We decided yesterday. Chester.'

'That was before …' She put her foot down. 'I'm going to run those bastards off the road.'

She shifted gear, making ready. Louis laid his hand on hers.

'Wait,' he said. 'Look what's up ahead. By the gate there.'

No eggs in the box. He left Alice furious in the car, walked up the track, knocked on the door. He waited, footsteps taking their time. The door opened wide. She was wearing a dress the colour of cornflowers, no arms to it and the material flaring out just above her bare knees. Her shoes looked like flowerpots. Last time he had seen her, she had appeared upon the landscape completely correct. He found himself stuck.

'I wondered if I'd see you again,' she said, and peered round.

'The car's on the road,' he said. 'I was passing through, hoping for some eggs, but …' He caught sight of her left leg, wrapped up in crêpe.

'Blasted pothole,' she said, 'carrying down a trayful. Lovely morning, and I thought, sod the Land Rover.' She pushed her hair back, blinked into the sun. 'It's just a sprain, that's all.'

Louis looked about him. The house was different now, severe but like a keep, pasture fields rolling up to battlement hills, the animals secure upon them. This is what he and Alice needed, he thought, somewhere entrenched.

'Got the sheep, I see,' he said. She folded her arms.

'And this is where they're staying' she said. 'I didn't realise, the way you treat your livestock, moving them from pillar to post every day of the month.'

Louis turned to take in the view across the valley, her meaning unclear. The nose of the Humber peeked out at the end of the drive. Alice would be getting impatient.

'And how's the Rover?' he said. 'Still a piece of perfection?'

'I don't take her out as much as I used to,' she said.

But there was a time ...

She'd never given anyone a lift in Brandon, Manitoba, but once back in England, the need had leapt upon her as if a new biology had been calling. The grey two-piece, the lacquered hair, the artifice of make-up, had all given a solidity to the venture. Only her egg-blue nail polish illustrated the fragility of the scheme, but it did not deter her. The stranger in a car was, after all, her abiding memory of old England, the reason she had left and, she realised, the reason she had returned. The only difference now was that she was in the driving seat. What car had they ridden to the Beacon that night? She couldn't remember. Something small, something cheap, insignificant, like the man she had been with, whereas the Rover ...

It had lasted – well, until she found the reason for stopping. An early evening, the day's work done, she'd change into her suit, settle into the Rover and set out for the A1 and the feeders leading on to it. She ignored couples and students. She wanted men, solitary creatures, with the stoop of disappointment upon them, no future, only their dingy past ahead. And in no time at all – for time played no part in the proceedings, time was an irrelevance, there was only the Rover and its capacity for reassurance – she'd find one, the body half-turned as if in shame and a ragged thumb on the end of it. Her heart would start and, with the pulse banging in her ears, she'd ease up, roll down the far window and enquire, as calmly as she could, 'Can we be of assistance?', the expression cut from the same cloth that she and the car were wearing. Usually, they did not understand her right away, confronted as they were by this vehicle of such devoted respectability and the woman sat pristine inside it. She and the car appeared to them as if transported from another age, when the world had been better and they had lived amidst the clean shape of things, and the sight bewildered them. Then, as reality dawned, came the mutters of disbelief, the grateful stammers and the door would be swung open and she would inhale the long smell of defeat as they climbed in.

'Seat belt,' she'd say, 'and the window, if you would be so kind,' and she'd wait as they fumbled with the catch and seized the handle, as if they couldn't believe what was happening to them, where they were.

'Where are you heading?' she'd ask, not that she took any notice of the reply. She'd flip the indicator, glance up to the mirror, and ease out back into the traffic. Rhythm was everything.

She let them endure the silence for a while, the Rover steady, and she waiting. Night-time, daytime, it rarely varied. Once aboard, it was as though a change rolled over them, and they were perched upon a pew rather than a bench seat, inside a church as much as a car, looking down the length of the bonnet, not as to the road ahead, but as to a nave, and they unaccountably sat before it, all their deformities bubbling up. Caps came off. Hands were folded. They worried over the state of their shoes. Nothing was said, but an intoxicating politeness began to choke the ventilation. Time to let the air in. Directness was the best approach.

'You're a bit old to be hitching, aren't you?' she'd say.

It went to the heart of the matter. Once they answered it, reluctantly, awkwardly, sometimes with a smile, the grim descent into their downfall had been taken. And it thrilled her, her orchestration of it. She had returned to the skill she had first discovered as a young woman in the courtroom, that same feeling of controlled ecstasy glowing within her, as she directed the proceedings. Her hands had been on the wheel then, and they were on the wheel now.

And thus, at a steady forty miles an hour, Mrs Calvert upright, the Rover holy immaculate and the motion endless, words rose up into their knotted mouths. Sometimes she offered them tea from a Thermos she carried, bringing balm to throats unused to such demands. But wet or dry, their lips parted and out leapt scenes from their own lumpen interiors, tales of drink and adultery, theft and violence, drug addictions, spells in prison. They spoke and their spirits lifted.

What the Rover wanted her to do with these men wasn't immediately apparent. Weren't the stories enough, all the broken men of the roadside, and the damage they had done, standing on the lip of loneliness? They brought neither peace nor comfort to her, yet by speaking of it, they gave shape to something which had none. As a young woman she had sat in a car and heard thoughts that only men could fashion, seen her life smashed before her eyes. Now she heard them and batted not an eyelid. Would she have gathered such a harvest in any other car? She thought not. The Rover was the motor for everything that had happened to her since her return. It had stiffened her resolve, given her a sense of invulnerability that came very close to religion. Within its sturdy frame it was possible to look through the high windows and envisage an England that she had thought no longer existed. It lived in a world most people longed for and no one found, a world that would never change, that was immutable, reliant, that would carry her through life unscathed, however rough the waters. It was like a book of etiquette, showing her how to behave. So, she drove, beguiled by debauch, wondering as to the purpose of it.

And one afternoon, she found it, on a slip road, no thumb out, the man half-tipped to the ground like an old carrier bag, possessions tumbled about the grass. She slowed up, rolled the window down.

'Can we be of assistance?' she'd said. The man had looked up and stared at her. His suit, she noticed – and it was a suit, not a mismatch of colour – was of a better cut than most.

'I have seen this vehicle before,' he announced. She silenced the engine, the first time she had done it, couldn't explain why.

'I am sure you have not,' she said, supposing it was perfectly possible. 'You walk the roads?'

'Walk the roads!' He rose to his feet, an unsteady hand on the open glass. His fingernails were unnaturally clean. 'You are the second person who asked me that question,' he said. 'You best leave now. I nearly fell in love with the first.'

He was supremely drunk, soaked to the skin with it.

'That was foolish,' she said.

'I had to leave. He was young, and I was …' He sighed. His breath was unspeakable.

'The worse for wear,' she said.

'Not then. I was correct. I walked away. I gave myself grace, what little I had left.'

He licked his lips, as though the truth had made him thirsty. Suddenly she knew. She searched his face. It was broken and lost, long years of it. He had been ... what had he been? Not this. He tried to stand upright. He was drunk but he had a carriage, as the Rover had a carriage, as though he belonged somewhere else.

'That was correct, indeed,' she said. She swung round, zipped open the canvas bag on the back seat.

'Would you care for a cup of tea?'

'Tea!'

He lost his balance, fell back, laughing at her stupidity. She got out the car, walked round. A day of firsts.

'How long have you been like this?' she said.

'Why? Have you come to reform me, an angel with an American accent?' He giggled, waved his arms and legs inanely. She stood over him, looking down as though he were an insect under a microscope.

'An angel with a Canadian accent,' she said. 'What's your name?'

'Depends on the year,' he said. 'Sometimes I can't remember.' And giggled some more.

'Let's get you that tea,' she said. 'Hot and sweet.'

She opened the passenger door, helped him to his feet. He sat, hands on his knees, legs outside. She took up the Thermos flask, held the beaker out. He squinted at it.

'It's quite clean,' she said, unscrewing the stopper.

'No need for that,' he said. 'I possess a cup ... my very own.'

He fumbled his pockets, brought it out, a badly dented thing, handed it over. It burnt a little in her hand, couldn't work out why.

'It was his,' he said. 'He was a boy, you see, but so beautiful … I wanted to take his cock in my mouth. Do you see, the shame of it?'

His hand was shaking and he was blinking tears.

'The Rover doesn't mind,' she said. 'Me neither. We have driven further than that, the Rover and I.'

He drank. The sweetness settled him. She always made it sweet. It was the one thing they had in common, these men, their absolute need for sugar. She poured him a second cup. He held the mug as though it was the only thing he had left, both hands wrapped around tight. He had lost everything, and it was swimming, half-remembered, inside him.

'Where to now?' she said.

He stuffed the mug back in his pocket, pointed down the road.

'The backbone of England,' he said, 'and all its knobbled vertebrae.'

'How about coming back with me?' she said. 'There's a job, if you want it, on a farm.'

'You mean to Canada?'

'I mean not a hundred miles from here. Just a smallholding really, fifty ewes. A bull, a farm.' He shook his head, struggling to understand.

'What will I have to do on the farm?'

'Be an outdoor type.'

'I am an outdoor type. Do you have a dog?'

'A dog?'

'For the sheep.'

She was galvanised, her face suddenly released. She took his hands, held them up to her waist. He had been strong once, but his arms were bird-bone light.

'Why would I need a dog?' she said. 'I have you.'

He slept most of the journey, laid out in the back. When he woke she was turning off, up to the darkened house. She drove round, unlocked the back door, marched him straight into the kitchen. She switched on the lights. A moose's head, the size of a small boy, rested on a low dresser. Cups hung from his antlers.

'I got him in an auction a week after I bought the place,' she told him. 'Nowhere to put him, but he needed a home. You and him both.'

'I am not sure I really need a home,' he said. 'Once I am shot, of course it'll be a different matter.' He took out his mug. 'May I?'

He hooked the handle through, patted the moose on the head.

'There, there,' he said. She liked that.

There was no bed for him that night. He slept in an armchair. If he snored she couldn't hear it. In the morning she sat him down at the table, faced him over a bowl of withered apples.

'Rules of engagement,' she said, pulling the bowl towards her. She had a cobweb in her hair.

'No drink. Not to speak of.'

'None to speak of,' he said. 'It's the only way.'

'Upstairs is out of bounds. The bathroom is on the half-landing. You may use it by arrangement.'

'Arrangement. Absolutely.'

'I'll give you twelve pounds a week, plus all the food you can eat. All the food is kept in the big fridge in the pantry, every bit of it. I don't like food going off, the waste. And I don't eat meat any more.'

'Don't you?'

'Not any more. I listen to the radio in the evenings. One thing that never sat with me over there was their accent, so bloody reasonable …' She stopped. It was crazy what she was doing, and they both knew it.

'Can you tell me why I am here?' he said.

What could she say? That she was going to save him?

'I told you, for the sheep.' He looked unconvinced.

'What do they do, the sheep? Or rather, what do you do with the sheep?'

'They live a life. I pay a farmer down the road to have his rams cover them. They get serviced. They have their young. They live. They die. I sell their wool. Unlike the rest of the farms, they don't get taken away, one moment happy in the fields, the next bowling down the A1 on their way to God knows where. They should have passports, those poor buggers, the travelling they do.'

It was a long speech, and he felt the anger in it.

'Do you like them?' he said. She considered the question.

'I regard them as humans with severe brain damage. They are here, as I am here. You feed them, inoculate them, wash their bottoms. They need looking after, every step of the way. This morning, however, we look after you.'

They drove into Scarborough. She bought him a second-hand bed, a Loom chair and a lampstand. A charity shop furnished him with four good shirts, two pairs of working trousers and a fisherman's jersey. By the end of the day he had a room of his own next to the back door, and the sole use of the downstairs lavatory. She'd bumped a chest of drawers down two flights of stairs for his clothes. He'd offered her assistance, but she'd dismissed it. Time for the sheep.

He was nervous of them at first, their heedless, stubborn ways. The Wolds had things upside down, the sheep held in the valley, crops grown halfway up. They rose at half-five, a big breakfast, then in and out the best part of the day, always something to do, sheep to move, sheep to feed, sheep that had strayed into other flocks. Mrs Calvert cared for the sheep more than she liked to let on, but he could see it, the way she tugged at their ears, scolding them for their determined capacity for self-harm. They made a beeline for getting stuck, ditches, fencing, wherever the opportunity arose. She'd sit in the Land Rover, watch him tussling with their bulk.

She kept chickens and a precise vegetable garden, sheltered by three walls. There was always work to be done. He did not feel for the land, though he knew, in an earlier life, had he lived it, he would have done. Had he lived an earlier life? It was somewhere in his memory, like a landscape rolling before him, huge and misty and marvellous. He'd got lost in it, that's all he knew. It was hard to remember anything else. He saw the sheep and remembered her words – They are here, as am I – and he believed it of himself, food to eat and land to walk upon and not a lot more. He never became ill, though he had bruises up and down his body most weeks, the battering the sheep gave him. He washed his own clothes and bed sheets, hung them out, brought them in, folded them away. He thought he might never leave, expected to fall down one day and fade into oblivion, wanted for nothing more.

They kept themselves to themselves. Within her own community she was neither disliked nor avoided, contact to a minimum. It was as she said. In the evenings they listened to the radio, sat in the armchairs too large for the room, too low for the leg, dark and strange and ugly. The house was full of it, heavy furniture, meagre windows, no memories there. She thought of her mother, alone in that little house, even when she lived there with her, but she did not talk of it. She talked of Canada and he talked of the road. Whether they listened to each other was questionable. Very often it was their own voices they were hearing. That said, he grew to know Brandon, Manitoba, its straight flat lines, the banks of its broad river, the screams coming from the hog processing plant, and she learnt of the road, the geography of walking, the erosion of spirit. But life before Canada, of that she did not speak. It was the same for him and life before the road. He was a mystery to himself, as she was to hers, as to where the truth lay. He did not know his. She was afraid that she might know hers all too well.

The second year she bought him a horse. He stroked the mare's flank, laid his head against her neck, spoke to her as though he had known her all their lives. The horse bared her teeth once, then snuffled in acceptance. From that moment on, Percy and horse were inseparable. He refused to give her a name. Horse, he said, and the animal shuffled towards him, head lowered. He rode her everywhere, up into the hills, across the fields, to the local shop. The demands of the mechanised road were no longer relevant. Even the monthly trip in the Rover became an imposition.

'Why don't you get rid of it?' he'd say. 'You don't use it any more, not like you used to,' and though she agreed that it made sense, she could not. It was like the horse was to Percy, personal. The Rover relied on her and she relied on the Rover. Were the Rover not there, she feared that all that she had secured might break loose, and she would become bereft again. So she kept the Rover in the barn, where it now stood, with this other man, this Louis, wanting to see it again.

———

She blinked back. Louis was speaking.

'Don't take it out much? With potholes like that, I don't blame you,' he was saying. 'I could fix it, if you like. Two ton of gravel, a little hard core. Wouldn't take me more than a morning?'

What could she say? There had been a time when she thought about him most every day, wondering whether she'd see him again, the pleasure she'd find. Now ...

'I thought you'd come about eggs,' she said. He acknowledged the discrepancy.

'A man can dream,' Louis said.

She beckoned him in. They passed a door, the single bed in partial view, the sheet made up and a mug on the floor. Did she have a man in there? Louis felt let down. Then he was by the back door and she was taking down a set of keys hanging from the hooked udders of a tin pig.

'I don't know why I bother to lock it,' she said. 'But I do.'

They walked out into the yard, water caught in the flag-stones from a recent wash. She unlocked the doors, swung them back. The Rover was sat in its two-tone livery. Louis didn't know where to look.

'Did I tell you, it's what my son rode in from the hospital, when he was just a baby,' he said, the words catching in his throat. 'Just a baby,' he repeated, 'looking out from the back, like he was lord of the manor.'

It wasn't true, but he said it anyway, like it had existed. Soon he would be back in Epping, on the porch with his feet up, waiting for his son to walk into the clearing, a school bag on his shoulder.

'How is he?' she said, trying to remember the boy's name. Louis cleared his throat, pretended he hadn't heard.

'Actually,' he said, 'we're thinking of moving, upping sticks, the three of us.' He left out Lot. There was no point in telling her about Lot.

'Yes?'

'Like I said, the last time we spoke, we need space, somewhere suitable.' He turned his back on the Rover, wished he hadn't asked to see it. It was the wrong sort of car for this conversation. 'I was wondering if you knew of any land going round here, or if you had any yourself that you didn't need. Land for, what do you call it, a settlement. Just the three of us at first, then ...' His voice trailed off.

'I don't quite follow, Mr Priest,' she said. 'You want to buy?'

Louis did not answer. His eye had caught movement on the hill to the back, the rider and the pale horse threading their way down through the sheep, slow and careful.

'Just like a western, isn't it,' Mrs Calvert said, proud how well they rode. 'Only no homesteaders, at least not yet. And in that regard ...'

'Foolish to ask,' Louis interrupted. He cocked his head. 'Is that the Humber hooting?'

And he was gone, no eggs, no goodbyes, not even a glance back to his old love. She followed him through the yard, watched him breaking into a run, heard the engine growl and the car lurch on to the road. She went to close the barn door. Percy was coming into the yard.

'I saw a man running,' he said. 'I was worried ...'

He had grown protective of her, and she liked it, despite herself.

'Nothing to it,' she said. 'He wanted to look at the Rover, that's all.'

She stuffed the keys into her pocket, gripped them tight. 'Do you ever feel unbalanced, Percy, feel you want to be seized by ... a madness?'

'You know I do.'

'I think he was, just then, seized by a madness.' She took the keys out again, tossed them in the air. 'Let's run the Rover out,' she said. 'We owe that car, you and me.'

Alice gave a start. Louis was hopping one leg to the other, trying to get the door open, like he was going to wet himself.

'What's up,' she said. 'Someone after you?'

Louis scoured the track back up.

'You ran all the way?'

'Downhill,' he said. He climbed in, banged his breastbone. He was biting at gulps of air, like they'd just been at it. She waited.

'Well, get a fucking move on.'

She threw the Humber in gear, tailed it on to the road. Louis's chest was going up and down like a pair of old bellows.

He looked worn and leathery and sunken in. She took her foot off, hoping it would calm him down, drove slow for a couple of miles.

He started sudden, waving his arms.

'The side road back there. Pull up for Christ's sake!'

He stumbled out the car. What was the matter with him? She let the Humber idle, then reversed around the corner. Louis was knelt on the ground, his left arm holding on to the pole, the hacksaw limp in the other. Just an ordinary speed limit.

'What is it?' she said. 'The blade broken?'

Louis didn't reply. She couldn't understand it. His face was falling down. For a moment, she didn't know who he was.

'Louis?'

He tried to raise his right arm. It flapped against his side, like a broken wing.

'Not seeing straight,' he said. 'Can't …'

His words were coming like he was underwater. She clambered out, knelt beside him. He tried to put an arm around her, but could not. He looked up at her. His eyes were swimming helpless and there were spit bubbles on his lips. She had a sudden picture of him wearing a nappy.

'Let's get you back in the Humber,' she said.

It was hard. A Polo slowed down, but she waved it away on the kick of instinct, regretted it the moment it disappeared. She opened the rear door first.

'Do you want to lie in the back?' He shook his head. When she moved off, he was leant up against the passenger door, watching her like a creature wounded.

'Say something,' she said.

'Whisky,' he said.

The bottle in the glove compartment was empty. The first opportunity, on the dual carriageway, she pulled up outside a steakhouse.

'I got someone taken ill,' she told the waiter. 'Could you sell me a brandy?'

She came back with two stiff ones and a handful of peppermint creams, courtesy of the manager. She tipped Louis a wink, drank hers back in one, showed him all was well. He found it difficult to concentrate. Half of it went down his front.

'I'll get you a straw next time,' she said, 'then you can suck on a whole bottle,' and wiped his mouth clean with her sleeve. His face was still all over the place. She wanted to hold him, but was afraid. She thought she should take him to a hospital, but was afraid of that too, the dam it might break, the waters that might overwhelm them.

The drive back was a test of her patience, Louis mouthing she hadn't a clue what. She couldn't make sense of it. He'd been firing on all cylinders before Miles had pulled the plug on them, had gone on for ever that afternoon, bucketloads of come and a force of energy on him like he was marking his territory all over again, like he was getting them both ready for whatever the fuck was going to happen. Even this morning, despite last night, he'd been all fizz, popped out early to say goodbye to the donkeys, a funny thing for him to do considering, but had come back gabbing on about them like he couldn't stop, their versatility, their patience, like what if they bought a troupe of them themselves, found a place for them to pull wagons and carts and dig wells ...

'Dig wells?' she'd said. 'What the fuck are you on about?'
'Us,' he'd said, 'a place to call our own,' and had grabbed hold

of her and would have fucked her all over again if the landlady hadn't barged in asking who was going to pay for Dougie's room. He'd got up and peeled off a bunch of notes, the bulge nodding in his trousers like it had a spring in it. She had been expecting to find out more on the way back, but now … Everything was falling apart.

Back in Peterborough, she went round to their old drop, hoping Owen would help them up the café stairs, but no lights, and no answer to her banging. She drove to the flat where Biddy and Miles lived, but their Hillman was gone from out the front. She hadn't a clue where Douglas lived. She sat outside the café, wondering what to do next. Louis had woken up twitchy, trying to open the door, couldn't work it.

'Fuck horses,' he said, agitated sudden. 'Donkeys are the thing. They carry the same load as you do. You look a donkey in the eye and …' He slumped back in his seat, exhausted. She took away his hand, kissed the back of it.

'We better get you upstairs,' she said. 'No horses, no donkey either.'

'Piece of piss,' he said.

It took a while for her to work it out. No chance of him doing it on his own. She found rope in the storeroom. She sat him in one of the café chairs, tied him to it. It was easier that way, turning him round, dragging him up the stairs, one step at a time. Louis liked it, joined in her grunts of exertion, body noises together again. When they got to the top, she started for their room.

'Window,' he said.

She pulled him to the big bay, untied him. He pushed her hand away, twisted himself round into one of the armchairs.

'Piece of piss,' he said again.

The headlights cheered him up, cheered her up too, like they were back on familiar ground, like if they could just get past tonight … She took off his boots, wrapped a blanket round him, put a shot of whisky in his hand. He took it down, started coughing.

'Do you want some water?' He nodded. She brought a peeled egg with it. He closed his fist around it, sat following the lights bat back and forth, like at a tennis match. She stood alongside him, stroking his head. She could stand there all night if need be. He fell asleep, the egg dropping from his hand. It rolled across the floor. Alice couldn't take her eyes off it, the ripples that had swept over them, thick like cream. Come dawn, she lay down on the floor beside him, like it was a forest floor, noises all around her. When she woke, Louis was still asleep, and Fish was outside looking up. He had a hooray neckerchief wrapped round his throat, like he'd joined a motor club. She ran down the stairs two at a time.

'There's been an accident,' she said.

'I'll say,' he said. He pulled at the knot. 'Where is everyone?' He looked up. Louis was leant against the window, hands flat out, like they were nailed to the glass. 'What's he playing at?'

He barged his way up. Louis was slumped back in the chair. There was a puddle on the floor, not whisky.

'He's had a bit to drink,' she said.

'I'm not standing for this,' he said, and jabbed a finger at her. 'What's more, the police have been looking for you.'

'Police?' The shutters were coming down. 'What about?'

'Wanted to know your whereabouts, a most particular date. Know what I did?' He tapped his nose. 'I checked our records, told them you were here all day, serving customers. That was special of me, wasn't it?'

He folded his arms. She looked out the window. Denise was dragging her leg across the tarmac. They had tried and they had failed. Time to go.

'Why don't we check on the egg situation,' she said, 'before we open.' Fish laughed.

'I think I deserve a little more than eggs,' he said. 'They'll be back, you know.'

Alice felt a reckless surging.

'Not able to oblige this week, Mr Fish, if you get my meaning. Just the eggs this time. Give me five minutes. I'll open a fresh batch.'

She drained the brine from the tin, filled it with the gunk Owen used to unblock the drains. Fish couldn't believe it, the best he'd ever had, his necktie fit to bust. Back upstairs, Alice flushed the contents down the pan, wrapped the gun in a blanket, loaded up the Humber. Ten minutes! Ten fucking minutes! Louis had woken up again, had heard her packing, recognised the sounds.

'Where we going?' he said, not greatly interested.

'Outpatients first,' she said.

He took hold of her wrist. The words came out of the side of his mouth like he was afraid of dropping them, but they were his words, and she listened to them.

'Do you think I've lived outside it all, to end up like a kennel in a dog?'

She wanted to laugh, dared not, loved him for it.

'What then?' she said. 'Chester? Aunty Lot? You need rest.' The grip faded.

'Not Chester. Not like this.'

314

She carried him downstairs into the car, his hand gripped on her breast but she didn't care. In the kitchen, Denise was spreading sandwiches. Mr Fish was crouched behind his desk, clutching at himself. She went back into the storeroom, took all she wanted.

The Humber started straight off. They had half a tank of petrol, a crateful of peeled eggs, and the gun. She poked the bonnet out, turned south. They could handle it, couldn't they? It's what they'd done all their life together. This time, she was on her own. Was what wrong with that?

It took her longer to reach than she imagined, stopping for accidents, sickness, Louis exhausted by the very act of moving. She pulled up, outside. There was an Austin Allegro in the drive, another shit red-cherry-colour, front-wheel drive, eleven seconds sixty mph acceleration, thirty miles to the gallon, on a good day.

'Trust them,' she said. 'More aerodynamic going backwards than forwards. You stay put.'

She got out, took a breath. Last time they'd been here, she'd wanted to fuck him on the hall carpet. She walked round the back, the key not in its place. She tried the handle, kicked the door. Finally, she stood herself in the porch. The stained glass still gave her the creeps, like standing in a bloody church. She put her finger on the buzzer, kept it there till he came. He was different, all shoulders and bone. How many years?

'Hello, Dad,' she said. 'Remember me?' He looked around, like it was a trick.

'Should I?' he said. 'Last time …'

'Last time I took my records back. You were all asleep. I had my boy with me.'

The man's eyes flickered.

'I don't remember that.'

'You shut the door on him. He didn't think I saw, but I did. I couldn't believe it, your own grandson.'

'He was a stranger on the landing. Why wouldn't I?'

'He was just a kid, Dad.'

'All sorts live round here these days. Now, if that's all you've come to say …'

She stuck her foot in. None of that.

'I need your help, Dad. I got a man out there, the one I ran off with. He's not feeling well.'

Her father stepped out on to the path. He could see Louis, head drooped down. 'She's dead, you know, your mother.'

'I didn't know. What did she die of?'

He kept his back to her.

'Is that all you can say?' he said.

'Was she very ill?' He turned. He'd been a good-looking man, tall, lines like a carving, and right there, they had come back to him a little.

'She didn't die in tip-top condition, if that's what you mean. Something burst in her brain. It was all over in a day.'

'When was this?'

'Four years this October.'

She couldn't think of what to say, what she felt, what she didn't. Colour caught her eye.

'Is that when you got the Allegro?' she said. 'All aggro, that's what we all called it, British Leyland's own goal.'

He didn't bother to respond. No one wanted to talk about the Allegro. Louis was trying to open the passenger door.

'She never stopped thinking about you,' her father said. 'Put her pension in your savings book, regular as clockwork. Is he all right in there?'

'I'll fetch him out. Why was that, the pension thing?'

'You were her daughter. What else was she going to do with it? Are you going to help him or what?'

She hauled Louis out of the car. Her father stood aside as she guided him over the threshold.

'He just needs to lie down,' she said.

'He needs more than that,' he said. 'The phone's still in the hallway, where you never rung.'

'He's not having any, all right? We won't be here long. Until he gets back on his feet, that's all. It's not too much to ask, is it?'

She helped Louis into the front room, sat him on the sofa, swung his legs round. Louis closed his eyes, not like before, but like he was content, pleased to be comfortable. Her father was standing in the doorway.

'We haven't eaten for days,' she said.

'You got a nerve,' he said. 'Soup?' He beckoned her away out of earshot. 'There's a commode in the garage, for when Margaret had her hip replaced. Don't want him to get caught short on the carpet.'

'For Christ's sake, Dad. Put his soup in a mug. Be easier that way.'

She did a quick tour while he got ready in the kitchen, brought blankets down, pillows, rescued the commode from out under a roll of netting, parked it next to the armrest. Her father came back with the tray, soup in three mugs and crackers with cream cheese on top.

'My old room's different,' Alice said. 'Everything I left behind, gone.'

'We didn't keep it preserved in aspic, hoping you'd come back unchanged.'

'I have come back.'

'Not unchanged.'

'Some would dispute that.'

For the first time, she detected a smile of affection breaking out. She handed Louis a mug, relieved that he could hold it. He wasn't talking, but he was doing something, gathering himself in, getting ready to get better. She sat in one of the three-piece armchairs, her dad in the other, Louis smack in the middle. Jesus, they were almost a family.

'We're not going to be here for ever, Dad,' she said.

'I should hope not. You can light the gas if you want. He needs to be kept warm.'

She knelt down. It lit itself, for Christ sake. She had to say it.

'I had no choice,' she said. 'I hated it here.'

'We know you did. Cracker?'

She took a biscuit. He'd put a gherkin on top. She picked it off, the others too. As if Louis would be up to a gherkin.

'This son of yours,' her father said. 'Chester.'

'He's with his aunt. He'll be joining us soon.'

'What's going on, Alice? You on the run or something?'

'Or something,' she said. She looked into the fire. 'You grow up thinking everything's going to be all right and then suddenly you look out and it's all wrong, everything you see, everything anyone's ever told you, it's all bollocks, jobs, class, money, family, this country, so proud of itself and it gets more bollocks every fucking day, not better, and our lives just get harder and harder to live, 'cause if you take your foot off, they'll catch up with you and bring you down. Like this fire … I mean look at it? Doesn't it say it all … Now I'm really pleased it's here to keep him warm.'

She was almost in tears. Louis was staring at her like he'd understood every word. Her father wiped his mouth.

'I don't get it. What's wrong with the fire?'

'Nothing, Dad. Go to bed. I'll sit up with Louis for a while.'

She got up. He got up. Would they kiss? He touched her shoulder, held it there, turned about. She followed him out, watched him as he climbed the staircase, first one way, then the other. Louis wouldn't be far off his age.

'Do you play the records ever?'

She looked up. He was leant over the banister.

'Course I do,' she said, wishing it was true

'We liked the records,' he said, 'listening to the noise coming through the floorboards. Always dancing, you were, thump, thump, thump.'

And he was gone, his door pulled firm. It fell quiet. In the hall, Alice and all her younger Alices stood in front of the big mirror, buttons checked, lips coloured, indiscretions masked. Last time she'd stood like this, she had wished herself naked, but no more. She was floating, not quite there.

It took her a month to sort out the plan, another to fix it. Louis got stronger by the day, the commode back where it belonged by the end of week three. The weather was warm enough for him to sit by the French windows, lean his face to the sun. They kept the fire on all the time, room like a greenhouse. It was his feet in the main. That was strange. Louis had never felt the cold before; now he huddled up like an old man in a bus shelter. Dad was more accommodating than she'd thought possible, kept quiet about them, like she'd asked, caught the bus and shopped for three. While he was out, she hunted down her old passport, long out of date, and his own, not used for years. She went to the post office, picked up the renewal forms. They still had the passport pictures Eddie had taken. She left Dad's passport in the sink one night, forged the referees, apologised for the state of it, and sent them off, his and hers, a day apart. They came back three weeks later, same day. Who gave a toss?

Now she was Alice Rogers again and Louis had a passport in her dad's name. She took a driving test, passed first time. Of course, she did. She was *good*. She'd jump-started her post-office book by then, eight thousand pounds, another five her mum left her in premium bonds. A week later she left Louis behind, drove the Humber to Aylesbury. Charlie was two sizes up, but squeezed into the same pair of overalls.

'You'll never guess what I'm after?' she said and kissed him big. He patted her arse. She should have smacked him, but what the fuck. It was good to smell proper grease again.

'Don't tell me,' he said. 'Something Swedish.'

'Worse than that. A motor caravan, not a VW, something with a bit more room. We're off travelling.' Charlie scratched at his groin, handled it all, no shame.

'Does Louis know?' he said. 'I can't imagine …'

'What am I?' she said. 'The little woman? Put this up for scrap, get what you can and ring round. Don't worry about innards. I'll be ripping them out. Call me when you find it.'

'How you getting back?' he said.

She looked about.

'You're loaning me that Maxi. I mean who'd want to buy that?'

<hr>

Charlie rang three weeks later: a 1982 Sherpa Highwayman, seventeen and a half feet long, inside shot to pieces thanks to a chip-pan situation. She was glad about the damage. Most motor caravans were decked out like constipated bungalows. She drew up plans. Louis had begun walking proper again, the back garden first, then the stairs, left hand banistered like glue, the right still rubbish. She'd sit at night and draw him what she'd been doing. Skills were coming back to her, how to measure up, how to get the eye in, how to handle the drill like it was a six-shooter.

She kept the ladder leading to the space over the cabin. That's where the gun would go, and the crate of eggs and the tools she'd saved from the Humber. Sleeping was easy. Sleeping was going to be a futon, rolled up and strapped up in the same place, ready access, blankets bagged from the charity shop. No pillows. She'd stuck a curtain rail over the divide between the driving and the living, hung two folds of red damask from it, pinned them on either side with heavy cord sashes. Standing back, it looked like the entrance to Aladdin. Just say the word.

She left Louis with Dad while she was working. They played cards. Snap was best, good for Louis's co-ordination, concentration. He got a craving for the ready-made shepherd's pie Dad bought at the supermarket, the mashed potato soft as wallpaper paste. He had it every day, never seemed to tire. Come six o'clock, when she finished up for the day, he'd be spooning it in like it was ice cream. Where had her Louis gone? She didn't know. There was this other Louis now and it surprised her, how much she loved this one, how much she wanted him close and happy and fed, all the things she'd never thought about before. They had just *been*. It was more complicated now. Then in the morning she'd stand and look through Aladdin curtains, see the seats and the big windscreen and the imagined view ahead. That's where she'd find her Louis again.

One morning she took him down to the postbox, to see how far he could walk, the same postbox where she'd run to meet her best friend Maisy, desperate to get out the house. It was hard to credit, this pillar on the corner, important to her again. She laughed.

'Wash funny?' Louis said. He talked out the side of his mouth now. She was getting used to it.

'I used to walk here every day,' she said, 'wonder if I'd ever get out. Then you came along …'

She walked him back. Dad had parked the Sherpa out on the road, like she'd asked him, the back door open and the steps put out.

'Go on,' she said. 'Try it out for size.'

Louis pulled himself up the step. An old chaise longue, moth-eaten at the head, stood underneath the smaller of the two side windows. To the right of the door a Baby Belling was attached to Dad's upended army trunk, the lid removed and three shelves in place, one for the bread and cheese, one for the tin plates, and a third for the potatoes and whatever. The trunk lid was hinged under the big window for a table flap, her dad's name and number still stencilled on the top, Capt. Rogers 876785, and two canvas chairs slung up either side. Opposite the Belling stood the only area boxed off; behind it, a stand for the bowl and the commode to shit in.

'It's all bolted down where it needs to be,' she said. 'Sit up front. See how it grabs you.'

Dad was in the kitchen, busy by the fridge.

'I'm taking him for a spin,' she said. He straightened up, milk bottle in hand. There was a tray on the table, three mugs, a plate of biscuits, and a clutch of paper napkins. It was part of the routine now. She twirled the keys around her middle finger, trying to keep it light.

'How long?' he said. 'Ten minutes or the rest of your bloody life?' She couldn't think of an answer.

'He needs therapy, Alice,' he said, 'stimulus.'

It was all she needed.

'I'm the therapy,' she said. 'I'm the stimulus.'

Back in the Sherpa, she joined Louis up front, started the engine.

'You know what I heard on the grapevine?' she said. 'The police are running trials with speed cameras. They're going to mount them on stilts, like a Billy Smart Kodak. It'll take pictures, read number plates, everything. What say we search out the first one, shoot the little cunt right between the eyes ...'

She reached across, took his hand. Louis was laughing.

She swung out on to the road, no prisoners.

EIGHT

T HERE IT WAS AGAIN! He heard it everywhere, that laugh, looked for it, though never found. He walked the forest, his feet big, like he'd taken root. He had grown so much over these years. He wasn't like a normal, didn't stand like a normal, talk like a normal. Even the look in his eye was different, like he was looking on to different landscape. When he walked, he walked like he was wearing a cloak, carried his face like it had a long beard hanging off the end of it, like his hands were holding a big stick. Sometimes they *were* holding a big stick. A big stick was useful in the forest.

He didn't see Angela much. She lived two miles away, had grown older than him, by a good distance. He'd hear stories, tawdry round the edges. She was a girl beset by them. Other stories came to him too, like garbled radio waves, spinning in his head, and he trying to string them together. Lightning had struck York Cathedral once, and there had been an earthquake in Wales, felt up and down the country. There'd been storms all over, trees uprooted, and gales thrashing, the hand of destruction sweeping across bold like a painting. Pictures had been taken of the *Titanic*, lost funnels looming the murk and the dead still there. Cattle were being burnt all over England, bodies wreathed in smoke and their legs pointing straight to heaven. Good Christians won't get Aids, someone said, and it shamed his ears just to hear it. They were piling those bodies up too. He wanted to grasp it all, could not. They were building a tunnel to France now, like a new limb grafted on. He wished it was a road, not a railway, wished it was a bridge not a tunnel, so they could see it, the two lands and the sea and the wealth of the journey in between. He wondered at the M25, now completed and circling the capital, the noose of traffic tightening, imagined Louis and Alice caught in the net, driving round and round, going crazy. The last coypu had been trapped in East Anglia and he saw him circling round and round, crazy too. Everything's a cage, his father had said.

Chester was out in front, splitting logs. Again, he heard it! Not a laugh at all, but another sound familiar. Long before he could see him, he knew who it was coming. He knew the thrum of the engine, the heft of the rider, knew the way he rode, back straight, arms straighter, knew the thick black goggles he would wear, and the red spotted handkerchief he would have tied in a knot around his neck, knew even the reason behind the visit, the only reason they came. They'd had a long winter, well into April, and with these warm weeks ahead he was beginning to replenish their stock.

He straightened up, one hand on his back, looking down the track, waiting for the rider to emerge. He had the strongest feeling that, as the sound grew closer, the more removed he became from the ground under his shoes and the axe in his hand, as if soon it would all be split apart, that the forest would fall to one side and him on the other, and that would be an end to it. It was like when the ambulance had come bouncing down the track bringing Aunty Lot back, its peculiar blunted shape like an alien craft there to lay its hand on the Hovel and change things. Hogan's motorbike would be like that, its Cyclops eye like a winged messenger, bringing a new permutation of laws and demands. He was Cortez, Hogan, smiling in a muffler.

Then he was in full view, the Triumph snorting as it passed over the rutted ground. Hogan parked it lengthways to the porch, set it back on its stand, took off his helmet. His hair was long and grey and peeled back over his skull. They hadn't seen him for over five years.

'Chester,' he said, and looked him up and down. 'My, my.'

Chester leant the axe up against the pile, wiped his hand.

'You still have the bike then.'

Hogan looked back.

'The only thing constant in my life.'

'And whose fault might that be?'

Chester turned. Aunty Lot was stood in the doorway, knotting the apron strings round her waist. She'd have the frying pan on before he'd stepped over the lintel. Hogan laid his helmet and gloves square on the seat.

'Path still good, I see,' he said.

He'd helped build it years back, a pretty patterned thing. Lot swept it most days. There weren't many brick paths in the forest.

'Show him round, Chester. Show him what we've done.'

Chester showed him round, the woodshed made from long undulating offcuts, the pen for the pig they had once owned next to the generator. Best of all was Chester's workshop hidden round the back, odd shapes of coloured Perspex and skip-claimed window frames: a planning officer's nightmare.

'Like one of those Picassos,' Hogan said, giving it a shake. 'Blocks of colour, all over the place.'

Inside the Hovel, Aunty Lot had laid the table for one. Hogan washed his hands under the tap and sat down. It was what was expected of him, he knew that.

'Come far?' she said, setting the sauce out. He indicated with his head.

'Scarborough.'

'Is there work round there then?' Her voice was deliberately light. Hogan swept the journey out of his hair.

'I've had it with muck-shifting,' he said. 'I was thinking of going home. Though I don't know who'd have me. Been years since I been back.'

Aunty Lot put the plate in front of him, sausages and a slice of buttered bread, turned it round so that the pattern faced him.

'Why bother,' she said. 'What's in County Mayo that's so bloody marvellous?'

'The fairies,' he said, giving Chester the look. 'No fairies left this side of the water. All your crop spraying has buggered their wings up.'

'Invite them over here, why don't you?' Aunty Lot suggested. 'Convicts and mailbags is all we get in Epping. Isn't that right, Chess?'

She slapped another sausage down on Hogan's plate, even though he hadn't touched the first two. Hogan sighed, began cutting them up into pieces, the knife and fork incongruous in his oversized hands. They watched him eat, Aunty Lot with her back to the stove, Chester sitting on the sideboard, his legs dangling down. They said nothing, waited for the explanation for his appearance, but the food came first. It was Lot's way of doing things, feeding the men first.

Hogan ate, his mouth working careful. Light was slanting in through the open door, warming the three of them. Hogan wiped the plate clean with a last tear of the bread and pushed the plate back.

'The thing is,' he said, 'they've been seen.'

Chester slid off the sideboard. Aunty Lot came round, closed the door with her foot, as if fearful of the news escaping.

'You saw them?'

'Not as simple as that.'

He pulled a half-bottle out of his pocket, set it down in front of him. Aunty Lot fetched two glasses.

'Three, don't you think?' Hogan said.

'Getting your feet under the table pretty fast, aren't you?' she said. She placed a third next to the others. They weren't dirty, but they weren't clean either. It was how she ran the place. Hogan tipped the whisky in.

'Good job you don't have any ice,' he said. 'I can't abide ice in a drink.'

'Hogan,' Lot said. 'For God's sake.'

Hogan took a glass. Aunty Lot joined him, resigned. That's how it was with the men she knew. Food, drink, then whatever you could take.

'You remember that man up at Scammonden,' he said. 'The one that had a run-in with Louis?'

Lot pulled at her apron knot, retightened the strings.

'What of him?' she said.

'I met him in York, up by the cathedral. He was standing there, looking at it. He didn't recognise me at first, but after what had happened up there, I was curious, walked over, introduced myself. Even after we talked, I don't know if he remembered me all that well. He remembered Louis, though. After Scammonden, he'd lost it.'

'Louis had?'

'Jesus, Lot, will you listen? The man on the horse, what was his name?'

'Jonas.'

'I thought you'd remember. He wasn't calling himself Jonas in Scarborough, that's for sure. Wasn't calling himself anything that made much sense, no more preaching, no more horse riding, his head all over the place, he said, until …' he took another drink '… he met with this woman. Don't laugh. *I'd* met this woman, *Louis* had met this woman, long time before, when we came across her driving one of Louis's old cars. Anyway, this Jonas, whatever he's called, had had a tale to tell. He'd thought he'd seen Louis once before, a few years back, running away from the farm where he worked. Least, he thought it was Louis, but had said nothing at the time. He didn't know the connection, see …'

'Connection?'

'Between Louis and this woman, not only the car. Louis used to buy eggs from the roadside there, quite regular for a time, until he saw Jonas, and then he never came back. But last week, Jonas and this woman were in Scarborough, go there regular, he said. He was walking along, eating an ice cream, when he saw this couple on the beach. It was warm but there weren't many bathers. She was carrying this man towards the water, like he was a baby, one arm wrapped round her neck, and his feet dangling down, the sum of him nothing but a bundle of sticks, and she in this shirt, trying to walk to the water's edge and not lose her balance. So, he runs down, offering to help, and that's when he realised who she has a hold of …'

'Louis.'

'… only very weak, almost gone. So he offers to help and this woman brushes him away, tells him he's an interfering prick and why doesn't he eff off back to the ice- cream parlour, so he backs off and watches her as she walks out the sea, holding Louis in her arms like she was walking a tightrope and he the balancing pole, carries him out until the water's up to …' he tapped his ribcage '… here, and then she lowers him in, keeps him on his back and starts to swim with him, holding him like a lifeguard does, her body underneath his, only they're swimming out to sea, and not in, Louis almost lifeless, and her legs going like pistons on a frog.' He stopped, wetted his lips. He was taking his time, telling it well. 'She swims and swims, far out, like they were never coming back. Then they stop and, for a moment, he thinks she's going to hold him underwater where no one can see, and he gets all agitated, jumping up and down, waving his arms, and then she turns, and they swim back, real slow, the woman strong and determined. They reach the shore and she carries him back out, and the thing was, and he said this twice, she was completely beautiful, her whole body bathed in a sort of glow, like a Venus, water streaming down the shirt like she was naked, seagulls swooping round her head and this man in her arms, like he weighed nothing, like there was another pair of hands holding him up. Back to the towel they go and she lays Louis down and pats him dry, and Jonas can't take his eyes off her, the way she is busy over him, rubbing his feet, smoothing back his hair, whispering to his ear … they could be alone on a desert island for all she cared. It was like no one else existed. But then she looked up from the beach to the promenade and he could feel what she was thinking, that it was going to be a long haul. She'd just swum seven leagues there and back, with a man strapped to her, and she was done for. So he took his chance, stood in front of her again and said, "Why don't we make a chair with our hands, carry him like that," and she looked at him, and saw him for the first time. "I've got a car up there," she says. "If you could help me get him up?" So they stand Louis on his feet and make a cradle with their hands and scoop him up over the sand, up the steps and along to this dirty white brute parked up. She opens the door and it's like a front parlour in there, and they sit him down on this sofa thing, Louis not asleep and not awake neither, like he's somewhere else. And just as he's about to tell her, she says, "Have we met before? Your face … ?" and he's confused. Met before?

'"I don't think so," he says. "Least, not you." And that startles her, and he's worried that the full story might be too much, that she has enough on her hands as it is. So he only tells her the last part. "He came to the farm some time ago. Ten miles down the road from here …"

'"Where we buy the eggs, on the hill?" she said. "We haven't been there for a while. This is the first time for …" He said she looked over to the sea then, like there were memories floating there. He tried to lighten the load.

'"You've chosen the weather for it," he said.

'"It?"

'"Your holiday," and the woman had laughed.

'"This is my life's work. Louis and the Beast." He hadn't understood. "Life on the road," she said. "First one breaks down, then the other." And she straightens up, anxious to be rid of him. "You still sell eggs? I might call in later, before we set down for the night," and as she says it, they both know she won't. Then she climbs in and off they go. Alice and Louis in a motorised caravan.'

Hogan settled back, glad the telling was over.

'How long ago was this?' Chester said.

'Two weeks? Nearly three? I came as soon as I could, as it's the first sighting in a while ...'

'You sure about that ... ?' Aunty Lot said. 'I often wondered if any of the others had seen them and kept quiet, like they'd been asked to.'

'I haven't heard anything like that. We keep in touch. The twins are working Leicester Forest East, Gil's gone home and Pete, Pete's got a little shop, Stamford. With a man.'

'Pete?'

'With a man.'

'With a man doesn't surprise me. It's the shop. A gift shop, you mean?'

'A clothes shop, second-hand, for the ladies, top of the range.' Chester kicked his legs impatient.

'Where is this farm?' he said. Hogan dug into his waistcoat pocket.

'I wrote it down. It's just off the A64. Here ...'

He laid it on the table. Chester stared at it, Lot too, both afraid to be the first to touch it. Chester moved it with his finger. Hogan's handwriting was neat and straight, like in a child's exercise book.

'What happened there, then? Scammonden?' Aunty Lot sat down.

'They built a road, Chess, that's all, a road and a dam.'

'And the most beautiful bridge in Britain,' Hogan added. 'A footbridge, no wider than a lady's ankle …'

'… floating almost …'

'It took a lot out of us,' Hogan said. 'Most godforsaken stretch of road in the country. There's beauty to it, I'll give you that, but at what a price. Now, you'd never know. Look down from one of the roads up top or from the bridge itself, and Jesus, it's a lovely thing, looping down in such a clean line, like a diver off the high board, leaning slowly into a curve, like you do on a bike. Pure fluid, the motion in its bones, and then, a little ways along, it cleaves in two, like a river, with an island floating in between, a tiny kingdom all of its own, then comes together again and climbs back up, to where the walkers cross and the bad part …' He pushed his chair back. 'Enough of all this. I'll take a wash if you've enough water. It's put a dreadful sweat on me, riding down and all this jabber.'

He patted Lot's knee, went out into the passageway. They heard the door to the bathroom close, the bolt worked across.

'You were there too?' Chester said.

She stared at him hard.

'Hogan might stay for a while,' she said. 'He could help on the allotment tomorrow. You were going to clear it, remember. He won't stay for long, not if you don't want it.'

There was worry in her eyes, whether the past or the future he couldn't see.

'Tell me,' he said. 'Tell me what happened there.'

First time Louis saw it there was a kind of disbelief at what he was seeing, the valley torn apart, huge jagged lumps blasted out of it, but still alive, more ruin to come. Scammonden was different. Scammonden was Genesis, imagined in the kneel of a prayer. Within it lay the possibility of near perfection.

'Sweet Jesus,' Louis said, 'this could be the death of us. Just look at her lying there. The land of the eternal hard-on. Oh, can you hear those banjos, boys,' and they rose up in a cheer, Pete and Hogan, Gil and the Brummies, for they knew the brutality in store. The road was going to rise up from a cutting a hundred and fifty foot deep on to an embankment two hundred feet high, the top of Scammonden Dam, a dam that had yet to be built: a dam, a motorway, five major rock cuttings, twelve million cubic yards of solid rock to move, six hundred and fifty thousand cubic yards of peat, and the worst weather in the country. Men had built motorways before, blown rock, put up bridges, laid track, but not in this climate, not with that soil. The ground told them all they needed to know about Scammonden. Waterlogged, and criss-crossed by deep gullies, once stripped of vegetation the peat could barely support the weight of a man, let alone a vehicle. It opened its mouth and swallowed what it found whole. Only the Muskeg and its Dinky Toy tracks was light enough to survive, and for fun, when their blood was up, they'd commandeer one and ride out over it, two or three of them apiece, bouncing up and down as they dared deliverance. 'Better than a jet ski,' Gil said, and they believed the boast, for if anyone had ridden a jet ski it would have been Gil, though everyone thought him mad to take the puppy with him. 'What if the little chap falls?' Hogan once asked, for Hogan, always in need, loved that animal almost as much as his master. 'Fat lot you know about a man and his dog,' Gil had told him. 'Don't you know if a dog gets into trouble in the water and his master swims out to rescue him, it's the man what drowns and the dog what survives? If he falls, he'll paddle his way back. No bog is going to get the better of my Patch, is it my precious?"

So they came like banished tribes out of Israel ready for the muck-shifting; everyone knew it was going to be the business. There was a bunch of Pakistanis up from Leicester, run by Wall-Eye, whose dad had been a dentist and who could pull teeth and set a broken jaw and wiggle his ears in time to Pete's cowboy guitar; then came Messrs Crawford and Stokes, the ex-squaddies out from Macclesfield, who put up a child's blackboard in the corner and ran the betting shop. Two huts down lived Hogan's brother and the Irish from County Mayo, a quintet of old lags who'd worked on the M1 and organised the weekly boxing competitions. Louis hadn't any time for the M1, first motorway or not. 'Straight as the Pope's penis, that road, and about as much use,' he'd taunt them. 'A motorway's got to be like a couple of rounds in bed. It won't get you there in a good frame of mind, if it don't have the slow curve to it.'

Before they could do any road-laying, they had to dig the peat out, five foot down on a good day, twenty foot on a bad, and no use to anyone, Hogan said, save the old fellow down below. They had to cut straight through it, run the plant out on the solid strata underneath and cut it out from the exposed vertical face, great lumps that bled a black and viscous blood. It didn't want to leave the earth, and it clung to the lorries that took it away. The only way of loosening its grip was to heat the flat of the trucks, so when the back tipped up, it slithered out, reeking of treachery. It had personality, that peat.

———

They knew it would be hard, but no one imagined that they'd still be there, three years later, the shanty town that would have sprung up, lashed down by timber and rope and steel, how they would be cut off from everything, week after week. It was hardly creditable, the last third of the twentieth century, fifteen miles from Manchester there'd be up to six hundred men, cold and starving, supplies running dry and no way out.

They gave the shacks names: Tandoori Nights, Stalag 62, the Cage of Consent. Pete had wanted to call theirs the Dry Chaparral: one, because Louis didn't allow any booze on the premises, and two, because it stood slightly elevated from the rest, confirmation that when it came down to it, Louis ran the place. An angry exchange, a question of ownership, a territorial dispute, all was settled up there. What was right for the road, that was his yardstick. No force was involved. He had no army to back him up. But he was Louis, and Louis had always seen to such sites, could measure their temperature, put in that curl that made the whole operation run smooth. Pete, eager for his name to be taken seriously, painted it on to a strip of wood, stuck it on a post outside, but it didn't last. One morning it had gone, and in its place, hanging on two chains above the door, was a sign with 'The Vicarage' painted in white. The Vicarage, the place on the hill from where the gospel according to Louis was preached, while the elements raged biblical outside.

That was the mark of Scammonden. They either worked or the weather put a stop to it. In summer, there were the dust storms, when the air choked and the sun was blotted out and a sort of violent blindness took hold. When the dust subsided, the rains came, not the rain that fell a few miles away in Huddersfield or Manchester, but rain that came at them like massed ranks of infantry, ready to mow them down. Two out of the three summers they had to bear it, machines, generators, sections of work washed away in wild tempestuous moments, a hand from heaven, a picking up and a throwing down, and puny men running this way and that. Winter lasted seven long months: sub-zero temperatures, the air filled with blizzard and snow and, when the sky had emptied, freezing fog would fall, and in its wake coverings of ice as thick as swaddling clothes. Concrete crumbled, scaffolding buckled under the weight, generators coughed their last. A man stepped outside and felt his spine shrink. He fell and his ankle snapped like a frozen twig. It never gave up, Scammonden. It fought them every step of the way.

Thus, the Klondike took root. Down by the machinery stood the site offices, where the orders came and the paperwork was done, where the pay got doled out. Up from them stood the stores and the workshops, then the shower units and the toilets and the recreation hut – two shacks spliced together, leather sofas, a Calor gas stove and a 21-inch screen with a varied signal. Next to that the canteen and, parked alongside it, Lot's mobile snack bar, the Pot Hole, which, when they were working, would trundle up and down the unforgiving length offering hope and sustenance, with a tea urn at the back as big as its petrol tank. Hope came in the disparity she'd make between their appearance and their claim to be men. Sustenance came in the polished metal trays below the battened-down window: shepherd's pie, sausage and mash, curry. At the end of the day's shift, she would bring the day's takings up to The Vicarage where Louis would be waiting. He'd take the bag from her, open up the drawstring and spill the coins out on the table. She was quick at counting, looked good with the coins, her long painted nails moving them into neat, accountable piles with deft determination, before setting the figure down in the little notebook she carried. Then Louis would box the money up in the cake tin kept on the top shelf of his locker. Could be weeks before Lot took it to the bank. Banks didn't figure much in Lot's thinking, and Louis's locker was as good as anything a bank had to offer. Quite how Lot got away with working on site, no hat, no accreditation, weaving her way through traffic that could crush her to death with one turn of a wheel, was a constant source of bewilderment, but she was Louis's woman and that was deemed enough. Things like that were what made Scammonden Scammonden. There was no fixed place for time and law there.

The brothel arrived the first September, the furniture van weaving down the access road, bare arms and hairdos waving out the window as if they were riding in on Wells Fargo, a cheer rippling down the sites as the news followed them through. Where they were from, the women wouldn't say. The Brummies thought they were from Nottingham, Hogan detected a strain of Cork City in one of them, and Gil, who only saw them from afar, said they carried themselves like 'ladies from London'. He was always polite, Gil. It was thought that if anything was to throw the Klondike off kilter, it would be the women, some matter of imagined territory, but there was never any bother on their account. They'd never had a brothel on site before. It gave the Klondike a sense of permanence, a sense of respectability, little steps up the back into a little seating area and the four cubicles with bead curtains. Soon, everything was organised, the fights, the drinking, the fuck-ing, all done on a rota. Only so many times a month with the women, only so much betting, only so much drinking.

Step out of line and Louis put the word out. You were gone. 'You should dress up like a sheriff, Louis,' Pete once joked. 'You'd look good behind a badge.' Its lanes were muddy, its dwellings ramshackle, but the Klondike was theirs under the big sky.

So Scammonden moved along, slow and painful, the men bent to the huge complexity of the task, seven miles of moor, six minutes of road, a motorway and a dam cut out of the unforgiving hills, with red-and-white bunting safety guidelines threaded throughout, so when the weather closed in, a man could haul his way to a rescue point – and wait for help.

It was the second year that the man came. They'd been working twenty-eight hours solid when the weather turned the air to powder, their lungs squeezed with the hurt of breathing and the machines all seized up. They were walking back up when they saw it, a tent stood up from The Vicarage, separate from everything, a bell tent, not boy-scout brown, nor camouflage army, but luminous white, with arched blue windows.

They stopped, the path under their boots hard and flattened. There was betting traffic coming in and out of the Cage, the next boxing contest fixed for Saturday if the bad weather held. They'd been talking about it on the way up. Now, with the tent ahead, the subject was forgotten.

'I have never seen a tent with windows before,' Brummie One said. 'Where the hell did it come from? Does Louis know?'

'You know what it reminds me of?' Gil said. 'St Paul's Cathedral, that tit on the top.'

A figure stepped out. It was difficult to gauge the stature of him at that angle. The Brummies thought him tall, Pete quite average. Hogan couldn't see any weight on him at all. His arms were folded and he was looking out over the settlement sky to the dying rumble below. The sky had cleared, but the pressure in the air told them they had about twenty minutes' grace. They were getting to know the moor.

'Is that a cloak?' Brummie One said, squinting. The sun was fresh in his eyes.

'More like a frock,' Hogan said.

'You mean like a priest?' said Gil.

'I mean like a frock.'

'Frock or cloak, he's wearing a hood,' Brummie Two said. 'Like an effing pixie.'

'That's not a hood,' Gil said. 'That's a halo the sun's given him.' He put a hand to his mouth. 'Hello there!'

The figure turned, stared at the bunch. They felt awkward, as if their feet had grown too big.

'Behold the men from Mars!' he shouted down, and opened up his arms. 'Have you found it yet?'

They looked at each other. What on earth … ? It was Gil who responded.

'Found what?'

'Whatever it is you're looking for,' and he disappeared back into his tent. They stood for a moment, fixed to the ground, unable to respond.

'What the fuck was that about?' said Brummie One.

'What the fuck is he about?' Hogan added.

'Whatever it is, Louis won't like it,' Gil said. Brummie Two sniffed, looked back to where Lot's van was parked, shutters down.

'Louis should be up here more often then, shouldn't he? If a man leaves his home unattended, no telling what springs up on his patch. It's how the pikeys work. One moment you've got a field full of poppies, the next you got a yard full of junk and screaming snot-nosed kids. Fuck like rabbits, pikeys.'

Pete didn't like that.

'Pikeys fuck just like you and me, Two. 'Bout time you got used to it. That man up there, he ain't going to fuck like anyone, not if he's a priest.'

Hogan threw his hands up.

'Who says he's a priest?'

'Well he's not Ministry of Transport, not in garb like that.'

'A contract man?' Gil put in.

'In a dress?' said Hogan.

'It's not a dress. It's a ...'

Gil stopped. No one knew what it was.

Hours later he came. They'd been forced out again, lashing down equipment against the rising wind, and were back inside, thankful for the rest. Louis was still shepherding a gang of vacation students away from the drains. None of them liked working alongside the students with their air of unwarranted comradery. Unkempt hair and a disdain for convention meant nothing to men like Louis's gang. A man who could knot a proper Windsor, dance a decent cha-cha to impress the ladies, that was what counted. The door swung open.

'And visibility was there none. That's it for a day at least.'

Louis came through, untying the strap of his hat. A lash of rain side-swiped the hut like a southpaw loose in the ring. The Vicarage took it cleanly, settled back in its ropes.

'Did anyone check the stanchions?' Louis asked, to no one in particular. He put his hand in his pocket, brought out Lot's money bag and a packet of tea. 'She'll be up later,' he said, 'if anyone fancies a haircut.' Which meant they were all due.

He sat on the bench, began pulling off his boots. The others looked at one another. Pete picked up the tea, moved to the Calor gas ring.

'Did you see the tent, Louis, just above us?'

Louis chucked his boots up near the door with the others, fed up with the day. The students had asked him all sorts of questions, where he'd come from, how long he'd been working on the roads, nodding their heads as if they understood what it was like to be a man like him. They had no right to ask him anything, least of all personal matters. One of them, curly blond locks, a marvellous specimen in the buff no doubt, had told him he was thinking about jacking university in, joining them, no ties, just working men's solidarity. He could have torn his hair out in bloody clumps.

'I saw it,' he said. 'Quite a welcome he's in for.'

He walked across, unlocked his locker, tipped Lot's money in without counting.

'Do you know who he might be?' Pete persisted. 'Kind of vexing, a tent put up like that.'

Another lash, harder this time, first one side and then the other. Brummie One stood up, straightened the little mirror. He and his brother were going out tonight, rain or no rain.

'Gil thinks he's a priest,' he said, combing his hair.

'I do not ... though it would make sense, with God knows how many cooped up here, have someone to draw the poison out.'

Brummie One spat in his hand, patted his hair down.

342

'The girls do all the poison-drawing I need. They had a bigwig down there the other night. He was a bit coy about where from exactly. One of the girls had to go to him. Rover three-litre, top of the range.'

There was a hammering on the door. The handle rattled, someone outside wrestling with it, pulling and pushing, not knowing which, before the door burst open and a man catapulted in. Brummie Two looked up from his phrase book. He was learning French. No one could understand why.

'*Fermez la effing porte, s'il vous plaît.*'

The man wore a black raincoat and carried a black umbrella, unfurled. The raincoat was bad enough. No one wore a raincoat round those parts. They inundated the floors.

'*Après moi, le déluge,*' the man said. He was tall, his head bent to the rafters running across the shack's width, an angular man with a face to match, long and curved. It was hard to tell his age. Young, Louis thought, the better side of thirty, but carrying himself older. The man stuck out his hand, the sleeve still running free with rain.

'The name's Jonas. Pleased to make your acquaintance.'

It was Louis to whom he made the remark, singled him out right away. Louis took the hand, regarded the puddle forming at his feet.

'Dangerous to go out in this weather. A man can get blown off his feet and not get up too easy.'

'I thought it only polite, to come down as soon as I saw you all gathered together. Hope I haven't spoilt the view for you, settling my little ship in port.'

'Ship? If it's the Ark you're building, the dam's not ready yet,' Louis said. 'Come back in a couple of years.'

The man wiped the rain from his hair. Indoor man, outdoor man? From the colour of his skin Louis thought indoor, although … He looked to the man's hands, but the cuffs of his raincoat kept them hidden.

'Arks go where the current wills them,' the man called Jonas said, 'and as you can see, my Ark has already found its mountain.'

'You're a surveyor then?' Hogan asked.

The man twisted his head around, smiled.

'Seeing to the alignment anyway.'

'One of Philpot's men?' Pete asked. They were all standing now, uncertain where to put themselves. It was their hut for Christ's sake. He took no notice of the question, his look on the bunks and the lockers at the back. To the men, the room appeared to close in on them. Something had been stripped away.

'There's a lot of you here,' he offered.

'Like the Tower of Babel we are,' Hogan admitted. 'It's how it is, muck-shifting.'

The man nodded, more water on the floor.

'Muck should be washed off,' he said. 'Especially in these conditions. There's observance to be made.'

'You mean, you're here to run the clock on us?' Brummie One said.

The man put his hands together over his nose, looked down for a moment. It was the nearest thing to a prayer any of them had seen for years.

'I mean the paying of respect.'

'Is this religion we're talking of?' Gil asked, prepared to be absolved.

'I am not from any church, if that's what you mean.' Brummie One remained suspicious.

'You're a Ministry man?'

The man smiled.

'I am my own ministry, as you are yours.'

The Vicarage was shaken by the scruff of the neck. Louis held on to the table to keep his balance. The man had bent his legs and ridden with it. Fairground people did that, Louis thought, on the Waltzer.

'Hope you tied it down tight,' Pete said.

They all looked to the window. The tent was rocking backwards and forwards, like a tooth being pulled.

'I better go back,' the man said. 'Looks like the Ark wants to fly, not sail. See you later.'

They followed him to the doorway, watched him stagger up, bent double to the winds. They could hear canvas cracking above the howl, like a whip. He reached the top, and, clutching on to the guy ropes, fought his way round the side until he disappeared out of sight. They waited. The tent was tossing to and fro on the sea of the storm.

'What you go and give it a name for?' Hogan said. 'A name better than ours.'

Louis made no reply.

'He's a plant of some sort, but on whose behalf?' Two said. 'Health and Safety, that's my bet.'

Still there came no sign of the man, the tent flapping wild, like it was signalling for help. Louis turned, decision made.

'Hop up there, Pete. The bastard's probably neck-deep in bog.'

Pete jammed his hat down, ducked into the wind. They trooped back in. Louis poured out the tea, pleased with the way the encounter was panning out. Whoever he was, if he had to be rescued, that would be the end of it. Whatever power he'd come with would have been blown away with him. The Ark. Hogan was right. It was a good name. He wondered whether he could appropriate it.

They spooned in the sugar. They sipped at their tea. The door flew back. Pete rushed in. He swept his hat off his head, banged it against his thigh, his face bust with excitement.

'You'll never guess what he's got up there. Only a horse! A four-legged horse, with teeth like a piano! Oh! If this don't beat all.'

A horse! Louis made light of it, but word covered the site like flood water. A horse! A horse, dirty white, with his own canvas lean-to and enough straw for a circus. A horse! When the weather improved the Ark had no end of visitors coming to see for themselves. What was the horse's name? No one seemed to get an answer. He was a big bugger, calm, but with a face that seemed to stare right at you. He stood in his lean-to with his horsey head looking out over everything. A horse! What the horse was doing here, what the man with him was doing here, was anyone's guess, for he wouldn't say, or if he said, it didn't make any sense, but the point was, he was here, in a tent pitched right above The Vicarage. You didn't pitch a tent, or an ark or whatever you wanted to call it, right above The Vicarage without a reason, without it being some sort of declaration, a challenge to Louis's run of things. The Vicarage had been pipped, pipped at a post no one knew existed and no one knew why. But pipped it was. Before the weather cleared, Messrs Crawford and Stokes were considering the odds as to who would walk away with the crown, Louis or this man Jonas. It was hard to factor in, a horse.

The storm blew out under thirty-two hours, Scammonden's slate wiped clean, the days ahead the clearest they'd had for months, the whole plain alive to men and machine and rolling under the heat. That week it was from afar that they took stock of the newcomers, the silhouette of the man and his horse climbing up an embankment or trotting down the huge gash of the valley, the gait so unfamiliar to the eye that it became the first thing they saw. They couldn't take their eyes off them, the man easy in the saddle, the reins loose in his left hand, the horse impervious to the outsize wheels and the sudden blasts of horn. They'd look out their cab window, or rest up on a shovel, and there he'd be, coming into the frame as if he was bringing news from the past. On he would come, weaving his slow, careful way, and then he was upon them and it appeared that he wasn't bringing anything much at all. He'd pull up, lean down, pass the time – remarking on the weather, their occupations, then, conversation concluded, touch his forehead to the moor, flick the reins, and move on. But the purpose of him? It was all The Vicarage could think about.

Lot got the first wind of it. She was parked up on the access road, halfway between the skeleton of the Scammonden Bridge and the dam embankment under a mile away. It was the second week, five in the evening, the weather still miraculous. Gil and Hogan were up there, drinking soup. They'd been watching him for a good half hour, nosing his way through before he changed direction, sidestepped the horse up over the packed soil.

'Looks like you got a visitor,' said Gil.

Lot straightened her apron, fluffed up her hair. It took a full five minutes for him to get there. Not another word had been spoken. She was waiting on a presence. She saw how he urged the horse up the last twenty yards, skittered to a halt, brushed dust from his shoulders. He was like a soldier, she thought, carrying orders. He nodded to Hogan and Gil, but addressed his remark to her.

'Tell me,' he said. 'What is it like to be the only woman here, the responsibilities?'

Lot looked up into his face. She had never spoken to a man on a horse before. His hands were lain across the animal's neck, as if it were a great endeavour he was steering and not a horse at all. She tried to ignore the animal, with its huge, patient eyes and its sense of belonging elsewhere, but found it impossible. Hogan's bike was one thing, but here was a living creature carrying a man she wanted to know. The world she knew was suddenly quite overcome. The man's eyes stayed upon her. There came to her a longing of enquiry and she wished she were alone and not smelling of cooking fat.

'Not the only woman,' she said, her voice unsettled, 'but you probably know that by now.'

She started checking the tray lids. The suggestion of immorality embarrassed her.

'But the only woman who …' Lot took the bait.

'Gives them sustenance? I doubt if that's true.'

'… who offers wholesome food. Do you have a bowl?'

She could clatter no longer.

'Soup comes in a cup,' she said. 'Likewise, the curry. The Ritz it isn't.'

She turned her back on him, banged about more, wishing him gone, wishing them all gone. The man had to call out over the noise.

'I was thinking more of tea for the horse.'

Hogan laughed.

'It's for working men, that tea,' Gil snorted. 'He'll need a bucket, not a bowl. Does he have a name?'

The man made no reply. More clatter. Then Lot kicked open the side door, stood on the steps holding a teapot with a belly the size of a football in one hand and a chipped enamel bowl in the other.

'One lump or two,' she said.

The man smiled.

'Milk will be just dandy,' he said.

'And for yourself?'

There, she'd spoken to him direct, woman to man, questioned a need. She was almost level with him, complete in her own right. She was Louis's woman, but she wanted to be more. It had travelled a long way that smile, seen much, brought as much with it. It wasn't so much a smile as a seeking out. She felt a burning within her, a desire to do something good, nourishing, within the complexity of love.

'Jam sandwiches,' the man was saying, patting a coat pocket. 'Though the grit that gets in them here! Never thought a moor could be so hard to breathe in.'

Down below the dust had risen, filling the valley with layers of dirty brown. Nothing could be seen or heard, no sound either, just the breath of the horse and the shake of his big head. She came back with the milk, set the bowl down as if it had always been that way. Close up, Lot saw that horses had much larger heads than she'd imagined, made her wonder what went on inside them, the room they had.

'Quite some outfit this,' the man said, looking out. 'And you and me, the only civilians here.'

He twisted back to her. He was younger than her, Lot determined, but then everyone was younger than her. On site, Lot made certain she was the oldest woman they'd ever fancied. She wished herself young again, or properly done with all that. This halfway house of illusion …

'I think you're forgetting the girls,' she said.

'Are they civilians? They've certainly been hardened in battle.'

They watched as the horse drank the tea, heavy lips drawn back across the big teeth.

'Does he have a name?' Lot asked.

'He does.'

'Is it a secret then?'

'No, it's a name.' He touched the animal's neck. 'Are you here every day?'

'This spot? I travel about, like you. I feed them, keep them going. And you … you're going to … ? We'd all love to know.'

Hogan and Gil stepped forward, anxious not to miss the answer.

'Me and the horse, we're going to make them feel a hunger they never felt before.' He pulled on the reins. 'The horse thanks you kindly for the tea and trusts you'll be here tomorrow.' He clicked his tongue, moved off.

'What the fuck was that about?' Hogan said. Gil was staring at the horse's slow descent.

'Wouldn't even tell us the horse's name,' he said. He shook his head, started on down. Lot went inside, bent her knees to the little mirror hooked to the back of the door, bared her lips. She'd get some sugar buns in. Horses liked buns. She'd find his name out all right.

That's how it began, the man and his horse and Lot on the access road looking down. She gave up trundling up and down the valley. She prepared her food, tanked up the tea and parked up on high, the man and his horse standing to one side, like they were an attachment. The horse drank his tea, munched his bun, the man looked out on the work below, nothing else there save the words that passed between them, words that only he and Lot and the horse with the big head heard.

And by degrees the men began to gravitate to this polar setting, hitching a ride or, finding their loaders and dump-trucks drawn below, walking up the last stretch, not so much, Lot realised, for the strength of her tea or the heat in her curry, nor for the man and how he spoke to the moor, but for the horse. It was the horse they came for, the big horse standing quiet and still, and somehow knowing, as if the horse was looking on something they could not see. Scammonden was taking shape now, the dam, the curve of the road and the carve of the valley, moving into motorway form, emerging from something that had never been. Machines toiled, wheels churned, yet here stood true horsepower, hand upon hand of it, unflinching, unable to speak, looking out over it all. They'd stroke his muzzle, hear him whinny and stamp, and follow his eyes. And though they could not fathom it, what they saw moved them from the song of the road to the song of the moor. Creation, Louis had been right about that, but what was good for the road was no longer the question. The question was, 'What was right for the moor?' And if the man said it, they did not remember it, for the horse seemed to speak for him, and what the horse said was this – that peat was a preservative and what they did on the moor seeped into the moor, changed its character as well as its physique, and that their actions, if left unlicensed, would corrupt the moor, and that the moor had suffered enough. They had to tread rightly in their boots, and treat the moor as they did the animal that stood before them. Look the moor into the eyes, the horse said, and suffer the moor to look into yours.

A new routine at work took hold, one outside Louis's remit, one that appeared inescapable. The horse began taking his tea on the hour, a sugar bun and a bowl of tea, and men from the Klondike would engineer it so a body of them could come and witness it, a silence falling as Lot emerged with the teapot and basin, the milk ready to hand on the step. She'd set the basin down, pour the milk, pull the bun from her apron pocket, place it by the side of the bowl and stand back. It was nothing really, a horse and a bun and a bowl of tea, but it was the theatre the horse brought to the time that held them, that look of his that first travelled around them, then the stare at the bowl, lastly the bun, no one daring to breathe a word. To think a horse could deliberate so. Then he'd lower his head, pull back his lips and show his big white teeth. Sometimes he would eat the bun first, sometimes drink the tea. Occasionally he'd drink half the tea, pause for a moment, eat the bun, then finish off the tea. It was a rare and splendid moment, and they'd clap politely, not too loud, for they had no wish to disturb him. They had no wish to disturb anything.

For the Pot Hole, the coins were rolling in. The horse was free but there was still food to be eaten and soup to be drunk, and the men would gather and eat and wait for the horse's moment on the hour to come. It was a social event. Lot would bring the bag to The Vicarage and Louis would spill out the coins and watch Lot count them and note them down, and each day the stacks grew a little taller and the words between them became thinner. And one night, Louis waiting on the porch, she came up late, stood before him, out of breath. She had her bag with her. He could see the weight of the coins.

'I'm not stopping,' she said. 'It's an expensive business keeping a horse. He had to call the vet out last week to look at one of his hooves.' She shook the bag at him. 'Might as well put this to some use.'

Louis stuck his hand in his pocket.

'Two-timed by a horse. I'll never live it down.'

'Is this jealousy I'm hearing? And you not given me a second look since our wedding day.'

'Our wedding weekend,' Louis countered. 'Two nights, if I remember correctly.'

It had meant nothing, a joke, the wedding a wager. The men were always trying it on. She had to give as good as she got. One night, Louis chucking his charm around in public, she'd said she'd only go to Scarborough with him if he married her. He called her bluff, drove over the next day, registered the marriage there, put the banns out, wouldn't come near her for three weeks, everyone busting a gut, thinking she wouldn't go through with it. She couldn't back out, and, if the truth be told, she liked the idea of cocking a snoot at it all, religion, ceremony, the rules of courtship. Time up, he drove her over, married her in the council registry office, two witnesses pulled in off the street, barely able to keep straight faces. He'd booked the honeymoon suite and had a vintage

Bentley waiting outside, all plumed and ribboned as though it was a real marriage. They'd left their bags in the room, walked to the cliff-top gardens, admired the settings, spent time on the sands, had their photograph taken, eaten tea and cake, once held hands. She'd been amazed how well he got on with everyone, the deckchair attendant, the man with the beer-drinking donkey, the woman behind the whelk stall, the way he moved amongst them, as if he'd done it all his life. He was as she'd always hoped him to be away from the gang, a natural gentleman. For two days she had imagined herself the woman for him. The line in his eye, the cut of his chat, had long assured her of that, and there it seemed to have taken form, but when they came back and had fallen into the old routines, she'd understood she was no more than the Euclid or the ten-ton loader, a part of the motorway engine, and she the quirk that all such engines possessed.

'You had to make sure of the bet,' she said. 'Otherwise, it would have been the one night, I think.'

'I've never laid another since.'

'I put you right off, right?'

'Put me off betting, Lot. No cause for complaint where you were concerned.'

'Makes me sound like a men's hostel. And here was me imagining you saw me as flesh and blood.'

'Lot ...'

He watched her walk up, pull back the flap in the tent, duck in. She'd done that before, he thought, done it any number of times. He went to his locker, took out the cake tin, put it on the step outside. By the morning, it had gone.

Down at the Klondike, the traffic began to change. The weather came and the weather went, but the vigour in the muddy streets seemed to drain away, as if its energy had been sapped, its elasticity worn out. The Brummies voiced it first, coming back from the furniture van one evening.

'The place was empty,' Two exclaimed, his face flushed with a mixture of bewilderment and satisfaction. 'No one there at all. They were that pleased to see us, we had two for the price of one. Just like Tesco's.'

'Been like that all week,' his brother added. 'They're thinking of pulling out.'

Life at the Klondike was slowly shutting down; the drinking contests were suspended; no one knocked on The Vicarage door in search of arbitration – there were no scores to settle. At the bookie's, Messrs Crawford and Stokes folded up their children's easel, no fights, no boxing, no wagers on the weather, no takers at all. One Sunday night, under cover of darkness, the furniture van and the six women inside it were driven away. Anything like that, they had to drive over to Huddersfield or Rochdale. But why drive to Huddersfield or Rochdale when you had the horse? The Micks built a proper shelter for him. Winter was coming and, when the access road became unreachable, he'd have to take his tea and bun under decent cover. The squaddies ran a cable up from the Cage for the heating and lights. Wall-Eye arrived one morning with an embroidered rug emblazoned with the sun, sang to the animal while he laid it across his back. It was a fitting adornment. The horse was on a crusade, purpose and destiny in every step. The Vicarage kept themselves apart. At the close of day they'd see Lot walking up past them, up into the tent. It was hard to say what went on in there. It seemed unlikely, the obvious thing. One thing was clear. Louis's writ was running on empty. He'd look from The Vicarage and see deserted streets and lights out. A ghost town was taking shape.

A month later, he bit the bullet, brought in two rule-breaking crates of beer, five packs of untipped and a box of unsalted, gathered the boys of The Vicarage together.

'If we don't put an end to it,' he said, 'we're finished.'

'You mean you're finished.'

Pete's directness surprised them. Louis refused to rise.

'He's a clever bastard, no doubt about that,' Hogan said. 'He's done it without firing a shot.'

'It's my belief he's putting something in Lot's tea,' Brummie One said, his mouth full of crisps. 'No leg-over for three weeks, and I'm not missing it like I should be.' Brummie Two banged open a bottle on the edge of the table.

'He's got accomplices,' he said, 'like a what-you-call-it … a fifth column.' An idea struck him. 'What about those bastards from Cornwall? They don't eat anything from the Pot Hole. Did you ever wonder why?'

'There's nothing wrong with Lot's tea,' Gil countered. 'I was in Bradford last week, visiting a lady friend. No complaints from her.' Louis was sharp.

'It's not the man I worry about. It's the horse. How do I fight a horse?'

'Paint it a different colour,' Gil suggested, knowing it to be a foolish suggestion, looking for another. 'Or you could race it.'

There was a stir.

'How do you mean, Gil?' Louis said, interested.

'Across the moor. The horse against the Muskeg. You might win that.'

'You could dress up for it,' Pete said. 'Like a cowboy.'

'Would you leave off about dressing up. A race … ?'

Hogan stood up.

'But why would he accept?' he said. 'He doesn't need to. He's the new religion. He holds communion. With that trick with the horse, he's even got the wafer and the wine. He doesn't need to *do* anything,' and though they went round it, they found no answer to Hogan's observation. Two hours getting nowhere, Louis swung the door open, fanning in fresh air. Lot was walking up late, money bag in hand, slowed down when she saw him in the doorway, the night cold and settled, the wind playing with the light they'd strung outside. She could see the boys sat round the table, empty bottles and crisp packets, smoke clouds pouring out into night. She wore the man's overcoat Louis had bought for her a couple of years back. Made her look like Greta Garbo, he'd said, the Greta Garbo of meat pies and mascara.

'What's this, Louis, a council of war?'

He moved out, pulled the door to. He was in his shirt-sleeves. He lived for moments like this, the bitter wind on his chest and Lot standing there in her overcoat.

'What else do you expect me to do?'

'A council of war.' She repeated the words, sparked by the idea. These were her men of old. She'd slept with two of them: Louis, and once, when they both should have known better, with Hogan, though no one else knew. He'd been big and funny, and not much use, but that was part of his charm.

'What's the plan then? Nothing bad for the horse, I hope.'

It warmed her, to see them again, together and animated. She'd missed them, despite her leanings. She had seen in the man and the horse a sort of salvation for her. She'd walk back at night as if she'd come away with the promise of a break in her life, that the tent and the horse were visions of something new. And here was the Louis of old, acting as if the cold couldn't touch him.

'The horse! How do I fight a horse? Do you know his name yet?'

She wanted to embrace him, feel his hard, unforgiving body, tell him to his lips that she did not know the horse's name.

'Why fight them at all?' she said. 'He's a good man, trying to do good.'

'Not for the road, that's for sure.'

'Is that all you care about, the road?'

'Why shouldn't it be? It's all what's left of me, after I've gone. What's he doing, messing with it? I need to make this road perfection. You of all people should know that.'

'Some would say it's blasphemy, even to consider such a possibility.' Louis brushed theology aside.

'The best they can do then. And if they lay the road without a drink or a woman or a brawl waiting for them, it won't work. They'll have nothing but servitude in them.'

'And decency, we say goodbye to that, here of all places?'

Louis ran his fingers across his breastplate.

'I saw a TV show once,' he said, 'about religious paintings, the Virgin Mary and baby Jesus and all that carry-on, how all the models for the painters were women from the furniture vans of yore. Baby Jesus feeding on a tart's milk.'

Lot was surprised.

'You're an artist now, Louis?'

'Isn't every man jack of us here one? This motorway, this is our oil painting, our Virgin Mary. There she'll lie, framed by the moor, full and swollen, running on a vision. And he'll bring her down to earth! We're rising her up to heaven, man.

You know what they all need after a week's graft: a night buried in drink or a pair of thighs, their wages chucked in the air, fall where they may.' He pointed to Lot's bag. 'Not into his pocket.'

'He wants nothing for himself.'

'His blessed horse, yes, I know. It will do no good, this ridden-in morality. You know what this road is going to be? The only motorway in England running east to west – Hull at one end and, once it joins Manchester, Liverpool at the other, the greatest trade route you could think of, Moscow to New York and this wonder the link in between. The men who built Suez, the Panama, they suffered cholera, yellow fever, dysentery, but when it was done they'd brought worlds together, continents, centuries, civilisations. This is the same. This road is reaching for the stars, and thanks to your man and his horse, we're walking around on tiptoe, like we're afraid to wake the …'

He let the word fall.

'And after this one, what?'

'How do you mean?'

'After this road, what then? You've said it yourself, there'll never be another one like this. What then? Peru?'

'I've no idea. That's why I need to …' he looked up '… regain the hold of it.'

She thought then she might never see him again, wanted to tell him as best she could, dress it up a bit.

'You're right about one thing. Without the horse … ' She gulped at the air, the coat suddenly damp and heavy on her. 'Whatever happens, this is it for me. No more road sites. Don't look so surprised. I'm getting old, Louis. Whatever it is, I'll never find it here.'

She waited for him to contradict her, but he didn't. She turned to go, a shaft of inspiration lighting her way. He was Louis and she had married him for all the wrong reasons, but there lay a loyalty between them for all that.

'What's better than a horse, Louis? What always beats a horse? Did Scarborough teach you nothing?'

Louis disappeared two days later, the night the weather fell back upon them, and the Klondike battened down tight. There was talk that he'd set out across the moor ready to be swallowed up by the land he could no longer govern, and though no one wanted to, many believed it to be so. Where else could he go? What else could he do? Men searched the gullies and ravines for signs, found nothing. The moor kept its secrets close. The weather lifted, the work resumed. And with Louis gone, the horse became almost luminous. He ate his bun, he drank his tea and he looked out over his conquered territory swarming with the beetle life of men. He stood in his horseshoes and they wondered at his shining strength, the purity of his intelligence, how it all gathered in this stilled momentum. The horse spoke, not simply to the hidden corners of these fallen men, but to the small creatures they had been and the excited innocence that had once surged within them. They looked at the horse and imagined him rearing up, stallion magnificent. They saw him paw the frontier air, thunder down the dusty valley, outlaws fleeing from his fiery mane. He knew what was right and he knew what was wrong. He was a horse, a horse for good. There was no escape.

Then one clear day, Hogan was with Pete and Gil laying open catch-water drains, their hands so bruised it was getting difficult for them to work their fingers. The heat had been upon them all day, and they were sat, looking down the scarred flat of earth where the motorway would lie, and the great steep of the embankment below as it prepared itself. It was a sort of miracle, that embankment. In years to come it would hold back four thousand million gallons of water and hold up a six-lane motorway. Hidden beneath the steadiness of its slope lay a science of gauges and pressure cells way beyond their understanding. Still, it was a dam, built of clay and sandstone, and this they knew and understood. They had built it and knew it wasn't finished with them yet. A mile away, the sweep of Scammonden Bridge had sprung up, a rainbow straddling the battered gorge. They were smoking a refreshing cigarette, taking it all in. Seeing the bridge in place was the first indication of the true beauty of the beast. They saw the moor differently now, and they were different men upon it. Before the horse they'd stamped their boots upon the face of it, regardless to what went on inside, how it moved and trembled underneath. They had work to do but thanks to the horse they had heard the moor breathe.

'It's like a fairy tale, that bridge,' Hogan said. 'You know, like in a kids' book, like you could walk across it to another world.'

Pete said nothing, gave him a little nudge.

'What is it?' Hogan said.

'Over there,' Pete said. 'Coming down the access road, left-hand side. The fairy with the hat.'

Hogan looked. A figure appeared to be wobbling down the slope, legs oddly loose and the figure rocking from side to side, as if he was drunk. Then he realised it was not simply a man, but a man on a donkey. A man on a donkey and both of them wearing hats. They recognised the hat at first, then the figure, single-minded in the saddle.

'It's never …' said Hogan.

'It sure is,' said Pete. 'Dang me if it ain't.'

The news ran through. Louis was back! On a donkey, a donkey with a grey brushed coat and with the name Pearl written out in seashells across the brim of her hat. Slung across her back were saddlebags and a leather bucket, and the saddlebags clinked as she stepped out on hooves that were painted gold.

The men blared their horns, banged their shovels, lined up on the road as Louis and the donkey ambled past, Louis staring straight ahead, as though he couldn't see them, and only the view between the donkey's ears, the cut of the valley and the highway ahead, bore him any significance. He rode steady, past the spot where the horse and Jonas looked down, until he was standing halfway across the dam, a good sixty men bunched around, all work suspended. Louis was back!

He pulled up, slid off, slid off as if he'd been sliding off donkeys all his life. He scratched Pearl's ears and patted her flank. He kissed her nose. Her front hooves stamped the earth in pleasure. He walked round and pulled at the leather straps, released the saddlebags, laid them on the ground. No one spoke. They'd watched their westerns. They knew all about saddlebags.

Louis unhitched the leather bucket, and opened the saddlebags, revealed the clinking to be bottles of Guinness, which he set down, then placed at their rear bottles of champagne, with tops the colour of the donkey's feet. Like a toy army it was, the soldiers on parade and the officers in their plumed hats. Louis opened up the bottles, filled the leather bucket first with the Guinness then with the champagne. The mixture fizzed and frothed. They could smell it in the air. Louis raised his voice.

'That there is Black Velvet, and Pearl here can drink a bucket of it without drawing breath. Who thinks he can drink faster than my Pearl? I bet no man.' Voices in the crowd warmed Louis's heart.

'A donkey. You think I can't outdrink a donkey?'

'A lady donkey at that.'

'Bloody waste of porter.'

The donkey moved up, no hesitation. A ring was formed round her and the bucket. They heard the steadied slurp, stood transfixed at the brown ears twitching back and forth, the tail whisking, not from side to side, but up and down, as a pump. Drink over, the donkey raised her head, shook the big dark drops from her lips. Louis spoke again, strands of orchestration running through his fingers.

'Once a day she has her Black Velvet, and once a day she'll have it here. The man who outdrinks her … I'm putting up last month's wages. Any man who does the same …'

The competition lasted one week, then two. Guinness was a familiar to all, champagne too, but not such a volume of it. When they drank the Black Velvet down it was as though their bodies had sprung a leak. Foam burst out their nostrils, violent belches erupted, hot and gassy. They could drink the stuff down all right, but they needed pause to rid their insides of the turbulent balloons that seemed to threaten the very safety of their skin. Pearl, bucket consumed, stood impassive, folds of Louis's winnings gathering in the band of her hat. The Cage regained its custom, the blackboard bearing chalk names of the next hopeful. Five days later, the Irish held their first official boxing match for two months, a Cornish carrot-top set against Wall-Eye's younger brother, the ring roped up and arc-lighted a quarter of a mile away, on a flat-bed of peat. Pearl rode the winner back into town. She was a winner herself. When the furniture van returned, there was a queue of thirty. Life coming back to the Klondike.

But what of the horse? What did the horse think? He stood on the rise, looked down across a plain of vanished influence. He drank his tea and ate his bun, but he drank and ate alone. Lot waited until he was done, but then she left him too, resumed her Klondike trundling. She had a business to attend to. No one ventured up to keep the horse company. They pitied the horse, felt for his loneliness, and the shadow it cast across the landscape, but they had a motorway to build, a moor to conquer and a conscience to wrestle with. They left the horse to stand on his own feet. He had four of them, after all.

The contest went on, but in a different form. No one could better Pearl's drinking speed, that much had become clear. Now it became a question of who could get closest to her time, which man amongst men would emerge as nearly as good as a donkey. It aroused fierce competition. Form and ritual were all. Pearl moved up to her bucket, the new competitor to his. Louis stood between them, ready for the Raising of the Lids. The Raising of the Lids promoted as much excitement as the drinking itself, for while every man began as he ended, as if his life depended on it, Pearl took her time before taking her first draught. It was as though she had come to recognise the immensity of her competitors' limitations, though whether it was kindness which held her back, or delight in humiliation, no one could determine.

And thus it remained until the hour the horse came down. He'd stood, week on week, white and lonely, with only the weather for company, Jonas sometimes saddled up, but mostly unmoving by his side, as though, like the horse, he no longer knew what purpose they served. It had been a heat of a day. Louis had the buckets prepared. Pearl stood impassive in her hooves. Her rival flexed his wrestler pecs, bare-chested. They were all ready for it.

Louis was in the act of Raising the Lids, when Pearl lifted her head, and looked over the scruff of her back. Picking his way off the slope came the horse, his steps light but deliberate. The crowd parted. The horse threaded through, Jonas follow-ing, like a man might with a plough. Men took their hats off as they passed, bowed their heads. The horse had a face like a saint.

Jonas laid a hand on the flat of his companion's neck.

'The horse has come to see what all the fuss is about,' he said. Louis held the lids high, as though they were cymbals. The air filled with percussion.

'Is that his name then?' he said. 'Cloth Ears? Deaf to all around him.'

A shiver of disapproval ran through the horde. It was not right for Louis to treat the horse so. The horse was good. They were shamed too, for hadn't they shunned the horse, turned away from his big head and his big eyes and the stare that had corralled all their misdemeanours? Doubt shuffled in their boots. How could they have ignored the Big Stare! And now he was come amongst them again.

Louis pointed to the buckets, anxious to regain ground.

'It's Pearl against all-comers,' he said. 'He's welcome to try, if you think he's got the bottle for it. It's not exactly teacups at dawn.'

'A contest, you mean?' Jonas asked.

A gasp went up. The donkey versus the horse! Now there was a match. She had a drinker's experience, but a horse's stomach must be twice the size of a donkey's. And the throat on him! If he had the temperament … The men closed in, straining for the answer.

'There's two ways of looking at Scammonden,' Louis said. 'The horse's way, and Pearl's way. Who empties the bucket first has the last word. Only one set of shoes for this road.'

The word went round. Machines were abandoned to the dust. The crowd thickened. The boys from the Cage wiped their easel clean, started chalking up fresh odds. Jonas spoke out loud.

'No betting,' he said. 'It's not money he's playing for.'

Not money! Of course, not money! As if the horse would play for money! And in truth, it was not even the road the horse was playing for, but the men themselves! This was God's dice in play, thrown under their own sky.

Jonas moved the buckets further apart to give the beasts room. Pearl moved on to hers, the horse on to his. Louis lifted the lids.

Later, it would be disputed when the donkey began her drinking, her last drinking as it turned out, for all eyes were on the horse, and the manner in which he hung his head above the bucket, like a teardrop waiting for the fall. Light rose from the bucket's black mirror, a dappled reflection that played upon the horse's closed lips and his long, velvet muzzle, a caress of something close to faith. His lips parted. He licked the light from around his mouth, took it within. A quiver ran down his back.

Movement turned the men's eyes. Pearl had her head buried in deep, the lap of her tongue steady like a pendulum. A sigh went up. It was a sound they all knew, the lure of the full glass, the desire of the open throat, the sweet pleasures to be found in the company of drinking lips. It was as good as fucking, drinking with other drinkers, better some would claim. It is why they loved her. Pearl's tail grew vigorous. She had a belting thirst on!

The horse stared down. He had not moved. What he saw in the bucket, no one knew, only that the inside was black and still, a beckoning into the unknown. Would the horse be afraid of the unknown? It did not seem likely, but there he stood, as though suspended, while his rival drank, oblivious to his equivocation. She was a drinker. That is all she knew, and all she needed to know.

The horse stretched his neck, shook his head to the sky. A call came from his throat, not a whinny, nor a neigh, but something like a shudder conceived deep inside him, moving beyond the men and their motorway, beyond his own horsiness, and it held them uneasy. Pearl halted mid-drink. Froth dripped from her mouth. She looked at the horse and the horse looked at her. They had been together on Scammonden for a while now, yet this was the first time they had met, the first time an exchange had taken place. What could it be? They were beasts, but a horse was a horse and a donkey was a donkey. What did they share? What separated them?

The horse moved forward, so that his front legs stood over the bucket, and his back legs splayed like a broken chair. Out of nowhere, his thing appeared, thick and long and with a dome shining on the end like a polished doorknob. Had they seen it before? No one could remember, but it was uncanny, the way it appeared, like their very own, but impossibly heavy, and not even stretched. Everyone knew what it was for, the multitasking of it, but it was difficult to take in, a thing like that. Pearl shook her head and went back to her drinking, her rhythm back on trim. Louis rubbed his hands. There was no way the horse could beat her now. A muttering went up. The crowd agreed. The contest was losing its edge.

Then it happened. Before the year was over Pete would have written a song about it, three heroic verses and a vulgar chorus, but he rarely got asked to perform it. The event was celebrated, though. Every time a bunch of them were getting stuck in and rose up for the gents, it was celebrated. There was an envy about what the horse did that couldn't be washed away. For blow them all, just when they thought it was all over, didn't the horse's hose spring up to life and start pissing the whole deck of cards, not just pissing as any old horse might, not giving a toss where the play landed, but pissing in an arc so ferociously perfect that it splashed down right on target, smack into the mouth of his untouched bucket. Oh, they'd all pissed into buckets in their time, but this! The sound echoed down the valley like a roll of drums, like it was Agincourt or the Valley of Death, like the world might turn on this moment. On and on it went, like there was no tomorrow, like it was seven rounds in the ring and the bell ringing for them to stop and the horse taking no notice, but looking from right to left at their gawping faces like butter wouldn't melt, while the steam and the stream and the sound of his monstrous flow ravished their champagne and their Guinness and wiped their own book of records clean with the sacrilege. They all knew what he was doing. This wasn't about the champagne or Guinness or the prowess of his throat. The horse was running in a different race altogether, and they stood silenced at the nerve and the sparkling brilliance of his aim. And then he stopped. Right up to the moment when the champagne and Guinness and his own contribution were wavering on the lip of the bucket, ready to spill out on to the ground, he pissed, and then he stopped, like a tap. His great thing, whatever it was, penis, cock, they didn't want to give it names, retreated inside, job done, his bucket now twice as full as when the competition had started. Pearl's head had all but disappeared as she neared the finish.

'I think you'll find …' Louis said, but got no further. The horse span round and, with one great kick of his hind legs, sent his bucket clean into the air. It landed upside down at Louis's feet, his clothing mostly drenched.

'I think you'll find,' Jonas said, 'that he has emptied his bucket first.'

'That was not the way to do it at all,' Louis said. He felt an idiot saying it.

'Your words, not mine,' Jonas said. 'As if he'd fill his stomach with such stuff. He's a horse. His needs are honest horse's needs, earth and shelter and companionship. Same as her needs should be an honest donkey's needs. Same as all your needs should be honest men's, and not …'

And then he and the horse walked away.

Had the horse won? Had Pearl? Had the horse cheated? He'd emptied the bucket, but they all knew what had been meant by the wager. But whose fault was that? A wager was a wager. It was some clever horse if he'd figured it out on his own. And the pissing like that! He'd always acted so polite, with his tea and his bun. But they were men. They appreciated such marksmanship. Take some training surely. Pearl might have won, but no one could say what it was she had won. No one could say that the horse had lost either. Lost what? Not dignity. Not nerve. The horse had been the horse and the donkey had been the donkey. They were beasts, beasts against them all – the captivity, the demands, the indignities …

The arguments went around the camp. They did not feel cheated, nor did they feel satisfied. One thing was certain. No one was interested in drinking against Pearl again. The horse had kicked the fizz out of that one. Thus, they went to their cabins, puzzled. But when they woke, they found the horse gone, broken loose from his moorings, gone to the treachery of the moor. Little work was done that day, as they roamed the ravines in search of him, but no sight of the horse could they find. It was the drink, the expectations laid upon him. A horse like that, the very fumes could have done for him. Even The Vicarage felt bad about the horse. No victory at all. Louis took it worst of all.

Jonas and the tent packed up soon after. Lot barely spoke a word, her heart shrunk up. Louis drove Pearl back to her home on Scarborough sands. When he returned he found Lot gone too. Scammonden lay incomplete, but for Louis the thrill had gone.

'I can't bear the thought of seeing this finished,' he told Hogan. 'Best fuck of my life, this beauty. Want to remember her that way.'

He scouted for new work. Two months later he found a job down south, roped in a new car for the journey, an A55 Cambridge Farina Mark II. The Vicarage packed their bags with him as usual, but their ties were slackening. The day they left, Louis took them down to where the water still ran, rolled up his sleeve, stuck an old medicine bottle under, let the moor gurgle in. Back in the car he turned the engine over.

'Tune up those banjos, boys,' he said. 'Time to play a different tune.'

The story hung over them the rest of the day, Hogan clean in his socks and the beer he'd brought no use at all. When he went to bed, Chester laid his lips on Aunty Lot's cheeks, first one side and then the other, felt them worn and feathery and, for the first time, distant, as if they had retreated, afraid of exposure.

Then she was standing by his bed, one hand fingering the shirt laid over the back. It was dark, but no longer night.

'Don't go,' she said.

'What?' He squinted. 'What do you mean?'

'Don't play me for a fool, Chess. Don't you think I don't know you after all these years.'

He struggled up. He had an erection, dragged his blanket into a heap.

'You're everything to me, Chess.'

He didn't know what to say.

'What else can I do?' he said. 'He's my father and she's …'

She took the shirt up, folded it neat, draped it back down.

'Your mother, yes I know. I shouldn't say this, but I was glad when they both went. It was just you and me then, all I ever wanted. Ever since I saw you, when you took me to the den, you were all I've ever wanted. There. I've said it now. Don't kiss me goodbye then. Leave it like you haven't gone away, not for good.'

THE MORNING HE WOKE and felt himself in it, the instant his eyes opened. Would he know where to go? Psyche had searched for Cupid, but Cupid was in heaven lying in his mother's royal bed, groaning with pain. Louis? Was he in pain? News from Scarborough beach suggested he was. His mother rode out the water like a goddess, seagulls diving haloes round her head. A white gull had plunged into the water where Venus had been bathing, bringing her the news of her ailing son. Pleasure, Grace and Wit had disappeared from the face of the earth, she had been told. Everything had become ugly and dull and slovenly. Was that the lie of land that he must travel through? It seemed to him he had lived a fantastic yet captivated life, held in by doctrines and practices that existed only in the Hovel and by the clearing. He would mark the difference soon enough.

He got to his feet. There on the wall stood the Brebis with the big eyes and the road behind her, rising to the land beyond. In the foreground the donkey was still tied to the tree. Black crayons Alice had used for the outline, pots of poster paint and jam jars to mix them in, his mother's painted footprints still marked on the floor. He followed them up to the wardrobe, brought out the paintbox. In eastern Tibet, a painter had drawn fantastical beings with human bodies and animal heads, the supposed attendants of the temple, his son beside him, amused at the monstrous forms looming up inside his father's frescoes. When the boy died and entered the bardo, he met the terrible creatures whose images were so familiar to him. Far from being frightened he began to laugh. 'Oh, I know you all,' he said, and wished only to play with them. Chester felt the same, stood in front of them, smiling.

'Well here we are,' he said, 'you and me.'

He spat on the depressed square of white, picked up a brush, licked it loose, then worked the point in. He raised the brush to where the donkey stood, leant his elbow against the wall, and painted out the rope.

'There,' he said. 'The road to freedom.'

In Greenland they'd worn a set of woollen underclothing, one or two sweaters and trousers made of blanket material. It wasn't Greenland, but the weather would come, some day. He packed a satchel with two pairs of trousers, a spare shirt and all his socks, eased open his door. Where Hogan had lain his head was not certain: not the kitchen and not the porch. Outside the Triumph stood cloaked in black. There seemed to him a lightness to the air, as though the gravity of the forest had been lifted, as though every step taken would be momentous, a moon-leap, dust on the ground, and only footprints left. A giant leap, wasn't that his mother's phrase? Whole sentences rattled in his head. Greek sailors were very reluctant to cross the open sea, even with the help of the sun and the stars to guide them. They skirted the headlands and rocks they knew, wary of shoals beneath the surface. Living things pass through a period of childhood and youth, and are filled with memories of ancestral history. The true traveller has his mind set unflinchingly to its aim, indifferent to the phantoms and obstacles and mirages and enticements of the road. Wesley had found salvation round the next corner. He'd woken with the passion of his own campaign on his lips. 'You are all fine fellows,' Captain Scheldrup had told the Greenland expedition, 'but I am afraid you will not all see London again. One of you will go through a crack in the ice. Plonk!'

A journey would never be complete unless the leaving of it was correct. Which book had said that? He couldn't remember but he remembered the promise he'd made to Aunty Lot. He grabbed a spade, caught the bus. He walked down the aisle, his body thrilled at the swaying movement of it. He sat by a window, face out, streets he'd known gathering momentum. He'd cycled to college down there, gone to the cinema a couple of times too. Any minute the bus would pass the turning into Angela's street, her house third down on the right. He could see it now, the blue front door, the upstairs front room. His rabbit. He'd never dug him up … A group of men climbed aboard, men with purpose, calling the driver by name, offering up early-morning jokes, their bodies not trembling with uncertainty like his, but oiled with knowledge of their world, their actions grooved like a carpenter's hand. Chester filled his lungs, counted them all, seventeen men, men with closed eyes and open newspapers, men who had washed and shaved and held women …

A tap had come on the shoulder again.

'Here we go, mate.'

He picked up his spade, marched over. It was early, even for allotment faithfuls. He didn't need to do this. Hogan would do it. Hogan would be only too glad to do it. In the strip three lots down, a young woman emerged from the owner's hut. She squinted to the sun, then caught sight of him. Angela.

'What the fuck are you doing here,' she said. 'Checking up on me or something?'

She stood defiant, dark hair dyed blonde, shirt tied in a knot above her jeans, eye make-up on the run, skin paled by the wilful race she ran. She was working in a tax office, good money, an affair with her line manager and in a great, obstinate mess.

'I didn't know.'

'No. You're just Chester, the Epping stalker.' She put a hand out. 'I didn't mean that. Couldn't go home last night. Trouble waiting. Cup of tea?'

He'd never imagined her making tea. She took him back. Inside was more than a shed. It had a stove like a drain and a lamp hanging from the crossbeam. There was a table with chairs and a tea caddy and a Primus and a tin of dried milk upon it. She pointed to the armchair in the corner, a jacket over the back and a cushion and blanket in a heap on the floor.

'Home sweet fucking home eh?'

Chester sat at the table. Birds were singing. She straightened his hair, fingers on his temple.

'Biscuit?'

She opened the tea caddy, took out a packet.

'Help yourself.'

Chester prised a biscuit out. It came apart in his fingers. He was annoyed at the clumsiness. He took another, eased it out carefully. It was somehow important, to hold something unbroken in his hands, as if it represented the whole bearing of his journey. It was only a biscuit, but it had a name stamped upon it and the rim seemed like the edge of a whole world, fresh and clean. He was holding something perfectly formed, and he wished for a moment that it was himself he was holding, the whole of him, instead of the part that he was, or a spring-cleaned Hovel with Aunty Lot carpet-beating out the back, or life itself, hold it all still for him to see and feel and touch. If he could carry in his mind something whole, take it with him, bring it out at will, how well he could live off that, whatever happened.

Angela sat before him, the light falling immaculate upon her. Never held a woman and yet there she was, breathing the same air, their chests rising and falling in the same swim of life. Suddenly it seemed a sacrilege, to hold something so idiotic as a whole biscuit in his fingers. He cracked it in half, spoke with his mouth full.

'I've something to tell you,' he said.

'Don't tell me. You're already married.'

'They've been seen, Alice and Louis. I'm leaving, see if I can … find them again.'

'Seen where?' She was excited, her own troubles forgotten.

'Scarborough. A couple of weeks back. Louis was … something's happened to him. She was carrying him, like he was an invalid. Hard to imagine, Dad a …'

She nodded, like she could picture it.

'Sounds, you know, like a stroke, like what my gran had. Lived for years after though. Where the fuck's Scarborough?'

'Up the east coast.'

'You find them? Then what?'

He shrugged his shoulders. She pushed her chair back, swivelled round, made room for herself on his lap. He shifted her bulk. Her back was resting against his arm, almost an embrace. He said nothing. She was warm and fierce. They both knew it.

'You're not coming back, are you?' she said. 'Your childhood sweetheart's not sweet enough for you, is she?'

She brushed the hair from his forehead again. His hand pressed into her back, conscious of the strangeness of it. He had a woman in his hands, a woman with her whole life within her. She ran across his cheek with the back of her fingers. It was easy.

'There's this man in the office, Chess.' He squeezed his eyes shut.

'I don't want to hear about it.'

'It don't mean nothing. I'm crazy about him, but I'm not stupid. It won't go nowhere. It's like, I can't help it, like there's nothing else for me. I don't want much, but not just this, you know. But I don't know where to look.'

How could he tell her where to look, with all the mysteries of her on his lap?

'You know where to look,' she said. 'Even when you don't. That's why you're like a little worm in my head, why I can't get you out of me, why ...'

'Angie.'

'Don't call me that. That's what he calls me. I bloody hate it. They go on holiday next week. The Algarve. I was think-ing of turning up there, give the bastard a heart attack, get a proper tan. He's way smaller than me, too. I'm fucking a married midget.'

He turned her face to his.

'Don't,' he said. 'Look for miracles instead.'

She stared at him. His eyes were sudden bright. He felt his arm press into her, his fingers grasping a fold of her flesh.

'There's miracles everywhere,' he said, 'lying all around. You have to look for them, that's all.'

'But none here in the forest, right?'

He lifted her off, animated.

'Who knows? There's a fork. I've got a spade. Let's dig for one. Take it back home.'

She looked at him, half-amused, half-angry, wholly uncertain.

'What, in this?' She shook at the knot. 'This is brand-new Debenham's.'

'Take it off then.'

She sized him up. That was the thing. She never got him. She'd tried, God how she'd tried, but she never got him. Just when she thought she had him, he turned a corner. Miracles.

'You and everybody else,' she said.

She pulled open the belly knot, threw the shirt on the chair. Her brassiere was pearly white, roses round the rim.

'Which is easier, the fork or spade?' she said. He pointed to the fork.

Clouds covered the sky. She knelt on a length of torn sacking, levering out stubborn couch grass, angry with herself. What the hell was she doing?

'You saying this is what I should do to get in Dad's good books?'

'Why not? Wouldn't need the Algarve for a tan neither.'

'Can't go there anyway now, the state of my nails.' She sat on her haunches, looked back at her handiwork. 'Looks good, them weeds gone.'

'They'll all come up again.'

'Like your common or garden prick.' She ran her hand over the ground she'd worked on, pulling at one she'd missed.

He watched her return to the weeding, fingers dug into the earth, dark roots of her hair coming up through the blonde, the length of her back and the hip sway of her. The sun came out, warming their bodies. They worked in silence, he upright, she on her knees, the fork awkward in her hands. He could work the spade and not take his eyes off her. She was a miracle all by herself. He could see them coming here day after day, week after week, see it becoming their allotment. In time there'd be a family, a baby, miracle on miracle. She could feed it here, bare her breasts here, happy to do so. He'd carry the baby on his shoulders. They'd grow settled together, the forest gathering its limbs about them. Every night he'd hold her and every morning he'd wake with her by his side. He could be a man on a bus, a man cycling to work, sitting at a desk, learning. They were working the earth, never been so close. Soon, he'd never see her again.

He stuck the spade into the ground.

'If I asked you,' he said, 'would you run around the allotment naked with me?'

'What?' She stopped, looked up.

'If I asked you to.'

'Is this some sort of joke?'

'I'm serious.'

She stood up, faced him across the waste of grass.

'You want me to run around Dad's allotment with you?'

'Without any clothes on, yes.'

She folded her arms. It's what she did at the office.

'Then what?'

'Then we put our clothes back on and we go our separate ways.'

'What's all this about?'

'I want to remember you, everything about you. I want to be me in front of you, and you in front of me, like for once there's nothing else, nothing in between.'

She stared at him. He wasn't afraid, that was the marvellous thing.

'Just run round?'

'We don't have to run. We could walk, in fact walking would be better, like it's serious, who we are. I'm Chester and I'm leaving and you're Angela and you're staying. We're saying goodbye, all we want is … I don't know …'

'To be who we are.'

'That's it.'

She studied his face. They were the same height and nearly the same age, and they'd known each other most of their lives.

'God, you scare me; ever since I've known you, you've scared me. You want we do it now?'

They walked back to the shed. Angela handed him the fork. Chester stacked it behind the door. He took off his shoes, slipped off his trousers and then his underwear, kicked them across the floor with his foot.

'You're whiter than a creepy-crawly,' she said. Her hand went to her belt. 'This isn't the first time I've taken my clothes off here, you know.'

'Yes, it is.'

They stood motionless, the naked boy hands awkward by his side, the young woman wild and tender.

'If Tarzan would step outside,' she said, 'Jane will join him in a jiffy.'

He stepped outside. A pair of bullfinches were swinging on a sunflower feeder, their breasts pink and plump in the sun. He heard her boots drop to the floor. There was movement, the creak of a belt, an intake of breath, and then she was standing by his side.

'Well, here we all are then,' she said. 'I thought you'd have a tattoo, knowing your mum. I'm going to get one too. Something that tells everyone to fuck off and leave me alone.'

'Stick that on then. "Fuck off and leave me alone."'

They laughed. He'd never felt so happy. She was feeling it too.

'Where do you think? Front or back?'

She span round.

'More room on the back.' He put out his arm. 'Can I take your hand?'

She put her hand to her mouth. The whole symmetry of her rose.

'You've got me stark naked and you're asking if you can hold my hand? You should be a monk.'

She held it out. They started walking. The ground was uneven, stones sharp under their feet.

'Not as easy as it looks,' she said. 'We should have kept our feet on. Remember when you lit the cake? You were looking at it like you were pushing your life out, and I knew then you'd do it, that you'd go off, push your life out, and that it would burn somewhere, somewhere real bright without me ... and I thought, God, if only I could be like that, dedicated to something that was mine ...'

She stopped.

'Look at me.'

'I am looking at you.'

'Not the eyes, Dumbo. Look me up and down, look at it all. It's got me in a lot of trouble, this body of mine. Now it's like it doesn't matter. Christ, I've never been like this.'

There were tears in her eyes.

'I'm pregnant, Chess,' she said. 'Would you fucking believe it. All the fucking spermicides in the world and I'm pregnant.'

Chester felt a door opening, and a light shining through it. 'Is it this man in the office?'

'How the fuck should I know?' she said. 'What am I going to tell them at home? Dad'll kill me.'

'Tell him it was me.'

'Don't be bloody stupid. You'd be lying next to your badger within the week. Big on respect, they are.'

Chester sensed the motion in him changing gear. When Wesley rode with Grace Murray, they had stood the hard travelling together, twin souls for courage. There had been terrible Welsh mountains to scale and such rain and wind as to rob them of reason, but still he spoke and still he brought new hope. Finding Alice and Louis was just the beginning.

'Don't tell them anything, then. Come with me. First stop Scarborough. Help me find miracles. You and ...'

He laid a hand flat to her stomach. She was worried she might faint. She'd never had a hand on her like that, like it was listening to every part of her.

'What, now?' she said.

'This minute.'

She looked at him steady. There was a size to him, but it wasn't that. Or maybe it was, standing like an oak, like there were leaves and branches to grow, like there was a spread to him that would cover them all. Or maybe it was like he was willing her to spread, that she was an oak too, if only she would give herself the space ... Why shouldn't she? There were lots of reasons why she shouldn't. But why shouldn't she?

His hand was still pressed on her. She took it off, kissed the back of it.

'Better put some clothes on first?' she said.

The ride was seamless, like a magic-carpet ride. Angela stuck out her thumb and a car stopped, '76 Triumph Dolomite, and then all sorts, more foreign than Chester expected, modern too, a Volvo 440, an '87 Volkswagen Scirocco, a Hyundai Pony, like there was a different breed of car out there he hadn't reckoned on, electric windows, cassette players, and drivers with engines they didn't have to wish on. No rust neither. Rust had always been a big thing for their cars and now it wasn't there any more. Lots of things weren't there. They were riding over his father's skin, towards Huntingdon and the A1, the stages writ clear in his mind. Stump Cross came and Stump Cross went. It had been like dinosaurs when Louis had taken him there, machines like great lizards crawling along the surface of the earth, chewing up trees and grass, tiny men running alongside, blowing on little brass horns, but now, blink and it was gone. And he had a woman with him. He was conscious of her, more than the road. Sometimes they sat in the back together and she placed her hand over his, laid it on top, flat, like a body might lie on another. Other times he sat up front and she'd lean forward, hands over his seat and the breath of her like a feather on his neck, like he wanted a touch that wasn't there, that wasn't allowed. Everyone thought they were a couple and he supposed they were in a way. He didn't know what sort of couple, maybe never would. What was wrong about that?

A couple of hours in, a sporty Renault Turbo, the driver with holes in his pig-skin gloves, dropped them by a café, the A1 only just begun. They hadn't eaten all morning, not even brought the biscuits, she'd been so fired up for the leaving. Chester had suggested she wait until the coast was clear, go home and pack some gear, but wouldn't have it. She'd tapped her bag and kissed him cheeky on the cheek.

'Got all I need in here,' she'd said. 'Driving licence, cheque-book, banker's card and six fifty in cash.'

Chester hadn't even known what a banker's card was.

They went inside, sat by the window, the traffic constant and full of promise. They were travelling together, everywhere about them the place they should be. It was weird, the café, more like a cinema outside and inside, two men ran the place like on a stage, all mince and gestures, one blond, the other dark, tanned like an Italian. They sang to each other, slapped each other's hands, like they were playing tag, bawled out the orders to a three-cornered hat in the kitchen. The dark one made conspirator eyes at Angela as he took their order: bacon, egg and chips. Chester had seen him before, couldn't think when.

The food came brisk, piled up and smelling good.

'Chess here thinks he's seen you before,' Angela told him.

'Maybe in Epping?' Chester offered.

'Epping!' The man put his hand on his hip, called out. 'Have I been to Epping, Douglas?'

'Not in my lifetime.'

'Couldn't have been me then,' he said, and smoothed a napkin over Chester's lap. 'I was dead before I met this one.'

Then, back on the road, Chester remembered the night in the forest with the fish and Pete on his bed and the man he saw. Of course he'd be here, guiding him through without knowing it. Hadn't the books taught him anything?

They motored on, the day bright, cars gleaming, a Ford Sierra, a Peugeot 504 Estate, an eight-wheeler ball-breaker, bent on playing leapfrog, the road's power increasing in intensity. Chester could feel it under him, conscious of its magnetic pull, the way it held England together. He wondered whether it did for Scotland in the same manner. Was it the road that had made the Union possible rather than a king, that without this road it could not have happened? England, Scotland, they could bend this way and that, but it was the road which bound them together.

What was nationhood? Geography? People? Funny clothes? Or was it bits and pieces of stuff, like the clutter in a home: walls and bridges, canals and roads. America was held together by the buffalo trails, the great herds moving north to south, east to west, millions of beasts barrelling through the hills and over the great plains. They were the first roads on that continent, their routes followed still. Apart from the highways the Romans left, motorways were the only purposely built direct roads in Britain. After the Romans bunked off, roads went all over the place. Simple ownership decided. Bigger populations, greater demand would have straightened them out eventually, but the Industrial Revolution gave us steam and trains, and we didn't need straight roads any more. We had iron ones. But then the railways got ripped out. Time to strap on the roads again. That's how Louis had told it. He loved their shameless dominance. 'Nothing I like better,' he'd say, 'than the sight of a farm being bulldozed, everything pushed aside for six lanes of muscle and trim. Better than a catwalk, the promise on that.'

An old Datsun Cherry took them off the A1, on to the A64 towards Scarborough. The last car to pick them up was a four-cylinder Fiat Panda outside York, the smell of toffee in the air. They'd been travelling for seven hours, unsure how it would end. He saw the sign, but it was half a mile gone before the meaning lit him up: free-range eggs, the farmhouse stark on the hill, and a long drive from anywhere.

———

When Mrs Calvert opened the door, it was as if she was back in Brandon, her son, all grown up, coming in from the lake-front. She hadn't expected it, seeing a reflection of her own kind, the long frame, the lock of hair, the similar flick of the head. How old was he? It was the first thing she wanted to ask. But you couldn't start a conversation with a question like that. And the girl behind him. She was trying to hide it, but she could see it, plain as the nose on her face. Four months, five? She squinted at him, the light fuzzy round his head. She prepared to dislike him, dragging a woman in her condition around the country.

'Yes?' she said. He ran his fingers down the strap of his satchel.

'I was wondering,' he said, hesitant, 'if this might be the place a friend has told me about. He met someone who works here, a man had news of my mother and father.'

She stepped back, surprised.

'You mean Percy?'

'I don't know his name, only that he knew my father, had seen him recently, had seen them both. Alice and Louis.'

'Louis?' She could feel herself fluttering, like the start of the pulse of something.

'You know him?' She gathered herself.

'I know a Louis, yes. He used to buy our eggs.'

'That's him!' He turned to the young woman. 'Straight from Epping, Ange.'

Mrs Calvert gripped the door handle, a sudden flood come over her. She'd had a son once, running into excitement like this, as though the world could solve things unexpectedly, as through an unseen hand.

'You're Chester, aren't you?' She caught his startled look. 'Your father and I met a long while ago. When I was driving … Percy met him, you say, him and your mother?'

'In Scarborough. A few weeks back.'

So that's what it was.

'Percy's not here, I'm afraid,' she said. 'He left over a month ago, said the itch had come over him. Took the horse with him, promised he'd return. It was after …' She paused, catching the boy's bewilderment.

'He didn't just come for the eggs, you know, your father? Come, I'll show you.'

They followed her through the house. There was a door half-opened, a single bed, and a bedside table. Out in the yard, she led them to a barn, unlocked it.

'Recognise this?' she said and pulled back the cover. The Rover stood there, livery perfect. 'You took your first ride in this car, barely a week old, your mother in the back and your father behind the wheel. That's why he came here the last time, to see it. Then he …'

She stopped, thinking it through. Then he saw Percy, and he ran off. Chester hadn't noticed.

'And this was … ?'

'Years ago. Five? Couldn't take his eyes off it.'

The girl patted her stomach.

'I bet this one doesn't get to ride in a car like that.'

Mrs Calvert took her in. She was an angry, defiant thing, a bundle of contradictions.

'You never know,' she said.

Chester looked at the car. No, you never knew. Most people would call finding this car again a coincidence, like finding Percy was a coincidence, but he knew there weren't such things as coincidences, only the otherness of the world coming into play, like the ancients knew: beyond reason and explanation, divined only by the mechanics of mystery. Men put on white coats and called themselves scientists, yet what they described were just a means of removing another veil, to gain a glimpse of something we could never fully see, never fully grasp. The Rover was part of the other. It had carried him as a baby. Alice had sat in the back, Louis in the front. How many other times had he ridden in it?

'Could I hear the engine?' he said. Mrs Calvert shook her head. It wasn't a plaything, her Rover.

'Later, perhaps,' she said. 'She needs to eat first. Where are you heading for, after here?' Chester looked to the hills.

'Scarborough. That's where he saw them, on the beach. Perhaps they still visit. Perhaps others have seen them, seen their car. I don't even know what they drive.'

She weighed them up. What was their real story? Did it matter?

'Well you can stay here the night, if you like,' she said. 'The bed's small but … I don't suppose you two mind that.'

And the boy and the girl looked at each other as though they'd only just met. Sweet really, Mrs Calvert thought.

In the morning they made their thanks, caught the bus to Scarborough. They looked down along the sands, saw the man with the donkeys, the donkeys with the hats. He was an old man and most days he walked tired in the sun, the children running around him like flies. He had liked the children, but they flustered him now. The donkeys were never flustered, but he was so. Chester introduced himself, asked him as to Louis and Alice, and the old man remembered them, told Chester of a time when they had come in a party, four or five of them. 'No, what am I saying?' the old man said, remembering. 'There were seven of them, seven riders for eight donkeys, Louis taking *that* one, Pearl's sister, you know,' and Chester nodded, encouraging him to talk more, although he did not know, and the old man obliged, for it was early and the day's work not yet started, and it felt good for his voice to be heeded again amongst the young, and went on to tell them that he'd seen them once, maybe twice since, the woman rather than the man, last summer, or maybe this, too many faces to remember, right? He was getting old, he confessed. The donkeys were wearing him out, although what would become of them, if he packed it in, didn't bear thinking about. If they didn't earn their keep, who would pay for their winter feed? And Chester, thinking of the beach, and the summer yet to play itself out, and thinking too of Angela, and how, when it got too much for her, she could lie on the beach and keep an eye out, feeling safe and cared for in the salted air, told him the story of his missing parents and offered to look after the donkeys for him, brush their coats, walk them with the children, see to their feeding, do all the work going, him and his girl, offered themselves up with Angela standing next to him, hands clasped Madonna over where her child was growing. That morning, when she stood up out of bed, he'd noticed the swell of her right away, like a sock to the eye, it was so *there*, as if, once out of the forest, her pregnancy or the baby inside was no longer afraid to show its face, like they were all happy to show it. And the old man took them up, for he remembered Louis and liked the thought of helping his only son. They agreed on terms. They would do all the work and he would sit under the umbrella and keep an eye on the cash box. They could keep a third of the day's takings and pay for his lunch. What could be fairer than that? Nothing, said Angela. Nothing could be fairer than that, and kissed him cheeky on the cheek. They stayed with him, most of the morning and the whole afternoon, learning the ropes, walked back with the donkeys, helped bed them down for the night, a stable behind the railway station and a scrub of land poached from the old goods yard. They said their goodnights, kipped down, her in a scanty bed, Chester on the floor again, even though the bed was big enough, and she had bought herself a pair of pyjamas.

They woke early for the donkeys. Chester still had straw in his hair from the night before and her body laughed inside her bedwear. The old man was at the stable already, feeding the donkeys apples, talking into their muzzles, told them of a couple of rooms the other end of the building, and they moved in within the hour. Chester bought his own pyjamas and they dressed and undressed separately, both conscious of what lay nearly visible, what they'd once shown each other, what they had to hide. Angela slept in the bed, Chester at the foot of the bed, still on the floor. They closed their eyes to the smell of the hay stored below and in the morning woke to the donkeys braying for their apples and fresh water. Chester and the old man would walk the donkeys down around eight o'clock, get them ready for the day ahead. Even if the weather was bad, they would walk them down and get them ready, because come rain or shine there were children who needed the beach and a beach which needed the donkeys.

This is how Chester worked the beach. He raised children upon donkey saddles, gathered the reins and walked the donkeys, first one way, then the other, up and down, mile upon mile. The donkeys were not slow, they were relentless, never seemed to tire out. Only at the close of the day, on the walk back up, did their toiling show, and Chester felt the same way. He spent the days, eyes fixed on the beach and the myriad of shapes and sizes: couples in the water, women far out to sea, anomalies. He saw a hundred Alices and saw her not at all. He wasn't sure who Louis might be.

Angela found part-time work selling parking tickets. Lunchtime she'd walk down with fish and chips for three, bought from the chippy round the back of the station. If the weather held, she'd warm the swell of her on the beach and, if not, sit on the benches, hoping that she might spot Alice and Louis first. She wanted to mean something to Chester more than an Epping girl in need.

Once a week, on Monday, the donkeys' day off, they'd catch the bus back to the farm. Chester would hang out by the egg stand, waiting for the car that never came, the flicker on his mother's face he never saw. Angela spent the day helping Mrs

Calvert: not the farm, the paperwork. She'd been super-brilliant in the tax office, had a hold on numbers like nobody's business. They didn't mess you around, figures. Only one thing riled. Mrs Calvert took it for granted that she and Chester were like a proper couple, like they'd done everything young couples did, screwed and argued and made peace with each other. And what were they doing? Wearing pyjamas every night. Chester wore underpants under his. She couldn't take it any longer.

'Remember the allotment?' she said. 'You getting me to take all my clothes off?'

He didn't reply.

'I'm not asking you for anything, Chess, but pyjamas every night? I mean, what are we afraid of? You hold me and I'll hold you. Who knows, one day, miracles.'

The summer went, months of lights, days of rain and sun, nights of miracles. Their ideas changed, their certainties. They would not find Alice or Louis on the beach. That had been for Percy to see. They lived in a glorious limbo, within a certainty of their own making, an innocence tested, uncertainty part of the plan. Chester had tasted the world of men and women, Angela growing proud with him. Their time in Scarborough was closing. The donkeys retired September 30th, the old man taking them to the Welsh border country, to winter on his brother's farm. They could come if they wanted to, he told them. The donkeys had become attached to Chester. He made them feel young, the old man also. Proper milk on the farm, he said. Rich and creamy, just right for a baby. Proper meat for the mother too.

Chester knew all about Wales. Wales sounded about right, hills and valleys, and close-knitted towns and the Brebis who lived there. Six months ago, Angela would have paled at the thought, but she was changed now. She imagined Wales, liked what she saw. After the baby was delivered …

They decided to tell Mrs Calvert. Chester had given up on the eggs. Selling eggs to strangers had emptied his heart. They caught the afternoon bus up for the last time. Angela nearly didn't go. She wasn't due for another ten days, but she felt heavy, wanted to save her energy.

There was a county-council Land Rover by the gate, posts being dug in either side. They walked up, Angela's feet splayed like a duck. Mrs Calvert answered the door, her face clenched, like she'd been punched in the face.

'Do you like sheep?' she said. Chester fumbled for an answer.

'He had a painting of one above his bed,' Angela said. 'Not many men can say that.'

She thought Mrs Calvert would find it funny, but she did not. She was puzzled. She liked Mrs Calvert. Mrs Calvert liked her.

'What's up?' she said.

'Phone call,' Mrs Calvert said. 'Suspected foot and mouth, not six miles away. They're culling in two days, earlier if they can find the men. All my sheep. Bloody madness. Do they look ill?'

She walked them out to the field where they stood. The sheep saw them coming, formed a huddle.

'I don't understand,' Angela said. 'If they're not ill …'

They could hear shots, a mile away, steady and rhythmic, like in a line.

'They don't wait … they kill them just in case. They did it to all the cattle, now they're doing it to all the sheep.'

'But surely … they can't just …' She held her belly, helpless. 'They look so …'

What was there to say? There was no sense any more, what was right, what was wrong. Sheep were barely sheep any more, caged up and driven up and down, hundreds of miles, week after week, just to kill them somewhere else. Cows were grown in sheds. What sort of world grew cows in sheds? The sheep had moved to the edge of the paddock, their black faces lifted up, expectant at the gate. One of them bleated, then they all joined in, a chorus running back and forth, calling to one another. Mrs Calvert turned away.

'They'll all be dead tomorrow,' she said. 'They know. Animals always know.'

She groaned a chasm. The baby kicked Angela hard. She blundered forward, barely aware of what she was saying.

'We'll take one,' she said. 'We're going to Wales tomorrow. We'll take one.'

'Tomorrow?' Chester couldn't believe it. 'Ange, we can't …'

'Why not? They got hospitals in Wales, haven't they, doctors? The farm has land for donkeys, sheep too probably … enough for …' She broke off. What was she saying? Who was saying it? Chester was as puzzled as she.

'It's not our farm, Ange. They wouldn't let us.'

'Not Wales then. Somewhere else. The moors.'

'Not ours,' Mrs Calvert said. 'They're rounding them all up.'

'Further up then,' she said. 'Or down.' She looked to the man who knew maps. 'Chess?'

Chester took pause. They were running out of control, his control anyway. This suddenness, stubborn, unreasonable reminded him of …

'Even if we wanted to,' he said, 'what would we take her in, from here?'

'We could borrow the Land Rover. You wouldn't mind, would you?'

Mrs Calvert studied her. Part of her youth had gone. Impending motherhood had not taken it, but this had. She was making a stand, a noisy, unreasonable stand, borne out of nothing less than conviction. This wasn't a knee-jerk. She was facing the world, conscious of consequence. She was serious. This mixed-up muddle of a girl, pregnant, uneducated, was deadly serious.

'They'll know something's up,' she warned her, 'me here and the Land Rover gone.'

'What about the other car?' Angela said. 'You know the ...'

'My Rover? With a sheep in the back?'

Angela clapped her hands. The conspiracy was taking hold, getting better.

'We could put a shawl over her head, like that kids' book. No, that won't work. Chess, help me out here.'

Chester held his ground, uncertainty washing over his feet. There was a sheep, right at the front, hadn't taken her eyes off him, the spitting image of the Brebis on the wall. But then, when he looked at the others, they all looked like the Brebis on the wall. Mrs Calvert was wrestling with the practicalities still.

'In broad daylight, they'll spot you right away,' she said. 'They'll be watching, all the farms, keeping on the lookout. It wouldn't be the first time a farmer's ...'

Angela wouldn't let go.

'Tonight then, when everyone's gone to bed, across the fields, on to the road that way.'

'Just as bad,' Mrs Calvert said, 'headlights creeping out on the hills after midnight.'

Chester dug his hands into his pockets, cleared his throat. It seemed to him that all choice in the matter had been removed from him entirely.

'Who said anything about lights?' he said. It could have been Alice talking, and in the dark he wondered where they might be.

T HEY'D GONE TO WALES first, to look for the Brebis. The Brebis would set Louis right, then the speed camera. After that, Scammonden perhaps, at last, and if he was ready, Chester. It was all doable.

They didn't find the Brebis, though Alice found the wall, the bricks patchworked a different grey to the others, discovered it by chance one early morning, two weeks in, parked heedless above the bend, but did it anyway, walked Louis down, and sat on the wall together, rolled them both cigarettes. She was a proper smoker now. It was something to share, tobacco, skins, lighting up. Lighting up brought their heads together, gave them an opportunity for them to kiss, like it was a language, like there were all sorts of ways to light a cigarette and kiss, kisses of memory, of hope, forgiveness. The hill dropped away steep more than she thought possible. It was a wonder they hadn't tipped headlong into oblivion that night. On the other side a copse of thin beech and, through them, a glimpse of green and hill.

'She'll be out there somewhere,' she said. 'How long do they live for, Louis?'

Louis formed his lips. He was speaking better, though he had to gather his face together beforehand. When the words came, it was like he was trying to spell the words at the same time, as if remembering the order of the letters helped his mouth in the shaping of them.

'For ever,' he said. 'Like in the Bible.'

Were there Brebis in the Bible? There was a Lamb of God, she knew that much, hadn't a clue what it had done. Was that what he meant? She wanted to ask him, but you couldn't push it with Louis, not in his present state. He spoke and then settled back. The language he used – there was only so much of it.

She got to her feet. 'What say we head for the hills, park up there for a night, see if she doesn't make herself known? We've only just arrived. She might not have heard about us yet.'

She drove up, found a spot looking out. They did mostly nothing the rest of the day. Why should they? It was great to see him with his feet up on the chaise longue and the back door open, something cooking on the Belling and she drinking cider with him, stroking his legs as they stretched out over her lap. It was all she wanted, Louis, and now she had it. The last two weeks had worked out well. Summer hadn't packed up, and they'd swung into a routine. Difficulties would come later, winter, breakdowns, health, but she wasn't concerned. They could do it. They could do all of it. She had Louis, and Louis had her. Therapy and stimulus, her father had said, and she gave him a dose of both every hour going, and then some. Twice a day she walked him up a path, along a road, through a wood. If he fell over, too bad. She waited until he picked himself up. If it got too much, they sat a while, shared a roll-up, had a snooze. She wasn't going to act like his nurse or his coach. He was an animal on the move, doing the best he could, and so was she. In the evenings she made him read to her like they'd done years ago, news out the local paper, adverts, stuff for sale, part-time work going, Louis squinting with the reading glasses she'd had to buy him. It was good for his co-ordination, and he looked something else in specs, like a schoolmaster who'd lost his books. They made her laugh.

Keeping him clean was important. It was warm enough to stand him outside, wash him down head to toe, and it comforted him, to see her hair plastered back, her top half wetted, and the steady touch of her. It was the whole of the right-hand side that was fucked, and she took extra-special tender the full length of it, trying to nudge it all awake. She encouraged him with her breasts. She'd lie in his lap and let him drag the right hand floppy over them, hoping it would trigger something. Back and forth it went, like it had never been there before, like it hadn't a clue what it was doing, like it was dead. It wasn't dead, but it wasn't alive neither. He wasn't up to making love any more, but neither was she. Louis's turn had put that fire out, like a bucket of water.

That's how they'd travelled that summer. Petrol was the biggest expense, but she wasn't worried. Thanks to her mum, she had nearly ten grand in the post office. The Sherpa was a greedy bastard and had bugger all in the way of acceleration, but still, it suited them, sitting high up, looking at the road below and the country going by, and Alice not certain what was going on in Louis's head. There was a different Louis living with her now. At night they'd park out of town, listening for the owls and foxes, the coughing of the sheep, and if possible, somewhere they could clock the motorway traffic. He'd once loathed the sight of them, but now Louis never tired of watching the cars and neither did she. It was their drug and she wanted nothing more. She didn't crave a house or a garden or a television. She didn't care about the news or who thought what. She didn't give a fuck for any of it. It was all pointless, always had been. Only roads made sense. She began to see them, not as part of a puzzle that Louis had thought should fit together, but as an entity in themselves, a republic of roads, a land for men and women on the move, where nothing is witnessed or understood, except the road itself. The purpose of a road was not to deliver or communicate or to ease access, but to show them the terrible meaning of time. Louis would die and she would die, and if she had her way, someone would come along and chop her up and feed her to the dogs. She'd be gone, just as everybody will be gone, and that would be that. She couldn't understand it, what people wanted. She couldn't really understand why they built roads, although she was glad they did. Human endeavour remained a mystery to her.

They stayed in Wales those winter months. The Sherpa was lagged and sealed and, when she lit the heat, warm as toast. They walked along seafronts, sat on benches. There were local cinemas to go to, pubs to visit. They could drive for three hours or lie in bed, what the fuck. They could look out the window, enjoy the smallest of events, a robin attacking a paper bag, an umbrella blown out of a woman's hand, a sheep butting a phone box, every moment tied to the moment of them. Alice saw it all as a beginning. All he had to do was to get better.

The first seizure came in a grocery store, Louis crashing against a vegetable stand, the staff all sympathetic and knowing best, offering to call an ambulance, thinking the worst of her as she shooed them away. How could she explain? They didn't want an ambulance or a doctor. They knew what medics would do, ask questions, give them forms to fill, strap them down any way they could. No one understood. There was nothing of any consequence but the presence of each other, nothing in front, nothing behind, nothing in between. Only one suggestion would she make, but whenever she did, he'd shoot it out the sky.

'We can rest up in Epping,' she'd say, 'if it's all too much. Lot's cooking and all that,' but he'd shake his head, like it was going to fall off.

'The road to recovery,' he'd say, 'is mighty bumpy. Wait until it's flattened out a bit. I don't want him to see me like this. Not with all this muck on.'

Spring came, and they'd been at it just under a year, a new back tyre, and the exhaust patched up with wire she'd nicked from a building site, and Louis coming out of it a drop, his right foot happier and the muscle by his eye stronger, and his hand making a claw when she opened her blouse and offered him some. They toured up and down looking for the speed camera, never found it, but who cared. Louis was on the mend! She had money in the bank but that wouldn't last. She started calling in at farms, huddles of houses, introduced Louis as her dad, told them that he was getting on, wanted to see as much of the countryside as he could, and she hoping to pick up the odd job as they journeyed along. It was half true and it served them well. People liked the idea of it, a daughter looking after her old man, bless his heart. Work was found, small slices of it: hedging, digging, lugging sacks. Everyone told her how strong she looked, how healthy, how they admired what she was doing. One or two tried to fuck her. At night she'd climb down and weep under the stars, not out of self-pity, but for the intensity of the closeness she felt, the rootless beauty of her love.

She was strong, but the driving took it out of her, more than she'd thought. The Sherpa was a heavy drive, constant on the arms, needy too, rust, oil leaks, worn seals. She could spend a whole afternoon under the chassis, only to go back again a week later. She was competent, but it sapped her, cost them money too. Louis started having little breakdowns as well, nothing big, but disappointing, like a step backward instead of forward, a sudden fall, a sudden seizure, something just giving up inside him, and his speech smeared over his face like a badly washed windscreen. They came as a surprise, always, like they'd both unremembered the last one, all bumps forgotten. She'd sit him on the chaise longue, speaking well to him, willing it to pass, drive off as soon as she could to somewhere new, as if that would help. He started to get taken short. She'd pull off his trousers and the stink would come, and it would hurt him more than it did her, turn his face away, like it wasn't happening. For the first few times it hurt him and then ... it didn't hurt him any more. It was life. If the weather allowed she found it easiest if he shat standing up, she facing him, holding him half-upright in her arms and the shit dropping into the kiddies' paddling pool she bought and down his legs. She didn't mind. Shit meant nothing to her. It was a smell and a substance that was all. She washed him down, patted him dry and pulled up his trousers. Pyjamas he had now, though he insisted on trousers in public, colourful like he'd never worn before, clothes that made him look a bit of a swag. Louis in pink! Imagine that!

Still no sign of the speed camera, she bought a camera of their own, started visiting ancient stones, great lumps stuck crooked in forgotten places, meadows, hill forts, moorlands, strange, alien shapes stuck in the middle of nowhere, no one knowing why and no one giving them a moment's thought. They raised Louis's spirit. He'd stand next to them, hand on the surface, like he could feel them breathe. She'd take his picture and set out the canvas chairs, so he could look at them for as long as he liked. 'If you wait long enough,' he'd tell her, 'you'll see them move. Like Stonehenge,' a glint in his eye recalling something that, as far as she could remember, had never happened, the fuck that never was. Later, she'd stick the photo on the Sherpa wall, next to the others. The Polaroid was their only luxury.

It was after one such visit that Louis went blind in one eye. He'd tried to grab the wheel, his vision all jumbled up, and she'd slewed off into a hedge, needed a farmer's tractor to pull them out. It frightened him, the blackness. More than anything else, it frightened him, frightened her too. The café swam into view, the notes she'd taken, Owen leaning over the sink, and what they'd done for him. For the first time she thought of the help she could ask, just for a short while. She'd start with the café. She'd walk in natural, like any other motorist, see the lie of the land.

They were Thetford way at the time. She'd been working with the pigs. It took them two days. That was the pace of them now, plenty of stops, plenty of her chat, plenty of dozy, idle hours. She parked up, pulled a hat down over her head, walked round to take a look. The name was different, the office where Fish had sat ripped out, more room made for the eating. The kitchen doors had gone likewise. Dougie and his Italian were flitting about the tables like caged songbirds, Owen stood at the back, lording it over a griddle, flipping burgers in a hat. Her feet stayed rooted. She wanted to lay herself open, but couldn't, couldn't face them, couldn't bring herself to show them the Louis he now was. They weren't part of it now. They'd joined the other side, or was it that she and Louis had finally left? Whatever, they'd pity him. Worse, they'd pity her. Anger consumed her, anger with them and anger with her, for the very thinking of it.

She backed the Sherpa out in a fury. There would be no friends, no notebooks for making contacts. No web of like-minds poised over the country, ready for the call to arms. They'd go west for a while, Wiltshire, Gloucestershire. There were plenty of stones in Wiltshire, work too with luck. He'd sit by the stones and watch them move. His eye would like that, tell the other one what it was missing. They could call in on Charlie, get him to give the Sherpa a once-over. Or not. She'd see what the next day brought. Maybe the camera, maybe not. There was no great rush.

And then, much later, she noticed, quite unable to say when it had started, that there weren't the months and seasons any more, not for them, just a succession of days, the rhythm she'd counted on pumped out of their lives like an exhaust. And the days, they were simply a sequence of light and dark, hours of concentration, hours of drift, much like what Armstrong and Swigert had experienced, the Sherpa no different from a moon-craft, living within a gravity of its own. Outside looked like they didn't belong in it at all, like it was dangerous even to breathe it.

She gave up on jobs. Older instincts kicked in. Take the gun. Just looking at it steadied her. She still had the eye, could snatch a rabbit's life with just one swing of the barrel. She got into the rhythm of it, got a kick of seeing them flung into the air, hanging them up, pulling the skin clean over its body like there was nothing she couldn't do. Rain on the windscreen, snow on the roof, sun on the steps. Cold, hunger, warmth, food, that was all. Sores appeared on his legs. She didn't wash him as often as she should, herself neither. Once, her jeans off, she was surprised to see her ankles swollen up, her skin flaky round the ankles. Louis didn't want her naked next to him any more. She had imagined her body would always bring him comfort, but now it did not. It disturbed him, got in the way. For the first time, her body was of no use. She couldn't bear to look at it either. She bought long white nightdresses, buttoned to the neck. Out in the open she looked *Macbeth*-infected, full of lurid potions. She longed for someone to talk to. She wasn't dead yet. She had to be steady, that's all, stand firm. She'd be stopped every now and again, police, traffic wardens, served some papers. She took no notice, chucked them out, moved away. No one cared. One day he had a fit, rolled on the floor, legs kicking like a badly shot fox. She wrapped about him tight, didn't move for two days.

'Perhaps you should see someone, Louis,' she said after. 'Pills or something.'

'You know what'll happen. What's the point of me, all hooked up, in hospital?'

'And if I can't cope?'

He took her hand, his grip shaking feeble.

'Then roll me down a hillside. I'll take my chances in the undergrowth, along with the worms and badgers …'

She realised she was getting weaker, had to do something about it. Louis was finding walking hard, didn't want to do much, a few steps, that was enough. That was OK for him, but her … it was a matter of survival. She thought of a wheelchair for him, couldn't bear the thought, like she would be behind him, murmuring pap into his ear like he was an invalid. He wasn't an invalid. He was Louis, couldn't walk well, that was all. People who pushed wheelchairs looked so smug too, being good. She wasn't up to being good, wanted nothing to do with it. She bought a galvanised wheelbarrow instead, hacksawed out the rise between the handles, laid the inside with foam rubber, then cushion seats from armchairs. Louis could trot as far as he wanted, his steps were like that now, too small for a proper man, then lie back idle, feet dangling between the handles and his head bobbing up and down like a stuffed Egyptian. It was great. They were still connected, not divided like prisoner and warden, but held together like they'd always been, by arms and legs and the wealth in their eyes. She could talk to him or not. He could look left or look right or stare right at her. It was another form of driving, the wheelbarrow, out in the open, in the elements. Louis liked the roughness of it, the hunch on her shoulders, the brace of her legs, the grip of her hands. She was doing work as he knew it, manual, strenuous, and damn the weather. He revelled in the looks they got, a man in a wheelbarrow wrapped in mummy pink and his woman trundling him along, no more embarrassment on her than if she was wheeling a sack of sand. It was a fuck you, a hands-on, look-at-us fuck you. 'Insides need shaking up,' he'd tell her, and wait outside while she pulled the barrow off the roof. And it worked for her too. There was purpose to her body again, her arms, her legs, her back. She rediscovered vigour. When she needed a break, she'd find a seat or a stone or a wall and park him alongside, feed him a ciggy or a bottle of cider with a straw stuck in, rest up a while. She'd come back and lie on the chaise longue, her flesh aglow, flashes of forgotten sex flickering up and down. They didn't last but it was good to know, they were alive in her somewhere. She got rid of the nightdresses, slept in her underwear. No, she wasn't dead yet.

Sometimes though, she couldn't remember why she was alive, what the reason for it all had been. It was another Sherpa foul-up that reminded her, police out with their notebook, front tyres fucked, brake lights buggered and Louis, up on the verge, asleep in his wheelbarrow. Who was she? How long had he been like that? What were they doing? It was his last wish, to see France before he … She showed them their passports. The passports helped. Driving licence? In her hand, all legal and proper. Made her want to vomit, their fingers all over it, but thank Christ she'd done it … They drove her under escort to a garage for the tyres, then to the station, where they charged her.

They didn't know what to make of them, kept them in for hours. Something wasn't right, but they couldn't see what. Louis fell asleep. Alice drank tea, flipped through magazines, hadn't looked at a magazine in years. And there it was, June issue, the *Police* fucking *Gazette*, a colour picture of the little bastard, all horrible and yellow, the first prototype, sneaked up unofficial, not forty miles away, standing by the hard shoulder like a robot nob. It was like all they'd ever asked for handed to them on a uniformed plate. She could hardly stop from the laughing, folded her arms, mouth tight, doubling up on contrite. She was sorry about the tyres and the brakes, but sometimes, her husband, in his condition, the demands on her … She ran her fingers through her hair. They lent her a comb.

Four hours later she'd paid off the garage, was sat in a lay-by, waiting for midnight. Two o'clock in the morning, that would be the time, three at the latest. She slept for a couple of hours, took Louis out for a shit. The night was clear, just like she'd always hoped, just like all their best nights had been, long and pure and full of promise. She drove beautiful, more beautiful than she could ever remember, the Sherpa moving surprising smooth under her hands. They weren't new, the tyres, but they freshened the Sherpa up, Louis swaying in his seat like in a cradle. She found herself singing to him, forgotten soul coming up like stacked-up forty-fives, all the while the roads unfolding, like on a map. All she had to do was to count off the junction numbers and watch the clock.

They were on it, five to two. She pulled on to the hard shoulder, switched off the lights. If she'd had the time, she'd have sprayed the Sherpa black, made it invisible. Lunatic dangerous, but she'd have done it. She got out, stood in front of it. It had a box for a head, and big mirror shades where its eyes hid. It was worse than she'd imagined, worse than speed limits, worse than a seat belt. It had a kind of life about it, like it was alive, not alone alive but like somewhere would be its brothers and sisters, a whole tribe, ready to swarm. This was just the start. One day there'd be one-legged nobs fucking every road in the country, fucking your every move. What choice did they have?

She clambered in the back, took down the gun, checked the breech. She walked round, pulled open the passenger door.

'Come on, Louis. It's time.'

'What?'

'Our big day, sweetheart.'

She helped him down, set him upright, the noise of the road on his boots. The motorway stretched straight, not another car in sight. She wanted so many things.

'See it?'

He didn't understand.

'There, Louis. Look!' She angled him steady, his eye following her arm. He saw it bottom to top, understanding flooding in as his sight rose – the black pole, the square head, the blank eye staring right through him. He put his hand out.

'Gun,' he said.

She wanted to jump up, climb on his back and ride him like a chariot, that he should know in an instant what to do, that they were still Alice and Louis, that he'd been there all the time, just as she'd thought. Nothing had been said for so long, yet he had stretched out his hand knowing that she'd have the gun, knowing that this was what they would always have done: thick like cream, perfect like an egg.

'All yours.'

Louis took hold. The sudden weight unsettled him. Alice laid a hand to his back. He raised the gun. Memory tried to swing it.

'Eye down the barrel, Louis, finger on the trigger, from your cock upwards, like you taught me.'

Her voice was cracking. Like he taught her! She had run away with him and they were still running.

He shook her off, took a step forward, unexpected firm. He settled the gun in the pit of his arm.

'One small shot for a man,' he said, 'one giant …'

The recoil catapulted him back, like he'd been wired to a rubber band. The camera was bent at the neck, mouth gaping and its insides smoking. Louis was lying on the inside lane, laughing. She ran over to pick him up.

'Better get out of here,' she said.

'Before we go,' he said, held out his arms. She didn't hesi-tate, out on top of him. Fuck the cars. He took her head in his hands, raised it up.

'When I die …' he said. His eyes were big and serious.

'No, Louis.'

'Look at me.' He licked his lips like a thirsty man. 'When I die. Scammonden. Dig a pit on the moor, wrap me in a coat, like we did the badger. Chester will help.'

'Chester?'

'It's too late for him and me now. We should have …' He shook the thought away. 'Bury me deep. Take some doing, mind. It comes out in wedges, but there's a dreadful suck to it.'

'I can dig, Louis. You know I can.'

'As deep as you can. No disturbances. I want my voice to carry. I've company to keep.'

———

He was done. After that, they gave up talking, their sentences perfunctory, reduced. Did she drive all day, drive all night, after that, drive all year, day in, day out? It felt like it, like they were driving towards the end, like there was nowhere else for them to go, just the roads and the lights blinking for the last turn-off, but it was months rather than years. Louis focused his attention on what lay outside, not the road, but the verge, hoping to bag the next one. Shooting the camera had skewered his reason. He pointed at objects that excited him, the words staccato in his mouth. They gave him erections that slid out shiny, like a dog's. He was almost animal now.

When it came, he'd been counting wind turbines. He could watch turbines all day. The turbines were like stones for Louis;

they moved with the elements. That morning he'd counted twenty, all lined up along the faraway hills.

'Let's count them again,' he said. 'They're …'

He shrank back, clutching at himself, his right arm flapping at the windscreen. On the opposite side of the road, a rider on a white horse was walking towards them, tall in the saddle. There was a pace to them, like they'd come a long way, like their journey had not yet ended. The man tipped his hat as they passed. Louis slumped in his seat.

'Jesus Christ, I'm done for!' he said. 'He's come for me!'

He clawed at his chest. There were rattles in his throat and his face was wandering lost. Alice pulled on the handbrake. The Sherpa swung across as she leapt out her seat.

'Louis?'

She was kissing him, rubbing his hands, his good left arm. Colour came back. He struggled up, the last call of strength. He yanked at her blouse. Her breasts fell loose in the throes of life.

'I killed the horse, Alice! God forgive me. I killed the horse.' She pulled the hand right in, held it hard.

'Louis …'

'I killed him. What will he think?'

His hand was clawing at her, digging for an answer.

'Will I meet him, when I get there?'

'God, you mean … ?'

'What if He's a horse, Alice, have you ever thought of that? What if it's a horse world, and what you do in life to horses is how you're judged? I killed a horse, Alice. I killed a horse!'

He was sat back up again, his face wild.

'You've been dreaming, Louis.'

'I didn't mean to, God knows I didn't, but he'd won see, won although he'd lost, and I knew if he stayed, that would be an end to it, end of Scammonden, end of me. It was anyway, I wasn't to know that, didn't have the sense to see it. It was just to lead him away, out on the moor. He was a horse, for Christ's sake, should have loved the freedom, but would he go? I'd lead him out and slap his rump, but he'd just follow me back, time after time. There was a shovel lying up top, where we'd set some posts in, and I started wheeling it around my head, to give him the frights, God knows I didn't mean to, the shovel, you know like a caber and there he was, careering right into me and it went slap against the head, really hit him, like his eyes were going to pop … God, Alice, the look on his face. We searched the next day, but … the peat must have took him … The horse … I killed the horse.'

He thrashed about trying to escape.

'Quiet now. He must have run away, if you didn't find him.'

'On his knees he was. He got to his feet, but he knew he was done for … and the look, Alice, the look … like he forgave me and had inside him all the understanding of me and who I was and what I had done … such a beautiful face, like a painting long ago … He knew me. God, he was a horse and he knew me …'

He fell back. Cars were hooting. She climbed back into her seat, parked the Sherpa on the verge. Louis was dead. She leant across, pulled him upright.

She'd take him where he wanted. She'd dig it deep. She'd take him to the top, where it looked out on everything, bare herself to it, the moor, the dam, the road, mark it out and cut it easy like a cake, her skin whipped and her flesh hot, cut the slices thick and wet, stack them ready. She'd dig it wide and deep, revelling in the dirt and sweat, mark her body with it, drop the barrow in, lay the cushions comfy, fold him down on that, his feet dangling over, his hands on the side, ready for the ride. And she'd leave her clothes close, the flowered number he liked, and stand there Alice naked, like the last thing he'd see before she covered him up. It was going to be bloody wonderful.

'I should strap you in,' she said. 'That would be the sensible thing to do.'

She swept his hair away from his eyes, rested his head back.

'Fuck that, Louis. Thick like cream. Perfect like an egg.'

She pulled back her dress, laid his hand on her bare skin.

'There you are,' she said. 'Hold on to that.'

They placed the Brebis into a pen next to the barn. She was two years old, Mrs Calvert told them, good teeth and a strong climber. He drove the Rover out, unbolted the bench seat at the back, dragged it out. He laid a ramp up to the door. Mrs Calvert couldn't bear to look. Inside, her Rover looked indecent.

She made them dinner instead, chicken pie and baked potatoes, stewed rhubarb for afters. Chester and Alice didn't speak much, but things had to be spoken.

'What'll you do after you've …' Mrs Calvert said. Chester licked the back of his spoon.

'Drive back, I suppose,' he said. It was what she had hoped for.

'Better not,' she said. 'They see the back taken out and they'll put two and two together. I could get my licence taken away. Better keep the car a while. Wales, is it? I could arrange for the seat to be sent there, for when the baby comes.'

She waved their protestations aside. Midnight they took the Brebis out. Chester arm-locked her head, Mrs Calvert's hands on her rump, Angela ready by the door. It was only a short distance, head in first and then all three of them grappling her rear. She had no choice in the matter.

They took their partings quickly. Mrs Calvert went back inside, turned out all the lights. Chester started the engine, waited until his eyes had opened to the dark; no moon but the clouds high enough for the light from the ground to rise. Mrs Calvert had shown him the route: up the top, along the high track, down the old bridle path and on to the road a mile and a half away. There was nothing to it.

He set off, over the yard, climbing quickly, second gear, then third, then down to second again, only the glow coming up from the track to guide him. It was steeper than he thought, the weight of the Brebis sliding back and the Rover slipping on the dew, and he geared down fast, then pumped back into second again, worried about the engine's pitch, how far it might carry. Who knew if anyone was out there?

Up ahead he could see the line where the land fell away, where the track along the ridge crossed his path, where'd he'd turn and become a silhouette on the skyline. The light would be brighter there, a sort of day for the night, and when he came to it, it felt as though he should use the indicator, so much like a road did it look. He turned, the ground cart-rutted, Angela bouncing in her seat like she was welded to the frame, and then, unexpectedly, a calm coming over them, the hill falling fast on either side, the flat long and stretched and below clusters of the unknown. The Rover nosed up refreshed, and for a moment Chester wished that someone *was* watching, the Rover carrying them proud, like the ship Essex had stood on, sailing for Cadiz, carrying history. No one would see this. It would only exist as a tale to tell, like an ancient's story to be handed down. If he'd worn a hat, he'd have rolled down the window, flung it overboard.

The descent took him by surprise, the sudden, hurtle-depth of it, first the grass rumble, then the land coming up like roller coasters as they dipped headlong into speed and the engine shaking crazy in his hands. He cut the ignition, the wheel breaking free of his grasp, and the Rover flying down, their bodies helpless inside, all the thoughts he had mad and useless. He wanted to press himself into Angela, tell her everything, feel the weight of all their unsung years together ... but there was rage against the glass and claws digging into the metal and his hands with nothing to grip but his own inability ...

'Hold on,' he said.

The Rover jumped clean out. Chester stamped on the brakes, pulled hard, back wheels rubbering the road, Angela slammed into him, and the Brebis all in a heap. It was done. They were sat facing east. Angela had an arm round his neck.

'Fuck me sideways, Chess. I didn't think we were ...'

He untangled themselves, got the engine going.

'Nearly over. A mile or two more, then the lights. A mile or two, no more.'

'Never mind the lights. She's shit herself.'

He let the clutch out. The Brebis was back on her feet, muttering. He could smell her breath and the oil in her coat, the other stuff too. He started forward, caution on the pedal, lights still off. Were they moving slow or swift? It was hard to gauge, but he knew what thirty mph felt like, even in a tank like this. He settled in. The Brebis stopped complaining. Angela sat back in her seat. The dark was easy, when it was all over.

He flicked on the lights. Hedges flashed dark-olive enormous. White lines blinked on the road like a runway. Angela sighed, thankful. He took her hand, kissed it. All he had to do was point the car.

For a while the traffic was almost absent, the road wide and silent, but then the motorway asserted itself, blue signs on stilts or hung overhead, bold numbers and simple maps, like their passage was ordained, like they were nothing but movement, all four of them. The traffic thickened. The A1, the M1, which one was it? Chester knew, but only if he didn't think.

Before he knew it, they were on the motorway itself, the M62, the Rover purring and the lanes filled with great wheels. Angela's belly sat beside him like a swollen moon. He was on his father's road, heading west. He thought he would know it, but he did not. There was nothing to see. It was just a motorway, that was all, all there ever would be. When the turn-off came, he nearly missed it, he was looking so hard, but he made the jump across in time, started the long climb. Scammonden Dam lay silent in the valley below. He couldn't see it, but he could feel it. Louis had left his life there, somewhere in the muck. If he could only dig it out.

He swung the wheel again, smaller roads, higher and wilder, the Rover straining as they reached the top. He took his foot off, fighting for breath.

'You OK?' Angela said.

He nodded. The moor was like a cathedral without walls, without a roof, flat and bare and touching the sky. What sort of angels flew here?

He let the Rover drift, then cut the engine, switched off the lights. They sat in the dark, all motion ceased.

'Help me get her out,' he said, 'then we'll ...'

He was used to cold, but it was colder than he thought possible, a chill of emptiness that took all geography away. He opened the back door, grabbed the Brebis's bewildered head. She didn't want to leave. Angela tucked her shoulder behind the Brebis's rump, pushed hard, like in a scrum. The Brebis jumped out on to the grass. She sniffed the air. They followed her to where the moor sloped into black. Far down, the motorway glittered in fabulous loops of light, molten ribs of steel parting like liquid lips, and a world of darkness in between. It was shining and bright, but it looked as if it had always been there, sort of eternal, like you could fly right into it. Chester took a step nearer. The Brebis turned, four feet firm, looked at him, weighing the measure of it all. They stood, staring at each other, the man and the Brebis. What could the Brebis know of him? Did she know *everything*?

Angela cried out, bending double, like she'd been kicked.

'Christ, Chess ... whose stupid idea was this ...'

She sank down on to the grass.

'Fuck me ... out in the middle of nowhere ...'

She lay back, her dress pulled up over her hips, legs splayed, pelvis bucking. Below, the motorway was moving. There was a radiance to this life, Chester could see it. It rose and fell and breathed, out of the moor and into the cars. Everyone he had known was on that road, Hogan and Percy, Aunty Lot and Mrs Calvert, tiny lights cresting the hill, on their way to the city beyond. A child was coming. Afterwards they would move to new ground, find their purpose. Somewhere on the moor, there were stones where ancients had worshipped, dances done, matters of moment, something very near holy. He held no fear. There was the road and the child and a woman and all he had never known.

Out of nowhere, a mess of white slid past the Rover, brakes pressed. A door opened, a woman running out, bare legs and a dress flapping above her boots. Angela was propped up on her elbows, staring down. The woman was dancing round the Rover, tearing off the wing mirrors, grabbing them with both hands.

'It's coming,' Angela cried. 'Sweet Jesus, it's coming.'

Chester looked from one woman to the other.

He took a deep breath.

The Brebis shook her head and thundered off into the night.

About the Author

Tim Binding was born in Germany in 1947. He is the author of *In the Kingdom of Air*, *A Perfect Execution*, *Island Madness*, *On Ilkley Moor*, *Anthem*, *Man Overboard*, *The Champion* and the children's book *Sylvie and the Songman*.

A NOTE ON THE TYPE

The text of this book is set in Adobe Caslon, named after the English punch-cutter and type-founder William Caslon I (1692–1766). Caslon's rather old-fashioned types were modelled on seventeenth-century Dutch designs, but found wide acceptance throughout the English-speaking world for much of the eighteenth century until replaced by newer types towards the end of the century. Used in 1776 to print the 'Declaration of Independence', they were revived in the nineteenth century and have been popular ever since, particularly amongst fine printers. There are several digital versions, of which Carol Twombly's Adobe Caslon is one.